WHITE DOVE

SHADOWS IN DRAB AND GREEN: BOOK 1

WHITE DOVE

KATRINA NOWAK

SCRIBBLE
& SPARK

Published by Scribble & Spark Bookworks

SCRIBBLE
& SPARK

ISBN 978-1-7320381-0-3

First Scribble & Spark Bookworks paperback edition, April 2018

Cover design & interior formatting by Mark Thomas / Coverness.com

For my awesome husband and my beautiful children

White Dove of the wild dark eyes
Faint silver flutes are calling
From the night where the star-mists rise
And fire-flies falling
Tremble in starry wise,
Is it you they are calling?

-Joseph Mary Plunkett

FLASH-FORWARD

August 1, 1914: Near Kilcoole, County Wicklow Ireland

The girl crouched atop a bed of straw, peering out into the night. Her breathing was rapid, and she could do nothing to slow it because it kept time with her pounding heart. With each breath, the straw beneath her bare feet moved ever so slightly. The rustling noise was soft in the night but deafening inside her head. She pleaded with her heart to slow, for she was being hunted and her breathing would give her away.

Her cache lay behind her, within arm's reach, carelessly piled in a heap among the hay. The donkey kept watch over the nineteenth-century German rifles that her pursuers wanted so badly to find. He slowly chewed his hay and nudged the butt of one of the Mausers with his nose. He snorted curiously. It was not often that he had visitors after sundown.

The salty sea breeze whipped across the meadow and carried into the open barn the distinct sound of a tree branch snapping. Her attention turned to the tree line. The straw rustled. Was it a British soldier coming for her?

The moonlight shone brightly above. It was the same moon that had guided her hours before as she met her gunrunner amid the waves of the Irish Sea. That same pale light now silhouetted a lone man as he made his way across the rolling Irish field. He looked ominous, but the light of the moon revealed that he carried no large firearm.

The girl reached for a Mauser and a cartridge. She knew little about rifles, but enough to understand that these dusty weapons—smuggled to Wicklow in the name of a free Ireland—were antiquated. She carefully loaded the rifle, as she had seen her father do years ago, and aimed the barrel out the open window. Only the muzzle protruded.

She could hear her father's voice, and for once it was not faded or obscure in her memory. *Take yer time, Nora. Choose a spot well ahead of 'em. Settle yerself. Take aim. And just wait for 'em to cross.* Of course, he had been talking about the game that teemed along the Shannon. She was poised to kill a soldier in the King's Army. Only hours before, this would have seemed absurd. But the events of the day had made her question everything she thought she believed. She chose a spot just to the left of the hedge line, and waited for the man to come into her view. Her finger made contact with the trigger. The metal felt like ice despite the warm August night. She slowly increased the pressure but did not squeeze it.

She waited. A second felt like a minute. Two seconds, like a quarter hour. She blinked. The man did not cross the imaginary line she had drawn between the muzzle and the hedge. She peered to her right, careful not to reveal her position. Her heart suddenly stopped. He was no longer there.

She pulled the rifle inside the barn. Standing slowly, she shouldered the weapon and steadied it across the open barn window, aiming it again toward the tree line. Her grandfather's old pendant hung heavily around her neck, its sharp edges reminding her that she was following a path he would have forbade. She took a step forward and kicked hay over the three rifles that lay on the ground.

The donkey snorted again, and his breath blew the hay off one of the barrels.

She listened intently but heard nothing save the whipping sea wind, the pawing of the donkey, and her own racing heart. Still shouldering the weapon, she peered further out the window. The summer grasses blew to the left and then the right like waves on the ocean yielding to onshore winds. The moon searched for the soldier like an enormous spotlight, but in vain.

Could the soldier have chosen to search the cottage instead of the barn? Did she have time to run to the shelter of the trees beyond? She didn't want to leave her rifles behind to fall into British hands. Many of her compatriots were also stranded and hiding throughout the Wicklow countryside, biding their time to make their way back to the Dublin safe houses. If the soldiers found her, it would put all of them at risk.

As her eyes scanned the meadow, the sound of a deep voice behind her took her breath way.

"Nora," it called in the distinct accent that marked Irishmen of the Pale. "Come child, 'tis not safe here." She swiftly turned and saw a face she recognized—a cocky smile that revealed a missing tooth. "Will be no easy task to get us home, but I've got a plan."

Only now did Nora recognize that the barrel of her Mauser was pointed directly at the man standing in front of her. Though he had dared to call her a child, she lowered it anyway. But she moved it slowly to allow him to sweat.

He tossed his head to the side, and his jet-black hair parted on his forehead, revealing dull gray eyes that hung with a fatigue uncommon for a man of just twenty-five. For the first time, he appeared to Nora to be human. Out here, he had no requirement to be braver, smarter, or more confident than every other man around him. He didn't need to keep up an insufferable facade.

"Glad you don't mean to shoot me," he said.

"I almost did," she replied.

"I know, I saw you." The man smiled.

"Are you ready for a bit of an adventure, Nora, in the name of Ireland?"

Now, it was Nora who smiled. "Always."

CHAPTER 1

Nine days earlier

July 23, 1914: Ballynote, County Clare, Ireland

The sun rose peacefully and brilliantly. Its gentle rays brought the green meadows to life and chased the darkness from the shadows of the ancient stonewalls. Until the first opaque light broke across the fields, the birds had sung short, solo songs, but now one call could not be distinguished from another. The chorus grew more chaotic as the sun peered over the horizon and pierced the landscape with a magnificent burst of light.

The summer wind off the River Shannon blew Nora McMahon's long auburn hair across her eyes, blocking her view of the horizon, but she did nothing to tame it. It had been wild for sixteen years and would stay wild today. She sat perched atop a boulder in the back field, the largest of the many stones that littered the landscape. The smaller rocks had long since been harvested to reinforce the boundaries that kept the small herd of sheep corralled, but the larger ones remained. They had sat here for perhaps a thousand years and would for a thousand more, witnesses to the story of millennia—and the story of Ireland.

The sun's peaceful rise across County Clare felt like a taunting irony. Everything in her world was broken and chaotic. The scattering light made her feel small and insignificant, yet her troubles seemed so great that she didn't know if she could shoulder them. Her grandfather's voice echoed in her head: *The Lord will guide you, Nora. There's not a thing you can do but follow.*

That voice. But where was she being guided? Closing her eyes, she remembered how his thick country brogue had made his words sound more like a poem or a song. Until just a few days ago, she had felt that he had been guiding her and her twin brother along his carefully chosen course. He had always given them a leash so that they could explore, but lured them back with his wise words and kind heart if they strayed too far. It seemed to them a voice and wisdom of ages past, and she knew of no other soul in 1914 who spoke that way.

But today she did not recognize her path, and she didn't trust anyone to lead her. A strange energy was growing within her, and she was uncertain she could tame it without her grandfather's guiding hand. He, like her parents, like the dreams of generations before, was now lost to the ages.

From her perch, she could make out the little island of Inis Cathaigh. Its lush green shores, cradled by the River Shannon, were also awakening to a new day. She lightly touched the Apostles of Ireland pendant that hung around her neck. It had always watched over her grandfather, but now it cast its protection—or its curses—over her. She didn't know which. The pendant felt heavy around her neck, and she had a hollow feeling where it rested on her chest.

Nora's mother had been a McMahon, a family who had lived on the island for generations. Her grandfather surely would have happily lived out his old age there had his daughter not been caught up in the rising and orphaned his two young grandchildren. He had blamed Nora's father—a Cullen born with their characteristic wild streak—for luring his daughter into an early grave with dreams of a free Ireland.

Nora realized, for the first time, just how precarious their situation had always been. Only her grandfather, the larger-than-life Eamonn McMahon, had kept them safe. His good McMahon name, which he insisted his grandchildren take to protect them from anyone who knew their parents' story, had ensured the children kept the lease to their plot after their parents had been executed for their crimes. But their landlord—known in Ballynote as "the Crook Ainsley"—despised this arrangement. Without their grandfather, they were just children of traitors—regardless of their name—and Ainsley was bound to exact his long-awaited revenge and cancel the McMahon contract.

Just the sight of the Crook, trailed by half a dozen perfectly groomed and obedient red and white setters, was enough to draw a cold sweat. Ainsley's English ancestors, like many of the landed gentry in Clare, bred the setters to hunt the game along the Shannon. But the Ballynote tenants suspected Ainsley kept his dogs around to harass and hunt another type of prey—the Catholic type who couldn't manage to make rent on time. Nora recalled these hushed rumors whenever she heard the yelping of excited dogs in the dead of night—and when the money tin on the top kitchen shelf stood empty.

While her grandfather was alive, the three were biding their time waiting for change to come to Ballynote. It was only a matter of time, he would say, before a peaceful revolution would free them from Ainsley's grip. But with Eamonn McMahon's untimely death, Nora and her brother, Seamus, had run out of time.

Nora was awakened from her wandering thoughts by riders in the distance. They approached her farm at a steady canter, a far too hasty pace for this early in the day. And yet there was no ominous trail of red and white setters behind them. Standing on her rock, she trained her eyes on the fork in the path to see if they veered off toward the Sullivan's barn or took the turn toward her farm. When the horses slowed to a trot and turned sharply up the path to her little cottage, dogs or not, she leapt from her perch and ran to wake Seamus.

There was reason to be concerned about the riders. They were behind in their rent. By now, word of Eamonn McMahon's death had spread, and the Crook would be looking to collect the past months' payments.

As Nora burst through the door of the small cottage, a heavy weight returned to her chest, stopping her cold. In her alarm at the riders, she had momentarily forgotten. Stepping into her dark home, she was again face-to-face with how her life had changed. The cottage was always dark and damp no matter the time of day, but today the candles from the bedroom where her grandfather lay served as the main source of the light. The following evening was to be his wake and the next day, his final journey back to the island.

She turned her head to avoid looking at the corpse as she went to the room where Seamus slept. It was dark and windowless, with seed potatoes piled along all of the walls. Seamus slept on the floor among them.

"Seamus," she whispered, although there was no need to be quiet. "Seamus! There are riders comin'! They seem in a hurry."

Her brother immediately sat up and looked around. His almost white-blond hair was as unruly as Nora's, and his face bore the same smattering of freckles. His feet were dirty from a summer of running around barefoot, and they poked out from his makeshift bed under a thin blanket. He looked confused, but he nodded and reached for his shirt. They weren't expecting any visitors. He stood, a full head taller than Nora, and as they passed the room with the candles, he, too, turned his head away. "For the love of God, can't you put a curtain up?" he said sharply.

She took no offense. She knew that he had seen plenty of corpses before, but the sight of his grandfather touched a long-suppressed memory for both of them. The old man's face was frozen in the same contorted agony that their mother had worn as the magistrate's representative cut her body from the tree and let it fall in a heap to the ground. That young, arrogant magistrate's son had been shipped in from Dublin to destroy her life. He'd smirked as he sentenced their parents to die.

Eamonn had wanted his grandchildren to see the bodies and to remember.

4

"The Cullens have a wild streak," he had said. "Pray to God that you are both spared from it. Dreams of an age long passed have claimed too many in this family. Never forget what you have lost to foolish fantasy." From that day forward, Nora and Seamus had become McMahons, and Cullen was a name only uttered as a whisper.

As she hung a sheet over her grandfather's doorway, hiding away their awful memories for another day, she nervously asked, "Seamus, where's the money?"

Seamus looked frantic as he peered out of the open door for a sign of the riders, but the cottage was nestled beneath a small knoll that blocked the view of the path. He seemed not to hear her.

She eyed the shelf above the fireplace for the tin can where her grandfather kept any money they had. The shelf stood vacant, even though Seamus and their grandfather had just been up to the Ennis market the week before and had earned a good sum for the sale of their first potato crop and seven of the finest lambs the farm had ever bred. Their sale had made enough to pay the rent and buy some time to come up with a plan.

"Seamus!" She was desperate to interrupt his thoughts. "They are coming for it!"

"I know!" he snapped. "But you can forget about it because it's gone."

Her muscles quivered with fear and her face flushed. That familiar crescendo of anger.

Seamus must have seen her dark emerald eyes flash with anger. "I gave it to the pilot and the priest. There's just a small bit left. Not nearly enough." For a moment, they stared at each other—Nora's fiery green eyes locked with Seamus's soft, pale blue gaze. She took a deep breath and clenched her fists so Seamus wouldn't see that her hands were shaking. She peered out the door and wished they still had her father's old flintlocks. Anything to keep the Crook at bay.

Seamus read her mind as she eyed their makeshift holsters, nails that still stood hammered into one of the low wooden rafters. "What would we do with 'em, Nora? Just get us killed. They'd be no match for the Crook's gang."

"Why didn't you tell me about the money?" She spoke slowly and deliberately to feign the calmness she wanted to feel. *Why did he always behave like he was in charge?* She corrected herself. "Why didn't you *ask* me?"

Seamus shook his head. "Didn't expect there to be much of a discussion. Did you want me to sell our lambs just to fill the Crook's filthy pockets?" He began to pace the small room along a well-worn path in the dirt floor, but never took his eyes off the open door. "Grandda raised those lambs. Thought it was only right that we use the money to bring 'im home."

Nora took another deep breath. She couldn't stand that he hadn't consulted her. He was always acting as though he were older and entitled to making all the decisions. Even when their grandfather had been alive. Nora looked at the floor, but she still felt her brother's stare. They both knew he was right.

"We still have the herd, Nora. As long as we have that herd, we are goin' to be fine." But his hands were clenched into fists as he waited for the riders to come into view.

"Aye." She felt her anger dissipate as quickly as it had flared, but in its wake it left a mounting anxiety. They were not prepared for the Crook or his agents, yet they had both known they would eventually pay a visit. "'Tis a stroke of luck that we have such a herd this year," she said, and watched as Seamus grimaced at the reference to luck. Irish luck had always been more of a curse.

Their attention focused on the door as the thunder of hooves approached. The first of the horses reached the crest of the knoll, followed by three others. Though they were close, Nora was so nervous she could not make out their faces, but they looked too young to be the Crook or his agent's posse. As they neared the cottage, the riders slowed and pulled to a halt. Unexpected laughter came from the front yard, and without warning, a shadow lifted from her. She forgot that her grandfather's body lay only yards away.

That laugh was unmistakable, as was the beaming smile now spread across the face of Colin Kildare. It had been months since she had seen or heard from him, but the echo of his laughing across their yard cast the same spell over her as it had for as long as she could remember. She hoped her brother hadn't noticed her grin.

"Halloo McMahons!" he called in his deep voice and jumped off his horse. Upon hitting the ground, he fell backward and sat on the ground. Nora pulled her long auburn hair across her face to hide her smile. She wondered how much he must have drunk the previous night to still be tipsy. He was clearly enjoying his first trip home to Ballynote since leaving to work in Dublin the previous year.

"McMahons!" he called as he sat on the ground, reins still in his hands and his horse watching him curiously. "I come with news."

Seamus ducked out of the cottage door and approached his old friend. He, too, seemed lightened by the arrival of this inebriated surprise. "Colin, I pray it be good news, otherwise you can put yer arse back on yer horse and head back to Dublin!" Seamus seemed unaware that perhaps he was not the only one who was happy to see Colin, or that maybe—as Nora silently hoped—Colin hadn't come only to see him.

Seamus pulled Colin to his feet and the two friends embraced for a long time. Finally, Colin pulled away. "I don't know if it's good news or bad news, but it's an excuse to drop by to see the likes of you."

Embracing Seamus once more, he nodded to Nora with a half smile and a wink. Again, she felt a small burst of energy run through her. She had so much to tell him. He whispered cautiously to Seamus, but the whipping wind carried his words to Nora's ear. "And I've got something for you—straight from Dublin."

Seamus managed a small smile. "At last."

Colin's companions also dismounted, and as soon as they removed their caps Nora recognized two of Colin's younger brothers, who had grown tremendously since she had seen them last. The fourth rider was a stranger to her, but it was apparent that the boys were all closely acquainted. Nora guessed he must be a fellow member of the Gaelic League, and that Seamus knew him from the meetings that he sneaked out each Sunday afternoon to attend. She knew in her heart that this group embodied the "wild streak" that coursed through her Cullen veins and that she should avoid them; but these boys and their dreams sparked in her an energy and a passion that she could not ignore. Their dreams were hers—they were dreams of freedom.

"Nora," said Colin. "It's been a long time." He smiled at her and winked, but it didn't feel sincere to her. There was something different about him that she couldn't quite put to words.

"Silas Smith," the fourth rider said. He lifted his summer cap slightly off his head, and the wind blew his red hair all about his face.

"Nora McMahon."

Silas laughed as he replaced his cap and brushed the hair from his eyes. "I know who you are. Seamus has mentioned his little sister more than a few times."

Nora folded her arms across her chest and furrowed her brow. *Little sister?* "He's not a day older than me. He could be younger for all I know!"

Colin appeared to suppress a laugh. "She raises a good point, Seamus," he said. "She could be a few minutes older than you." He patted his chestnut horse and released it to graze on the moss that grew along the path.

"If she's older than me, maybe she should grow a little bit," Seamus teased.

"How come you never bring Nora to the Gaelic League?" asked Silas. He, too, led his gelding over to the moss. The horse eagerly teethed at the greens, causing foam to form around the bit.

"'Cause she's a girl," said Seamus. "And I've never seen you bring yer sister."

Colin interrupted. "Eh, that doesn't matter," he said. "A rebel is a rebel, plain and simple." Nora smiled. *Some things don't change—even after a year away*, she thought. *He still sticks up for me.*

"She'd be lost. Doesn't have the wild streak," said Seamus.

"Fook she doesn't," said Colin. "She's a Cullen—despite yer Grandda's attempts to hide it. You all have it runnin' through yer veins red as blood."

Colin changed the subject. "Where's the ol' man? He'll want to hear our news too. It concerns us all."

When neither Nora nor Seamus moved to fetch their grandfather, Colin asked, "He found out about the League, didn't he?" He grinned. "All he needs is another generation of rebels under 'is roof. Is he speaking to you?"

"No," Nora heard her brother say. She cringed. Each time her grandfather's demise was voiced aloud, it felt like a knife reopening a wound. "He's dead."

Colin's grin fled, and he straightened himself awkwardly, as if shaking off his inebriation. For the first time, he looked Nora in the eye and held her gaze. Clearly he was in disbelief. Everyone had been. Her grandfather had been an old man, but his strength and stubbornness had tricked everyone into believing that there was nothing he couldn't conquer—death included.

The three looked from one to another, but none of them spoke. Colin's brothers stared into the stony pathway and kicked a few stones about.

The sound of a parcel hitting the ground caught Nora's attention. A paper package had dropped from Colin's waistband. It was a curious, small bundle tied with butcher's string. She instinctively bent to retrieve it, but Colin quickly reached out his hand to stop her. His touch felt cold and distant and not as she remembered.

Seamus swooped down and grabbed it. He clutched it to his chest and looked at Colin with a mischievous smile.

She tried to steal Colin's attention back. "What's yer news, Colin?"

Colin's little brother piped up. His voice still sounded like that of a child, though he had grown tall and broad like his older brother since Nora had seen him last. "Some important heir in the Balkans was killed by a terrorist. Shot in the throat right next to his wife. Some place called Sarajevo. It's all the talk around Ennis these days, but news never spreads fast to the likes of Ballynote."

Colin nodded. "Aye, 'tis true. The word in Dublin is that there's going to be a war and there's nothing those blokes in London can do to stop it."

CHAPTER 2

July 24, 1914: London, England

"There can be no war. There can be NO WAR!" Viscount Eldridge boomed.

Edward rolled his eyes and tried to bite his tongue. When his father couldn't make a logical argument, he inevitably just shouted. He managed to keep quiet only for a moment. "Typical of you to shy away from adventure," Edward said, looking down at his brightly adorned captain's tunic, polishing a gleaming button with his white gloves, then nodding in satisfaction. "It's just like you to shy away from our responsibility," he added, in a tone that he knew would cut to his father's core. He was pushing the limit, but he had grown tired of listening to his father's circle and their thoughts on foreign affairs. Though he was just twenty-five, he and his friends prided themselves on having political acumen their fathers had either long forgotten or never attained.

"As we speak, the Kaiser is preparing an army for mobilization. So is Franz Josef! Even the Tsar has an army primed for orders! And you would have us sit here on our hands and watch it unfold. Thankfully, our fleet is exercising. At least Churchill is taking responsible action!" As he made this point, he could hear the laughter of his younger sisters enter through the open window. The light summer curtains blew gently in the wind, billowing out as if filled with the girls' delighted shrieks. He was irritated at their timing. Had the air not been ringing with their girlish play, he was certain his argument would have resonated with his father. He raised his voice to compete.

"Father, we have a chance to be a part of something—England has made a promise to protect Belgium! This is a calling your silly dinner parties and balls certainly do not satisfy." He tossed back his crop of thick brown hair. Exasperated, he added, "If I have to dance with another Lord's homely daughter pining for a husband I think I will explode!" He could hear his youngest sister, Agnes, squeal in delight. Why was he the only one who felt so impatient with life in the Eldridge household?

"A few days on any front, and you yourself will be pining for homely dancing partners and silly parties!" Viscount Eldridge snapped. A painful look swept over his father's face, and Edward found himself holding his tongue to see if it was a bout of indigestion or if his father meant to continue the insult.

The Viscount took advantage of Edward's hesitation. "Do you know how excruciating it is to watch my firstborn son—and heir to my good name—echo the insanity being argued at Westminster? If a war is what you want, look to the Irish—there's a call to arms! Anything to rid that island of its bloody papists!"

Edward had returned to polishing his buttons and did not give his father the courtesy of making eye contact with him. He slouched in his chair and hoped his father noticed. "I'd rather not lead my men into a fight against their own brothers."

"I fear for any men led by the likes of you!" his father bellowed. "Gerald—now there's a boy with a good head on his shoulders. No pining for war—though he would serve if called. You could give your younger brother a positive example for once—perhaps forbearance!"

Edward did not expect his father would be so cruel. Usually the viscount found more subtle ways to express his preference for his younger son. For Edward, the sounds of the girls playing was becoming too much against the tension building in the parlor. He stood in a brazen display he knew his father would interpret as insolence. At well over six feet and with a broad and muscular build, he towered over his short and rather rotund father. His height and thick hair sharply contrasted his father's physique, and Edward took some comfort that he in no way resembled the man.

Though never a picture of health, today Viscount Eldridge's pale complexion appeared rather purple as he raged. The usual perspiration pooled along his balding forehead. But what his father lacked in physical presence, he made up for in impeccable dress. Though his waistline expanded year after year, his tailors kept pace with his girth and supplied him with ever-larger shirts and trousers, all in the latest—and most expensive—fashion. Even in his crisp new uniform, Edward was dismayed that he still felt underdressed.

As he stood, his father took notice and raised an eyebrow. Edward hadn't the courage to walk out on him, and he felt a twinge of inadequacy because he knew that his brother would have. Gerald innately knew how to react to every situation—when to back down, when to stand up for himself. And he was constantly praised for his keen reading of all social situations. Edward never could seem to find his balance.

The viscount must have sensed Edward's indecisiveness and delivered another blow. "You have had every opportunity to become a man of consequence. You have lived a life unimaginable in any other time in history—the best education in Europe delivered to you by poets and philosophers of pedigree! In the summer—only leisure and parties! And how do you repay me for this upbringing? I wonder if perhaps an encounter with the Kaiser's army could drill some sense into you!" The perspiration began to trickle down the sides of his face and cling to his fashionably trimmed sideburns. His mouth, parched from a few hours' respite from his beloved scotch, retained small specks of froth.

"We'll be lucky if you stand your ground long enough to get one shot off at the Kaiser's men!" his father hissed. "Besides, it is certainly premature to be talking of a war! The gun smoke has barely cleared from the assassination. The best outcome is a resolution that tames the Balkans without igniting the Tsar. Yes," he added thoughtfully, "that would be a best-case scenario. And as for your Belgians, I could not care less! The war we need to fight is to our west, not the east!"

Edward dejectedly watched his father storm from the room. He had waited too long to make his own dramatic exit, and now it was too late to make the lasting impression he had wanted. He lowered his eyes as his father walked past him and into the parlor to depart for his cabinet meeting. His ears still attuned to his father's words, he hoped to detect a hint of remorse in the viscount's voice, but instead he heard him deliver his parting shot.

"Talk of military action on the continent at a time when we lack a Secretary of War due to idiotic Irish mutinies and, not to mention, our own government is divided. How preposterous!" His father spied the morning edition of *The Times* on an end table and snatched it up, then turned back to his son. "God help us if war comes, because if you return, you will return to a different world. Even with victory, there will be no certainties."

With that, Viscount Eldridge walked briskly through the door to the parlor and called for his butler. When the gaunt old steward arrived in the parlor, the viscount did not look up from *The Times,* which he clutched tightly in his chubby hands, but simply stated, "Francis, please summon a carriage! I mean to depart in fifteen minutes for Parliament. Tell the driver that there is no need to wait in Westminster for me, as I expect the meetings will last well into the evening."

Francis politely dropped his head and said, "As you wish, sir." The few remaining hairs combed over the butler's balding head dropped across his brow, and he flicked them back into place, smoothing them across his freckled scalp. As he exited the room, the wayward strands bounced up and down with his gait as if waving good-bye.

Hearing his father order the carriage, Edward immediately left the salon via the opposite door and began to climb the back staircase. He wanted to get away from his father, away from the joyful sounds of the girls playing, and away from thoughts of his brother's charm. He wondered if there was no longer any comfort to be found in his own home.

He walked past his father's prized bust of Admiral Lord Nelson, who had presided over the upstairs hall for at least two decades, and entered the large set of doors to his bedroom suite. He began removing the layers of his new uniform and laid them on the chaise for the servants to press and hang in the armoire.

His mother had commissioned an artist to complete three paintings of him in his dress uniform before he left for training. The sittings had thus far been dull and had kept him from several social engagements, but he knew his mother was proud of him, and he wanted to please her. He had seen the first painting—a young officer in regimental dress with a stern look on his face and a stare that seemed to focus somewhere far in the distance. The artist had captured the uniform well, but the man depicted had looked like a stranger to him.

When I return a war hero, he thought to himself, *Mother'll remember that Gerald is not her only son!* He chose a fresh day suit and stood in front of the mirror. It fit him well, and he nodded in satisfaction. *And when I am a decorated officer—over to Ireland to solve the problems there. Even Father couldn't disapprove of me then.*

Pleased at these thoughts, Edward bounded down the stairs and called for Francis. He was eager to get on with his afternoon plans without his father taking notice. Although he was bored by the summer schedule his mother painstakingly scripted for him—afternoon tea with preapproved daughters of parliamentarians, attending cricket matches, tennis, lectures in philosophy and law—he found ways to amend the schedule to make his activities more appealing. He traded tea and tennis for rowdy sessions of scotch and politics with boys and wide-eyed young ladies too curious and vivacious to make his mother's list. It helped him to pass the time but was decidedly unhelpful in achieving the goal his mother had set out for him—to find a suitable wife among the eligible aristocracy.

His choice in the matter—a beautiful girl called Elizabeth with a refreshing mischievous streak—was notably absent from his mother's list. If he was his brother, he could simply saunter into the parlor with a confident manner and congenial personality and announce his choice to a chorus of praise from his parents. But he was not Gerald. He did not have the heart to tell his mother or the courage to tell his father, and so had decided to convince his family to decide that Elizabeth was *their* choice before they learned of his secret romance.

Elizabeth's mother was American. That was not a disqualifier—it was in vogue to have a foreign relative, and it made for the type of pretentious conversation that his mother loved to be a part of. It was instead Elizabeth's father who posed the gravest threat to Edward's plans. Lord Philip Clarendon was a boisterous peer in the House of Lords, known for frequent outbursts. But his real sin was his wholehearted support for a war on the continent while petitioning for peace with Ireland, specifically via a vote in favor of Home Rule. Politics put Lord Clarendon squarely at odds with Edward's father. The two could politely oppose each other in Parliamentary debates but engaged in vitriolic exchanges when not governed by protocol. It was no secret that the two men despised each other.

Everything about Elizabeth that made her interesting also made her forbidden. She had inherited her mother's odd Yankee manners and her father's crazy politics. Edward found this intriguing and strangely alluring. He attributed her mischievous nature to her unique pedigree. She was tall—almost as tall as he was—which made her stand out among the mostly petite and trim ladies of society, but which also added to her an overwhelming presence.

She had long brown hair that was cut in layers and gave the appearance of a waterfall when she wore it down. And when she wore it up, it accentuated her sharp jaw and long neckline. She was, undeniably, one of the most beautiful young ladies in London. Women were snooty toward her—perhaps because she was educated in America and scoffed at the stuffy London attitudes—but men couldn't keep their eyes off her, which Edward had to admit, only increased his desire. He longed for the day when he could walk down the streets of London, his arm in hers, and revel as she caught the eyes of other men. For now, their liaison was only known to their mutual circle of friends, and only when they stole away could he put his arms around her and feel as though she was truly his and his alone.

Edward's carriage rattled toward Lord Gibbons's Grayside residence—a member of Parliament whom his father could get along with—to the weekly book club formed by his eldest son, James Gibbons. The purpose of this club had nothing to do with literature, and everything to do with facilitating prohibited liaisons among its participants. As he watched the London streets pass out the coach window, Edward plotted how to devise a meeting between his father and hers in order to secure her an invitation to the Eldridges' early August dinner party.

Each year, the Viscount and Viscountess Eldridge threw themselves a party on their wedding anniversary, and Edward thought that this might be just the atmosphere in which to introduce his parents to Elizabeth. His mother had always placed confidence in coincidence and made difficult decisions based solely on intuition. He hoped to engineer a parallel between the celebration of her thirty years of marriage and the introduction to her future daughter-in-law.

Today the book club was supposed to discuss the poetry of William Butler Yeats. Elizabeth had suggested this lunatic venture, otherwise Edward likely would not have participated. Along with most of his peers, he saw Yeats for what he was—talented indeed, but a dangerous and radical Irishman who promoted a backward Gaelic language and continued to inspire folly among young Irish men, who fantasized of independence from England.

But Yeats's writings mesmerized Elizabeth, who spoke with wonder of childhood trips to the theater in Dublin, where her godparents lived. She had seen the controversial *Cathleen ni Houlihan*, and did not shy away from debates with her peers over Irish politics. Edward attributed her charity toward Irish nationalism as something surely inherited from her American side, and therefore harmless and part of the free spirit that he loved.

He had no intention of discussing Yeats, and instead planned to entice Elizabeth to engage in other free-spirited and forbidden activities in lieu of discussing "the Irish question," as it had come to be known. As he made his way to the Grayside mansion, absorbed in plans to steal off to some dimly lit back room with his sweetheart, the war he coveted was far from his mind, and the world it would destroy was more a part of him than he could possibly imagine.

CHAPTER 3

July 24, 1914: Ballynote, County Clare, Ireland

It was not the raucous Irish wake of generations past, but Nora took comfort in the sight of dozens of her cousins and neighbors getting tipsy enough so that when Seamus got out their grandfather's old fiddle, the cottage came alive with dance and song. She and Seamus had no food to offer, yet the cottage teemed with dishes brought from as far as Ennis. Summer pies bursting with berries and sugar pastries like Nora had never seen filled their kitchen, and the smells of cinnamon and nutmeg evoked memories of holidays on Inis Cathaigh. Each guest brought his own make of whiskey, and the sounds of the clinking filled the room as friends and relatives toasted the late Eamonn McMahon. The light from the fire shone off the brass flasks as they were passed from guest to guest. Nora couldn't help but wish that the Irish had wakes for the living instead of the dead. Her grandfather would have loved this party.

Throughout the evening, she kept one eye on Colin. For a few years at least, his flask had been his constant companion, tucked into his waistband so that his right hip protruded slightly. He often absentmindedly rested his left hand on it, as though he were in a duel and readying himself to draw. Countless childhood hours at Mass had shaped his politics and inculcated the requisite guilt and fear for his everlasting salvation, but the clergy had never managed to beat the left-handedness out of him.

Every minute or two, he flipped his unkempt blond hair out of his eyes with a quick nod, then brought the drink to his lips with the bedeviled hand. Seamus shared a swig between repeated performances of the only jig he knew until the whiskey was gone. When the flask was empty, they commandeered Silas's stock, leaving him annoyed and sober. Such was the fate of slow drinkers.

The women spent the evening trying to steal Nora away for private conversation, but she was not interested in their small talk. Trivial discussions of the hardships of motherhood and marriage were boring, but this night they were trying to outline her future, which was worse. Predictably, they seemed to believe the mere suggestion that she should immediately settle down and marry would convince her. It seemed everyone was interested in her becoming just as miserable as they appeared to be. "Every one knows what happens to orphans in Clare," they warned. If her choices were a hasty marriage to their choice of a local boy or the dangers of being young, single, and poor—she would happily take her chances with the latter.

As much as she kept an eye toward Colin, when some well-meaning neighbor didn't corner her to strike up a conversation about husbands, she also kept an ear toward her brother and his constant talk of politics. She knew he was up to something, but as much as she tried to pick up information as she bustled around the cottage waiting on their guests, he must have known she was listening and tempered his conversation while she was within earshot.

She caught Colin's eye twice but made no conversation. Each time, he hung onto her glance for a brief moment before diverting his eyes and feigning interest in the discussions going on around him. She felt his silence like a pang in her chest. It created a great curiosity inside of her. What had transpired in the previous year that made him so detached?

She was used to being the center of his attention. Perhaps he saw her differently now that he had grown accustomed to city life. Whatever Dublin life was like, it had stripped him of his playfulness; he walked about as if an invisible chain hung around his neck. Her only comfort was that when their eyes met, she felt the same energy that she always had, and from the way his cheeks flushed when he looked away, he must have as well. Just why he wouldn't hold onto her gaze remained a mystery. What was he keeping from her?

As the evening wore on, Nora became acutely aware that guests would soon depart. Suddenly afraid of the silence that would follow, she scurried about the cottage offering guests more and more food and drink in an attempt to force them to stay. Perhaps some would spend the night, keeping her company as she stood a silent watch until daybreak, when she would have to say her final good-bye to her grandfather.

Just as she felt her powers to keep her guests engaged wane, there was a soft and raspy knock at the open door of the cottage. It sounded as though a tree had reached out with its branches to scratch against the door. But in the place of a bough stood an old, stooped man dressed entirely in black. Nora was oddly unsettled at the sight of him. He looked as old and as tired as Ireland herself, though his white beard could not hide the last stubborn red strands from his long-ago youth. Nora had never seen him before. With his long black coat and loose black pants that could not hide an emaciated frame, he certainly looked dressed for a funeral.

Seamus, now the man of the house, walked over to the door. With their grandfather's fiddle in one hand, he reached out with his other to greet the stranger. "Evenin' to you." He had none of Nora's reservations.

"Evenin'," said the stranger, tipping his cap.

When he said no more, Seamus continued, "I do believe you've got the wrong funeral."

The stranger dipped his head inside the cottage. "I fear I've got the right one. I saw the light from yer cottage and heard the music and knew I was happenin' upon an old-fashioned Irish wake. I wanted to stop and pay me respects. I pray the deceased not be the great Eamonn McMahon."

The chatter from the room began to die down, and eyes cast over to the corpse, still laid out in the small bedroom. When Seamus only cast his eyes downward, the stranger crossed himself and bowed his head. "God rest 'im."

"Aye, God rest 'im," said Seamus.

"You look to be the man of the house. And a lot like the last man of this house. God rest 'im, too. Might I come in?" asked the stranger.

"Of course you can," said Seamus. The old man appeared gaunt and tired. Seamus couldn't deny him the comfort of a warm cottage brimming with delightful food. "You knew my da?"

"Aye, in another time I knew him well," the man answered. A certain sadness clouded his voice.

Seamus gave the old man a genuine smile. "A wake is nothin' but a party in disguise. And all are invited. Especially if you knew me da."

As the old man entered the room, Nora could immediately see the hardness of his skin, like a hide exposed to the elements for too long. The light from the candles scattered about the cottage and cast shadows on the stranger's stark facial features, making him look as though he, too, were not long for this world.

All of a sudden, a young cousin broke the silence, crying out, "I know who you are! I've seen you before! You're the traveling storyteller that comes about every once in a while."

Nora's heart leapt. "A storyteller? Not possible," someone said. "There hasn't been a storyteller in these parts in fifty years!"

Her grandfather had told her about these men. They were legends throughout rural Ireland, and every once in a while someone claimed to have seen one, but never had she seen any proof they still existed. And this one claimed to have known her father.

"I've been known to tell a story or two," the stranger said. His voice was that of an old man, but still clear and deep.

The discussion among the guests had all but stopped as eyes focused on the thin old man dressed entirely in black. "For a bite to eat and a night's rest I might share a tale or two with you," offered the man. "Seems we've got the requisite crowd already assembled." He twisted his old black hat in his hands. "And I believe we know that the deceased himself would have enjoyed a good story."

Seamus gave Nora a sly grin. How could they resist such an offer? "Sounds reasonable to me," he said judiciously, though he clearly thought that only one night's stay was quite a bargain in exchange for some entertainment.

I would have let him stay a week! Nora thought. Her suspicion of their new guest had vanished.

The room erupted in applause as the old man slowly looked around for just the right perch, finally making his way to a corner of the hearth near the fire. Nora quickly found a chair for him by tipping one occupied by her ten year-old cousin, jettisoning him to the ground. She brought the storyteller some water in a cracked glass.

"Have you anything a wee bit...stronger?" he asked, to the delight of the guests. Nora blushed. Several guests immediately reached out with flasks for the old man to take.

"Well," he said, "the generosity here is such that I may stay two nights!" The guests again were delighted and began to settle in on the floor and table— anywhere they could in the small, crowded cottage—to hear what the storyteller had to say.

Nora sighed with relief. The guests were now captivated and would not be leaving anytime soon. She'd get a reprieve from the looming solitude after all. Renewing her waitressing with vigor, she ensured that the guests had ample to drink as they settled in for a story.

The storyteller accepted sips from the flasks that had been handed his way, slowly tasting each and smacking his lips as if he relished the burn the alcohol left in his mouth. "Yes, perhaps two nights," he repeated as he swirled the contents of one flask.

For several moments, he looked about the cabin at the faces of each of the guests settled in for a tale, almost as if looking for someone in particular. "What shall we hear tonight?" he finally asked, to no one in particular, though he spoke in a way that allowed each member of the audience to feel as though he was speaking to him or her alone. He let the question go unanswered. The room dripped with an eager silence. When the old man seemed certain that he had trapped his audience under his spell, he continued.

"Shall we hear of Saint Patrick and the exodus of the serpent from Ireland?" There were no replies as the guests looked at each other to see if anyone would speak up. You've heard that one, I see," he said. "How about the origin of the Cliffs of Moher? That's always a good one." Again, no one responded.

His eyes settled on Seamus for a long moment, and he said, "No, no. Those won't do tonight." Nora felt his gaze shift to her. She could feel her heart beat inside her chest.

"There's another story that needs to be told. One of mourning, but also of passion and fire and fate." Nora could feel her cheeks burning as he continued to eye her. "A story of Ireland herself," he said in a whisper. "Her past and her destiny and the ways in which they are intricately connected." He broke his stare and again surveyed the room. It seemed like a full minute passed in silence until he spoke again. "Did you know that there are living guardians of this transition—the transition between history and future?" No one spoke, and the storyteller said, "Yes indeed. Yes indeed."

Keeping his voice at a whisper to invite the guests in closer, he said, "And there is one here tonight who is a keeper of this destiny."

The guests looked at one another. The adults were grinning, awaiting the entertainment of the story, but the children were mesmerized, looking around the room to see if they could identify this so-called guardian.

"I have met a few such people in my lifetime," the old man said, "scattered across this land by the wind. Seeds disbursed by storms and gales but also by soft summer breezes—the ones that fall gently through open windows on July nights just like these." His words rolled from his tongue in rhythmic phrases with an accent that was not of Clare or Cork or even Dublin, nor up to Galway. It was an accent of ages past that even the oldest among them could not recognize.

"These guardians hold within them the memories of days gone by, protecting them and nurturing them until the day comes when the future must inherit the past." He took a swig of whiskey from the flask still perched next to him. The light from the fire flickered across his pale cheeks and reflected is his soft eyes. "It takes a peculiar person to bridge the past and the future, one who seems to understand events before they even come to pass. They are ordained by fate itself."

He looked around the audience. "And who is it among you? How will you recognize such a person, how will you know? Is it you?" he said, looking at a small boy, whose eyes were large and wide. "Perhaps it is you?" He pointed at Nora's little cousin. "But I will advise you all, pray that it not be you," he added ominously. "Because the journey to guard the past and reveal the future is dangerous—deadly, even."

The guests looked around, relishing the excellent entertainment. "Almost always deadly," he said quietly, allowing curiosity to build. "Because giving rise to the future can require great personal risk." He took a sip from a nearby flask. Nora couldn't help but notice that their storyteller was again focused intently on her twin brother.

"And how does one inherit this burden?" he asked. "How does it pass from one to another so that the past and the destiny are protected? So that they will eventually meet? We will find out. But first, we must go back almost a thousand years to the time of Pope Adrian IV."

Scowls emerged on several faces, and the eyes of the storyteller flashed. The light from the flames made them shine. "So you know of him? Good!" he said. His gaunt cheeks turned upward and pulled his mouth into a smile. "Because this is precisely where our story begins!"

Nora, satisfied that her guests were content, at last settled in to listen to the storyteller. To her surprise, Colin sat down beside her. Even in the old days, when they saw each other frequently, he rarely got close to her unless they were alone. And even then, he was a gentleman, though Nora suspected this was inspired mostly by a combination of his unwavering fear of mortal sins and his knowledge that she was not as concerned by them. She eyed him curiously, until, to her relief, he finally returned a longer gaze. He retained some features of the boy she'd known, but in so many ways he had changed. His voice was deep and his shoulders strong. His clothes were no longer comically loose—he had grown up. She wished that sitting next to him were as natural as it had ever been, and that time had not stolen away her childhood love and turned him into a man she didn't know. He nudged her with his elbow in a playful way, and Nora surmised that he must have felt a distance between them too.

"It's almost like yer grandda planned this entertainment for us," he said. He brushed his hair from his face and brought his flask to his lips. She could smell the whiskey on him. As much as she hated the smell on Seamus, she loved it on Colin. It reminded her of the adventures they used to share. "Perhaps it's his parting gift to us," he said.

It was known for many miles that Eamonn McMahon had had a knack for storytelling. There was something about the old Irishmen who nurtured old Irish traditions. As they aged a combination of memory and history flowed from them to others by way of mesmerizing stories. Some tales were more embellished than others, but all carried a core of truth.

"Pope Adrian IV!" The storyteller's voice cut through the tiny earthen cottage and stole Nora's focus away from Colin. "The only English-born pope that Rome has ever seen. A popular fellow," he continued, but winked dramatically to convey more than a hint of sarcasm to his audience. The guests seemed relieved to learn that the storyteller thought no more highly of the infamous pope than they did.

"And in the time of Adrian, there was a great fear of the rogue nature of the Irish Catholic, or so Rome called us. We weren't inclined to adhere to doctrine when for centuries we had practiced a religion that connected a passion for Christ with a passion for the land around us. And why not? Is the land we stand upon not in itself a gift from God to be honored and loved?" He let the question hang over his audience long enough to see them begin to nod in agreement and continued with his story. "We were rebels!" he said, and a large, toothy smile emerged across his face. "Still are," he said, and winked, to cheers from the crowd.

He held up his hand, and the room quickly became silent. "But the Catholics of Ireland could not be controlled by Rome as other peoples across Europe were, and—as we all know—a deal was struck between Rome and the King. The Normans who had invaded England in the previous century would continue on into Ireland to capture the rogue spirit of the Irish Catholic—and perhaps take large swaths of the most precious land on Earth for the Crown as well."

The guests were already captives of the storyteller and prisoners to the words his ancient voice wove. Even the smallest of children knew of Pope Adrian and what grew into English claims to Irish lands and politics, a legacy that continued to the present. The old man continued. "And in the year 1169, which interestingly was years after the death of Adrian, the Norman Gilbert de Clare entered Ireland on invitation to assist in a local war. Thus began the English conquest of Ireland. And of course, the army of King Henry II followed. This is the history that we all know, that we learn in school."

He paused to take a drink and then wiped his beard with a long black sleeve. In the light of the fire, he looked even more ancient, so that some among the audience began to whisper questions: *Was he from the time of Henry II? Had he even witnessed these events?* Such was the trance he had so quickly woven between the walls of the old cottage on the midsummer night.

"But the history they teach you in school is incomplete," he continued. "You see, in 1169 and under the King of Leinster, who had extended this original invitation, and on the outskirts of modern Dublin, lived a family who had for ages been stewards to the local king, Diarmait Mac Murchada. There was no royalty in their blood, no claim to the heritage of Brian Boru, just a loyalty to the Mac Murchada clan and a peculiar genetic tendency toward red hair. And in this generation, the family consisted of seven sons followed by a single daughter. Atop the heads of each of the seven sons was a crown of hair of the brightest red. Now, we all know that across this island, red hair is plentiful enough; but this red was so deep, it seemed an unnatural color. So red that if you took summer berries and mashed them into a paste, it would not be as red as these sons' hair. And when the mother finally had a daughter after giving birth to seven sons, she was surprised that in addition to having a child of a different gender, the child had hair not the color of the brightest red but of the whitest summer flower."

Nora shot a quick look toward her brother. His white-blond hair glowed in the light from the fire. Again, she could hear her heart beat quickly. He seemed to take no notice that the storyteller was describing hair like his.

"The child was considered an omen of something to come," the storyteller continued, "For why, after seven children with red hair born to parents with red hair whose grandparents had red hair, would there be a child with hair almost as white as snow? But even more peculiar about this child—" he paused, and Nora watched the old man fix his eyes on her brother, then frown. "We'll get to that later," he said, "the peculiarities of this child. Just know that as she grew, it became apparent to all that she was indeed a special girl, perhaps not of this world. She spoke with the wisdom of an ancient monk but approached the world with the energy of a child. She embodied everything that was beautiful about the world around her. She had the peace of the rising sun, the fury of the wild Irish river, and the mystery of the ancient wells that littered the countryside. She was, all at once, the cool summer breeze, the brisk autumn nights, the whitest of the winter snows, and the greenest of the spring meadows. To all around her, it seemed as if she had descended from the lush rolling hills themselves a witness to all they had seen.

"And this youngest daughter with seven older brothers, this girl with the wisdom of ages before, grew to be a beautiful young woman who attracted the attention of all of the young men in the village. She was as beautiful in spirit as she was in features. But despite many suitors who pursued her, she refused to allow her father to meet with any of the families to arrange a marriage. And being his only daughter and such a special child, the father could not disappoint her, so he allowed her to stay unmarried long after her twentieth year.

"And when the armies of Gilbert de Clare arrived in their village seeking quarters, her family was obliged to house the soldiers—because after all, they had come at the behest of the King of Leinster, to whom her family owed much loyalty." The storyteller paused to take a swig of drink, and the audience remained silent, enraptured. Nora again eyed Colin, who stared intently in the direction of the old man. Even he, always skeptical of folklore, had fallen under the spell. The only sounds were the crackling of the fire and the distant barking of dogs.

The storyteller cleared his throat and continued. "The soldiers quartered at the home of the family with seven red-headed sons and one fair-haired daughter for many months. And after some time, the father noticed a change in his daughter. No longer did she wear her ivory locks tied tightly to the back of her head, but instead her long hair cascaded down her back, aglow in the light of the moon. She was indeed breathtakingly beautiful. The father noticed that she stole away during the nights and returned just before daybreak, when the doves began to call their morning songs.

"This behavior continued until the army of Henry II arrived at the outskirts of their village and threatened to oust the soldiers of Gilbert de Clare. When the soldiers quartered in their home left for battle, the ivory-haired daughter disappeared with them.

"The father was beside himself with worry and, being a trusted steward of the King, went directly to him to ask him to intervene, saying, 'My daughter has disappeared with the soldiers that quartered in our home, and she must come home!' For how could a child that was Ireland herself be lured away by a foreign-born soldier who would steal her away from her home?

"The King listened sympathetically, but he was powerless to intervene, for he knew that the daughter had not stolen away for a forbidden romance, but for a much nobler purpose. But he also knew that he could not reveal that purpose to the father, for it would break his heart more than an affair. The secret endangered her very life. As I mentioned before, this daughter with hair as white as the snow had another peculiarity about her."

At this, the storyteller abruptly stopped speaking. At first it seemed as though the guests thought it was part of the performance, but when he did not continue his tale, they began to slowly break out of their trances. A cool breeze floated through the open door and windows of the little cottage. The warmth from the crowded room and the fire in the fireplace seemed to dissipate. Nora felt a chill crawl down her back—a chill that a mere shift in temperature could not inspire. The sound of barking dogs filled the air, followed immediately by the bleating of sheep from the pasture and shrill and eerie laughs from the bridle path.

Seamus leapt from his perch by the table and ran out the door. Silas followed close behind. Colin, seated so close to Nora now that his knees had been waywardly leaning up against hers, jumped to his feet and tore from the cottage after his friends. A murmur of confusion rose from the guests, and the storyteller stood up from his stool. The spell he had spent that past quarter of an hour casting had been abruptly broken.

Nora leapt to her feet and charged toward the hearth. She reached above the fire for a torch, lit it from the embers, and then ran after her brother toward the pasture. The cool July night was alight from the stars, but its beauty was lost on Nora as she raced toward the frenzied sound of the dogs.

She ran up the hill toward the ancient stone fence that corralled their small herd. In the light from the torch, she saw the outlines of three figures stopped outside the fence: Seamus, Colin, and Silas. Slowing, she approached the fence, holding the torch far out in front of her.

29

Then, in horror, she stopped. Where were the sheep? Frantically, she looked toward the far end of the pasture, but it stretched black and empty under the brilliant, starry sky. Her eyes widened. The last of the dogs were scurrying back toward the bridle path, and she recognized them immediately—the dreaded Ainsley dogs, their telltale red-and-white coats vivid in the torchlight. She jumped up onto the top of the fence and hastily made her way along the stones toward the bridle path, trembling at the thought of losing the livestock. But still she saw no sheep, even as the path came into view. She abruptly stopped and reversed course, heading back toward her brother.

"Seamus!" she called. "What are you doing just standing there? We have to go after them! They've stolen our herd!"

Her brother stood still, as though made of the same stone as the old fence. Colin slowly brought his left hand to his face and held it there, and she knew he was emptying his flask.

"Seamus!" she screamed again, agitated at his inaction. "Seamus!" Her voice cut into the night.

"Look down, Nora," Colin said softly—too quietly for the panic she felt. Holding her torch high, she peered down into the pasture from atop the fence. At first she saw nothing, but as her eyes adjusted, the torchlight revealed dozens of small mounds scattered about the field. She moved the torch from out in front of her face, and the light of the rising moon reflected off the white-coated mounds. The bodies of their sheep lay strewn about exactly where each had fallen. She gasped, but let no other sound escape. She watched as Colin, the moonlight silhouetting his tall figure, climbed over the fence and walked up to one of the warm carcasses. He put his hand to the body, and when he stood up again his hand was red with the blood that still drained from a gaping wound. Nora heard the voice of her brother from behind her. "Mauled," he said. "Those fookin' dogs."

A silence hung between the four, and Nora was vaguely aware that the rest of the guests had flooded from the cottage and were making their way up the hill. She looked behind her and saw their storyteller, stone faced, his ancient sad eyes fixed on her.

"No," came a voice, soft and steady, but laced with fire and anger. It was Colin. "The bastards slit their throats."

CHAPTER 4

July 24, 1914: London, England

Edward's carriage pulled up into the drive at Grayside just in time for afternoon tea. He checked his gold pocket watch; it read precisely four o'clock. He held it in his hand as the carriage navigated the bumpy drive. The golden chain bounced along with the carriage wheels, the precious metal soft in his palm, until the delicate links slipped between his open fingers and into his lap. It was a beautiful gold watch, passed down from his grandfather upon Edward's graduation from Oxford. His grandfather's initials were engraved on the backside, and Edward had recently had a jeweler engrave his own initials below the original ones. EABE, for Edward Albert Burke Eldridge, the future Viscount Eldridge.

His mother was a Burke, and all his siblings carried her maiden name as a middle name—a common naming convention. Albert, the name of which he was most proud, was after Prince Albert himself, who had been a close friend of his paternal grandfather. A Lord Eldridge had sat in Parliament for centuries, many befriended by various monarchs, but his grandfather the Viscount Eldridge had been especially close to the Prince Consort, so many male cousins in the Eldridge line bore the name Albert.

The name Edward, of course, came from the current Viscount Eldridge, his father. But the younger Edward disdained the name as he disdained the man, and had instructed everyone to call him Albert instead, so great was his wish to distance himself from his father. To his dismay, only his younger brother Gerald had taken up the habit, and then only to annoy him with the moniker "Big Al."

The crusade for "Albert" came to a quick halt when Edward had met Elizabeth. She had been dressed in blue when he first met her—"Alice blue," she called it, after a hue worn by President Roosevelt's eldest daughter. Though Roosevelt was out of office, the Alice blue craze continued all across America, particularly in the wealthy New York enclaves. Edward, for one, couldn't have cared less about Alice Roosevelt, but he admired how that pale blue dress shimmered and made Elizabeth's gray eyes glow.

When he finally mustered the courage to ask her to dance, he had told her, "Call me Albert," at which, she had laughed in a loud and most unladylike Yankee way. The ballroom had looked up from their scotch and politics to identify the source of the snorts, but Edward, in his trance, had only seen the way the Alice blue silk rippled when she laughed, how the light from the chandelier shone on the fabric as they waltzed across the dance floor, so that the dress fell like a brilliant waterfall on a bright summer morning.

"I simply cannot call you Albert," she had said, between bouts of laughter. "You see, my father has a horse named Albert, and I assure you, he is poor company." She wiped a tear from her face. "Quite gassy, if you know what I mean."

At this, Edward also laughed. "I do," he said. After that, all mention of Albert had died, though his brother Gerald, quite amused with himself, refused to abandon "Big Al".

The driver pulled up to the carriage entrance and pulled the horses to an abrupt halt. "Shall I wait or return for you later, sir?"

"I do not know when my engagement will end, and therefore will require you to wait," he replied, quickly slipping out of the carriage. He strode toward the door already held open by the butler, who welcomed him in, handing his top hat and coat to another servant tending the foyer, and then showed him to the library where other guests had already gathered.

As he rendered the requisite polite greetings to the other members of the group, all of whom had ostensibly gathered to discuss the works of W.B. Yeats, Edward's eyes immediately focused on Elizabeth. She was wearing a stylish yellow dress that flattered her figure, and his eyes couldn't help being drawn to the long lines of her neck as they descended to soft shoulders cupped by a lace trim that emphasized the forbidden parts it was meant to cover.

As usual, he found her radiant, and she returned his smile as he entered the room. Tea was quickly served, and the servants retreated to other duties. Free of the watchful eye of the older generation and their spies, the upcoming society members breathed easily and settled quickly into casual conversation about anything but Yeats.

Edward had come to talk politics, but to his dismay, society gossip monopolized the conversation. As a group, the children of aristocracy proved to be a reckless generation, who threw the formalities of their upbringing to the wind in search of adventure and vice. As such, their behavior was constantly butting up against scandal, to their collective delight and to the chagrin of their parents, who were helpless to control their children's behavior but intent on corralling it.

Jane, the second daughter of Lord Fitzherbert, sat between Elizabeth and Edward. Most of her vibrant red hair was pulled back tightly into a bun as if to give off heirs of propriety, but several locks had been purposefully pulled away and allowed to fall in large, loose curls around her face, which suggested that there was a more impish side to Jane Fitzherbert. She took on her usual role as a lady in the know with exuberance as she relayed the exploits of her older sister,

Beatrice.

"As you know," Jane began, holding her audience captive as they anticipated the latest gossip, "Beatrice is approaching an undesirable age. For years Mother has paced at night wondering whether or not Beatrice will ever find a gentleman that meets her tastes. And it just so happened that last week, Beatrice asked me to chaperone an encounter with the son of the German ambassador!"

"A German?" asked Elizabeth with a flash in her eye. "Perhaps Beatrice is more daring than we've given her credit for!"

Beatrice had been a frequent topic of conversation at their weekly meetings, mostly because Jane was eager to become engaged to Lord Charlton, son of the Earl of Monmouth. Custom dictated that Jane's engagement be delayed until the engagement of the eldest Fitzherbert daughter, and the group had long speculated in jest that Jane herself might reach an "undesirable age" long before her sister found a husband.

"Sounds like a scandal in the making," added Elizabeth. "With the prospect of war with Germany, a forbidden relationship is quite daring indeed. But what you haven't considered," she added with a smile, "is that war might separate Beatrice from the only potential suitor she's ever had, leaving you destined to be an old maid."

Edward sighed. Elizabeth loved to egg Jane on. He rolled his eyes and begrudgingly participated. "Well, perhaps old, but definitively not a maid," he said, much to the delight of the group.

After smoothing her dress and brushing a loose lock of hair from her face with only a hint of embarrassment, Jane retorted, "Well, I find myself in good company among this gathering, I dare say." And then she added, with an exaggerated glare at Edward, "And let those without transgression cast the first stone!"

Not fazed in the least, Jane then fell back into her story, as if remembering that she had not conveyed all of her gossip. "The outing had some promise, but for the most part was quite boring," she said. "I did my best to linger far ahead of them as they wandered through Hyde Park—you know—to allow as much illicit behavior a possible," she added with a smile. "But of course, all Beatrice was interested in was talking politics. From what I could tell, she was more keen on discovering information about the prospects of a German-Austrian alliance in a war with Serbia than she was on discovering the prospects of a German hand up her skirt!" The group laughed, and she smiled in apparent satisfaction.

Edward shot a glance toward Elizabeth. She had been exposed to intense political discussions her entire life, but she seemed happy to eschew politics entirely when away from her parents. He knew it was probably impossible for her to avoid the tension that political discussions brought to her household, with her father a member of the House of Lords and her mother the daughter of an American senator. But what Edward recognized and others did not was that Elizabeth's society antics were a game to her, and she found the other high society ladies dull and superficial. Though she laughed at Jane's antics, Elizabeth was, when not in the company of her female peers, profoundly serious about current world events.

It was Edward who broke the laughter, using the German ambassador's son as an excuse to launch a more serious topic. "Tell me, Jane," he started, "Did your sister's German have anything to say about Kaiser Wilhelm's likeliness to provide military support to Austria?"

Jane rolled her eyes. "Of course you would only be interested in the war," she sighed.

Elizabeth glared at him. He wasn't expecting this.

Meanwhile, Jane was prattling on. "Don't you know, Edward, that I have more serious things to worry about, such as my prospects for becoming the next Lady Charlton! Nevertheless, he did say something about his father being in Berlin for a series of political engagements, but that they would return soon and perhaps then he would have a chance to escort Beatrice to a diplomatic function."

"This makes sense," said Edward thoughtfully. "The Kaiser just embarked on a cruise in the North Sea, but not before meeting with his diplomats, and, perhaps more importantly, the Austrian ambassador to Berlin." He shot a glance toward Elizabeth to see if she appeared impressed with his sophisticated knowledge of the Kaiser's comings and goings, but she still appeared annoyed. Why was she so loath to discuss such consequential events?

He tried harder. "Many in London would be keenly interested to know what was said at those engagements before Wilhelm departed. The future of Europe likely rests on the decisions made."

"When do you think the ambassador's son will return, Jane?" Elizabeth interjected. But the conversation had moved on.

"How do you know this?" James asked Edward, ignoring Elizabeth's question to Jane. "About the Kaiser?" He had entered into the conversation now that it had moved on from Beatrice's marital status and taken a more interesting turn. He removed his glasses and placed them gently on the cherry wood table next to him. Without his glasses James's dark eyes appeared much smaller, a look that was exacerbated by his constant squinting. Next to his glasses lay a gold-embossed copy of the works of W.B. Yeats, which by now James likely understood would remain unopened.

"I assume parlor conversations have become much more interesting these days," James continued, brushing his dark brown hair to the side of his face. He grew his hair long on the top and had a habit of brushing it to one side and then the next, which resulted in the hair on top of his head perpetually sticking straight up, not knowing which part to follow. "My father is loathe to share anything with me, most likely because he doesn't want to explain his pacifism."

"Agreed, James," echoed Edward. "My father leads the 'Little Englanders' in shying away from any conflict. It certainly makes it difficult to engage in any rational conversation with him."

"From what I've heard," added Jane, reluctantly moving the conversation past her own troubles, "talk of war is premature. My father believes the Austrians will not provoke a military conflict. It is no secret that Franz Josef was not fond of his nephew, and especially deplored the Duchess of Hohenberg." Edward saw movement from Elizabeth's chair as she fidgeted with her hands. The glare had left her face and she instead seemed suddenly attuned to the conversation. "Why would he start a war over their untimely deaths?" Jane blathered on. "He certainly prefers the new heir!"

Edward watched with delight as Elizabeth finally entered the fray. Jane's lack of understanding of a world that so affected her had pushed to over the edge.

"Jane, it's a matter of principle for the Austrians. The heir to the throne was murdered! Their entire empire rests on Austria's ability to control the Balkans—a folly they continue to pursue." Elizabeth shook her head. Though she tried to hide her dismay at her friend's cursory understanding of the topic, Edward detected she was not entirely successful in managing her tone. "It's an assault on Franz Josef's empire—its very sovereignty, as he sees it. Mark my word; Franz Josef will go to war. And soon—before summer's end."

Edward smiled. This was the Elizabeth he had come here to see. "I believe the lady is correct," he said, eyeing her coyly. "The Austrians, misguided as they are, will declare war, and Europe will become quickly entangled. And I couldn't be happier at the prospect."

"And that's where I disagree, Edward," Elizabeth snapped, to his surprise. He hadn't expected that she would turn on him, too. "Austria will not show restraint, and there will be consequences, this I recognize. But I certainly don't welcome a war. It will be a war that England will not be able to avoid."

Edward pondered this point. He had certainly heard it often enough. "It will take Europe no time to defuse the violence," he said. He felt like he was preparing to repeat the discussion he had just had with his father. "It will be a quick, decisive victory and will settle the passions of the Balkans once and for all," he replied, adding, "And likely will subdue German imperialism at the same time." He was sure that a girl as bright as Elizabeth would recognize the opportunities that war would provide.

"And if it is not decided quickly, my dear Edward," she replied, "are you happy to sacrifice your youth and the world we know for a world we cannot predict? Would you die for this? Would you wish any one of our friends dead for this cause?"

An uncomfortable silence fell over the room. For the first time, the idea of a tangible cost to his coveted war struck Edward. He had certainly considered that some men would be killed, but in his mind they had been faces with no names, generic men with no identities. They certainly hadn't been anyone he knew or loved. "I am happy to fight for a noble cause," he finally replied.

He pursed his lips and locked eyes with Elizabeth, trying to glean from her stubborn gaze what she was thinking. Her big gray eyes were expressive but gave him no hints. Jane's red curls lay still around her face as she looked from Edward to Elizabeth. James nervously parted and reparted his hair. But none of the four spoke. After a moment, Edward smiled and then reached for his tea, if only to alleviate the tension that was building in the room.

CHAPTER 5

July 24, 1914: London, England

The conversation quickly turned back to the more trivial and less controversial happenings of London society, but the idea of war still weighed heavily on Elizabeth's mind. She knew that when war came, Edward and all of her brothers would immediately be called to join their units. Edward and James—and her brothers for that matter—saw war as an adventure. Although she had always sought adventure, she was cautious about welcoming a war she knew no one would be able to control.

Before long, the Grayside Book Club meeting began to go its separate ways, never having once mentioned any literary works. The meeting's disintegration was hastened by James's decision to break out scotch and cigars when they had exhausted all new society gossip and talk of war became too gloomy. Elizabeth knew her father would detest the idea that she smoked, particularly something as vile and unladylike as a cigar. When James left to escort Lady Jane to her awaiting carriage, Elizabeth found herself in the library with only Edward

"Elizabeth," Edward said softly, so that the retreating party would not hear, "Would you join me in the garden for a walk?"

"Are you going to try to convince me that I should support your war?" she asked. She tried to sound playful but couldn't mask the somberness in her voice.

"Nothing of the sort," he said. "We needn't discuss politics at all."

"Well then, my answer is no," she said, finally capturing a playful tone. "Politics is the only thing I wish to discuss with you."

Edward raised an eyebrow and she knew she had confused him. "I just don't want you to go into the discussion thinking you can convince me. I don't want to waste your time." she clarified.

"No time with you is ever wasted," he replied.

She rolled her eyes at his predictable response. "You must know by now that your high society manners have no effect on me. After spending all those years in America, I can see right through your etiquette." She took the ends of her hair in her hands and slowly paced the room as she absentmindedly played with her hair. Through the floor-length windows, she could see that the day was slowly beginning its transition to evening. Another day was coming to an end, and nothing had been done to slow the march to war. She could feel with her whole being that her time with Edward was coming to a close.

"Do you mean to tell me there are no gentlemen left in New York?" Edward woke her from her thoughts with a playful jibe.

"There are gentlemen," she said, "but they give ladies the courtesy of telling them the truth. They are driven by different motivations than the English."

"All men are driven by the same motivations, whether they are English or American or even German," said Edward. "That, my dear, should be obvious to you."

She let go of her hair and put her hands on her hips. The orange rays of light that filled the room cast shadows across the wood panels along each wall. The shadows contorted Edward's face and made him look much older than he was, and more sophisticated. She thought it made him look even more handsome. "I meant that American gentlemen aren't bound by the same trappings as English gentlemen," she said, recovering from her momentary distraction. "They have no titles to inherit, no entitlement to position in society. And so they have more freedom—freedom to vote their conscience, freedom to have an unpopular opinion, freedom to speak their minds."

When he didn't speak right away, she knew that she had overwhelmed him with the pace of her speech. She could always score points quickly in any discussion with her quick Yankee tongue. Not giving him the opportunity to organize points for his own argument, she continued.

"But so far as motivation goes, if you are speaking of pride, of ego, of power—and of women, for that matter—you are right, Edward," she said. "Men all have the same motivation. Which is why we are sure to be at war within the month."

Though they remained deadlocked in a quasi-argument, quasi-debate, they stepped out together onto the veranda. It was a beautiful summer evening, awash in orange streaks of sunset and filled with the calls of birds across the gardens.

"It's unfair," said Elizabeth soberly. "Our days, our lives are so serene. A few hundred miles to the east, war is about to break out. Thousands face a looming destruction. And to our west, Ireland is a tinderbox waiting to ignite. It has been for generations with no change. No hope for better. It's no different today than it was when my poor cousin in Dublin was forced to put down that violent uprising in the south. And yet—" she put her arm around Edward's waist and rested her hand on his hip. "Look at that beautiful horizon. There is nothing but a peaceful and rich future that awaits us, if only we weren't so foolish as to disturb it. What others wouldn't give to view this horizon, to participate in this future that is ours for the taking." She leaned into him and closed her eyes so she could force herself to remember what it felt like to be next to him. How straight he stood, how he smelled of French cologne, how the bristle of his whiskers felt against her cheek. She knew he would be leaving London soon. She saw no way to avoid the war that was coming.

"You don't think we deserve it?" he asked. "Our families for generations have worked to build this life, have served our country, have sacrificed on her behalf. Isn't it part of our inheritance?"

Opening her eyes, she felt a twinge of sadness. There were some things about Edward that she could never quite reconcile. The fact that he felt entitled by the mere fact of his aristocratic birth was particularly difficult for her. Though it did not diminish the love she felt for him, it left her wondering if, when years from now their youthful love no longer distracted them from each other's quirks, she wouldn't resent this trait. "The world is changing, Edward," she said. "We will inherit the future we make, not the one that others carved for us. And—" she couldn't help herself. "—the service of our parents doesn't entitle us to anything."

He wrapped his arm around her as well. "Sometimes I wonder if you aren't a full-blooded American, my darling."

"Interesting," she said, trying to insert some playful banter into their otherwise serious conversation. "I know for sure that you are entirely English," she said. "There is no doubt in my mind. And yet I love you still."

"Why?" he asked.

Without hesitation, she looked up at him. "Because you aren't perfect," she said. "And you don't try to be."

"How odd," he said. "I love you for precisely the opposite reason. Because you are perfect."

She frowned, pretending to be annoyed at his comment, but at the same time it almost took her breath away. "That sounds like something an American boy would say," she said.

"How would you know?" he asked, and he sounded not entirely in jest.

She released him and walked slowly down the steps of the veranda. She looked over her shoulder, and he followed. When they reached the back lawn, they looked to the residence to ensure they hadn't caught any attention from within the mansion. She grabbed his hand. "Come on," she said, and they ran for the cover of the gardens, which were in full summer bloom.

The summer sun lasted well into the evening in July, so they had no hope of hiding among the shadows of the greenery as they might have during the autumn, when London's high latitude held the sunset at bay until late in the evening. Still, she led him to a row of trees where they might steal some privacy.

She pulled him quickly behind a large cypress tree and looked once more toward the residence. All seemed quiet. Some of the rooms were being lit even though the sun remained strong. The fragrant scent of the conifer reminded her of the garden parties she had attended as a child, and she allowed Edward to wrap her in his arms. She felt too tall around most men, but not Edward. He had strong, broad shoulders that made her feel small when he held her close to him—which she relished. His body pressed hard against hers, and for a brief moment, her eyes locked with his. Their faces were only inches apart, and when he hesitated, she slowly brought her lips to his in a soft kiss. There was something so alluring about a forbidden kiss, even one with familiar lips. He leaned into her, taking the kiss as an invitation for another. After a moment, she put her hands on his chest and ever so slightly pushed him away.

"More to drink?" he asked with a smile.

She stifled a laugh. "No thank you. I have more serious business with you tonight."

"More serious?" he inquired, looking at her quizzically.

She leaned up against the tree and slid down to a seated position. Once on the ground, she removed her shoes. "I hate these things," she said, tossing them aside. Her pretty yellow dress was soon covered in the needles that littered the ground. Almost everyone she knew would have been alarmed by what she knew were gauche manners, and though she knew Edward noticed, she loved that he didn't care.

"Do all American girls run around with no shoes?" he asked her. He knelt but didn't sit on the ground with her.

"All half-American girls do," she said.

"Which half tells you to do that?" he asked and smiled.

"The smart half," she replied. "The half that thinks shoes should facilitate motion and not inhibit it."

She motioned for him to sit with her, but he shook his head. "What's your serious business?" he asked. "If it is removing more articles of clothing, I suppose I can participate."

"I want to know your true thoughts on whether or not England will go to war," she said.

He sighed. "I get to be with you alone for two minutes, and this is what you want to do?"

She nodded.

He sighed again. "We had all afternoon to discuss such things, and all you wanted to do was incite Jane. You are crazy."

She threw her head back and laughed, not in the ladylike way that Jane seemed to have mastered, but loudly and fully, though she knew that everyone except Edward found it to be unfitting.

"Why do you do that in their company—laughing and carrying on about silly trivial things when I know you to be much more serious about such things?"

She shook her head. "To keep myself from going even crazier than you already think I am," she said. "It makes the world and its current state bearable. If you spend all day analyzing this or that, it all becomes so heavy. This life—the parties, the gossip, the matchmaking—it's just an escape, don't you know that?

He rose to his feet and stood thoughtfully for a moment, then relented and sat next to her, first clearing a spot among the needles and debris beneath the tree. She moved toward him and he ran his hands through her curls, seeming to gather his thoughts. "I think our prospects for war are decent," he said finally. "We have alliances and promises that I believe we must maintain. It remains to be seen how Parliament will uphold those promises, but I believe that we cannot avoid a conflict if France becomes involved."

He kissed her forehead in an absent-minded way. She loved how natural it was to be with him when they could escape all the rules. It felt freeing, and she couldn't help but think about how much easier life had been when she was in America. Edward continued going through his thoughts aloud. "If France can stay neutral, however, I find it difficult to believe King George will involve our military."

"So we have to hope France stays neutral," she said, pensively. "And what of Germany? Would they commit to defend the Austrian empire?"

He suddenly stopped stroking her hair, as if he had had an epiphany. "That remains the question. The question that everyone wants to know the answer to. But why are you asking me, instead of your father? Surely he knows as much as anyone," Edward said.

"I've asked him," Elizabeth said. "But I value your thoughts as well."

"And what does your father say?"

"That we must defend those who can't defend themselves," she replied. "He's right in the thick of it—begging for a war. But oddly enough, he wants war on behalf of the Serbs, who just want their own freedom, or potentially the Belgians, who stand to be overrun. It's the same reason he supports Home Rule for the Irish. I guess that makes him quite unique in Westminster."

"None of this is good news for me," said Edward.

"I know," Elizabeth replied. "You'll be going to war."

Edward laughed. "That's not why. It's much more complicated than that."

Elizabeth leaned back into the tree and pushed her bare feet through the needles along the ground. Small sensations like this reminded her that life didn't need to be so difficult.

Edward continued his thought. "If your father is begging for war on the continent and peace in Ireland, I've no chance of convincing my own father to take him on as an in-law. There's nothing my father despises more than the Irish."

The idea that her father's unpopular position on the Irish question could affect her relationship with Edward hadn't occurred to her. "Perhaps he will find me charming despite my father's political leanings," she replied in jest. "Though some of them are my views as well." She emphasized this to remind Edward that she, too, had a soft spot for Ireland.

"I shall agree to disagree with you on both Germany and Ireland, because I find you so otherwise enticing," Edward said, smiling. "But you can keep trying to convince me about your Irish…there must be some reason why you find that place so enchanting. And as for my father, there's no doubt he will find you charming, my darling. A man with a beating heart could not help but find you charming. But this may be a game better staged for our mothers."

"I agree," she said. "If we leave this to our fathers, the only chance we'll have to be together is if we run away."

"They'll find us," he said.

"We could go to America," she said.

"Are there any viscounts in America?" he asked.

"Not a one," she said. This thought made her oddly happy, but Edward was unable to hide his frown even to please her. She stood and began to clean the needles from her dress. They had been away from the manor for too long. Someone would be sure to notice they were missing.

"Can we agree to try our mothers before trying anything drastic?" he said, as he rose to his feet. He spoke in a lighthearted way, but Elizabeth knew that he was quite serious. Edward would be indescribably out of place in America.

He turned her again so she faced him, and this time he brought his lips to hers. As he caressed her cheek she felt his hands to fall to the body of her dress.

She playfully backed away. "Surely you must know that I won't fall for your charms so easily."

He visibly sighed. "No, I didn't think so," he said.

She smiled at him—a smile that she hoped said that she wanted to stay, but knew they should be headed back.

"No one is expecting us," he said, as if trying to lure her mind away from wherever it had wandered. His eyes looked up into the canopy of trees. "Privacy like this is nearly impossible to find."

His words sounded ominous. How many more chances would they have to be alone together before he left London? "I know," she said, eyeing the veranda through the trees. "But Father said he would be home by nine o'clock. I need to know what was discussed today in the House of Lords. It's not every day that England debates a war."

Wanting to let him know that she still wanted to be near him, she took his hand. "Do I bore you?" she asked.

"No, Elizabeth," he said as they emerged from behind the trees. "I'll take you just as you are." Then he added, "your crazy politics and all."

As they walked slowly up the ornate steps to the veranda, Elizabeth looked up at the ivy that adorned the outer brick walls and saw silhouettes in the library. She didn't care what others thought of her, but she knew that if they were spotted, her illicit activities could get back to her father.

Edward sensed her hesitation to continue climbing the stairs and said softly, "Don't worry, my darling, I've planned ahead." He laid his hand one last time around the curve of her back and gently kissed her cheek as he guided her up the stairs.

As they reached the top stair, James's outline came into view, along with a smaller figure that Elizabeth immediately recognized as Emily, James's fifteen-year old sister, who looked pleased to have been invited to facilitate mischief. Elizabeth breathed a sigh of relief and was grateful for Edward and James's discretion at having another lady present. James and Emily escorted their guests to the parlor, where a servant assisted Elizabeth into her shawl and another had Edward's coat and hat in hand.

Elizabeth's coach pulled up, and she bade good night to James and Emily and looked at Edward for a brief second before adding, "It was a pleasure to see you again, Edward."

"The pleasure was all mine, Lady Elizabeth" he responded, and it was such a predictable response from any student of the formalized education they had all endured, that Elizabeth silently mouthed the same response in unison, and Emily burst into a giggle. Before she could stifle it, a footman was assisting Elizabeth into her carriage.

CHAPTER 6

July 24, 1914: London, England

Francis was unloading his father's carriage in the stable as Edward came up the drive. The gas lamps in the parlor and adjoining sitting room cast light through the embellished windows and heavy Parisian drapes and shone onto the drive. Even before he entered the residence, he heard his father's booming voice echoing into the yard and his mother's soft and even replies inserting calm into the viscount's outbursts.

Edward walked into the parlor, his footprints steady and rhythmic across the stone floors. His younger brother and sisters stood just outside the partially closed door to the sitting room, peering inside. Agnes put a finger to her lips, motioning him to be quiet. Playfully, he took exaggerated tiptoe steps, and she smiled. She was just seven years old—certainly too young for the conversations taking place—but eager to feel a part of the adult world.

As they listened to their father's shouting, for a brief moment Edward pondered the little girl, blond hair in plaits, holding a handmade doll fashioned to look like her. The image of a delicate child in her summer nightgown contrasted strangely with the coarse cries of his father, which told Edward that Europe had taken a step toward war.

For the first time, he realized that his sister's youth would be entirely shaped by the decisions made in the days to come, and he might be gazing for the last time upon the remnants of the innocent childhood she would leave behind. In this moment, he grasped what she stood to lose if the war that came was not quick and decisive. He swept her up into his arms and held her as he and his other siblings listened to his father's rant.

"And despite the overwhelming sentiment among peers," boomed the viscount, "we may not be able to avoid this monster after all!"

Edward took a deep breath, partially in trepidation, but also in elation that his predictions had been correct.

"Last evening, those two-faced Austrian diplomats who have deceived us for the better part of a month, issued a decree, nay, an *ultimatum* to Serbia, that simply emasculates the nation. The Serbs will never adhere!" Heavy footfalls suggested that the viscount was pacing about the sitting room, unaware that his four children sat just outside in the parlor, listening intently and passing nervous, excited glances among one another.

"Now, darling, all is not lost—" she began.

"Not lost?" He shrieked so loudly that Edward thought little Agnes would start to cry. "My dear! The stated purpose of this decree, according to the Austrians, is 'to beat Serbia to death'—the Austrian minister used those exact words to Grey this very day. And poor Sir Edward is at a loss, and it is a rare day indeed that I hold any sympathy for the man. But what is he to do? The middle ground he sought has disappeared before his very eyes, and with it perhaps the entire government! We are teetering to avoid a schism at best, without the prospect of a war! And those scoundrels, led by that imbecile Lord Clarendon, are probably just giddy with themselves and the opportunity for conflict. Mark my word—" his father's voice quieted, and a chill ran up Edward's spine. "Lord Clarendon" was Elizabeth's father. "England will be forced to take a side," his father continued. "We will be at war before summer's end."

A long pause ensued, and Edward pressed his ear to the door to glean why the conversation had suddenly stopped. He heard his mother's voice. "If you had told me a month ago that we would be at war by summer's end" she said, sounding weary and reserved, "I would have certainly assumed you meant a war with Ireland. How quickly events can turn," she concluded. Edward peered around the door in time to see his mother dab her eyes with her handkerchief. "And to make matters worse," she added, with no attempt to mask her vanity, "the mood at our anniversary party will be quite dull this year. What a shame!"

Edward could practically hear his father roll his eyes, but he felt no sympathy for him. His father had spent years encouraging his mother not to concern herself with the stresses of politics and had robbed her of the sensitivity to fully comprehend the turmoil that was about to encompass her dear England.

As the conversation in the sitting room began to wind down, and the viscount could be heard pouring himself a glass of scotch, Edward motioned for his siblings to quietly ascend the back staircase to the chambers on the second floor. Gerald, just two years his junior, led the group, followed by his fifteen-year-old sister, Anna. As always, Gerald looked disheveled. His brown hair went every which way, he sported a three-day old beard, and his shoes were scuffed and worn. Even still, to Edward's dismay, he was extremely popular in all social circles and had a charm with women that was unmatched.

Edward went last up the stairs, still carrying little Agnes. She had a lone tear falling down her cheek, but she did not move to wipe it away, nor did others follow it. He wondered just how much she understood. He squeezed her tightly.

When they reached the top of the staircase, Gerald leaned on the marble bust of Admiral Lord Nelson that had stood as the centerpiece of the hallway for longer than any of them could remember and turned toward Edward. "Does this mean you will be off to join your unit, Big Al?" he asked excitedly. Lord Nelson tottered on his mahogany wood stand under the strain of Gerald's weight. Gerald could do few things calmly. In this way, he reminded Edward of their mother. It was this constant exuberance and energy that made him so damned likeable. His brother's annoyingly attractive face was practically bursting with excitement.

But Agnes's plump face had gone white. "But surely you wouldn't go to a war, would you Edward?"

Edward shot Gerald a stern look then turned back to Agnes. "Don't worry, my sweet," he said. "No one is going anywhere right now. Father was just upset. He will be better in the morning. Let's get you ready for bed."

He passed Agnes to Anna. He wasn't certain if Agnes believed him, but by the look on Anna's face, he knew entirely that Anna understood his lie. When the girls had entered the back chamber, he turned to Gerald. "For a Cambridge man, you are quite dull," he said. "What's the meaning of scaring the girls?"

"I thought you would be excited," he said, his hand slapping Nelson on the shoulder.

"I am," Edward replied. "In fact, I've never felt so excited in my life. I hope to be ordered to my unit immediately. Well, immediately after Mother's ball, that is." He paused, reminded of his afternoon with Elizabeth. The war that he felt so surely was coming was inconveniently timed.

Edward looked to Lord Nelson, who appeared less and less stable on his stand as Gerald became more fidgety. He took a step back, not wanting to get blamed for the old admiral's demise if his brother got any more excited. His father loved that ridiculous bust.

"On a different matter entirely, Gerald, what do you think are the prospects of getting Mother and Father to agree to an engagement with Lord Clarendon's daughter?"

"Father's least favorite member of Parliament?" asked Gerald. In an unexpected bout of luck for the admiral, Gerald threw both of his hands into the air, significantly reducing the risk of Nelson crashing to the floor. "The man who wants war with Europe but peace with Ireland? What an odd fellow, but what a beautiful daughter." Gerald said. He scratched his unkempt brown hair, then his three-day old scruff, both of which somehow managed to look exceptionally good on Gerald while such grooming habits barely passed as "slovenly" for everyone else. "Although I must say, she's a bit odd as well, particularly if she fancies you." Gerald added.

Edward refused to show any sign of offense in an attempt to keep his brother's teasing at bay.

"I'd say your chances are nil," Gerald continued with a tone of sympathy that Edward knew was sincere. "You'd probably have better luck trying to marry a German."

"You may be right," Edward answered gloomily. As he thought, he looked back toward Nelson, whom Gerald had once again enlisted as prop to lean on. "And that's why I'm going to need your assistance," Edward said.

"My assistance? What can I do?" Edward could see the spark in his brother's eye. He had to be careful about how he described the task to Gerald, lest his brother proceed with a little too much enthusiasm and sink the entire effort.

"I need you to convince Mother. Father cannot say no to her. And she cannot say no to you."

"I still think you should start looking for a fräulein to fall in love with. Your chances are better, Big Al," Gerald said. He turned to the statue. "Even Nelson looks incredulous" Edward studied the cold, white bust and couldn't disagree. The sculptor had done an exquisite job of capturing a look of eternal skepticism, though Edward was not sure this had been his aim. For better or for worse, the hero Admiral Lord Nelson existed in the second floor of the Eldridge mansion in a perpetual state of doubt.

"But you'll help?"

Edward cringed as his little brother smacked him hard on the shoulder.

Any onlooker would have assumed it was Gerald who was the older, wiser brother. "Al," he said, a wide smile plastered on his too-handsome face, "you've come to the right place."

CHAPTER 7

July 25, 1914: Inis Cathaigh, County Clare, Ireland

Nora closed her eyes and let the rocking of the boat move her body back and forth with the rhythm of the lapping waves. Water from the River Shannon continually splashed into the boat and soaked through her faded yellow dress, pooling at the bottom of the boat and dampening her shoes. As the old leather soaked in the water, they seemed to shrink around her feet, reminding her how they didn't quite fit. She could feel her toes pushing hard up against the edge of the shoes. Most days she preferred to forgo footwear, but wore her best for this occasion. The water felt cold against her skin, and goose bumps formed along the backs of her upper arms and legs. Even on a summer's day, the breeze from the ocean was uncomfortably cold.

She was sitting backward in the boat, watching as the shores of Ballynote slowly became smaller and the distance between her and those familiar rocks lengthened. The events of the previous night were swirling in her head. They had no hope of any sympathy for the loss of their herd—as the major landowner in Ballynote, the Crook was the defacto judge and jury for any disputes, and Nora imagined that he was probably reveling in the ruin he had caused. But while she was in despair at losing the sheep, it was the old storyteller who occupied her thoughts. He never had finished his tale.

She found herself recounting his words over and over in her head: *And there is one here tonight who is a keeper of this destiny.* Was it just a story? Had he said what he said merely for effect, or had he meant it? And why had he seemed fixated on Seamus?

Her brother sat facing her with one hand on their grandfather's coffin, as if to steady it in the rocking boat. Apart from the pilot, they were the only souls on board. The loneliness of the journey seemed overwhelming. Was it a premonition of things to come? The old wooden steamboat creaked as the pilot steered it directly into the waves. The wood beams were permanently soaked from years of rainy journeys across the Shannon.

Seamus also appeared to be lost in thought. His soft blond hair was almost white, just like the girl from the story. But there was nothing remarkable about him. He had fair blue eyes to match his ivory hair and, like Nora, bore a smattering of freckles across his face. He looked just like any old Ballynote farm boy.

She wondered what he was thinking about—pleasant memories of this voyage, or more sorrowful ones? While she had no memory of bringing her parents' bodies to the abbey, she knew her brother did. He had spoken about it from time to time when they were children, whenever something about the air or the weather or the sounds of the water triggered the memory. Though she could not recall that river voyage, she did distinctly remember standing in the cemetery outside Senan's abbey and watching as dirt was thrown onto the simple wooden coffins that held her parents' bodies. She recalled the abrupt splattering noise the soil made as each shovelful hit the wood, slowly hiding the coffins from her view. In her mind, she could still hear the hymns, the voices of the mourners all but drowned out by the melancholy notes of the recorder—a sound so sorrowful and so joyful all at the same time.

These were the sounds of Ireland—they played the memories of her youth and tied her so inextricably to this misty, green, stony, rain-soaked island. She could imagine no future for herself outside of Ireland, and it distressed her to think that with the loss of their herd, she might have lost control over her future. She was at the whims of fate and luck, wherever they brought her. And she knew enough about "Irish luck" to be fearful.

What was the supposed "luck of the Irish," anyway? Was it her grandfather's painful and untimely death? Their sheep and only source of livelihood slaughtered by the Crook? Perhaps it was the Irish luck that had driven so many of the Irish to risk the voyage across the Atlantic in hopes of a better life.

As if sensing her thoughts, Seamus suddenly opened his eyes. "Nora," he said, "we've both got to leave Ballynote."

She nodded. This was the stark truth: with no sheep and no money, they could not stay on the farm. She heard Seamus take a deep breath. "And I think you should go to Boston." His voice seemed distant, as if it were coming from miles away. The sound of the wind and crashing waves nearly drowned out her brother's words, but Nora knew that was not the only reason his voice sounded so detached. He was already distancing himself from this place, and this was his plea for Nora to follow him. His words made her angry, though she didn't quite know why.

"You will have a warm home and can find a job. Maybe even finish school," he offered. His voice still sounded small against the whipping wind. "Grandda would have wanted you to go," he continued, though he must have known he was making no headway with his stubborn sister.

"That is a lie and you know it, Seamus!" she shouted. She was certain that her words were not lost amid the wind and waves. While it was true that Eamonn McMahon had offered many times throughout Nora's childhood to pay her passage to Boston to live with her McMahon cousins, each time she had refused, and each time he had accepted that refusal. He would never have forced her to go. "Grandda knew that me heart is here in Ireland. I can't imagine bein' anywhere else," she said.

"Aye," said Seamus. The wind blew his cap off his head and he caught it and tucked it under his arm. His hair whipped across his face. "But things are different now," he said, yelling to be heard.

"I can work a field as well as any man," Nora said. "I can find a job, we'll not starve—"

"I'm not just worried about you starvin', Nora," Seamus cut her off. "Don't you see?" he said, softening his tone. "I'm worried that you won't have a life that makes you happy."

"Since when have you cared about that?" she asked, still letting her stubbornness get the better of her.

"Come now, Nora," he said. "I'm yer brother and might be a perpetual pain in yer arse, but I still care about you. Sometimes, anyways."

Nora wouldn't let herself smile at this peace offering.

"I don't want to see you married off to some boy you don't love because we are poor and Catholic and you need to in order to survive," Seamus continued. "And I don't want you to raise poor children who will struggle for land and freedom and who have no chance of a better future. We have to break this cycle, and by God, America might just be the way to do it."

"I'd rather be poor and in good company than be Irish and in America," Nora said. She looked up at the gray sky. Small rays of light broke through the gray sky, shining onto small swaths of the river and making the water appear a brilliant blue green.

"Do you ever think about how we got to be this way?" asked Seamus. "Everyone in Clare and all across these parts have always been Catholic, but surely we weren't always all poor. We are ruled by a government in a faraway capital that stole our land just to rent it back to us. We are prisoners in our own homes, in our own country."

"But it is *our* country," she said. "It doesn't have to be this way!" Over the sound of the wind and waves she could hear gulls squawking in the distance, but above their little boat, only doves darted silently about under the low cloud layer.

"Precisely! We deserve better. But don't think that Americans don't understand our troubles! They've lived this as well, and they shed themselves of London! Maybe they can teach us something."

"Seamus, we need you here," she said. She tried to make her voice sound grownup, but she feared it came across as pleading. He would never respond to that. Instead, he closed his eyes, hands still firmly clinging to the coffin, resting on his argument as if it were all-convincing.

The waves had intensified during their heated discussion and had spilled onto the floor of the boat, soaking their shoes and leaving the bottom of the craft covered in several inches of water.

"You know, Seamus," she said, swirling her feet in the water and making her own small ripples, "Not so long ago, Grandda asked me if I would not like to go to Boston to live with our cousins. 'Twas the year we lost our potato crop. And I was frightened that we wouldn't make it, and even guilty that I was a third mouth to feed. But I told him that everythin' around me was what made up me home. It isn't a full belly that makes home, but it is the fields and the clouds, the mist and the hills. And even the relentless rain. I love the smell of the spring when it finally comes to Ballynote; I love the breeze from the Shannon in the summer. And, Christ, I even love the cursed, bitter winters. I told him he could send me away but my heart would always be here."

"And what did he say?" Seamus asked, his eyes still closed.

"He said my love of this place was a blessing and a curse. A blessing because my soul had found its home on earth, and not all souls can be so lucky. But then he said it was a curse because if I were ever to wander, I would feel an ache that could not be satisfied."

Seamus opened his eyes. "I'll tell you about an ache that can't be satisfied," he said. "Try an empty stomach after a hard day's work and a government in London dinin' on the finest the world has to offer while working their arses off to deny the same to the Irish. That's an ache that can't be satisfied!"

He again closed his eyes, then snidely added, "I wish to God Grandda had asked me if I wanted to go to America! I wouldn't be on this creaky boat with empty pockets, a four-day old corpse, and a pasture full of rottin' sheep carcasses!" The gulls continue their incessant calls over the waves.

"You can't leave, Seamus," Nora implored. "Ireland needs you!"

"Fook it does," he replied. "There are plenty of other poor farmers to rot away in Clare."

Nora felt her heart sink. "But what if you are the one?" she asked, immediately regretting broaching this subject with her brother. But the idea had weighed on her all night, ever since their storyteller had left them in the field with their sheep.

"What one?" asked Seamus.

"The one," she replied. "The guardian. Your hair is light and all the rest of us have red hair. And the storyteller couldn't take his eyes off you last night."

Her words hung between them until Seamus let out a loud laugh. "Shite, Nora, that's just a fookin' story! There are no guardians. There's only cursed Irish luck! If I'm a guardian, then you might as well be the Queen!"

Nora felt her anger return. She turned and stared out at the river. The clouds had crowded out the rays of sun, and the deep green water appeared almost gray with the dismal misty morning. How could a summer day feel so cold? She made up her mind that no matter what Seamus said or did, she could not leave her beloved island. For the first time, she wondered if perhaps their destinies were not intertwined after all. She had never imagined that they, too, might be separated. Was it fate or the Almighty that wanted so desperately to turn its back on her?

Seamus's hand was still on the coffin. "What really bothers you?" he asked.

She knew this was his attempt at breaking their stalemate, but she returned his gaze, not yet ready to forgive him. "I can read yer sadness, and I know it is more than our bickering." Closing her eyes, she could imagine her grandfather saying the same thing to her, and she felt less angry toward her brother. At once, Seamus seemed a man in her eyes. The events of the past week had forced him to grow up as well.

"I will not abandon Ireland, Seamus," she said. "If we all flee, who will fight for her?"

He looked off in the distance toward the mouth of the Shannon, which opened somewhere in the distance to the vast Atlantic Ocean. So many generations had journeyed across those waters, trading one set of troubles for another. It was the opening to an expanse not visible from their small boat, but out there somewhere nonetheless. Nora sensed that America called him like a Siren he could not force himself to ignore.

"You're doing it again," he said.

"Doing what?"

"Starin' at me with those wild eyes of yers. The way you always do when you are determined. I dare say you share the wild streak as well, Nora McMahon."

The small boat jerked as the pilot ran it onto its landing and turned to his passengers. "Last trip to Ballynote is at half six. Best be on the dock if you aren't wantin' to spend the night.

CHAPTER 8

July 26, 1914: Dublin, Ireland

Michael walked briskly through the quiet Dublin streets. The first rays of daylight were trying to creep across the city but were held at bay by the thick morning fog. It was still cool, yet he wiped a nervous sweat from his brow as he walked to his rendezvous point near Dublin Castle. He had to remind himself to maintain a walk, though many times he mindlessly broke into a jog, only to realize that he would look conspicuous to anyone who might be watching for him.

He passed just a few other pedestrians and kept watch on each out of the corner of his eye as he hurried past. He trusted no one—neither the milkman with his horse and cart, nor the drunkard leaned up against the wall outside the castle. His pocket watch read a quarter past six. He was late, but in all likelihood so was Cian O'Brien, the man he was scheduled to meet.

It had been, after all, a long night. Michael guessed he had traveled ten miles by foot since the previous evening, and probably twice as much by bicycle. His legs were starting to shake from exhaustion and lack of sleep, and he was keenly aware of his growing hunger, yet he felt strangely energized. Careful planning had paid off, and the message he carried was the one that Cian would want to hear—that everything was in place.

He had walked the route past Dublin Castle and toward home hundreds of times in his life, but this time he took side streets and doubled back several times just to make sure that he wasn't being followed. He wanted to be unpredictable. Ordinary soldiers might be predictable, but soldiers in the business of secrets were surreptitious. Or paranoid. He wasn't sure which was more accurate.

It wasn't so much the constabulary officers he hoped to avoid, but other, less obvious, prying eyes. Everything was riding on his ability to keep today's operation from the menacing members of the Ulster Volunteers. He knew that if anyone had tipped off the Ulstermen, they would be on the lookout for a dark-haired and stalky twenty-five year old, running about the streets of Dublin in the telltale dress of a blue-collar Catholic. He had seen his own mug shot, where he had smiled broadly in defiance, and wished he hadn't let his smile reveal his missing incisor. He would be easy to identify.

Certain that no one was trailing him, Michael approached the preestablished meeting place. His destination was a small alley just a few side streets from the castle. It was not busy, and it provided several logical escape routes if they had to flee. The winding streets around the castle would make it easier to evade anyone trying to follow them. He slowed to a halt, and then cautiously and deliberately leaned up against the gas lamppost and lit a cigarette—the signal. He inhaled deeply and held the smoke in his lungs, feeling an immediate, familiar calm, like an old friend returning after being away too long. He spit and took another drag.

The dawn sky was too cloudy to see the sunrise, but light was beginning to scatter across the sky and reveal an eerily gray horizon. Time passed slowly; his cigarette shrank. Never before had Michael felt so empowered, so vital, and so confident that he was driving a changing world. He understood the precarious nature of politics, timing, and chance, and he thought that this time, at last, he and his Irish Volunteers might be aligned with all three.

As the embers of the cigarette drew nearer to his fingers, he briefly considered the possibility that Cian's mission had not been successful. As he was debating whether to light another cigarette or to disappear into the shadows, Michael heard approaching footsteps. A dark figure appeared from one of the small side streets. The long, ambling gait and shuffling boots were unmistakable. "'Mornin' Cian," he said quietly.

"Mornin' to you, Michael." Cian's familiar voice emerged from the darkness. "What news have you?"

Michael pushed himself off from the lamppost and took a final drag on his cigarette. The young men were face to face, and Michael could see that Cian, too, was exhausted from the night's adventures. Dark circles shadowed his fair eyes, replacing the normal smudges of mechanic's grease as the most prominent feature of his gaunt face. He looked much older than his twenty-something years. "The lines are cut."

He saw a wide smile break across Cian's face. "I knew you could do it. As for me," Cian started, "checkpoints are up all the way to Howth and the *Asgard* entered the harbor a few hours ago. She's early."

"Her cargo intact?" asked Michael.

"Aye," said Cian. "She signaled with her flags and then ducked behind the island for cover. She's ready, at our signal."

Michael put out his cigarette with his boot. "The plans are set. The boys know they're drilling, but nothing else. Formations will assemble in both north and south Dublin this morning at exactly half nine. Then the march will begin, and they'll join each other outside the city. It should go off without a hitch, as it'll look just like last week's march, but with twice the amount of men."

"Those Ulster buggers will be too drunk to know anything's up," said Cian.

"Too stupid, you mean. They haven't a brain among the lot of 'em," said

Michael.

"How many of our boys do you expect will show?"

"Almost three thousand total. A fookin' army."

"All right then," said Cian. He reached out for a cigarette, and Michael reluctantly handed him one.

"I've got to do fookin' everything' around here, do I?" he said. "Cut yer telegraph wires, evade the British whores, dole out smokes?"

Cian ignored him and grabbed a match from Michael's breast pocket. "Best be on yer way. I'm headed out to the harbor to organize the offload. A couple of boys will be cyclin' out in the next few hours to ride ahead and direct."

"I'll see you at Howth," said Michael, "and you owe me a smoke."

"Aye, at Howth," replied Cian, "and I don't owe you shite." He disappeared again into the shadows.

Michael counted off a full minute. He looked to the windows above the alley. They were all dark with no signs of movement or candles. His cigarette butt smoldered on the wet ground. With one last look to the room above, he walked off in the opposite direction from which he had come, toward St. Kevin's Church. He soon passed from the wealthier areas surrounding the castle and into the tenements where Dublin's poorer Catholics lived. To an outsider, the differences would have been stark—well-landscaped residences quickly turned into overcrowded, broken-down buildings whose facades were all that remained of a wealthier past. Elaborate buildings, occupied by single families only eighty years earlier, now housed dozens of large families, each in tiny, one-room apartments. But Michael, who had lived his entire life in a world where unimaginable wealth surrounded abject poverty, barely noticed as he passed through the tenements.

ᔥ

Thump-thump…thump-thump…thump-thump. Michael began a mental count of how long he'd been knocking. He looked conspicuous standing on the stoop. "Come on, what are you waitin' for?" he muttered. At forty-five seconds, he backed away from the door. "They'd have no way of knowin'—" he thought aloud, but his own voice in the silence of the morning was unconvincing. An uneasy feeling crept over him.

He heard steps, and the door cracked open. He could not see beyond to know who was there. "Sunrise comes early today," said a soft voice from within the home.

"No earlier than yesterday you little shite!" he said. The door opened wider, and Michael quickly slipped in. A meek face met him on the other side.

"What the fook was that about?" he shouted at the young boy who answered the door.

"Protocol, sir. An' the code word. Just makin' sure—"

"Well make sure with someone else! Every constable in this city knows my mug and would love to have the chance to chat with me! Oh, there's that troublemaker, sittin' on the stoop with nothin' to do but get himself taken in for a good questionin' and a few black eyes!"

"Sorry, Capt'n." The boy's small pale figure shrunk at Michael's scolding.

"Just use yer fookin' brain! Or we'll all get arrested before we have a chance to make any real trouble. Now go and fetch me jacket!"

"Give the boy a break!" A girl of about twenty interrupted and moved in between Michael and the young doorman. "He's just doin' what he was told. And you ain't that important." She flipped her long brown hair away from her face so Michael could see the stern look in her eyes.

The boy took the opportunity to scamper off into another room, presumably after the coat.

"Gettin' in the way of discipline, Molly," Michael said.

"That ain't discipline. Discipline is followin' the rules—Patrick's rules, I might add. You're bein' nothin' but a bully."

Michael rolled his eyes.

"Here, have some coffee," she said. "You've still got work to do today. Here's hopin' somethin' can improve yer mood."

Michael eyed Molly's uniform, a plain drab skirt that signified she was a member of the women's auxiliary. Like all of the nationalists' makeshift uniforms, it was ill fitting. The women's uniforms were all designed as if the lone model had been a teenaged boy. They fell loosely on the shorter and younger girls but hugged the hips of most women so tightly that they left little to the imagination. Molly bustled by him with hips at least twice those of any teenaged boy he knew.

"Hold the coffee then," he said and winked. "Hike up that skirt instead. That'll improve me mood."

She tossed a cup down on the table and poured it to the brim with black coffee. She took no care as she poured, and coffee dripped along the table.

"No sugar?" he pressed.

"Not for you!" Laughing, she went off toward the kitchen. "You always were a dirty bastard Michael, ever since the day I met you!" She pushed the swinging door open with her tray, and Michael watched her hips disappear from sight. The door swung back and forth, revealing and concealing her. It was as if her backside were waving good-bye.

Michael shrugged and sat down. He didn't care that Molly had left him alone. He preferred solitude to the company of anyone who found him uninteresting. The small chair groaned with the weight of his square frame. He breathed in the coffee, which all but drowned the stench of cigarette that lingered on his clothes. The very smell of the coffee alerted his senses and helped him to forget that he hadn't slept in over a day.

The kitchen door began swinging again, and the young boy appeared, this time with Michael's uniform jacket in hand.

"Here you are, Capt'n," he said.

Michael said nothing, but grunted. The boy laid the green uniform jacket on the table and retreated without another word.

"Hardly a fookin' solider," he said to himself as the boy scurried away. He took a long sip of Molly's coffee, then immediately spit it out across the table and his pristine uniform jacket. His lips and tongue burned from the piping hot liquid. More laughter came from the other side of the swinging door: "Do take care!" Molly's voice called. "The coffee is quite hot!"

Michael swore under his breath and took a handkerchief from his tunic pocket. He began to blot the spilled coffee from his uniform jacket. Patches remained dark amid the deep green. He silently fumed.

The kitchen door swung open again. Without taking his eyes off his uniform jacket, Michael said, "Had second thoughts about hikin' up yer skirt, did you?"

The air hung with a silence, but Michael still did not look up.

"Nonsense!" came a familiar voice. "What's mine is yers! I need you to take a look at somethin' anyways. I've got some sort of pain in me arse, you see."

Michael shook his head and clamped his jaw to hold back a smile. "Wasn't suspectin' 'twas you, Timothy. And for the love of all that is holy, leave yer trousers just where they are!"

Timothy McNeill bounded into the room, plopped himself in the chair next to Michael, and did his best to feign disappointment. He was as unkempt as Michael was orderly. Where Michael's dark hair was trimmed and parted neatly down the middle, Timothy's dirty blond hair went every which way. It fell in wispy strands over his eyes, and he frequently blew it out of the way but never cared enough to comb it properly.

"Guess that arse pain will have to wait," he said. He grabbed Michael's scalding coffee and brought it to his lips. "Quite hot," he said. "But nothin' that Dublin's finest can't remedy." He reached into this tunic, produced an unopened bottle of Jameson whiskey, and began whistling to himself. He stopped his song abruptly to listen to the pop of the cork. "A beautiful sound, Michael. Beautiful."

"Kind of like your whistling," said Michael sarcastically.

Timothy resumed his song undeterred and gave himself a generous pour. He swirled the cup to mix the liquids before bringing it back to his lips. "Remedied." He tipped the cup back and drained it.

"Excellent coffee, Molly!" he yelled in the direction of the kitchen.

"Thanks love!" came the reply.

"You really have no way with women, Michael," said Timothy. He blew the hair from his eyes and held his bottle of Jameson up to the light to determine how much was left.

"Says who?"

"Molly Byrne," replied Timothy, now refilling the cup with whiskey alone. "And now every woman she talks to for the rest of the day."

"Eh," said Michael. He brushed his jacket for a final time and stood to put it on. "Can't have them all swoon over me. Just wouldn't be fair." Slipping the jacket on, he adjusted the collar. "Can't help but look sharp, now can I?" he asked.

Timothy stopped his whistling and looked toward his friend. "I dare say Michael, had I a skirt—"

"Fook you," said Michael.

Timothy finished his single malt. "That pain in me arse keeps gettin' worse," he said. "You sure you can't have a look?"

"Are you ready for today?" asked Michael.

"You love to change the subject when it's not going your way, now don't you?"

"I like to focus me mind when I lay all me cards on the table," said Michael. "And today I have laid bare every last card I have."

Timothy rose from his chair and put down his cup. "Now that you've ruined me morning whiskey," he said, "I suppose we can get down to business. I assume all went according to plan last night?"

"Just according to plan," Michael replied. His irritation had dissipated now that the topic had turned to matters of the Volunteers. "I cut the telegraph wires myself. A sight to behold. Made an incredible mess of the lines. Good luck to those constable whores getting any message from the harbor through to Dublin."

"This time tomorrow, we'll be a force to be reckoned with," smiled Timothy. "In the words of Pearse himself, 'the only thing more ridiculous than an Ulsterman with a rifle is a Nationalist without one.'"

"Well then," said Michael, "call us ridiculous no more."

"Still got a job to do," said Timothy.

"Aye," said Michael. "I suggest we head down to the park. Patrick tells me you'll be leadin' a platoon."

"Aye," said Timothy.

"A shame you'll be second fiddle to me again," said Michael. "'Cause I drew an entire company—Company A."

CHAPTER 9

July 26, 1914: Road to Howth, County Dublin, Ireland

A little more than two hours later, Michael stood at the north side of Father Mathew Park and looked out at the gathering crowd. The Volunteers had come out in full force for the Saturday drill. They transformed the half-acre park into a sea of haphazard gray-green uniforms. Most of the Volunteers lacked the resources to purchase a uniform from the designated merchant, but they had outdone themselves in their resourcefulness, commissioning wives and sisters to assemble tunics and trousers that closely matched the prescribed versions. Still, at the sight of this unpolished group of boys and men, Michael had to force the dismay from his mind.

"They've had no professional trainin', Michael," came a loud voice only inches from his ear. "Stop judgin' them."

Michael jumped in surprise. "You know how to sneak up on a man, Timothy," he said. "I'd flatten you if it wasn't such a good skill to have these days." He brushed dust from his green jacket. It was impossible to walk anywhere in this damned city without getting his uniform dirty.

"Don't judge 'em just yet. They've got the best quality you could hope for in a group of disorganized men," continued Timothy. A wind came up across the park and blew the hair out of his eyes.

"And what's that?" asked Michael, looking up from his uniform to the chaos in the park.

"A keen sense of duty to Ireland! You are lookin' so hard for discipline that you can't see the obvious. And," Timothy added, "they'll follow the likes of you anywhere." The wind died down, and Timothy's hair once again covered his eyes. Michael frowned. Just how much could Timothy actually see with his hair always in his face?

"Lookin' like a group of drunkards just expelled from a pub..." said Michael.

"Doesn't matter," said Timothy. "They'll follow you. Just be sure to lead them like you are the one who is sober."

"Sober?" asked Michael.

"Didn't say you had to *be* sober, just that you had to act like it."

"I can do both," said Michael. "But they've got a long way to go."

"Aye, they do," said Timothy. "And that's yer job." He started walking into the park, flipping his head back every couple of steps to get a clearer view of where he was headed.

"And yers!" Michael called to him.

"Fook, I'm just a lowly platoon leader. You've got Company A, remember?" He laughed. "May the luck of the Irish be with you!"

❧

Michael slowly made his way to the forward-most company. "Mornin' Capt'n!" called a small boy. He looked to be no older than twelve.

"Good morning," he replied gruffly. He walked a few paces, then turned back to look at the boy. His pants hung off his skinny body, and his tunic looked like it was made for a much older brother.

The mention of the rank "Captain" had gotten the attention of the nearby men. "Morning' Capt'n!" called a chorus of other voices.

Michael did not reply, but kept his eyes on the boy. "How old are you?"

"Fifteen, Capt'n!"

"Are you sure?" he asked. A light breeze picked up across the park and blew the boy's baggy clothes all about, making his frame look even smaller.

The boy looked confused. "I think so, Capt'n," he said earnestly.

"Does yer da know you are here?"

The boy's eyes momentarily showed a flash of surprise, but then he collected himself. He lowered his voice. "Do you know my da?" he asked. The men around him laughed, and he shrank back sheepishly.

Michael did nothing to hide his annoyance. "Of course I don't know yer da!"

"I want to drill today," the boy recovered. "I can march just like anyone."

"He's better off here than runnin' around the streets causin' trouble!" said an older man.

Michael took two large strides up to the young boy and leaned forward so that he stared him directly in the eye. The boy stood tall and looked back at Michael, daring him to send him home. The two stood there for several seconds before Michael spoke.

"So long as you follow orders, I don't care how old you are." Michael looked out into the crowd that had circled around him. "That goes for each of you!" he said, addressing all the men. "I don't care how old you are or how smart you are so long as you learn discipline and follow orders!"

"Aye, Capt'n," came a chorus.

Michael wiped his brow. It was already stifling hot. He looked to the boy, who had cracked a smile. He frowned, and the boy corrected himself. Michael nodded in approval and walked on to Company A to find his adjutant. Sergeant Brennan was tall and stood with impeccable posture, making him easy to pick out of the crowd.

"Just a few coppers today, Capt'n."

"Aye," replied Michael. He scanned the park. Just as Brennan had said, he saw only a handful of the mounted Dublin Metropolitan police. Their dark blue uniforms stood out among the sea of green in Father Mathew Park. "They'll escort us to the city limits," he said.

His adjutant nodded and walked over a shady spot on the green. "Company A!" he yelled. "Fall in!"

From Brennan's reaction, Michael surmised that even he was in the dark about the day's true mission. The police atop their mounts looked bored while their horses lazily swished flies away with their long tails. They gave no indication they knew what was to come.

Sergeant Brennan finished assembling the company and turned to his commander. Michael strode toward the head of the company to receive his adjutant's report. Corporal Walsh fell in beside him bearing the company colors. Just as with everything else about the Volunteers, the flag was handmade by someone's sister or wife and stitched together with whatever scraps of mismatched fabric and thread could be spared, but it served its purpose.

Company A stood at attention amid the quieting chaos in the park. Within a few minutes, the remaining companies were assembled, and for a moment the park stood quiet. Only the summer breeze ruffling the green uniforms could be heard in the crowd of over a thousand men.

A bugle broke the silence with a piercing sound. Michael turned his head to the right and shouted, "Forward, march!" His company moved forward in step.

He could hear the company commanders behind him issue their orders to march as well, and within minutes, the Volunteers of Dublin North were marching eastward toward the sea. The rhythm of their boots echoed along the streets in a splendid demonstration of might. A small contingent of Volunteer leadership marched ahead of him, but he had a clear view of the route ahead. Behind him, the Volunteers filled the width of the street in a massive parade through the city. He figured that more than a thousand men had assembled, and once joined with the members of Dublin south, their numbers would easily reach two thousand, if not more. Michael was cautious to keep a steady but not grueling pace. It was nine miles to Howth, and the boys were expecting a far shorter excursion.

Precisely at eleven, they met the Volunteers of Dublin South, who had already assembled at the first checkpoint. Michael heard the murmurs from within the company when his men sighted the second regiment, but he made no attempt to quiet them. This change to the usual routine was unexpected, and he was sure that some of the men now understood that today's mission was far more than public relations and drill practice.

"No sign of the Ulstermen," he heard his adjutant mutter. "By now I would have thought they'd be here, throwin' rocks at us."

Michael glared at him, and Sergeant Brennan fell quiet.

"Are you trying to jinx us?" Michael muttered back. He cracked a small smile. "'Tis bad enough we've got Irish luck hauntin' us!"

Along the way, men and women of all ages began to line the streets, and the march took on a parade-like atmosphere. Children, many who were filthy and dressed in rags, lifted green flags and pieces of fabric and cheered. Though it was contrary to discipline, many Volunteers broke rank to shake hands and wave, and Michael begrudgingly allowed the behavior. He knew that the Volunteers desperately needed the public—particularly those from the poorer and most downtrodden sections of town—to be as engaged as possible in the spirit of the cause.

The late morning was hot, despite intermittent summer showers. Michael was grateful when the sea breeze began to roll in as they neared Dublin Harbour. Dublin North's Company A led the thousand-strong formation past their last checkpoint, where two boys in oversized caps pedaled rickety bicycles, cheerily pointing the way down Harbour Road.

Michael saw Cian pedaling ahead with the two boys. Through a break in the tree line, Michael could make out a small yacht just off shore, and he guessed that this must be the *Asgard*. She looked to be approaching the Howth village. Several of the men saw her as well, and one boisterously shouted, "Is she our gunrunner?" Michael took a deep breath as he heard cheers rise among the ranks. Company A had at last figured out what the march was all about.

The men were tired after a nine-mile march, but the adrenaline of realizing they were taking part in an actual operation provided more than enough energy to continue on through. As they neared the east pier in Howth, Cian turned his bicycle around and signaled to Michael, who approached him.

"Well done, Capt'n," said Cian. He looked just as exhausted as he had hours before, when Michael had met him in the alley, but his eyes shone with excitement. "We're right on time," he continued. "Take the three lead companies, and head down the pier with me. We'll need to clear the docks of any tourists or passersby. The rear companies are to guard the entrance to the harbor. No man shall pass through—not civilians, not the authorities. We'll use force if necessary. Let's move out, on the double!" he said to Michael, abandoning the bicycle at the corner of the street. He pointed in the direction of the pier.

§•

The first platoon hastily moved onto the East Pier, shouting, "Make way!" The few tourists and fishermen saw the approaching line of Volunteers and began to exchange nervous glances, but Michael kept his column of men advancing. For a moment, he locked eyes with a fisherman who looked from his nets to the formation, then back to his nets. Finally, in an exasperated motion, he tossed his nets—catch and all—into the water and scurried out of the way just in time to avoid being knocked into the water himself.

The *Asgard* was slipping toward the dock as easily and inconspicuously as vacationers pulling into a quiet fishing town for replenishments. But its hull held Michael's hopes for the future of Ireland. He assembled three platoons of men to meet it with him. As he called out his orders, a troop of young boys approached the pier. He began to motion to his men to shoo them away, but Cian took his arm.

"'Tis no use. Hobson brought them in himself."

"It's not a job for boys," said Michael. He couldn't understand why all the leadership insisted on enlisting everyone and anyone for this work. How could the Ulstermen take them seriously if they couldn't muster more professional ranks?

"Doesn't matter what you think, Michael," said Cian. "These boys are Bulmer's Fianna Eireann kids—he's convinced that these boys will carry the movement long past when you and I are dead from rebellion. You don't want to cross ol' Bulmer Hobson. He makes the trains run on time, and he's callin' the shots today. Try to be on your best behavior."

"Why am I always surrounded by kids?" Michael asked. "We're tryin' to run a militia, not a nursery school!"

"Quit your griping and get to work, Michael," said Cian. "It's not yer call."

"That crazy Bulmer," Michael muttered.

The yacht pulled into the pier, and Michael refocused on the task at hand. "Form an assembly the length of the pier!" he shouted. "The first man will grab the cargo and hand it to the next man, on down the line!"

From the ship, a woman's voice cried, "Tie 'em loosely, boys! We need to be able to move out on a moment's notice!" Michael whirled around to take a better look at the crew. A woman about forty years in age had shouted the command.

Cian, not at all taken aback by the presence of a woman, immediately tied a simpler knot on the cleat and leaned over the water, hand outstretched. "Welcome to Ireland," said Cian, shaking her hand.

"Nothing quite like this welcome," she smiled.

A voice with a distinctly English accent called from the bridge: "No time for small talk, boys, let's get 'er unloaded!"

Michael eyed Cian, who smiled. "We have friends where you'd least expect it."

"In fookin' England?" Michael asked incredulously.

"In fookin' England," Cian replied. "Now let's get to work."

"Aye," said Michael. He motioned for the Fianna Eireann boys to approach. "All right, boys!" he called. "I tried to send you home but was told that I couldn't. Are you ready to work?"

"Ready!" came their cheerful young voices.

Michael frowned. "Just don't drop anythin'—last thing we need is ammunition fallin' into the drink or rifles too damaged to fire."

The crew began lifting out wooden crates that were too small to be rifles, even unassembled.

"This first batch will be the ammo, boys. They'll be heavy—be careful! Hold them tight like they was yer baby sister!"

He handed crate over crate to eager young boys, who then handed them off to the men on the pier. Hand over hand, dozens of crates were passed down the pier and loaded into the waiting motorcars. As each car was loaded to the full weight it could bear, it pulled away and waited for the others to take on their cargo. When all five were loaded down, the lead car blew its horn, and once again the Volunteers parted, allowing the cars to exit. Cheers rang out from all along the pier.

"We're not finished yet!" yelled Cian, "Get back in line!"

"Back to the line!" voices rang out down the pier, and the men at once formed a disorderly line and readied themselves for more cargo. Hands on hips or over their heads, they caught their breath.

"Ready, boys?" Michael asked his young charges. The young boys looked as tired as the men but still were excited to continue the work. "Handle 'em carefully. They're not loaded, but they shouldn't be dropped."

The boys nodded enthusiastically, hands ready to take on the next load of cargo.

"How many we got?" Cian asked a crewmember.

"'Bout nine hundred," a bulky sailor replied. Unlike the men on the pier, he showed no signs of fatigue. A cigarette hung from his mouth, held in place through a large gap in his teeth, and he continued to smoke as he worked. "Mausers, all of 'em. Bolt action."

Cian frowned. "We was expectin' a lot more."

The sailor removed his cigarette and spat into the water. He lowered his voice. "'Course you was. But we split the cargo so as not to put all the eggs in one basket, if you know what I mean. Capt'n has instructions for the rest," he said, motioning toward the bridge.

"Aye," said Cian, his eyes focusing on the captain. "Let's get 'em off!"

Michael seized the first rifle from the ship, but he stopped in dismay when he saw the engraving on the stock. *M1871*. These were antiquated weapons. Not only would each round have to be loaded individually, but they used black gunpowder cartridges.

He handed the gun to Cian, saying, "Jesus Christ! What the fook are we supposed to do with old-fashioned rifles? We'll get one shot off for every three of theirs! And that's if we can manage not to jam 'em!"

"The Germans are preparing for war, Michael," Cian said. "We're lucky to have been able to buy even these." He passed the rifle back to Michael.

"Lucky? The Ulstermen brought in Gewehr 88's. Smokeless powder and rapid loading." Michael tossed the M1871 onto the pier in frustration. "We'll be outgunned in both range and rate of fire. Not to mention this black powder— it'll give our positions away every time!"

Cian reached over Michael and began taking rifles from the yacht crew and passing them into the eager young hands of the Fianna Eireann boys. "Aye, but think of the effect on the public. It doesn't matter what they are—it matters what they represent."

"Think of the effect on me skull when my round jams in the chamber and I take an Ulster bullet between the eyes!" Michael spit on the dock. "Can't fookin' catch a break! We risked our lives to bring in weapons like these?"

Cian said nothing in reply, but continued passing the rifles from the crewmen on down the line. "A better attitude would serve you well, Michael," he said coldly.

"A better rifle would serve me well."

"That I can't do," said Cian. "But they are issuin' better attitudes somewhere around here."

"The pub?" asked Michael. He reluctantly began passing the old rifles down the line.

"The bottom of the fookin' Irish Sea," said Cian. "Which is where I'm about to throw yer arse if you don't stop complainin."

"If you don't, the Ulstermen will, I suppose," said Michael. "And I'll sink faster with me new paperweight."

Cian' rolled his eyes and thrust two Mausers into Michael's hands. "Good. Until then, keep passing 'em down," he said.

Within a matter of minutes, hundreds of German Mausers had been passed down the pier to the awaiting Volunteers. Some shouldered them, and others passed them on to the men forming the barricade.

As the last of the rifles were passed to the hands of the Fianna Eireann boys, Michael paused and looked to Cian. "Why the fook are you so happy?" he asked. "You've got a smile plastered on yer face like you just kissed a girl."

"Shhh!" said Cian. "I'm enjoyin' the sight."

"What sight?"

"Irish Volunteers. Armed."

Michael sighed. "I'd feel better if they were Gewehrs."

Cian was about to respond when a commotion erupted toward the end of the pier.

Michael heard a voice from the shore, "Back off!" Then the distinct cry, "I'll put a lump of lead through yer skull!"

"We've gotta move, boys!" yelled the English crewmember. Michael and Cian hurriedly untied the yacht from the cleats and pushed it off the pier. Its sails unfurled as they met the harbor winds. The *Asgard* captain came off the bridge and yelled. "Kilcoole, in Wicklow. Six days' time!"

"Aye!" said Cian, waving. He turned to Michael, "Let's go!"

They took off down the pier toward the commotion and found the Howth harbormaster, demanding to be let through to the pier.

"Not a chance," murmured Michael to Cian. Then he shouted, "Hold the line!" The men moved closer together, ensuring that no one could penetrate. They had to give the *Asgard* enough time to get a good distance away before allowing any authorities on the pier.

"Here's the first test of your grandda's rifle," said Michael. "Let's see how she does!"

Behind the harbor master appeared a small detachment of the Royal Irish Constabulary, but they were so few in number that Michael immediately knew they would be no challenge. He smiled at Cian. "Happy to watch this one play out," he said.

"Hold the line!" Cian called again, an order that was repeated across the men by the adjutants. Michael gripped his newly acquired rifle and in a moment of fear realized that not only was it antiquated, but it was also unloaded. The automobiles with the ammunition had already departed. None of the weapons were loaded. He could feel his hands begin to sweat.

He watched through the barricade as the Constabulary talked down the harbormaster, who retreated in a rage to his vehicle. The Constabulary followed him on foot, making no attempt to confront the Volunteers. A cheer erupted.

"I'd say they did beautifully," said Cian. "Not a shot fired!"

"Not a one of 'em was loaded," said Michael.

"Doesn't matter," said Cian. "And I knew it wouldn't. It doesn't matter that they're old, and it doesn't matter that we've only got a few rounds to put in 'em. We're finally a force to be reckoned with."

Perhaps Michael had underestimated how effective the old rifles could be. A lone crate of powder cartridges remained on the pier, and Michael instructed the surrounding platoons to divvy up its contents. "One cartridge per man, no more," he said. "It's all we have till we get back to Dublin." The men eagerly attacked the crate, and within moments its contents had been distributed among the ranks.

Once the authorities were out of sight, Michael began calling orders to reassemble, and the platoons reformed into companies for the march back to Dublin. They seemed revived, excited—unperturbed by having to carry their new burdens on a nine-mile march home. At this moment, the harbormaster was probably attempting to notify Dublin of the shipment and bring in more constables. "Good luck cabling for help, boys," he said to himself. "May the luck of the Irish be with you."

Company A departed the pier in as orderly a fashion as possible, given their rudimentary training and the excitement of pulling off an illegal gunrunning scheme in broad daylight. At the entrance to the east side of the harbor, where the remaining companies continued to block the entrance, Cian jogged ahead of Michael's lead company. Evidently, he felt they would need a scout. As he ran past, Michael heard him say, "Orders are to defend ourselves if we run into trouble."

Michael clutched his rifle and nodded.

As the formations joined and began the march back down Harbour Road, townspeople again began to emerge from their homes to see what had transpired. Seeing men with rifles slung over shoulders and wearing the gray-green uniforms of the Irish Volunteers, they began to cheer, and the men began to yell back.

By now, Michael surmised with pride, the Constabulary had likely tried to order reinforcements, only to find that their telegraph wires had been cut. He anticipated an easy march home. But he was also keenly aware that they would all be watched like hawks from now on—not only by the authorities but also by the Ulster Volunteers. The stakes had been raised.

The crowds in the streets intensified as they approached the village of

Raheny, which they had traversed just a few hours before. The march again felt like a parade—children waved flags, and their mothers swore in delight at the expense of the British and Ulstermen. His men were beginning to tire now, after marching almost fourteen miles in the July heat with few breaks and no real sustenance.

❧

Michael was relieved when at last they came into Fairview, only a short march away from Dublin. In only a half hour or so they'd be home, and they'd made it without incident. Taking the same route as they had that morning, they turned onto Howth Road.

Without warning, as they rounded the corner, Cian stopped. Their route was blocked by what looked like a full battalion of grim men in plaid trousers, black jackets, and feathered tams: a contingency of the King's Own Scottish Borderers.

How was this possible? He had cut the telegraph wires himself! How had word traveled back so quickly?

Cian was fast to react and, increasing his pace, led the formations down an adjacent street. With any luck, the soldiers would not be able to regroup in time to cut them off. "Move along boys!" he called back to his company and hastened the speed of the march.

Michael followed suit, and the companies all began moving down Malahide Road at a grueling pace, just a small detour from the original route. "Keep up!" Michael called back to his men.

He knew that by sheer firepower, they outnumbered any force that could have been mustered by the Borderers. But he was not keen to get into a firefight with them. It would only lead to trouble and arrests. The Volunteers were a growing organization, but they were young and couldn't afford to be stripped of their leadership at such a crucial time as this. With the Home Rule bill poised to pass Westminster, the Volunteers needed to be organized and ready to ensure an undivided Ireland.

About halfway down Malahide Road, they saw the ominous colors of the Borderers as the soldiers poured into the street from an alleyway, again blocking their path. Cian was forced to stop the march, and as he slowed, Michael issued the order to halt. "Company, Halt!" Then, "Silence!" He wanted to hear any words exchanged between Cian and the Borderers.

Cian stood in the center of the road, gripping the rifle slung over his shoulder.

"Surrender your weapons!" called the Borderer's battalion commander. He was a plump, middle-aged man, and although he carried himself with the pomp of a career officer, his stature did not seem intimidating. *Just some aristocrat looking to earn himself more land.* Michael was determined that this commander would not gain any new honors from his service in Ireland.

A small uproar swelled from the men, and Michael once again commanded, "Silence!" He strained to hear.

"We are a militia on parade!" Cian was shouting. His face was turned away, and Michael closed his eyes as he tried catch his words. "Just last week a formation of armed Ulstermen walked these very streets unharassed."

Several of the local men who had joined them in the streets to get a better look at the impending confrontation spoke up and agreed. A red-bearded man with a thick Dublin accent cried out, "'Tis true, sir! Walked right past me home, they did!"

The Borderer commander remained uncompromising. "Surrender your arms, or we will forcibly take them from you!" he called.

From Michael's standpoint, there looked to be about a hundred Borderers blocking the street, and who knew how many in that side alley—probably not enough. Would they really try to disarm more than two thousand men holding hundreds of rifles? He wondered how long would it take them to figure out that very few of the weapons were loaded.

Cian made no response but turned his head as though preparing to order his formation to continue marching. At this, the Borderer officer yelled to his men,

"Disarm them!" The first rank of soldiers approached the formation, and Cian and the rest of the leadership fell back to join Michael's company.

"Do not fire," Cian said, loud enough so the first opposing platoon could hear, hoping the Borderers would take the bait and assume the Mausers were all loaded. Then, in a quieter voice, "But feel free to find other creative ways to use your weapons." Snickering broke out among the first ranks of Volunteers..

Immediately, the first platoon, led by Lieutenant Timothy McNeill flipped their rifles around and prepared to beat back the group of Borderers who were approaching. The soldiers did not brandish their weapons, although Michael knew they were armed. They were not deterred by the sight of the wooden butts. They kept approaching.

When the first rank was within an arms' length, the Volunteers rushed forward and began beating down the Borderers with the butts of their rifles. Michael took aim on the man nearest him, a short, stocky fellow with spectacles, and rammed the butt of his rifle into the man's head. Blood gushed from his nose as he fell back, stunned. Michael moved forward, repeating the same motion on anyone in his immediate path, his first platoon following his lead.

The Borderers began to retreat. The fat commander's face was now red with anger. "Advance!" he yelled. "Disarm them!"

Michael dug in his heels and prepared for another confrontation. He heard Sergeant Brennan yell to Company A, "Hold yer ground!" He waited, his rifle butt raised, but the Borderers stalled. He was close enough to see them exchange glances nervously between each other. Were trained men of the King's Army afraid of Irish riff raff? A smile broke across his face. The gap in his gums from his missing tooth, which he was usually so careful to conceal, was prominently displayed.

A few more seconds passed. They were refusing the order to advance. "Steady!" he called to his men. "We'll give 'em all we've got!" Now he was taunting them, begging the Borderers to advance on him. His men began jeering, and neither he nor his adjutant did anything to stop them. He took a few slow and

86

confident steps forward. The sound of his men's boots as they followed him echoed across Malahide Road.

He felt a man come up behind him, and turned his head slightly. Timothy— that sneaky bastard. "You left your platoon?" he said.

"Nah, just wanted a better view, that's all," Timothy said.

They heard a small cheer arise from beyond the first rank of the Borderers.

"What is that?" Michael said. "Where is it coming from?"

Timothy put his hand in front of Michael. "It's coming from them. It looks like they are cheering us on."

"Who?" He was unnerved. Just what was going on? Again, he showed the butt of his rifle.

"The second rank." Michael craned to see the men of the formation in front of them. Confusion was overtaking both sides.

"Kind of makes you sorry to have bashed in faces," he heard Timothy say over his shoulder. The cheer intensified. "Seems not all of them want this fight."

"Not at all," said Michael. "I'll bash faces all day until they leave us be!"

All around was chaos. Some of the Borderers had obviously stood down while others still brandished their weapons.

"Company, march!" Michael yelled. His order seemed to have caught the Volunteers off guard, but they straightened their lines and began moving forward. Again, the sound of their boots echoing off the houses made their formation seem twice as large as it was. A flash of light caught Michael's eye. From within the ranks of the Borderers, more flashes of light appeared. The sun was reflecting off fixed bayonets.

"Hold your fire, men!" called Michael, trying to keep up the farce. "They will not do us harm." The Borderer ranks again began moving toward the Volunteers. Michael held up the butt of his rifle and prepared his men for another round of clubbing.

The lines of bayonets halted. Michael's company did not. He felt sweat rolling down his face, but he advanced his men right into the line of Borderers. As he crossed through the first rank of opposing men, they stepped aside and let him through. A young man, his short-cropped hair poking out from under his ridiculous-looking cover, pointed his bayonet directly at him. It was too late to retreat, so Michael locked eyes with him and marched right on. The man dropped the bayonet and stepped aside, as the others had. Close behind him, his company was now marching right through the ranks of the Borderers as well.

As if on cue, all around him, men began grappling with each other, but only fists flew. Not a shot was fired. Michael smiled to himself. Bare-knuckled fistfights were an Irish specialty. He slung his rifle over his shoulder and joined his men, landing a right hook directly on the face of a stunned Borderer. The soldier's glasses flew into the street. Michael felt too sorry for him to finish him off with a second swing. The Volunteers fought their way through a few ranks of men and then watched as the rest of the Borderers fled in a disorganized retreat.

The yelling on the street was deafening. Cheers, profanity, and shrieks of delight filled the street. Michael spotted Timothy through the chaos and slowly made his way toward him.

His friend was frowning. "Why so glum?"

"I didn't get a chance to knock out one of 'em before they ran off! Think we can convince them to come back?"

"Be patient," Michael said. "You'll get your chance. Maybe not today, but soon."

"Promise?" said Timothy.

"Promise."

The mayhem slowly died down, and Michael could hear Cian's voice calling out over the disorder. "Assemble!"

"Back to work," said Timothy, and he rushed off to assemble his platoon.

Michael called for his adjutant. "Any injuries, Brennan?" he asked. The Sergeant ran to do a quick inventory and promptly returned. He had two swollen eyes—likely from direct contact with a Borderer's fist—but smiled as if he didn't notice or care. "Three Volunteers down, sir. One bayoneted. Two are already on their way to the hospital by motorcar—some local good Samaritan. The third is well enough to march."

"Very well," said Michael. "Did we lose any cargo?"

"About seventeen rifles," said the adjutant. Smiling, he added, "But we gained two Lee-Enfields."

Michael smiled back. "Almost an even trade, eh?"

By now the ranks, which had maintained some guise of discipline throughout the day, had descended into chaos. Wounded Borderers lay in the street, but no one stopped to provide attention. The villager who had been so willing to transport Volunteers to the hospital did not seem to have room for any loyalists and had disappeared as quickly as he had arrived.

Michael gazed helplessly at the gaggle of men that remained in the street. There was a mix of residents and Volunteers, and the chaos was mounting. He made his way through the crowds to Cian, who like Brennan had some bruising beginning to appear on his face. "What'll you have 'em do, boss?" Michael asked.

"Your guess is as good as mine," Cian replied. "All in all, a decent outcome to the day, all things considered."

Michael nodded in agreement, then looked ahead to the end of Malahide Road and a long stretch of hay fields.

Cian followed his glance. "I say let's get 'em back to Dublin, the sooner the better," said Michael.

"Agreed," replied Cian.

Michael made his way back to Sergeant Brennan and pointed toward the field. "Tell the boys to fall out and make their ways back to Dublin. All rifles are to be surrendered at safe houses by dark. All weapons will be accounted for."

The adjutant nodded.

"Lee-Enfields included," added Michael with a grin.

"Aye," said Sergeant Baker. He began bellowing directions to the men within range. In a moment, Volunteers were running across the open field back home to Dublin. Michael lingered and directed stragglers, though he felt more like he was herding drunken cattle. Within minutes, the crowds had dispersed, and only a few of Michael's men could still be seen making their way across the fields at a pace much more leisurely than Michael would have liked.

He looked back down the stretch of Malahide Road that, only a quarter of an hour before, had been the scene of an all-out brawl between two armed groups. Yet not a shot had been fired.

"A miracle," Michael said to himself. "A damned miracle that no one was killed. And dumb luck that we got away with running hundreds of rifles into the heart of Dublin in broad daylight."

Cian came up behind him. "Aye."

Michael whirled around, startled.

"The Lord is shining on us today, Michael," Cian said.

"The Lord or luck. Not sure which one."

The two men shouldered their Mausers and moved quickly into the fields toward one of the makeshift armories they had set up in the safe houses throughout Dublin.

CHAPTER 10

July 28, 1914: Ballynote, County Clare, Ireland

Nora walked slowly from room to room. Her footsteps fell softly on the packed dirt floors of her empty little cottage. Their few possessions had been sold, and she and Seamus had packed up what remained into makeshift sacks made from their bed linens. Nora's pack was larger, for it contained some dresses that had been her mother's, odd pieces of silverware, and some old tarnished jewelry. The jewelry had been passed down from ages ago, when the Cullen or McMahon families had fine things, but Nora did not know how long ago that was, or who had decided to keep them over feeding hungry mouths.

It was daunting to think of the path that lay ahead. Seamus had been right—he always was. They would both be leaving Ballynote. She breathed in the musty, damp air of the cottage that to her was the smell of home. As plain as it was, the cottage was comfortable, and the dark wooden walls secure. She gazed at the hearth—the central feature of their home—and lamented that all her memories of her parents were tied to the little cottage. She remembered her mother cooking at the hearth and her father coming in the doorway, ducking his head so as not to hit it on the low wooden frame. He always came in around dusk, dirty from a long day in the fields. His beaming smile broke through the twilight and seemed to light up the dark interior. With one hand, he removed his cap; with the other, he hid flowers behind his back—just picked from the back meadow. He would raise one finger to his lips, imploring the children to join him in his little game, as though this was an unexpected gift for their mother. She coquettishly accepted them day after day, always feigning surprise.

Nora recalled how he would fold his arms around her mother and lift her off the ground as if they were young and in love. Perhaps they had been. Maybe death had come to them before life stole the spark from their hearts. After leaving this place and all the small reminders of them hidden within the walls, would she forget what little she knew about them? Would she ever know their mystery—what precisely had driven them to do what they did? They must have known the risk. Why had they done it anyway? She looked long and hard at the fireplace and then back at the door, trying to burn their images and her fragmented recollections into her memory.

Seamus appeared in the doorway, and for a moment she wondered if she were dreaming. He looked so much like their father.

"Take a long look, Nora," he said. He bent his head slightly to come in, just the same way their father always had, "You shan't cast yer eyes on this place again in yer lifetime. Just in yer dreams." He walked over to put his arm around her. "But if you ever forget, ask me, and I will tell you about this place and about the time we left it behind us, on a new adventure to find our fortune."

She smiled at him, and leaned her head on his shoulder. "How do you know what I am thinkin' all the time, Seamus?"

"Because everythin' you think shows up in yer eyes," he said. "Those curious eyes of yers. Come—you must be off to Ennis. We can't have you miss yer train."

They picked up their linen sacks and headed toward the door. But Nora hesitated at the threshold, closing her eyes, hoping to burn into her memory the smells and the feeling of home. Finally, with no excuse to stay longer, she walked out the door for the last time.

Seamus closed the cottage and did not look back after he turned away. He had already severed himself from this place and time. She knew that was just how he was.

Colin was already in the yard, adjusting the saddle on his small bay gelding. Just behind him was a dark mare grazing idly on the moss. Seamus headed toward the cart and mule—the last remaining equipment from the farm—and threw his sack onto the wooden seat next to some grain he had packed for his short trip to Limerick.

In the days since returning from Inis Cathaigh, he had found temporary work in Limerick City, and coincidentally Silas Smith had found room for a boarder. Seamus had been only too happy at this supposed good fortune, but it troubled Nora. The arrangement had come together too quickly, and she was suspicious that Seamus had already been planning to leave Ballynote, even before their grandfather's demise.

As for Nora, it had been Colin who suggested that she might come to Dublin as a hired girl. She had but little choice in the matter, given her circumstances, but she was happy that Colin had presented it to her as if she had many offers on the table. "You know, Nora," he had said, "I could find you a proper place to work if you would want to come to Dublin. I'll take you there myself, but only if you wanted. I wouldn't dare tear you away from Clare if you had something else in mind."

She had waited to respond, as if seriously contemplating an answer, though she knew instantly she would find no better arrangement in Clare. When she didn't answer right away, he had said, "It's not so difficult for young girls to find work in the Dublin mansions, you know. They're always needin' hired help, 'specially girls comin' from the corners of Ireland, who aren't too proud to work for board. 'Tis not a bad start, Nora."

Colin's words echoed in her mind as she walked toward the small, dark mare with her linen sack. *No,* she thought to herself, *'tis not a bad start.*

Seamus walked up behind her. "You're a friend, Colin," he said. "Look after Nora. Check in on her from time to time."

"Aye," he said. "I'd be happy to. We have to stick together these days."

Nora eyed him, and he smiled back at her.

The young men embraced, and Seamus said softly, "Truly, I thank you. She's all I have left in this world."

"And what am I?" Colin asked. He playfully shoved Seamus, pretending to be offended. "I'm only the best friend an arse like you will ever have."

"That may be true, but take care of her nonetheless."

Nora fidgeted with her linen sack and finally succeeded in tying it to the back of the saddle. Seamus walked over and gave her a leg up onto the mare. He looked up at her, but his gaze was distant and detached. "Take care of yerself Nora. Write to me when you get there."

She knew her brother loved her, but she also knew the forces that called him to seek his own freedom were stronger than his affection for her. It was the same enchantment that had lured her parents to early graves. Freedom was an intoxicating temptress for all Cullens, it seemed.

"We just have to make it till spring," he said. "I'll come to Dublin just as fast as I can save enough money to have a life there. And we'll be together again." Seamus tried hide the quick glance he exchanged with Colin, but Nora saw it as clear as day. Ever since Colin had arrived in Ballynote, both he and Seamus had been acting strangely. Something was up.

"And don't feel alone," Seamus whispered to her. He didn't seem to notice her suspicion. "We are two pieces of the same fabric, and as long as we are both alive we'll never be truly on our own, no matter where we end up."

Nora kept note of the stares that Colin and Seamus exchanged as Colin turned his horse down the path. Nora's mare followed instinctively, stepping slowly and clumsily behind the bay. Seamus walked beside her for a few steps,

94

the wind whipping through his white linen shirt like a canvas sail on a ship at sea. The force of the wind held him back from her as her horse ambled away, and she felt a premonition that she was too afraid to let her mind explore.

"Good-bye, Nora," Seamus said.

Nora turned her head to take in the landscape one last time. The velvet green meadows, the rolling hills, and the rocks scattered about the fields. The pastures where their sheep had grazed only days before were empty, the stone fences serving no purpose now but to decorate the hillside.

It was a troubled landscape, but it was magical. These fickle fields had brought them so much pain that is was easy to overlook their beauty. Nora glanced toward the rock where she had watched the sun rise each summer morning and whispered a good-bye. The wind whipped up from the river, blowing her curly auburn hair into her face and hiding the tears that began to fall lightly on her cheeks and drip down onto the mare's back as she and Colin slowly made it down the bridle path to the road below.

CHAPTER 11

July 28, 1914: County Clare, Ireland

They rode along in silence for what seemed like an hour until Colin slowed his horse so it came into step with hers. The wind had long since dried her tears, but Nora's sadness was overwhelming. Even to Colin, it felt like a magnificent weight that crushed an otherwise glorious Irish summer day—the kind of day that came to Clare and cast its homesick spell on him only when he was leaving. He closed his eyes and listened to the horses—their heavy steps, the energetic snorts that showed their pleasure with the breezy summer day—and tried to think of some way to take the sadness away from both of them. Usually, he would just tell her a story or a silly joke, but he wondered if perhaps he no longer knew her in the same way. Would she still find him amusing?

It had always been Nora who started and continued conversations, with her incessant but sweet questions. But she had been mostly silent since he arrived in Ballynote, and he knew it was he who had changed. She must have sensed that he had fallen in love with something that rivaled his affection for her. Until going to Dublin, he had only seen life as a series of inevitable steps—childhood, adulthood, and death. Nora was what made Ballynote exciting. She had been the mischief and adventure that he sought. But that was before—before Dublin, and before he found another focus for his passions…Irish freedom. Ballynote had reminded him of what he had traded in a way he hadn't anticipated.

He opened his eyes. Her long hair was loosely tied back, but the pieces not tethered down whipped about in the wind. He remembered her as having bright red hair, but now that she was a little older it had faded into a soft auburn, and the freckles that had once dominated her face were much more subtle. When he'd first seen her the previous week, he had recognized just how grown up she'd become. Since that day, he had often recalled the moment she had stepped out of her little cottage and into the brilliant morning sun. Had she always been that pretty?

He hadn't wanted to see her because he knew he would be tempted to stay in Ballynote. But the whole reason he had gone back to Clare was to pass along his cousin's message to Seamus—he couldn't have avoided the cottage. And he certainly hadn't anticipated Eamonn's death. He just hadn't been strong enough to leave her behind, given all that had happened.

He went from scolding himself for bringing her back into his life to excitement at the thought of it. What troubled him was that he didn't know if he could manage these two lives in Dublin. He wanted Nora as far away from his mischief as possible—she wouldn't be able to resist getting into the thick of it, and he wouldn't be able to keep her safe. But as much as he wanted her away from trouble, he wanted her close to him. He had certainly made a mess of things.

She woke him from his thoughts. "Colin, what is Dublin like?"

As always, Colin thought, *a question.* He slowed his horse, and Nora's mare followed.

"Oh, it's a grand city," he replied. "Historic. Old buildings and churches, busy little streets with lots of bridges. Lots of pubs," he smiled at her. "Always something to see. Quite different from Clare."

"Do you prefer Dublin?" she asked.

He frowned. It was such a simple question, but so hard to answer. "Ballynote will always be me home," he finally said, "so much that I ache for it whenever I am away. But I suppose I'm glad to see a bit more of the world."

They rode on a little ways. "And if you get tired of the city," he added, "there's plenty to remind you of the rural Ireland you grew up in. Just a little way out is County Wicklow. Looks a little like Clare if you use yer imagination. Some rolling hills and the smell of the ocean. The old church of St. Kevin is there, tucked in the Wicklow mountains. Silas and I rode out there once, when he was up tendin' to some business." What type of business, he didn't dare say, and when she didn't inquire, he happily left it at that.

"Perhaps you can take me one day on a little adventure," she said. For the first time since burying old Eamonn McMahon, she spoke about the future. He smiled at the thought. "You're going to do just fine, Nora," he said.

Around midday, they stopped to eat the lunches she had packed. It was a simple meal of bread with the last of the carrots from the small vegetable patch she had kept. They let the horses wander about to graze and sat on the grass to eat and rest.

"Would you ever leave Ireland, Colin?" Nora asked. Though they had made their way away from the coast, the wind persisted, and she kept interrupting her meal to tuck the loose ends of hair behind her ears.

He'd never considered this before. "I don't even know where I'd go. I think I'd like to see America, someday." He immediately regretted broaching this topic. He stared down at his dry bread and reached under his shirt for his flask. He took a long swig and felt the burn on the back of his throat. She said nothing but watched him as she tried to corral her hair behind her ears, to no avail. It flew all about her as the wind whipped through the meadow.

He wiped his chin with his sleeve and tried to divert the conversation away from America. "But I don't have any desire to go to England, that's for sure, and run into even more of those bastards. In any case, it's up to us to be a part of Ireland's future, and I think we do that by staying put."

Nora appeared to listen intently. "But what's to be done for Ireland's future?" she asked.

"Ah, that's the question," he said. "What is to be done? Something for sure." This was a topic he could talk about all day.

"It's not an easy life that we live," he said. "You'll see that in Dublin. There is wealth beyond yer imagination there. But for the majority, it's poor. People work hard to survive just the same way they do out here. But there's got to be a better way. We aren't all destined to be poor and powerless."

He took another long sip from his flask and cautiously continued. "I decided long ago, Nora," he said, "that I couldn't change the circumstances of me birth, but that I could change the circumstances of me life, and I promised meself that I will leave this world a freer man."

He watched her as she thought about what his words meant. Her expression remained unchanged, but the gleam in her eyes revealed that she understood the consequences of what he had said, and gave away how intrigued she was.

Colin popped the last crust into his mouth and took another swig of whiskey to wash it down. Their eyes met for a long time. When she looked at him with those curious eyes, he felt as though she peered directly into his inner thoughts. He had forgotten that she did that when they were alone together; he had forgotten how he couldn't help but confess what he was thinking. He reckoned she already knew what he was about to say. "I made this promise not just to meself, but to Ireland."

She nodded but did not reply right away. He again wondered if he had made a mistake. He knew he shouldn't bring her into his new world, but at the same time, he couldn't hide it from her. She and Seamus had already paid a high price for her family's beliefs. Was it wrong to keep her from what seemed to be her destiny while at the same time encouraging Seamus to join the fight?

She broke their silence. "My promise is the same."

"You're too young to make that promise," he said. But he knew that wasn't true. He meant that she was too good to be a part of the world he had come to know since living in Dublin. He watched an enormous scowl descend across her face and he stifled a smile.

CHAPTER 12

July 28, 1914: County Clare, Ireland

As they rode into town, Colin realized just how much he had enjoyed the day with Nora, and he was happy Seamus hadn't insisted on accompanying them as far as Ennis. But his time with her was coming to an end. They were to spend the night at his uncle's home in Ennis before boarding their train to Dublin. And after that, he did not know when we would be able to see her again.

His cousin had arranged work for her with a wealthy Protestant family on the outskirts of the city. This alone was not a reason for him to stay away, but he hadn't yet told Nora who exactly she would be working for—and why he would have to make himself scarce. He couldn't decide if she would be safer if she knew who her boss was or if it was better to leave her in the dark. It was a predicament.

He forced it from his mind and dismounted, then helped Nora down from the mare. They led the horses up the path to the small stable in the rear of his uncle's home. The old farmhouse was dark. His uncle was probably off on his afternoon milk route, and his aunt was most likely still finishing up the evening dinner preparation at the local tavern.

"When is the last time you were in Ennis, Nora?" he asked, as they unsaddled the horses and led them to a small paddock.

"It's been a while," she said. "I came last in the fall with grandda when we sold the harvest. Haven't seen it in the summer months for years."

"There's more to see here than Ballynote," Colin said, "but it's not so pretty as the coast. Would you like to take a walk with me before me relatives arrive home?" Perhaps he could steal a few extra moments.

He could tell Nora was tired, but she agreed.

"Well come then," he said. "I can show you where we'll catch our train tomorrow." He almost took her by the hand, as he would have without a second thought when they were young, but they were no longer children and could no longer use their youth as an excuse to behave that way. He felt the burden of adulthood. Even the boredom that tormented him as a child seemed a fair price to keep society's customs at bay.

Ennis still showed the scars of the previous decades. During the famine about sixty years before, the starving homeless littered the streets and built ever-growing shantytowns along the roadside, as more and more farmers were forced off their land. Their small huts along the road still stood, though they were now only sparsely occupied. Of all Ireland, the suffering in Clare during the famine was beyond imagination. Colin had always detected a certain sadness about Ennis, no matter how long ago the blight had ended.

Politically, the town had been forever changed. Residents still cursed England for exporting food that could have curbed the suffering—and then turning her back and condemning the entire region to starve. Feeding, housing, and nursing the suffering masses—something within Westminster's capability—would have been expensive and politically inconvenient. Of all the members of Seamus' Gaelic League, those from Ennis were the most zealous in their fight for a free

Ireland.

Even before, Ennis had been a bastion of Irish nationalism. It was here that Daniel O'Connell had secured the first Irish Catholic seat in Parliament, and it was here that Nora's parents came to listen to the famous Charles Parnell raise hopes for an Irish home rule. It was also this city, where the simmer of nationalism was never quite quelled, where her parents decided that change would only come to Ireland if her people fought for it.

৯

The two walked along silently alone in their own thoughts. When Nora finally looked up, she saw the large stone steeple of the Ennis Cathedral rising high against the quaint town landscape. Almost as an afterthought, she grabbed Colin's arm. Her touch awoke him from his thoughts as well.

"Colin," she said, "will you wait for me for a moment? I've got some things I need to think about." She glanced toward the church.

"Since when have you ever spent a minute extra inside a church? Did you fall and hit yer head while I was away?" She scowled.

He prodded her a little. "Just sayin'—last time I was in the habit of spendin' any time with you, I believe you tol' me that Irish Catholics were allowed, what was it?" He seemed to delight in teasing her: "Ah yes—flexibility—when decidin' on whether or not to go to Mass."

"Aye," she said. "Flexibility. And I'll exercise some flexibility now and step into a church."

"When was the last time you were so flexible?" he asked.

"'Tis between me and the Lord," she replied.

"Right," he said, reaching for his flask. "I'll be flexible out here."

"You don't care to join me?" she said.

"I've spent an hour a day inside a church for the past seventeen years," he said. "A week shy of eighteen. I reserve me right for flexibility, right here, with me Jameson. But I'll wait for you all the same."

Her scowl faded to the smallest smile, and she let go of his arm to cross the street. She stepped quickly into the stone courtyard in front of the church and scurried up the steps. She heaved against the heavy wooden door until it finally budged open. A small sliver of light from the open door shone into the dark interior.

Nora stepped onto the wooden floors of the old church and let her eyes adjust to the darkness. Some light crept in through the heavy stained glass windows on each side, but most of the light emanated from the candles lit at the foot of the altar. It was the largest church Nora had ever been in, and she gazed with wonder at it vastness. As she slowly walked to the front of the church, her footsteps echoed loudly, as if their owner carried a heavy burden instead of the weight of a sixteen-year-old girl, and a small one at that.

Each time she entered a church, she wondered if she would finally understand the faith that her grandfather felt so strongly. Each time, however, God's presence escaped her. This church in Ennis was no different.

She could hear her grandfather's voice, already so distant in her memory: *Be still, and open yer heart, and you'll feel 'im right there with you.* But try as she might, she felt only emptiness. She feared that her heart might already be too hardened and her mind too headstrong. She wondered if not all souls could be saved. Maybe wild Cullen souls weren't meant for everlasting salvation.

She genuflected and looked up at the candles that adorned the sanctuary. Countless Irishmen had undoubtedly knelt in these very pews and prayed for freedom. The church had stood for over a hundred years—it had heard the prayers of the starving, of the grieving, of the oppressed. And yet the Irish remained subjects of the Crown with no relief in sight. Neither the Lord nor the British had gotten around to granting Ireland her freedom. It had never been clearer to her that freedom would never be granted—it had to be taken.

She thought of her life up to this moment—of the mornings in the field, of farming, of her grandfather and Seamus. She tried hard to bring to mind her intermittent memories of her parents. Her grandfather had assured her that her path was already laid out for her, and all she had to do was to let herself be guided. But her current path seemed interrupted and confused, and certainly not predestined.

She prayed in the same way that she always had—in disconnected thoughts interrupted by her own daydreaming. It was peace of mind and peace about her future that she wanted. *But what exactly is freedom?* she thought to herself. It certainly wasn't the end that her parents met, or the life that her grandfather had lived, or the countless before them who had lived and died under the rule of a foreign power. What was the solution? Violence hadn't worked—time and again it only led to more oppression and more suffering. But peaceful resistance put no pressure on the British. There had to be a middle way—a political solution.

As she tried to focus her distracted mind, she felt a warm, firm hand clasp her own, and she realized with a start that Colin was kneeling next to her. How long had he been there?

Their eyes met once again, and she slowly laced her fingers between his, conscious that the crucified Lord positioned above the altar observed this indiscretion, though try as she might, she felt no guilt. She could feel his hand tense, and she knew that he was acutely uncomfortable with this act of defiance, just as he always had been—whether they were in a church or lying together on the banks of the Shannon. She placed her other hand around the Twelve Apostles pendant that hung from her neck, and they knelt together in silence.

After a long while had passed, she looked over at him. His eyes were closed, and his face looked peaceful, as if he were sleeping. He had all the boyish features she remembered—longish blond hair that went in every direction, a smattering of freckles. He seemed a full head taller than the previous summer. She sighed. He had come home grown up, and she was still a child.

She released his hand and sat back on the pew. He remained there for a moment, then slid back next to her. "Never imagined I'd ever sit next to you in church again," he said.

"No?" She raised an eyebrow. "Not ever?"

105

"Right back to yer old tricks again," he said, and winked at her. "Only took you a few days." He stood up. "Let's go. If we stay here too long, we'll forget that it's a glorious summer day outside. 'Tis rather dreary in here." He looked up again at the crucifix that hung over the altar. "They chose a particularly gory version of the crucifixion for this church, didn't they?"

Nora followed his eyes to the crucifix. Was revolution possible without bloodshed? Peaceful sacrifice might still lead her to the same bloody end that so many before her had met. She wondered if her grandfather's hero, Daniel O'Connell, knew this as well when he implored people against violence.

She and Colin slowly left the church together, her thoughts just as confused as before. Exhaustion finally began to take its toll on her.

They meandered back toward Colin's relatives', both immersed their own thoughts. Colin looked down at Nora. "I really enjoyed spending the day with you."

"A rare admission for the likes of you," she joked.

"I'm just glad it's you going to Dublin to be a housekeeper and not Seamus. Otherwise I would have had to listen to his whinin' the whole way up. Depresses the horses, you know, all that complainin'." He looked back at her and winked again.

By the time they reached the small house, both his aunt and uncle were at home. As they approached the low wooden entryway, Nora stood back. The house looked cozy and inviting, but she hesitated to enter.

"Don't worry," he assured her. "They're nice folks. They won't be able to help themselves but like you. Yer reputation precedes you, you know," he said smiling. He walked right in without knocking, leaving Nora to wonder what sort of reputation she had with Colin's relatives.

"Evenin' uncle!" he said. "Aunt Maeve, how are you?" he asked, giving his aunt a kiss. Nora's eyes slowly adjusted to the dim light. The smell of the farmhouse reminded her of a damp, Irish spring day.

"Just fine dear," his aunt replied. "And who have we here?" She spoke in an excited way, not just with her voice but also with her vibrant brown eyes. She was a plump and exuberant little figure, and Nora wondered if this was just how his aunt always spoke or if she really did have a reputation to live up to.

"You know exactly who she is, Maeve," grumbled Colin's uncle. He slowly rose from his wooden rocking chair, but his back stayed crooked like a knotty old tree and he was barely any taller than he had been when he was seated.

Colin obliged his aunt. "This is Nora McMahon," he said. "Straight from Ballynote."

"Ah, the much-anticipated Nora!" Colin's aunt looked as though she might burst with enthusiasm. She plodded along the dirt floor in short steps and gestured with both of her hands. The small vases of flowers perched upon the kitchen table were constantly in peril as her chubby little arms flew left and right "So pleased to meet you! Such a shame about Eamonn's passing. Such a kind and gentle man. Surprised us all that he had passed. It's been ages since I've seen 'im. Was he ill?"

"No ma'am," said Nora, finally able to get a word in. "Farmin' accident. Cut 'imself plowin' the field for the summer crop. Never healed. After the fever hit, he was gone in just a few days."

"May he rest in peace," she said. "You poor child, headed up to Dublin all by yerself, no family or nothin'. Colin, you look after this girl! I want you to take good care of her, as if she were yer own kin." Colin's aunt produced a handkerchief from her apron pocket and dabbed her eyes. Nora looked closely, and she was amazed that Aunt Maeve had been able to produce real tears on her behalf. She found herself instantly liking the woman, though she had known her but a few moments.

"Jesus, Mary, and Joseph, Maeve," chimed in Colin's uncle in the annoyed tone of a husband who had lived for decades alongside an overly dramatic wife. "Give the poor girl some space. What's the meanin' of loadin' her down with all this sadness? You're going to do just fine, Nora. You're strong, just like yer parents. Come from good stock, you do. Look at me, now. Yes," he winced and took a labored step forward to reach of his cane. He squinted his eyes as if trying to focus them. "Yes indeed. You look just like yer mammy, God rest her soul. But you've got yer daddy's eyes."

He looked like he wanted to say more, but he paused and reached for his pipe. Nora observed him as he packed it with tobacco. He couldn't be much older than forty-five, but he moved in carefully planned motions, as if to avoid using the joints that caused him pain. Why was it that every Irishman seemed to age so harshly?

"Those eyes—" he struck a match on one of the old wooden beams along the wall. "There's a story to those eyes. Has anyone told you?"

"No, sir," she said. "They're just eyes." The farmhouse was so dark with its wooden interior that the light from the match seemed to brighten the room.

"Someday, someone will tell you about 'em. Won't be me, though."

"Aw, come on Uncle Lawrence," said Colin. He plopped himself in his uncle's rocking chair and leaned back, evidently comfortable enough at his uncle's to make himself at home. "Don't tease her. Everyone loves a good story."

"Didn't say it was a good story, me boy," he said cautiously. "Just a story. And one that can wait."

He turned back to Nora in his usual slow and deliberate way. "Just know that you'll always be something special, wherever you go," he said. "And don't let anyone tell you otherwise. You've probably heard yer whole life how you and yer brother weren't going to be anything because you were Cullens." Nora's heart skipped a beat at the name "Cullen." She hadn't heard it spoken aloud in a long time. Her face felt hot, though the dark and damp cottage was cool. Uncle Lawrence lowered his voice, and she drew in closer to him to hear. He smelled strongly of his pipe. "But I'm telling you," he said, "you can't help but be something, precisely because you're a Cullen. Remember that." He took a long puff and blew the smoke slowly toward the low ceiling, where it hung like a fog.

Just what he had meant, she did not know, but for the first time in many years, she felt fiercely proud that someone knew she was a Cullen and remembered her parents as something other than criminals.

As Uncle Lawrence blew breath after breath of smoke up toward the ceiling, Aunt Maeve exuberantly placed a dinner of chicken broth and potatoes on the small kitchen table. As with every Irish farmhouse Nora had ever been in, the kitchen table was the centerpiece of the main room, and though simple and unassuming, every guest who sat at it could be made to feel like royalty. The smell of the broth stewing in the big iron pot made her mouth water.

She sat as the guest of honor at the little table, which creaked under the weight of two extra plates. Aunt Maeve was the last to be seated. She rested her large bottom on a teetering little stool and settled herself at the table. She made the sign of the cross, folded her hands, and closed her eyes, evidently waiting for her husband to begin the prayer.

Colin's uncle began to speak. "While you were down in the country, Colin," he said, "there was some activity up in Dublin."

Aunt Maeve's eyes flew open, and her little mouth—usually bent into a contented little smile—frowned in disgust.

"Oh?" said Colin. He slurped his broth loudly. His aunt's face instantly returned to a smile, as she seemed to interpret each slurp as a testament to her great culinary skill. The tension over the missed prayer subsided.

"Yes," his uncle replied. He ate quietly, but bent over the table to reduce the space his spoon had to travel to meet his mouth. "Don't know all the details, but there seems to have been—an acquisition, shall we say. Did you hear anythin' of this?"

Colin's expression teemed with suspicion. Nora had no idea what his uncle was referring to, but it seemed obvious that he was trying to trap Colin into saying something he didn't want to reveal. Nora was silently rooting for Uncle Lawrence—she wanted to know what was going on in Dublin, too.

"Acquisition, you say?" said Colin.

He's pretending he doesn't know anything, thought Nora. *Thinks he so clever.* She would press him for more the next time his relatives were out of earshot.

"Seems they pulled it off," his uncle said. He studied his nephew, who continued to slurp.

"Seems I stayed too long in Ballynote," Colin finally replied, giving in a little. "How did you hear about it?"

Uncle Lawrence suddenly seemed less eager for a conversation, and he began to slurp his broth as well. From the look on her face, Nora assumed Aunt Maeve found his poor manners much less endearing. Colin's aunt rolled her eyes dramatically—several times—probably trying to make sure Colin and Nora saw how annoyed she was.

"I have me sources," Uncle Lawrence replied.

"Oh, he does not!" cried Aunt Maeve, unable to take her husband any longer. "He read yer mail! Yer cousin up in Dublin wrote to you—knew you'd be passing through Ennis!" She looked triumphant.

Colin dropped his spoon into his bowl and broth splattered across the table. Nora couldn't tell if his aunt had been more upset before about the skipped prayer, or now, by the wasted food. Either way, it was obvious she blamed Uncle Lawrence for both. Sensing he was in trouble with both Colin and his wife, Uncle Lawrence slowly reached into his shirt with his swollen arthritic fingers and produced a small, folded piece of paper. "Yer aunt makes a terrible partner in crime. Can't keep 'er mouth shut."

Colin snatched the letter from him, clearly annoyed. He quickly scanned the lines.

"Can you read it?" asked Aunt Maeve softly.

"Course I can," said Colin, folding the letter away.

Nora watched the whole scene intently. She understood none of what Colin's uncle was talking about, but she sensed that the acquisition was not merely something to do with the grocery business. She had to hold her tongue to keep from blurting out questions.

"I did you a favor," said Colin's uncle. He looked directly at his scowling nephew. "You need to be more careful with yer correspondence. You're lucky I was the first to read it."

Colin opened his mouth to protest, but stopped himself. The four sat quietly around the table for several moments in an uncomfortable silence. The setting sun began to extinguish the remaining light within the cottage, and Aunt Maeve nervously jumped up to light the gas lamp. Her plodding footsteps sounded like a drumbeat across the floor. The silence clearly made her uneasy.

Uncle Lawrence took out the last bit of tobacco from his pouch, and as he tamped in into his pipe, he addressed his nephew. "Best be careful when you get back, Colin. Do what you will, and do what you believe, but be careful, Colin."

Again Colin opened his mouth to speak, but held back. He picked up his spoon again and began to slurp.

"You too, little Nora," Uncle Lawrence said ominously. "It's only a matter of time—"

A matter of time for what? She thought. She couldn't wait to get Colin alone so he could explain what had just transpired. There was a lot more going on in Dublin than she had anticipated. And from the sound of it, Colin was not a bystander.

They ate the rest of their meal together in silence. Colin continually flipped his hair out of his eyes as he sat bent over his bowl and slowly finished his meal. Nora was so anxious to speak with him that she began to grow impatient. *Just finish up already!* She thought.

She could tell that Colin's aunt was also using every power she could muster to stop herself from pestering Colin for more conversation. After all, this was probably the most exciting bit of news the Kildares had received in quite a while—though its significance still escaped her. His aunt began to clear the table and shuffled back and forth with her usual exuberance. Nora instinctively rose to help, but Colin's uncle quickly grabbed her arm.

"Nonsense, Nora dear! You are our guest."

Aunt Maeve agreed. "I wouldn't have you do a lick of work, not in my kitchen," adding under her breath, "though the others are welcome to assist."

She cast a stern eye to her husband, who continued to chew on his pipe, feigning deep thought so as to avoid washing dishes.

She turned back to Nora. "You look simply exhausted from yer trip. You head right up to bed, child. You can have the loft all to yerself." She turned to her nephew, who usually shared the loft with his brothers and cousins when he visited. "Colin, there's room for you in the hayloft out in the barn. Plenty comfortable up there this time of year."

"Aye," he said. He spoke for the first time since the meal, and his voice sounded calm again, as if all had been forgotten. But Nora knew better. "I'll show you up, Nora."

He scooped Nora's small linen sack up off the earthen floor and a grabbed a small gas lamp stowed on one of the many small shelves. He nodded to Nora in an obvious request for her to follow him and began climbing up the ladder before his aunt could register a protest. Nora hesitated at the bottom of the ladder, keenly aware that Colin's aunt was standing feet away with her mouth agape.

When Colin arrived up at the top, he looked down, eyes alight, and beckoned her up urgently with his hand. "Come on!" he mouthed. Though she didn't dare to cast a glance toward his aunt, she couldn't escape the feeling of her judging stare as she clamored up the ladder.

Uncle Lawrence stopped the protest that was brewing inside his wife. "'Tis not a mortal sin to say good night, Maeve. He's practically a grown man."

Still aware of Aunt Maeve's disapproval, Nora peered into the loft, looking for Colin. Once her eyes adjusted to the darkness, she spied him in a far corner. She crawled over just as he lit the small gas lamp. Light broke across the loft.

He put his finger to his lips, and whispered, "Quiet." He lifted folded piece of paper for her to see. She understood. She sat next to him and took the paper from him, carefully unfolding it. His cousin's neat script was just visible.

"Me cousin knows I can't read," he said. "The bastard."

Nora scanned the letter and began to read it to him. "Me dear cousin," she began in a whisper. Then she stopped.

"Tell me exactly what it says," he said. "Don't leave anything out." He reached for his flask.

She sighed and did as he asked. "You piece of shite," she continued, and try as she might, she could not help herself from letting out a laugh. Colin almost spit out his whiskey.

"Shhh!" he said, though Nora could tell he, too, was trying not to laugh.

From the main floor, Aunt Maeve called up to her nephew. "It only takes a second to drop that sack off and get yerself to the barn!"

"Coming!" said Colin. "Keep reading," he said. "And for the love of Christ, stop swearin'!" He playfully elbowed her.

"While you are having a grand old time in Clare, drinking yerself silly, sleepin' all day—alone no doubt—we're in the middle of a fookin' war up here. Our German friends—several hundred—arrived in Howth today and are settling in splendidly. Get yer arse back to Dublin."

Nora stopped. She still had no answers to her questions. "Your cousin sounds charming," she said.

"There must be more," Colin said.

Nora turned the page over.

"P.S. I've got a job for you. A customer in Wicklow has some groceries that need deliverin.'"

"That's all it says, Colin. What does it mean?" she asked. "And who are these friends?"

"Mausers, I presume," he said.

"What?"

"Colin!" came another call from the main floor. "Do I have to retrieve you meself?" Colin ignored his aunt.

"The friends," he said. "They're most likely German Mausers. Somethin' better if we're lucky." His eyes smiled.

Nora wanted to ask the obvious, but Colin saved her the trouble.

"Rifles."

She felt the blood drain from her face "What on earth do you need hundreds of rifles for?" She hoped she sounded as unnerved as she felt.

"For Ireland." His face was alight with excitement, though Nora could tell he was trying to conceal it. All at once he looked to her the way he always had, when they were children in Clare. The spark she had missed in him had returned in full force.

"And just what do you aim to do with them?" she asked. She reached over and forcefully guided Colin's face so that he looked her in the eye. She wasn't going to let him evade this question. He didn't disappoint.

"Send those English whores back to London," he whispered, winking at her. He moved her hand away and began to make his way toward the ladder.

"But Colin!"

"Shhhh!"

He came back toward her. "You can pretend to be concerned all you want— but I can read yer eyes, and they tell me you're at least a little intrigued."

"I'm not pretendin'! Ye seem to be up to yer neck in trouble!"

"You're intrigued. Come on, admit it. As sure as you're sittin' there with yer wide, green eyes, you're intrigued." He bent down so he faced her as she sat on the straw mattress. "Thank you for reading the letter to me," he whispered. Then he leaned forward and gave her a quick kiss on the cheek.

"What was that for?" she asked. "I'm always reading to you."

"Wasn't for you, 'twas for me," he said. "Aunt Maeve is convinced I'm up to no good. She's going to give me hell the minute I get off that ladder, and I hate gettin' scolded for nothin'."

Nora finally smiled too. "I suppose I am in trouble too, then."

"Not yet," he said. "You're still 'little Nora.' Couldn't do a thing wrong." She felt herself start to scowl at him—she hated it when he teased her—but the scowl only encouraged him. "Did you want to be in trouble?"

He leaned over once more, and this time kissed her slowly on her lips.

"There, now you're in trouble too." He scurried over to the ladder and this time descended. "Good night, Nora," he whispered.

She unexpectedly sighed in relief as she watched him disappear from sight. This was the Colin that she remembered and had missed so much over the past year. She lay back on the mattress in time to hear him catch an earful from his Aunt Maeve.

CHAPTER 13

July 29, 1914: London, England

Gerald stepped quickly across the great hall of his parents' London residence. The stiff leather of his shoes sounded a purposeful rhythm across the tiles, helping him feign a confidence he did not feel. He, as his brother, adored his mother, and in his adoration had always enjoyed a respectful but honest relationship with her. In a few areas of his life, he omitted details—mostly pertaining to nights at Cambridge where perhaps he had entertained female guests of questionable character—but on the whole, he had open and frank conversations with his mother and trusted her with information that he would never relay to his father.

But he also loved mischief. So when Edward had presented him with a scheme to secure Lord and Lady Clarendon an invitation to this year's anniversary party, he accepted the challenge despite having to be less-than-honest with his mother. *She'd kill me if she knew,* he thought with a grin.

Lord and Lady Clarendon were well known in London society for their somewhat radical tendencies, which earned them more enemies than friends among their contemporaries, but also granted them near-heroic status among their children's generation. Gerald was no exception.

He believed that his own father was genuine about his politics, but Gerald found inconsistencies with his father's opinions. For example, Viscount Eldridge wanted to avoid a war in Europe but wanted with all his soul to crush the growing Irish nationalism in and around Dublin. These were common sentiments among members of Parliament, but Gerald saw this as shortsighted at best, and heartless at worst.

Gerald and Edward both knew that Lady Clarendon's American influence had certainly had a softening effect on her husband's politics. Having grown up under American democracy and with a liberal senator for a father, she formed her political views in a decidedly nonaristocratic way, and, through her husband, often sent shockwaves through the stale halls of Westminster.

In addition to backing his wife's unprecedented and outspoken support for women's suffrage—during a time when the suffragette movement was becoming quite an aggravation for the House of Lords—Lord Clarendon had taken another unusual stance on foreign politics. A very few parliamentarians strongly supported the Irish nationalists; and most recently, many others supported a war in Europe. But Lord Clarendon was singular and almost revolutionary with his fervent support of both: Irish Home Rule *and* a war with Germany. In the eyes of most parliamentarians, the views were incompatible. The pro-Irish were taunted as weak and, perhaps worse, sacrilegious. Those who wanted a war on the continent were patriotic, though the doves saw them as perhaps misguided. Some hawks wanted a war on both fronts. Lord Clarendon's views confounded his peers.

But Gerald found his logic principled, which was why he supposed he admired the man. Clarendon himself described it as "support for self-determination," which to him meant that the people of both Ireland and the Balkans should be able to determine how they wanted to be ruled. Whether the Irish wanted to be ruled by England or preferred self-rule, it was for them to decide. Similarly, if the Balkans wanted to be rid of the Habsburgs, that was a decision for those living in the Balkans, not for Vienna. It was this seemingly paradoxical position that earned Lord Clarendon the wrath of many in London's upper-class corners.

The political divide between the Clarendons and the Eldridges made for almost insurmountable complications with Edward's choice of Elizabeth, and the timing only added to the difficulty. Lord Clarendon and his father were particularly at odds during these tense weeks, and while his parents were eager to see Edward settled with an appropriate bride, Gerald assumed that from his father's perspective, Elizabeth would not fit the bill. His mother, however, had potential to be swayed.

꒰Ꙧ꒱

Viscountess Anita Eldridge sat before a large desk in the sitting room outside the library. Directly across from her sat one of her attendants, Alice, who feverishly wrote notes as Lady Eldridge dictated. Lady Eldridge also held a pen, to what purpose Alice could not conceive, but she waved it in the air as the ideas flew from her mouth at an astounding rate, leaving poor Alice flustered as she attempted to capture every last detail.

"And the hall shall be decorated with lilacs—no—lilies. I want white lilies at every entrance and at every table. And oranges. Can we get oranges this time of year? The duke and duchess simply adore citrus and, therefore I'd like to have platters brought to each table with oranges and perhaps even grapefruits. We certainly want to lay out the best. We have but a few opportunities to entertain the duke."

She paused thoughtfully, pen pointed directly at the ceiling as if she were about to strike up a band. Alice took advantage of the short pause to catch up on a few of the viscountess's directions before looking up and dreading the next round of instructions. As Lady Eldridge took a breath in preparation for another round of detailed imaginations of the anniversary party, she caught sight of Gerald as he stood in the doorway. "Gerald, my dear!"

Gerald had always been his mother's favorite, and to Alice she seemed genuinely excited to see him each day, now that he was home on a semipermanent basis from university. "How lovely to see you!" the viscountess continued. "Alice and I were just discussing floral arrangements for the party. Do you prefer white or pink lilies? I think white is more pristine. Yes, yes, definitely white. Thank you, darling, you've helped me to decide. Mark that down, Alice! Gerald wants white." The rapidity of her speech was astonishing, and Gerald's expression indicated he was pondering how long she had been dictating to work herself into such a frenzy.

At the mention of Gerald, Alice spun around, then quickly caught herself and turned back to her notes, pretending to concentrate on her paper. She hoped that Lady Eldridge did not notice her face flushing. With her pale complexion, her skin easily and instantly became blotchy and red. Gerald remained cool and collected as he sat down next to his mother. He stole a quick glance at Alice and smiled politely. She thought it unfair that he could act so casual around her, while she could barely look at him in public without becoming embarrassed. It certainly didn't help that he was assuredly the more attractive of the Eldridge brothers.

"Mother," he began. "I see your party arrangements are coming along swimmingly."

"Oh, Gerald," she replied with a sigh, resting her cheek on the hand that still firmly gripped a pen, "it is such a task, and simply exhausting. There are so many choices, and the party is approaching. And to make matters worse, the window dressings just aren't going to do. The color schemes are all wrong, and we haven't time to replace them. Such a shame." She looked cross for a moment.

"Mother, take a break," Gerald said before she could continue.

"I simply cannot," she replied in an exasperated voice. "There is just too much to do."

"Alice can continue the planning for the afternoon. She certainly can fill in a few details," he added, winking at her.

Alice stared at him while the viscountess's head was turned, and shook her head violently. "Surely this party is far too important for the likes of me—" she protested, but he cut her off.

"Ridiculous!" Gerald announced. "Alice will move forward with your directions. We can't have you stressed before such an important party," he added smoothly—so smoothly, in fact, that Alice could not tell if he was being sarcastic or if he actually believed what he said. "Besides, I thought perhaps I could accompany you to the charity event this afternoon." He smiled innocently.

"Charity event? I didn't commit to a charity event today!" Lady Eldridge's eyes darkened again.

Gerald looked at Alice, who caught his cue and nervously stammered, "Why yes, Lady Eldridge, don't you recall that we accepted an invitation to an event supporting the literacy campaign?"

"Literacy campaign?" said his mother, raising her voice and enunciating each syllable, as she often did when annoyed. "Surely not. Isn't this hosted by Lady Clarendon? No, surely not."

Alice thought quickly. "Has there been some mistake?" She felt her face getting redder and redder.

"Oh, Lady Clarendon!" said Gerald, as calm as ever. "What an excellent opportunity. The duchess will surely be there."

"The duchess?" The viscountess sounded intrigued.

"Why, yes," interjected Alice, going off script. "She and the duchess are quite close, I do believe." She felt her voice crack as she spat out what she knew to be completely inaccurate. The duchess despised Lady Clarendon's crazy ideas just as much as the rest of the upper crust of society. Even a nitwit knew this, and Alice was quite sure that the viscountess was no nitwit.

Gerald winked at her. "Perfect," he mouthed.

Alice waited in silence, fearing Lady Eldridge's response.

"The duchess, you say?" she repeated slowly, apparently intrigued. "Yes, I believe we did accept that invitation! Thank you for reminding me. I shall call Francis to prepare the carriage. How lovely of you to join me, Gerald. She has several daughters you know—the duchess." Her face lit up as she looked to Gerald, smiling. "How lovely, indeed!"

She turned to walk from the room. With her back safely to them, Gerald brushed past Alice, giving her a quick kiss on the cheek. Alice felt her cheeks flush.

Lady Eldridge turned suddenly. "Alice, I'll need you to carry out my instructions per our conversation." She paused. "Are you feeling ill, dear? Your face is flushed. No time to be ill today! There's work to be done!" And with that, she briskly left the room.

Gerald turned to Alice. "And you were perfect!" he exclaimed. "Thank you, my darling." He planted another kiss, this time directly on her lips, then pulled away to look at her. "You know, my dear, my mother is a horrible influence on you."

"Well that's not quite fair—"

"She is. Whenever you are around her you are perpetually nervous—all of her particular tastes are enough to make anyone exhausted. Don't take her so seriously."

"But Gerald!" she whispered, "the duchess will most assuredly not be at the event today. I'm quite sure she despises the Clarendons!" How could he expect her not to be nervous?

"Don't worry, little girl," he said. "I will take care of it." He walked from the room, then leaned his head back through the open doorway. "And you were simply perfect." He added in a low voice, "and I look forward to returning the favor." This time he walked out too soon to see the flush she felt surge back into her cheeks.

As Gerald again walked down the expansive hallway, he smiled at the echo of Alice's quaint country accent in his mind and laughed at the absurdity of what they were trying to accomplish. In a more sobering thought, he realized that he could be entirely happy spending the rest of his life with Alice, though he couldn't imagine a world where they would be together. That was the funny thing about privilege—it was no privilege at all. He had the world at his very fingertips, yet he could not even acknowledge the girl that he loved. As both he and his brother were finding out, membership among the country's elite wasn't kind to matters of the heart.

Hell, he thought, *if Edward can't propose to a girl of social standing just because our parents' politics differ, a life with Alice is beyond impossible.* And yet he knew he would continue to pursue her anyways, because he simply enjoyed being around her. *And that makes me a coward,* he realized.

The walls around him were replete with reminders of the life he was intended to live—or so his parents imagined. Fine art adorned every wall. Servants bustled back and forth from room to room, tending to the every need of his family. The Eldridge crest was displayed prominently—the same crest that would be bestowed upon heirs to the Eldridge name. *Assuming their mother isn't a member of the staff,* he thought dejectedly. But for all the riches and the opportunities that would come to him just because of his heritage, his life felt surprisingly empty. When he was away at university, he could distract himself with the various temptations around him, but when he was home he rarely had this escape. What distressed him the most was that he hadn't had the faintest idea what to do with the burden of privilege—it certainly didn't permit him to do the things he wanted to most—and yet he felt it was his duty to use his place in the world to do something worthwhile.

And until recent days, he had found no purpose, no calling. He had wondered if he would waste away in a perpetual adolescence looking for a noble path. And then the tiny country of Belgium had entered into the collective conscience of his country and given him a real purpose.

Prior to this month, he had never given a second thought to the small neutral nation nestled precariously in between two continental powers and wholly incapable of defending herself. *The Kaiser could take it in a matter of days,* he thought. Approaching the front entryway to the residence, he plopped himself on a velvet cushioned chaise to wait to join his mother for the short carriage ride to Lady Clarendon's charity event.

It would break his mother's heart to have two sons fighting on the continent, but he knew that England needed educated young men like himself in the military. He reasoned that if England were to declare war on Germany, it would be a quick and decisive win. No power could take on the combined armies of England and France. *It's finally a real purpose. A way to use my privilege for something besides my own pleasure,* he thought. Given his father's position, he would likely enter as a captain in the King's Army, just like his brother, and be given command of a company. He felt slightly better, though the idea that he was a coward for not acknowledging Alice still gnawed at him.

Gerald was awoken from his thoughts by the sight of his mother, her plump, middle-aged figure bursting through the doorway in a flurry of resolute energy. Several attendants followed, listening intently and looking just as nervous as Alice had as the viscountess rattled off instructions. He wondered how many times in his life he had witnessed such scenes. Viscountess Eldridge was unrivaled in her ability to direct—and to get exactly what she wanted.

"And the salon furniture should be rearranged so that the chaise benefits from the afternoon sun, but not so that it is too bright. I like to take my tea in the sunlight, but not such that I overheat." She paused to fan herself as if to emphasize her discomfort.

Then she abruptly changed topics. "And the girls' tutors—please have them focus more on their French lessons. I was appalled at Anna's French when the ambassador came to call. And since it appears we are about to embark on a closer relationship with Paris"—she emphasized this point—"it would *behoove us all* to work on our *diplomacy* with the French, beginning with *language*." Her voice got louder and her enunciation more exact as she continued. "And finally," she exclaimed, running short of breath, "schedule another session for dear Edward this afternoon. With the frenzy that is building this week, I am afraid his portraits will not be complete before he receives his orders." A look of dramatic despair fell across her face. "At least I will have you, Gerald, for comfort after your dear brother departs. I can hardly bear the thought of him leaving and being in harm's way. Praise heaven that it is destined to be a short affair!"

His heart sank a little. Meanwhile, she continued toward the massive door that led to the carriage road, where she paused poignantly to illustrate that no one was yet there to open it. Just then, Francis appeared with the viscountess's fascinator and summer shawl and opened the door. The midday sun flooded the parlor. Gerald donned his top hat and, taking his mother's arm, escorted her to the waiting carriage.

"We are so blessed to have Alice," she said in a melodramatic voice. "What would we do without her? She's the only one of the staff I trust completely. It's a shame she has no lineage. Any gentleman would be lucky to have her. She just has a sophisticated and sensible way about her—you'd think she was from a right and proper family."

Gerald sighed heavily and nodded. "An outright shame, Mother."

The stifling late July air hung heavily inside the carriage as mother and son took their seats for the short ride to the Clarendons'. Wiping his brow with a kerchief, Gerald said, "Mother, 'tis good of you to support the less fortunate."

His mother cocked her head and looked at her son. "Dear Gerald, I have never been an advocate for the illiterate," she said matter-of-factly. "We are supporting the campaign as a way to mingle with the duchess and others who are worthy of our attention. And don't pretend that you don't already know this," she added, her lips still pursed and eyes squinting from the late morning sun.

Gerald sighed. "But surely, Mother, all of the good you and Father do and the financial support you provide to charities is done with compassion, is it not?" He grimaced at the ghastly directness of his inquiry.

"Oh Gerald—" the carriage jostled, and she instinctively lifted her hands to her fascinator to ensure that her hair remained perfectly coiffed. "Gerald, dear," she continued, "we are not heartless, we just have to have priorities. Your father and I are quite busy with our social agendas, and each activity must support your father's positions but also be a benefit to his good name—which is your business as well! Nothing we do is simply willy-nilly."

Gerald, sitting directly across from his mother, purposefully did not inform her that a lock of her graying hair had come loose. He watched it bounce along as if dancing to the motion of the carriage. "But Gerald, your heart is young and it is in the right place. When I was younger, I was a passionate girl. I felt so strongly about certain ideals and felt such energy within me, but knew that if I devoted myself to these passions I would stray from the role that I was meant to play in this life." She gave him a little smile, almost as if embarrassed at having shared this part of her with him.

"And what role is that, Mother?" he asked, pressing her to continue.

"To be your mother, of course!" she instantly replied, as if this should be obvious to him. "And to be your father's wife and to support him and to promote him—we want him to be successful, now don't we?" Gerald knew better than to answer, though he wasn't sure he wanted his father to be successful if it meant letting Belgium get overrun by the Germans. "And through this," she continued, evidently unaware that her favorite son might disagree, "particularly as your father is a peer and has great impact, we are both fulfilled. That is a partnership, Gerald, and that is what women do. We are stronger than we appear," she said with emphasis. Then she lowered her voice and flashed a grin across her plump face. "And we don't always agree with our husbands, but we support them. That is what we do."

He looked out the window at the bustling streets of London as he pondered.

She had never opened up to him quite like this before. Then speaking carefully, he said, "And you see the best way for you to support father is to follow a social agenda that you don't have any passion for?" He hoped he hadn't offended her.

But his mother continued happily, "I am attending this event, and most others for that matter, for you, dear Gerald. And for Edward and your sisters. My involvement in these social circles eases your route to success. And I am happy to do this for you."

He smiled at her to be polite, but couldn't help but feel profoundly sad for his mother. Surely her life was more than this. He had never given her role much thought before, or ever really considered how she felt about the innumerable daily tasks she performed. She always attacked each endeavor with such energy and confidence that he had assumed she was impassioned—that she had found a purpose—and not that she was just performing a duty.

The carriage weaved steadily through south London, passing businessmen bustling through the streets and mothers who grabbed their children by the arms to avoid the unpredictable carriage traffic, all in the blazing July sun. Gerald was thankful for the breeze made by the quick pace of the carriage, as it brought some relief.

"Gerald, my dear, thank you," his mother started as the carriage approached the entrance to the Clarendon mansion and began to slow.

"Whatever for?" he asked.

She looked at him directly. "Thank you for sitting across from me and thinking youthful thoughts. It has given me just the glimmer of a memory of my youth, reminding me that I once was a girl and felt passion about certain things. Much more than a glimmer, and I do believe my heart might break. I had long forgotten that I, too, am capable of such emotion."

Gerald slowly put his kerchief into his breast pocket and said, "Mother, if you don't mind my asking, what were your interests before you and father were married?"

"Suffrage," she said quietly, almost too softly to perceive. Her eyes looked sad.

Gerald was surprised at this response. He never imagined his mother to be political.

As if sensing his confusion, looked him in the eye and explained, "I wanted someday to be able to be part of something real, something important. And I thought the best way that I could do that would be to voice my political opinion through a vote. Perhaps my role now, in supporting your father, in some way fulfills that." Gerald thought he heard her voice break. "But it's not quite the same."

Gerald felt his own heart break. His own dear mother had felt the same need for purpose as he did, and yet her supposedly privileged position had failed her. What had high society done to his poor mother? Aristocracy was certainly not a membership without cost. Today he had briefly seen a spark in her eye he had never seen before. Was it this passion that made father fall in love with her? How quickly after they were engaged did it disappear, once she entered a world where it was forbidden? Had her independence slowly left, or had it been suffocated? Was it still in there somewhere?

He thought of Edward's Elizabeth and her fiery defenses of her ideals. Would she, too, be silenced once she married Edward? *What are people when they suppress what makes them special in the first place?*

Instead of letting his mother see how saddened he was by her admission, he put on a cheery face. "Well then, Mother, we've come to the right place. In addition to supporting literacy, Lady Clarendon is also a strong advocate for women's suffrage. Perhaps she will make a better companion today than the duchess."

His mother smiled. "Perhaps, dear Gerald, perhaps."

CHAPTER 14

July 29, 1914: London, England

Lady Clarendon's event was a sight to behold, and unlike any social event Gerald had previously attended. In fact, there was nothing about it that resembled the carefully choreographed social gatherings he was accustomed to. A few of the same faces were there, but entering the Clarendon mansion was like stumbling into a different world.

The first thing that struck him was the commotion. Instead of guests sitting in quiet circles as butlers silently tended to their requests, the parlor was abuzz with chatter and high society ladies scurrying about, each seemingly having a task they were attending to. Viscountess Eldridge was taken aback when the breezy footman took her cloak and hat, and instead of escorting her to Lady Clarendon, simply pointed toward the sitting room where the hostess might be found.

"This is madness!" she said shout-whispered to Gerald, who, following the footman's casual finger, led his mother off toward the sitting room.

As they made their awkward way down a crowded hallway lined in green silk, the viscountess clutched Gerald's arm like he was the parent and she the child. The bustling guests pushed by as they hurried from room to room.

Yet with all the commotion, Gerald couldn't help but notice the general cheer that wafted about the large, sunny rooms. Every woman there, from the stylish young debutantes to the gray-haired dowagers, had a smile on her face, and some laughed as they assembled pamphlets, organized books, and chatted about this or that. With all the organizing and piling that was going on, not one lady seemed to notice that she was working. There was nothing but gaiety everywhere.

"Well, this is quite the pleasant surprise, isn't it, Mother?" Gerald asked cheerfully. But as he looked down and smiled at his mother, her large brown eyes opened wide and her lips pursed in the most disapproving little frown, as though she had been whisked from her pleasant afternoon carriage ride and thrown into a circus ring. He couldn't help but laugh. "Smile, Mother," he said to her, nudging her elbow. "This is what passion looks like in 1914!"

Her stubborn frown softened slightly, but her lips remained pursed. Gerald wondered if perhaps he had made a mistake in bringing her here.

"Gerald, I don't see the duchess!" she whispered nervously.

She certainly didn't fit in with these exuberant, joyful ladies. There was no one here for her to take charge of, and outside her element, she seemed like a lost little puppy.

"Now, I'm sure she's here. Come now," he said, "Here's Lady Clarendon." He had only met Lord and Lady Clarendon once before, and he was almost positive she would have no idea who he was, but having studied theater extensively while at Cambridge—by way of spending a many a night studying the physique of one of London's up-and-coming actresses—he strode off to make use of any acting skills he had gleaned from these dalliances, a reluctant Viscountess Eldridge in tow.

As he made his way through the ladies crowded around Lady Clarendon, he caught her eye, and at once her face lit up. She bellowed, in a most unladylike way, "Gerald! Gerald, how lovely to see you! Simply wonderful of you to come!"

She trotted—and ladies never trotted—right up to him, grabbing his hand with both of hers, and in that odd Yankee accent said, "I am just thrilled to have you here!"

Before Gerald could say anything, Lady Clarendon turned to Viscountess Eldridge and said, "Anita! I cannot tell you how pleased I am to have you. Thank you for accepting my invitation!"

His mother, mouth slightly agape, just stared. Her gaze went from Lady Clarendon to Gerald and back to Lady Clarendon, and then fixated on Lady Clarendon's hands, still clasped to Gerald's. *She has likely never in her life witnessed a woman shake the hand of a man,* Gerald thought anxiously, so he spoke for her. "And Mother is simply thrilled to be here. She is most passionate about literacy!" He beamed; his acting skills were blossoming. Those late nights with his favorite actress had proven worthwhile after all.

Lady Eldridge stared at Gerald, then sighed and said, "Most certainly. Such a pleasure to receive your invitation."

Gerald breathed a sigh of relief and passed his recovering mother off to Lady Clarendon, who grabbed Lady Eldridge's arm and led her into the throngs of women. Thus began his mother's foray into twentieth-century social movements.

As his mother slowly begin to fold pamphlets, he was interrupted by a tap on his shoulder. It was Elizabeth, who, even when dressed in a simple summer dress, was stunning. *How did a bloke like Edward ever attract her attention?* Grabbing him by the hand, she pulled him back into the quiet parlor. She had a beaming smile, not unlike her mother's. "Gerald, whatever are you doing here?" she asked.

"Running an errand, that's all," he answered.

"What errand would bring you here, with your mother?" she inquired flirtatiously. But Gerald could sense she knew exactly what he was doing.

A glance through the archway that led to the sitting room told him that his mother, to his surprise, seemed to be enjoying herself, chatting politely with Lady Clarendon as they folded papers. "I'm not quite sure," he answered. "But you'll either hate me or love me for it. Time will tell."

He nodded toward their mothers, now chatting excitedly. His mother picked up a pen and began pointing it in the air with large swooping movements. Other ladies took notice and began to gather around. A chorus of "Oh yes!" and "Marvelous!" arose from their midst. The viscountess had found something to direct.

He laughed to himself and turned back to Elizabeth. "I have a hunch that you're going to love me," he said.

CHAPTER 15

July 29, 1914: Dublin, Ireland

"But what will happen next?" Nora asked Colin in a hushed voice. She did her best to appear calm, but her eyes were wide with alarm.

"I'm not sure." He grabbed his knapsack and her linen sack from the rack above their seats. The morning train from Ennis had arrived in Dublin, and most passengers were disembarking. Colin grabbed an abandoned newspaper from a vacant seat and stuffed it into his knapsack.

As they emerged from the train, Nora was curious about the world she was entering, yet so nervous she felt sick to her stomach. The bustling station was like nothing she had ever seen before. *So many people!* Colin extended his hand to hers as she jumped from the train to the platform and held onto it long after she steadied herself.

Colin's eyes were directed toward the exit to the station, and he appeared lost in thought as he led her down the platform. She followed, jogging to keep up with him and darting around the myriad of passengers who all seemed in a hurry. The smell of perspiration filled the station as people scurried about, attempting to board the train to Dundalk, the last stop before heading north to Ulster.

"Me cousin could have been more clear when he wrote that we were at war!" Colin mumbled, as they quickly moved through the crowd to exit the platform. "Bastard."

Nora was mesmerized by the sheer number of people in the train station, all coming and going in different directions. She had never been around so many people. It made her dizzy. Sensing her confusion, Colin put his hand on the small of her back and guided her along.

When they had cleared the platform and emerged out into the bright July sun, he pulled her out of the way of the crowds and reached into his knapsack. He handed the newspaper to Nora.

She looked at him. "You ought—"

But he interrupted. "Yeah I know."

"Just how have you made it this year without someone to read for you?"

"Nora!" he said, impatiently.

She leaned up against the exterior wall of the station, unrolled the paper and read him the headline. "Three people shot dead by British soldiers on Bachelors Walk."

"Jesus Christ!" said Colin. "It's true."

Nora kept reading. "More than thirty others injured as soldiers shoot into crowd." She too was also in disbelief. "A fourth died later from injuries."

"Who did it?" asked Colin.

Nora skimmed down the page. The passengers leaving the station were distracting. An exasperated mother yelled at a chubby little child who was hauling a massive suitcase. "I ain't carryin' a thing!" she cried. "You carry yer own trunk! An' keep up or I'll leave you behind!" The boy dramatically collapsed and proceeded to wail. The commotion made it hard for Nora to concentrate on the paper.

"Looks like the 'King's Own Scottish Borderers,'" said Nora, pointing back to the paper and trying to ignore the screaming child. "Do you know of them?

"I do," he said. "Fookin' whores."

Nora looked down again at the paper in her hands. "It says they were confronting the Volunteers as they returned on the road from Howth and ordering them to disarm."

"Did the arms make it through?" he asked urgently.

Nora ran her fingers along the text. They were wet with perspiration, from the heat or her own anxiety she did not know. Her hands began to smudge the ink on the delicate paper.

"Well?" he said impatiently.

Nora scanned frantically. "Yes!" she exclaimed. "Only twenty rifles were seized!" Colin's face lit up again, and Nora frowned. "Why is it that only rifles seem to make you smile these days?" she asked.

He shrugged and took the paper back from her, shoving it in his knapsack.

"Stop smiling," she said. "You just said that yer cousin thinks we're practically at war."

He shrugged. "Come, Nora. We've got a ways to go yet."

"But Colin," she said again, almost yelling as she fell behind him, "What will happen now that the Volunteers have rifles?"

"Maybe nothing at all," he said, over his shoulder. "But that's not the point. The point is that if something does happen, we are ready." He slowed his pace until she caught up. "And it is a good thing, Nora—it is a good thing. We are on equal footing with the Ulstermen. What's more, we are ready to show the British our grit."

"But what might happen?" she asked. She practically had to run along the cobblestone street to keep up with Colin. Her ankles were unsteady in her ill-fitting shoes as she ran along the slippery stones.

"Home Rule," he said. The smile had not disappeared from his face. "Home

Rule might happen, Nora—and if it does, Ulster will not take it sittin' down. There will be a fight! And now we'll be ready." He was still grinning ear to ear. "And if the Brits don't give us Home Rule—we can fight 'em for it!" He stopped suddenly as a carriage rolled directly into their path. The driver cursed at him. Colin yelled in reply, "Watch where you're goin', you arse!"

Not skipping a beat, he turned back to Nora. "Nora, this is a good thing," he repeated. She was only half listening now, awestruck by the sheer amount of traffic all trying to cram itself down one narrow side street. "We've been trying to make this happen ever since Ulster brought in arms last year," Colin was saying, "and it's been damned near impossible after the Brits passed a law makin' it illegal to ship arms to anywhere in Ireland."

Nora paused, stopping dead in her tracks. A car loudly sounded its horn for her to move, but she stood her ground. "Why do you refer to the Volunteers as 'we'? You're one of 'em, aren't you?" She would not put it past Colin to be right in the thick of trouble.

He reached out into the street and pulled her to the side of the road to allow the blocked car to pass. "They'll run you right over, you know!"

She locked eyes with him. "Answer me." She knew he couldn't look her in the eye and lie to her.

"Ah no you don't," he said. "I know yer tricks!" She cocked her head slightly. It made her hair fall in front of her face, and Colin put his hand out as if to brush it away, then abruptly pulled back. He looked off over her shoulder, and Nora saw his left arm reach for the flask tucked neatly inside of his right waistband, a gesture she knew meant he was conflicted.

"You are, aren't you?" she asked.

He reluctantly brought his eyes back to her. "Yes, Nora," he said in a hushed voice. "But it's best you don't talk about it."

"Why not?" Nora asked, baffled. Colin's admission had released a curious energy inside of her, and she could feel her heart race. "Surely it's something you are proud of!" Her voice was getting louder.

"Of course, Nora," he said. But he glanced about the crowd uneasily. "Let's forget it for now? We can talk about it later."

Nora continued to push. "How could I possibly forget about it?" Why on earth would Colin have kept this from her, especially when they had talked of no other topic for the previous two days? "You don't trust me," she said aloud.

"No Nora," he said firmly. "I trust you absolutely. It's others I do not trust."

"Who?" asked Nora.

Colin hesitated. "The Parsons." He paused, then added, "Yer new employer."

At this she became quiet, as it hit her all at once. "They're Protestant!" she exclaimed.

Colin sighed. "Nora, of course they are. You think a Catholic can afford to hire anyone? To pay anyone wages? If they could, they would have been run out of this city long ago and robbed of all their wealth."

Nora felt embarrassed. How had she not put the clues together? Of course they would be Protestant. "Are they Irish at least?" she asked.

"The missus is a Brit through and through. Accent straight from London. As for the mister, he'll say he's Irish. Every last one of the Presbyterians will," Colin replied. "They all claim they are. But in truth, they're from England or Scotland, but they've been here so long they think they're Irish."

"How long?" asked Nora.

"Jesus Christ, Nora! How many questions could you possibly have?" he said, exasperated. When she fell silent, his face fell regretfully. "You sound like you're from some back county or something, where nothing ever happens," he joked, clearly attempting to apologize.

But he had hurt her feelings. They walked along the street in silence. The midday sun bore down on them. The tension grew between them.

"Fook," Colin finally muttered. He sidestepped into a small alley and abruptly pulled Nora in with him. The brick buildings were so close together that instead of feeling cooler, the heat from the structures radiated into the small space. He leaned over so they were looking face to face.

"Let's have it out," he said. "Look, I—"

"You're an arse!" she cried.

He burst out laughing, his hands still on her shoulders.

She hadn't expected this, and try as she might, she could not help but let a smile escape. The tension started to dissipate. His long, blond hair fell over his eyes as he laughed, and she absentmindedly reached over and brushed it out of the way.

"I am an arse, aren't I?" he said, gently taking her hand away. "Tell me off, then. We're friends, right? You can tell me whatever you like." He stood up straight and towered over her again. "And I can tell you whatever I like too, all right?"

"All right," she said.

"So it's settled," he said. "I'm an arse, and you—" he leaned over again and looked her in the eye. "Y'are the best part of my day, despite yer bloody questions." He put up a hand to stop her from responding. "And to answer yer question, the Parsons will fleece Ireland as long as they can keep their English privilege."

"Why did you bring me here then?" It made no sense to her. *Why would Colin agree to have her hired out to these people? People who probably detested boys like him?* But that wasn't the real reason why she asked the question. He never could bring himself to voice his affection for her, and as they neared the end of their trip and a life she was too nervous to imagine, she needed more than ever to hear it.

"Because you had nowhere else to go," he said. "And if you stayed in Clare," his voice trailed off. "If you stayed in Clare, who the hell would I have to ask me questions?" He smiled.

Just say it, she thought.

"Or get me into trouble?" he continued.

"You can get yerself into trouble," she said, egging him on. "You don't need me to do that."

He shook his head. "Nora, the kind of trouble I get myself in might land me in the drunk tank for a day or two. But the kind of trouble you'll get me in—a fookin' mortal sin." He winked at her.

"Are you afraid of mortal sins?" she asked. She had known the answer to this question for years.

"Don't flirt with me," he said. "You know I'm terrified of 'em."

"You shouldn't be," she said. "As soon I pray to God and he listens but once I'll start to fear mortal sins."

"Then I'll be afraid for yer everlasting salvation for you," he said. "And yer blasphemy," Nora saw that he couldn't help but smile as he said this. It wasn't what she was hoping for, but it was as close to an admission of his feelings that she was likely to get.

They walked further from King's Bridge train station toward the old city center. Instead of thinning, the crowds only intensified, and they seemed to spread out over a vast area. Colin and Nora were jostled among the throngs making their way toward the various bridges that crossed the river.

The temperature was hot, and Nora instantly missed the refreshing breeze that constantly cooled the soft hills around Ballynote. The River Liffey was not so generous as the Shannon, which always seemed to revive her on hot summer days with its cool Atlantic breeze.

Sweat was dripping from Colin's forehead down the sides of his face, and his shirt was already sticking to his back and arms. Nora grabbed his arm to keep from being separated. "I had no idea Dublin would be so crowded," she said.

Colin glanced at the masses around them. "It's not," he said, confused. "It's never this crowded. Something is happening."

A group of young boys ran past them, and Colin yelled to one over the noise of the passing pedestrians: "Hey there, fella!" The scene around them was no longer just heavily trafficked by groups of people walking—it was approaching chaos. "What's all the commotion about?"

"There's a parade on, don't you know!" shouted the youngest looking of the bunch, a thin boy in baggy clothes that looked like they belonged to a much older brother.

"Aye," called one of his dirty-faced companions. "And we's goin' to be marchin' in it. We're Fianna Eireann!" he proudly yelled. The group of boys, perhaps ten or eleven years old and all dressed in dark pants and lighter tunics, dashed off into the crowds, dodging from side to side between the pedestrians. Everyone now seemed to be moving in the same direction.

Nora now sensed urgency in Colin's step. "Come with me, this way!" They backtracked, heading north toward the Liffey, moving with the crowds, then darted the same way the boys had gone until they found a relatively empty side street. From there they followed the contour of the river deep into the heart of the city.

Nora had a hundred questions for Colin, but she kept her mouth closed as she followed along. They kept the crowds on the main street within their sight but avoided the overcrowded thoroughfare. Above her, on the side of the building, a small metal sign read "Henry Street." Almost simultaneously, Colin stopped. "Here," he said. "We'll cut by the post office. Let's see what's going on."

The crowds were noisy and agitated. Many people vigorously waved green, handmade flags and banners. Nora and Colin pushed their way toward the front to catch a view of whatever was happening on Sackville Street. All at once, a massive cheer arose. Nora stood on her toes, but all she could see was the backs of heads and a sea of green flags.

"What is it?" she asked.

"Here," he said. He placed his hands gently around her waist and lifted her up to stand atop the base of a nearby gas lamppost. She closed her eyes and was immediately brought back to Clare, when he used to lift her onto the banks of the Shannon after one of their many secret afternoon swims. She opened them again, and all around her children were also clinging to the lampposts that lined the street, trying their best to catch a glimpse of the massive assembly.

Now taller than Colin, she stood atop her perch and peered down the road.

"I see columns of men marching," she said.

"Aye," said Colin, "those are the Volunteers."

"And who are all the women and girls?"

Colin looked in the direction of the marchers, but he could not see past the front rows of the crowd. He grabbed the black iron post and pulled himself up alongside Nora. The jostling crowds pressed him up against her, and he put his arm around her to steady them. She could smell the faintest scent of whiskey on him—she loved that smell.

"Must be Cumann na mBan," he said, easily slipping into the Gaelic they had both learned as children. "The women's auxiliary. This is not a spontaneous march. The two groups don't usually coordinate like this. And look," he added, "here come our friends."

Following Colin's gaze, Nora saw dozens of younger boys, dressed just like the ones they had seen earlier, walking alongside the Volunteers. "Those are Fianna Eireann boys," said Colin. "They will be Volunteers as well in a few years' time."

Nora looked back down the road, watching the columns of marching men and scanning the ever-expanding body of people around them. By now, all of the lampposts were occupied by multiple passersby trying to get a better view. Nora had never seen a crowd such as this. Just listening to the noise and watching the sea of people made her dizzy. She leaned back into Colin, who had settled himself behind her. She noticed that he had not loosened his grip around her, though neither of them was in danger of falling off the post. His hand, still resting along her waistline, seemed so large against her small figure.

Just as quickly as the roar of the crowd had begun, it began to hush. One moment, thousands of people were shouting, cheering, and waving flags; then the roar abruptly softened to whispers of people hushing their neighbors. The columns of Volunteers, auxiliary, and Fianna Eireann had halted in place, and a black horse pulling a cart came into view.

Nora was about to ask Colin what was happening, but he quieted her and nodded back in the direction of the cart. All at once, Nora saw that on a platform atop the cart lay a solitary casket. Three other horses pulling similar makeshift hearses followed closely. This was not a parade. It was a funeral procession. People continued to wave their flags high, but the rowdiness had calmed into reverence.

The horses began plodding along Grafton Street toward the lamppost where Nora and Colin stood. "On their way from the Pro Cathedral, no doubt," Colin said.

"Aye," said an older man standing under them. His gnarly old hands gripped a tattered green flag. "All four of 'em will be laid to rest today at Glasnevin. And no sign of the King's Butcherers."

"They aren't so bold now, are they?" said a red-faced, scowling woman. "Let's see 'em come out and shoot private citizens today!"

"You won't be seeing them now," smiled the man. "Not when there are a thousand angry Mausers on the streets of Dublin!"

Colin nudged Nora and nodded.

The horses passed slowly. At the sight of the coffins, a familiar pit in Nora's stomach returned, and she thought of her grandfather, cold in the earth. The feeling was in stark contrast to this funeral, where the atmosphere seemed more cheerful than mournful. It was hard to connect these deaths with the rambunctious and almost party-like atmosphere in front of them.

"Are all funerals in Dublin like this?" she asked Colin.

He laughed, reminding Nora how young and naive she must seem to him. "No, Nora," he said. "I've never seen anythin' like this in me life."

As soon as the hearses passed, the crowd again began to cheer. The Volunteers followed closely behind, flanked on their sides by the boys of Fianna Eireann. Once again, the excited cheers of the crowd began to escalate to a frenzied state. Column after column of men—most wearing homemade versions of the green uniform of the Volunteers—passed. Nora looked into their faces as they smiled at the crowds. They, too, looked not much older than children. Few of them could be older than twenty.

These are the boys who think they can save Ireland, she thought to herself, then instinctively looked for any members of Cumann na mBan. But the few who had marched alongside the men had long since passed by. The Volunteers greatly outnumbered the girls in uniform.

"Come, Nora," Colin said into her ear. "Best be going now." Removing his hand from her waist, he jumped down from the lamppost. He held his arms up to her, and she leaned into him as he cautiously lowered her to the ground. When she fell against his chest, he steadied her. His arms felt strong around her, and she relished the feeling of being held close to him. It made her feel less alone in the world.

He grabbed her by the hand, and they found their way single-file through the crowds and back to the calmer side street from which they had come. Once they could again walk side by side, he released her hand. She sensed that their time together was coming to an end, and the nervousness she had felt earlier returned in full force. She had so many questions for him. Mostly, she wanted to ask him a question that would spark a conversation. The quietness only made her feel panicked. She needed his voice for reassurance.

As if he sensed her anxiety, he spoke. "So what do you think of Dublin?" he asked, a characteristic grin on his face. Sometimes he was so full of emotion that it seemed to radiate out of him, especially when he joked or laughed. But at other times, he was disconnected and reserved. She understood, then, that it was easy for him to share his lighthearted side, but he guarded his most inner feelings so fiercely that even those closest to him were not granted a glimpse

"It's a busy place," she answered. "But I presume today is not a normal day in Dublin."

"It certainly is not," he said. "This is a sign of change and of things to come. Dublin is about to come alive." A spark had been lit in his gray eyes.

❧

They walked on, drifting into thoughtful silence again. Nora knew that she had witnessed something consequential, but how much so she did not know. Perhaps Dublin itself did not yet know the importance of what had just taken place.

Colin gradually led them far south of the Liffey, into an area he usually only visited when delivering groceries for his uncle. The small row houses that had lined the streets near St. Stephen's Green gave way to the massive residences of Rathmines, each with a perfectly landscaped front terrace. The clanking automobiles that traversed the streets near the train station were replaced by horses and carriages, but not the types you would see in Dublin proper. These were well-bred animals pulling magnificent carriages, whose masters viewed the streets from upholstered seats and behind partially drawn curtains made of the finest velvet. People weren't riding in them because they couldn't afford automobiles—they were riding in them because the carriages were more luxurious than automobiles.

As Nora watched the passing carriages, she suddenly became aware that she was the only woman on the streets with her head uncovered. She awkwardly lowered her head each time a carriage passed.

"Nora," Colin said, "I'm bringing you to a new world. The Parsons—despite their political leanings—are in fact good people, and they will treat you fairly." She perked up at this—she had wanted to know more about these mysterious Parsons.

"But they live a life that until this day you probably never knew existed," he continued. "They live in comfort like you have never known, and you are going to feel out of place for a while. But promise me this," he said, stopping altogether and putting his hands on her shoulders. He looked directly at her. "Don't ever, ever be ashamed of who you are or where you came from."

She was hoping he would have given her more. But she knew that he had clammed up on the topic. Just what he was hiding, she couldn't tell. "I promise, Colin," she replied. Anxiety swept over her. She realized fully, for the first time, that she was never going back to Ballynote. She no longer had a home. But worse, she had been surrounded by her family all the days of her life, and she now found herself truly alone. The only one she knew in this whole city was Colin.

"Colin, how will I find you? You know, if I need anything." She was frightened by the frantic sound in her own voice.

"I'll come to see you now and again," he said, "I promised Seamus." She frowned at him. "Just teasin' Nora," he said. "I'd come to see you anyways. Just to see what the grand life looks like with a little bit of Ballynote in its midst."

"But what if I need to find you?" she said, her voice no less anxious than before.

"Kildare's Grocery, in the Liberties. Everyone will know where it is. You can leave a message with me uncle if I'm not there."

They approached a large brick mansion with a small carriage drive leading to two great doors surrounded by windows. Gas lampposts were placed symmetrically along the drive. Nora stared at the building. "This must be an inn," she said aloud.

Colin laughed. "No, Nora, this is the Parsons'."

"You mean to tell me that one family lives here?"

"One family. One family in each of the homes on this street."

Nora looked around. The mansion was magnificent. It stood three stories, and the grounds occupied almost half a block. "You were right," she said finally. "There is wealth here beyond what I ever could have dreamed of."

She began to walk up the drive, but he grabbed her arm again and held her back. She looked at him curiously, not sure what he wanted. His long blond hair was ruffled from the trip, much lighter at the ends from the summer sun, and his eyes were a steel gray. Mostly what she noticed about him was that he looked sad.

He stood there, again with one hand on each of her shoulders, and finally said softly, "Don't forget, Nora, don't ever be ashamed of who you are, no matter what. You come from a good place and have a good heart." Then, more lightheartedly, he said, "Not everyone can be from Clare, you know. We're the lucky ones."

She smiled at him and repeated, "I promise, Colin."

He leaned forward slowly. She closed her eyes and could almost smell the muddy banks of the Shannon as an often-recalled memory of Colin overcame her. But instead of a cool ocean breeze, she felt the hot Dublin summer, and she knew that she was far from that bygone moment, and far from home.

"Ah, you're doing it again," he said. "Tryin' to get me into trouble."

When he backed away from her, she felt her heart sink. This was not how she wanted the moment to end.

"You and yer mortal sins," she tried to tease, but she couldn't bring herself to joke with him.

"You catch me off guard every now and again, Nora," A warm breeze brought the smell of fresh flowers from the mansion grounds. "But not today. I'll have to go to confession on Saturday with me uncle, and me trip to Ennis with you is already going to cost me a dozen Hail Marys. I don't mean to spend me whole evening with Father O'Brien."

She frowned.

"But Sunday starts a clean slate." He winked.

"Don't flirt with me," she said.

"I wouldn't dare." He led her up the carriage drive, and a middle-aged man dressed in a black suit with a tall black hat met them.

"Halloo, Mr. Dunham," Colin said, shaking the man's hand.

"Halloo, Colin," said the man, grinning from ear to ear. "You've brought the girl, I see." Nora studied the man, whom she took to be the butler. He had a kind face and an energetic step, but Nora couldn't help but notice something odd about his reaction to her.

145

"Sure 'ave," Colin replied. "Nora McMahon, from Ballynote. Just arrived today."

"Nora McMahon, you say," he said. He put a strange emphasis on *McMahon*. "Pleased to meet you, Nora," said Mr. Dunham. "I'm Ronan, the head butler. Ms. Evelyn's been waiting for you to arrive ever since she heard from John Kildare that you'd be on today's train from Ennis. She's been looking for an extra hand for some time, so she'll be happy to have you. Come dear, can I take yer luggage?"

"No bag, sir," said Nora, projecting her voice to try to feign confidence. "Just me linen sack."

Mr. Dunham nodded but seemed conscious that he had embarrassed her. Too many years of serving in luxurious surroundings had sheltered him from the meager lives of most of the Irish, and from his own modest upbringing.

"Of course, me dear. Come, and I'll introduce you to the head housekeeper. Thanks, Colin, for bringing 'er by. " Colin gave him a quick nod.

Mr. Dunham turned for a final thought. "I suspect we'll be seeing you in a week or two. The Parsons will likely order a lamb for sometime next week, as they'll be hosting a delegation from Belfast."

Colin nodded, but said nothing.

"A delegation, Mr. Kildare," he said again.

"I heard you," said Colin. "I won't forget."

He turned to Nora. "Are you ready, me dear?" Without waiting for an answer, he scooped up her linen sack and began walking into the house. Nora followed. She turned back to look at Colin, and he smiled at her. His big gray eyes still looked sad, and Nora turned away before her own eyes teared up.

CHAPTER 16

July 29, 1914: Rathmines, Dublin, Ireland

Mr. Dunham led Nora through the great doors and she let out an audible gasp. The afternoon light shone into the entrance hall through the large glass windows. The black and white floor tiles sparkled, and the living trees in the hall blocked some of the sun's rays and cast leafy shadows on the wall. Nora was amazed at how high the ceilings were. They stretched up two full floors, which were connected by a lavish spiraling staircase.

Mr. Dunham let Nora marvel at the entrance for a few seconds. "Beautiful, isn't it?"

She nodded, but no words came to her.

"Come now, you'll be wanting to dress before dinner."

Dress? Her heart skipped a beat. She darted after Mr. Dunham. "But sir, this is all I have!"

He smiled. "Dear child, do not worry! Ms. Evelyn will give you everything you need." He removed his black top hat and wiped his brow. "Don't worry so—you will be taken care of here. Come now." Again, Mr. Dunham took off down the long corridor, and Nora followed behind, trying to keep pace. Her shoes, too small for as long as she could remember, dug painfully into her heels, but she did her best to keep a steady gait. She became conscious of how loud the worn soles were as they briskly passed through the hallways.

At last they reached another staircase, and Mr. Dunham turned to her. "This, Nora, is the servant's stair. You'll remember to use only this staircase in yer daily work, unless of course you are escorting Ms. Evelyn. The Parsons are fair, but they also require order."

"Yes, sir," she said. The back staircase looked just fine to her. They ascended to the second floor and down another long hallway that seemed to lead to the back section of the residence. When at last they stopped, Nora sighed with relief and checked her heels. As she had expected, the backs of her feet had gashes in them from where her shoes had rubbed. She hoped no one would notice.

Mr. Dunham knocked on a closed door, and within seconds, a stern face appeared at the door. A woman of about fifty stood in the doorway, the soft features of her face overshadowed by a persistent frown. "Yes Ronan, what is it?" she asked curtly.

"Mrs. Finnegan, please meet Miss Nora McMahon, the new housekeeper."

Mrs. Finnegan stared past Mr. Dunham toward Nora. She looked her up and down. Nora felt entirely self-conscious, reasoning that Mrs. Finnegan probably knew just from looking at her that she knew nothing about being a maid. And not only that, Mrs. Finnegan could probably tell that she didn't have anything proper to wear in her linen sack and that she'd never in her life stepped into a home as magnificent as this one.

Still, instead of cowering, Nora straightened her shoulders and looked Mrs. Finnegan right in the eye. She would not be ashamed of where she came from. She was, after all, Nora McMahon.

"Hmmm," was all that Mrs. Finnegan said. "Where'd you find this one?"

"Colin Kildare brought her by. You know, nephew of the grocer."

"Hmmm," she repeated. "Where did you come from?"

"County Clare," said Mr. Dunham, answering for her. Nora saw Mrs. Finnegan's scowl grow deeper as she slowly shook her head. Mrs. Finnegan and Mr. Dunham stared at each other in what seemed to be a silent conversation.

"Clare, you say," said Mrs. Finnegan, breaking the silence and turning to Nora. "So no schooling, I presume."

"Some," said Nora, indignant. It was the truth—she only had minimal formal schooling. But that hadn't stopped Eamonn McMahon from ensuring that his grandchildren could read and write like any wealthy Protestant child. Further, and unlike any Protestant children, Seamus and Nora also could read and write in Gaelic, just like their parents and grandparents before them, who had learned the forbidden language in illegal hedge schools.

"Ms. Evelyn needs to stop taking these charity cases, if you ask me," Mrs. Finnegan paused. "But it's not me decision, now is it?" She looked at Mr. Dunham, and Nora watched curiously as the two exchanged another tense glare.

"It'll be just fine, Louise," Mr. Dunham said, finally.

"Thank you, Mr. Dunham," she curtly replied. Mr. Dunham nodded, then quickly disappeared back down the corridor.

Nora stood there, as straight as she could, waiting for Mrs. Finnegan to speak. Finally, the woman said, "Now hear me. I have been in this business long enough to know a bad egg when I see one. Ms. Evelyn may have a soft spot for cases like yerself, but I do not. And Ms. Evelyn listens to me when I have an opinion about staff members. You have one chance, Miss McMahon, one chance! I have four rules for you. We'll see which one you break first."

Nora said nothing, but stood, listening intently. Anger began creeping into her, though she tried to quiet it. She instinctively reached for the pendant that hung around her neck and held it between her fingers. She relaxed her face, refusing to let any emotion escape. But she could feel her eyes glaring at Mrs. Finnegan.

"You will be polite!" she began. "And you will touch nothing that doesn't belong to you. Not a thing! And I will be watching you very closely," she said, emphasizing the last few words. "Third, there are young men who work these grounds. You will have nothing to do with them! No conversations, no smiles, no fraternization whatsoever!"

Nora took a deep breath. How could this woman judge her in this way? *It's hardly polite to judge,* she thought, *and the first rule is to be polite.* Perhaps the rules didn't apply to Mrs. Finnegan.

"And finally," the woman said, "you will be clean!" This insult stung Nora much more than the others. All at once she began to feel embarrassed. She looked down at her clothes and for the first time realized how dingy her dress looked. It was worn and stained. Holes had been patched up over the years, and it was probably a little small on her. She knew that it had been tight, especially around the bodice, for over a year now, but it never occurred to her that she should have something else.

Did Mrs. Finnegan notice all this? Worse, had Colin noticed? Colin understood her because they had grown up together, but he had lived in Dublin for a year now. He surely knew the difference now between a girl who dressed properly in new, tailored clothes and someone like herself.

"First thing's first," said Mrs. Finnegan, leading Nora briskly down the long corridor. "I'll show you to yer quarters. You'll be sharin' a room with Martha. Follow her lead—she is a good member of the staff. You will take a bath and dress in the house uniform. You will have one drawer in the armoire for yerself. In it you will find stockings. You are to wear stockings always," she added, slowing her step to look pointedly at Nora's bare ankles.

"You will pay for yer clothes out of yer first few weeks' salary." Mrs. Finnegan again adopted a surprisingly fast pace for a petite middle-aged woman. Her steps were short and quick as she hustled down the hallway. "And the cobbler will be by to measure you for shoes." This seemed fair. Besides Mrs. Finnegan, the Parsons seemed like not such a bad place to be.

They walked further down the corridor and, arriving at the last room, Mrs. Finnegan opened it without a knock. Nora stowed this away for later. No privacy could be expected here.

No one was in the room, but there were two beds against opposite walls and a large armoire with double doors. All of the furniture was a deep cherry color, and even the carved embellishments on the wood were perfectly matched. A small door led to a water closet with a sink, bath, and toilet.

Mrs. Finnegan looked at Nora and frowned. "What is the matter with you?" she asked. Nora instantly realized that her eyes were tearing up. "Nothing, Mrs. Finnegan," she said softly. "It's just that…"

"Just what?" Mrs. Finnegan interrupted.

"It's just that it's so beautiful." She looked about the room, with its furniture and drapes and even wallpaper—a soft lavender color. She could hardly believe that she would be living here and sleeping in a bed as grand as this one.

"Hmmph!" said Mrs. Finnegan. "Dinner tonight will be promptly at six. You will start work at half four tomorrow mornin'." Mrs. Finnegan turned around and walked out of the room, closing the door behind her.

Nora stared for a moment at her new quarters. On one bed lay a black dress with white trim. This, she assumed, was her bed. She walked over to it and sat down. She sank deep into the mattress and felt as though she were sitting on a cloud. It was a far cry from the straw mattress she had slept on her whole life.

From the bed, she could see out the window into a beautiful garden with roses all around the perimeter. She saw several gardeners tending to the flowers. "These must be the men I am to refrain from tempting," she said sarcastically to herself.

She began to explore the room and walked into the water closet and let out a small gasp. She found herself staring straight ahead at a face she did not recognize. It was a girl, almost seventeen years old, with soft freckles, long auburn hair, and eyes a curious shade of green. She gazed at the girl for a long time, eventually finding parts of her that seemed familiar. She had seen those eyes somewhere long ago, but couldn't place them.

A long-forgotten memory rose up. She closed her eyes and heard the sound of the rain beating against the walls of the cottage in Ballynote and the sound of thunder exploding around her. She remembered looking up into those same intense, green eyes as her father's comforting arms folded around her. She could hear him say, "Don't be afraid, child. The storm will pass."

She opened her eyes and smiled, and the reflection smiled back at her. She could not remember the last time she had seen herself in a mirror.

CHAPTER 17

July 29, 1914: Dublin, Ireland

The afternoon sun was stifling. There was no trace of wind from the nearby Dublin Bay, and the air hung heavily about the city. Colin sat on a bench in St. Stephen's Green, wishing for the cool afternoon breeze of the River Shannon. He often came here to think, particularly when his mind was unsettled. While he had enjoyed his trip home to Clare, he was feeling, for the first time, as though he might not belong there anymore. When he had first come to Dublin the previous year, he had wanted every minute to go home to the life he knew.

Had it been his choice, Colin would have stayed in Clare and lived the life his parents and grandparents had lived in generations before. But his father would have none of it. He wanted his sons to know something besides poverty and Clare, which to him were one and the same. So he had sent Colin off to live with his widower uncle and cousin in Dublin as a grocer's apprentice. Colin didn't mind the business, though he found it rather boring. Still, he had an active mind, and when he concentrated, he did quite well. When his mind wandered, as it always seemed to do, it wandered to Clare. And that was when trouble came. A missed order, a delivery to the wrong address, food spoiling when he left it out. As much as he wanted to, he could not force his mind to concentrate on the monotony of his uncle's business. He felt there was something greater awaiting him.

Until his last trip home, he had thought that eventually, if Irish governance were ever returned to Ireland, he would go home to Clare and start a life there. But Ballynote had felt small and quaint to him. The fields and stone walls and the smells were the same, but he found that he was no longer content there. He felt ashamed at outgrowing his home—if that was indeed what had happened. What troubled him was that he now questioned what it was that awaited him. It certainly wasn't being a grocer, although he could stand it for the time being. But if he wasn't ultimately going to return to Clare, what would he do?

As he watched the horses and carts trot by the green, scattering the small flocks of birds amassed on the ground in search of food, he reasoned that what had changed about him was that Dublin made him feel important in a way that he had never felt while in Clare. He felt as though he was at the very pulse of the changes that were taking place in Ireland—and caught up with the very people who were forcing the change.

The people in Dublin seemed to have some sort of effect, however distant, on what happened at Westminster. The frustrations of Dubliners menaced Parliament and forced the Crown's attention in a way that the rest of Ireland simply could not. Londoners knew nothing of the lives of people in Ballynote or Ennis or Limerick, but they knew about Dublin, and they were apprehensive about the passions that spilled out of the Irish capital.

Colin sighed and rose from his bench. He could feel sweat running down his back and thought with a smile what the passersby would think if he waded into the duck pond in the middle of the green. In Ballynote, people would find that a common-sense thing to do, but not in Dublin. *No,* he thought, *not in Dublin.*

A slight breeze drifted across the green. It was not enough to provide any relief—surely not as refreshing as a dip in the duck pond—but it brought up from his shirt a slight scent of something familiar. The train from Ennis, the funeral, the Volunteers—Nora.

She was a most peculiar girl. She was young, yet she gave the impression of someone much older and wiser. And though she was small, she could be intimidating, even to Colin. When she thought, she thought deeply. At times, she seemed to carry the weight of the world. And her eyes were the most curious shade of green—the color of the sea during a storm. Since he was a child, he had always felt inclined to protect her, but from what, he never was sure. He wondered if he had already failed in his promise to take care of her.

At around six o'clock, Colin resigned himself to return to his uncle's store. He had not been back since he left for Clare a couple of weeks before, and he was overdue. There was likely a pile of work to be done, and he wasn't looking forward to spending his next several evenings making up for his time away.

Rising from his bench, he slowly walked toward Grafton Street, passing under the giant stone Fusilier's Arch that commemorated the Dubliners who had fought in the Second Boer War. He and his friends always referred to it as "Traitor's Arch," in indignation over the Irish who willingly went to die in a British colonial war.

He vowed he would never fight at England's behest—it would be a slap in the face to all who had suffered at the hands of the English. Underneath the arch, the names of soldiers were carved into the gray stone. He wondered if England remembered their sacrifices, beyond this small commemoration.

He meandered down the small side streets toward the grocery, surprised at how short the walk seemed when his mind was busy. The narrow streets were alive and cluttered with shops and small children darting about almost every which way, some looking innocent, and others running with clearly stolen loaves of bread or vegetables from the South City Market under their arms. The newsboys called on the corners in vain, trying to sell their last remaining papers. The bustle of the small streets in old Dublin made it impossible to feel alone.

As Colin turned onto Combe Street on the edge of the Liberties, he saw a small, dirty boy of about eight loitering in the doorway of a darkened shop. His face was smeared with dirt and his clothes ripped and worn. He had a large bruise on one of his cheeks. Upon seeing Colin, the boys' eyes lit up and he ran over to greet him. Instinctively, Colin reached into his pocket and flipped the boy a shilling. Colin had learned long ago that a shilling here and there safeguarded him from pickpocketing children.

"Halloo there, Daniel," said Colin, ruffling the small boy's hair. "What happened to yer cheek, fella? Did you help yerself to someone else's pocket change?"

But the boy scowled at Colin. "Where've you been these days?" said the boy, indignantly. "Haven't gotten hardly a shillin' from no one in a week's time!"

"Sorry to hear that, fella," replied Colin. "I had to go home for a few weeks, but I suspect you'll be seeing me regularly for a while. How's the shop?"

"Dunno," replied the boy. "Busy, I suppose." He began walking alongside Colin as they neared his uncle's store. Colin became suspicious. Daniel didn't normally do this. Usually one shilling bought him off for at least an afternoon. Colin weaved in and about the crowded street, Daniel maneuvering between the other children to keep up with him. "Christ, what do you want, Daniel?" Colin finally said. "I'm out of coins, and I'm late for work."

"I've got a secret," Daniel said, almost tauntingly.

"Oh yeah?" replied Colin, feigning interest. He had always felt an affinity toward the little boy, so he decided to play along. "'Bout what?"

"Rifles" said the boy.

At this, Colin's interest was slightly piqued. Even little Daniel was caught up on the gossip. "Rifles, you say?"

"Maybe," said Daniel. Then he smiled coyly. "Maybe I'll tell you for another shilling."

"Maybe you'll tell me for the shilling I already gave you," said Colin. Then he added, "And if it's worthwhile, I'll give you *two* more."

Daniel was an easy sell. He looked over his shoulder, as if he didn't want to be overheard, and beckoned for Colin to follow him into a nearby alley. Colin sighed and followed the boy, half certain that Daniel was at that very moment concocting the very best two-shilling story he could think up. When they were out of earshot of any passersby, Daniel whispered to Colin, "You missed the commotion with the big gun run a couple o' days ago."

"I heard from a passenger on the train what happened," Colin replied. "A shipment of rifles into Howth was intercepted."

"Yes!" replied Daniel, jumping into the air in his childish excitement "But most of 'em got through! Too much confusion and panic over the shootings at Bachelor's Walk, and the boys got most of the guns in."

"So I heard," said Colin. He was slightly surprised that Daniel's story corroborated what he had heard on the train from Ennis. "But that was in the paper this morning, little fella," Colin said. "Hardly worth two shillings."

Having learned nothing new from Daniel, Colin turned to go back into the street. He tucked his hands tightly into his pockets so as to be able to catch Daniel if he tried to reach in and grab the coins he still had in his trouser pocket. But Daniel didn't make a move toward Colin. Instead, he stood defiantly and shouted to Colin, who was quickly walking back into the street, "And there's another run comin'!"

Colin turned and looked at the boy, who smiled broadly, showing off his two missing front teeth. This story was certainly worth two shillings. Colin walked back toward Daniel, a serious look on his face. All of a sudden, his cousin's cryptic letter made sense to him. *A customer in Wicklow has some groceries that need delivering.* He pulled his hand from his pocket, revealing two small coins, but his mood had turned more serious.

"When?" he asked sternly. "Tell me."

Daniel's face suddenly became grim, as he looked over Colin's shoulder.

Colin instinctively turned to look at the street. Perhaps they had been overheard by a passing warden. Before he recognized what was happening, Daniel grabbed the coins from Colin's hand and darted into the street, quickly disappearing among the crowds.

Colin, not worried about his shillings, broke into a run down Ash Street, into the heart of the Liberties and toward his uncle's shop. He navigated through the crowds and shopkeepers, as conspicuous as the children who pickpocketed and stole bread. He bumped into a woman holding two children and a basket of vegetables and barely paused to apologize as he raced toward the large green "Kildare Grocery" sign hanging over the small stone shop at the very end of Ash Street.

Not wanting to converse with his uncle about his trip, he decided to slip in the back in hopes of running into his cousin, who was sure to be able to fill in where Daniel left off.

He slowed to a walk as he entered the alley leading to the back door of the shop. Laundry hung from the windows of several second floor apartments and whipped in the summer wind like dreary-colored flags. Two tabby cats, fattened from a lifetime of eating scraps from the store, sat near the door waiting for an afternoon snack. At the sight of Colin, they scampered away and hid behind the steps of the neighbor's back door. Colin tapped his shoes to remove the little bits of dirt still stuck to the sides of them from his lunch in the meadow with Nora the previous day, and smiled. He was bringing small tokens of Clare to this dark alley.

He opened the door quietly and deliberately so as to slip in without being noticed. He was alarmed by a loud clanging. He looked up to see a large brass bell hanging from the top of the interior doorway. He saw his older cousin sitting in the corner reading a pamphlet. His carefully cropped dark hair was neatly parted to the side—tidy as always.

Not looking up, the cousin said, "New bell. Da installed it the other day."

"So I see," replied Colin.

"Did you get me letter?" his cousin asked. Even seated, his shoulders were back and his posture perfect.

"I did."

"So you know you missed the most exciting thing that's happened in Ireland since the great Charles Parnell got caught with his mistress?" said his cousin, finally looking up at Colin.

"Tell me what happened!" Colin said. He plopped down at the old wooden table next to his cousin. The windows were open on both sides of the bright back room, allowing a refreshing breeze to circulate. "How did the boys get by the constabulary?"

"Some genius cut the telegraph wire," said his cousin. "No way to communicate back to Dublin."

"Brilliant!" said Colin. "Who?"

"Michael Kildare, at yer service," said his cousin proudly. Michael slid his chair back from the table. The wooden legs of the chair creaked as they scraped along the floor. He stood and walked over to the corner of the room that doubled as a kitchen. Striking a match on one of the beams overhead, he lit the stove.

"That ole buffoon?" said Colin.

"Yours truly," said Michael. He rummaged along the shelf for a porcelain teacup. The entire kitchen was disorganized and ill stocked—a telltale sign that no woman had lived there in years.

Colin took a more serious tone. "How long have you planned this, Michael?"

"None of yer concern," Michael said. Colin knew his cousin reveled in finding ways to annoy him. Michael looked to be please with himself and awaiting Colin's outburst.

"It is my concern, Michael!"

"Is it?"

"Look, Michael," said Colin. "I'm not content just drilling and marching—" he started, then paused for a moment, making sure to choose his words carefully. He didn't want his cousin to think he was ungrateful for even the small role already played in the Volunteers. "I am proud to be where I am, but I want to do more. And I know you are in this up to yer neck, and I—"

Michael cut him off. "Yer neck is too skinny to be involved," he said. "When they hang you, you'll fall right through that noose! A lot of extra trouble for the King, to string you up twice," Colin frowned at his cousin, not finding the joke funny.

"When they hang *me*," added Michael, "I'll swing for days for all to see."

"You're not the only one around here who wants to fight for Ireland," Colin said, making an effort to control his anger. "You just happen to have the right friends who put you in charge."

"This is man's work, Colin, and you are but a boy. And the deeper you get involved, the more likely we are to hang, if this goes the way of every other Irish fight for freedom."

"I'm not a boy, Michael."

"You sure?" his cousin asked. "Haven't ever seen you in the company of a lady." Colin didn't reply. He put his knapsack back over his shoulder and began to walk toward the front of the store.

"Ah, come off it, Colin," his cousin finally said. "I'm just foolin' with you, and you should know that."

"So good to be back," Colin said sarcastically, as he passed through the tattered curtain that separated the back of the store from the front.

"So you do have a lady then." his cousin called after him. "Yer Nora?"

"None of yer business," Colin said as he walked back through the curtain, this time holding a red apple he had taken from the produce shelf.

"Well I sure hope she's yer girl," his cousin said. "You sat around lonely all year sulkin' over 'er, while you could have been out with me and the boys. We'd have at least found you someone pretty to take your mind off Clare."

Colin again said, "None of yer business."

Michael rolled his eyes and returned to the table. He sat down in his chair and picked up one of the accounting books that detailed the store's expenses, but Colin could see that he wasn't focused on work. He smiled to himself, happy that he'd successfully annoyed Michael. Usually it was the other way around.

Colin reached for the door handle, and Michael finally gave in and broke the silence.

"I wrote to you, didn't I?" continued. "I told you to come back."

"You probably needed someone to work yer shift while you went out and did something important," said Colin, sullenly.

"Not a bad idea," said Michael aloud. The tea was ready, and he rose from his chair again. "But no. Sometimes you are thick Colin. What did I say in the letter?"

"That we had a customer in Wicklow. And I had no fook of an idea what you were talking about till—"

But Michael cut him off. "Aye, a customer, in a few days' time!" He poured piping hot water into his teacup and dropped in dried tea leaves. "And I needed you back here so you could run some interference for us."

"Interference!" yelled Colin. He threw his knapsack across the floor in anger. "What do you mean interference?"

"I thought you'd be happy about it! If you want someone else to do it, that's fine," said Michael.

"Interference!" said Colin again. "How about a trap? If little Daniel on the street is telling me there's another run comin', then you'll need more than interference or a distraction!"

Michael became alert all of a sudden and put his cup down on the counter. His tea splattered. "Say that again," he said, bringing his burned fingers to his mouth. "Shite that's hot!" he muttered.

"Daniel knows. He told me just five minutes ago when I passed him on the street. Told me he'd tell me anything for two shillings. How many others do you think he's told the same to?"

The breeze in the shop somehow felt much warmer that it had a few minutes before.

"Where does he live?" Michael asked. He finally sounded serious.

"Not sure," said Colin. "Henrietta tenements most likely. He's always between here and there. No doubt he's never there except for night."

"You need to find him," said Michael. "Find out what he knows. And who else he might have told."

"Aye," said Colin. "I will." His anger hadn't subsided. "But I'm going to do more than interference,"

"Fook you are," said Michael. "You'll do what I say."

Colin gritted his teeth and tensed up his fists.

Michael softened and changed the subject. "Before you hunt down yer little snitch, tell me about Clare. How was home?"

"Fine," said Colin, curtly.

"Just fine? You've been talking about Clare for months. Surely it was better than just fine. How was Seamus?" Michael inquired. "Did you deliver the package all right?" He took a sip of his tea. "Seemed like a straightforward job, but I wasn't expecting that kink to be thrown in the plan—but we made the best of it, don't you think?"

Colin could feel his anger break out on his forehead as sweat. He knew the "kink" was Nora. He chose to ignore Michael's comment. "He's doing all right, considering. He was real close to Eamonn, you know. Like losing another father, it was."

"Was he happy with yer delivery?" asked Michael.

"Aye, can't wait to board that ship."

"Will be good to have a man in Boston," said Michael. "Now there's a real mission. A shame you passed that up."

"Nah," said Colin, shaking his head. "I want to be here when it all goes down. Not fundraisin' thousands of miles and one big ocean away."

"How'd you tell Nora?" asked Michael.

Colin took a bite out of his apple and slowly chewed it.

"Fookin' wimp," said Michael.

"Wasn't my news to tell!" A piece of apple flew from his mouth. "T'was up to Seamus, and he didn't want Nora to think he was abandonin' her. It's different now that Eamonn's gone."

"So he just lied?"

"In a way," said Colin. He wiped his chin.

"You'll take the blame for this, you know," said Michael. Colin took another bite of his apple.

"Don't remind me." Colin stared up at the rafters above. Only a few weeks away and he had forgotten how high the ceilings were at the grocery. In Ballynote, he could reach up and touch the ceiling in his parents' cottage.

"But it the end, it all worked out for the best," said Michael.

"Maybe," said Colin. "So long as she lays low she'll be just fine."

"Lays low?" Michael exclaimed. "What do you mean lays low?" He let out a laugh. "Oh no—do you know the favors I cashed in to work this little arrangement? And with no notice? I promised Patrick she'd be worth the investment. I want a weekly report everything that goes on over at the Parsons. She's a workin' woman now, Colin. One of the most important girls in Dublin!"

Colin felt his face get hot again, and for the first time, a little panicked. No one had said anything to him about this. "No, Michael," he said. His speech was low and clear. "She'll not do yer bidding. I brought her here so I could keep her safe. Keep her out of trouble in Clare."

"Exactly," said Michael. He sounded so nonchalant. It only added to Colin's anxiety. "We're offerin' her a step up in the world. Not too many respectable jobs for homeless girls in Clare." Michael smiled, and it made Colin eerily uncomfortable. "A spy is at least a little more honorable a profession than a prostitute."

Colin felt the simmering anger turn to a rage. He lunged at his cousin, his left fist cocked in the air. "Watch what you say!" he shouted. He grabbed Michael by the collar. He was only a few inches taller than Michael, yet he was much broader. He knew Michael would have trouble if they ever came to blows.

But Michael didn't seem concerned for his safety. "Calm the fook down, Colin!" His voice still sounded calm and calculated.

"You'll not bring her into this," said Colin. He held tightly to the thin fabric of Michael's shirt. The cotton was so worn that it slipped between his fingers.

"And why not, Colin?" he asked. "Why else do you think I was able to place her so quickly? Did you think that I was just doin' it out of the kindness of my heart?"

He hadn't once considered that Michael had a more sinister motive. The sudden realization drained the energy from his hands, and he felt Michael's shirt slip even more from his grip.

"Fook, Michael, she's just a girl. She didn't ask for any of this. Does Mr. Dunham know? He'd have never—"

"He knows," said Michael.

Colin felt his grip release entirely, and Michael let himself fall back into his chair. "I don't believe you. He'd never ever put Nora in harm's way, not after—"

"He knows. He wants her close, so he can keep an eye on 'er."

"But Mr. Dunham is already there. You already have yer man on the inside."

"I've got more than that." Michael muttered under his breath. He returned to the counter and added more tea to his cup of hot water, then gingerly swirled it, watching the water turn a deeper brown. "Ronan Dunham is suspicious. He fits the profile of a nationalist. Hasn't missed a Sunday Mass since who knows when; from rural Ireland. Old enough to remember yet young enough to fight. Nora—she's just a sweet little dove. Ain't no one goin' to suspect her. Plus, Ronan travels with Mr. Parsons. Nora will be there every day."

Colin shook his head. "I won't allow it."

"What do you mean you won't allow it?" Michael began to laugh. His eyes scanned the disorganized shelves for sugar. "Did you think you were in charge? Hell, this is even above my head! Yer girl is living with the parents of the Ulster Volunteer leadership, with a family that has close connections to Parliament. The thought must have crossed that small mind of yers. You had to know we was bringin' her here for a reason!"

Colin felt his face turn hot into again, though this time he felt humiliated. How had he not understood what Michael was planning? "You have no business—"

"Ireland is me only business!" Michael snapped. "And I will take any small advantage I can get!"

"She's not an advantage Michael! And I will send her back to Clare before I put her in any danger."

"You brought her here," Michael started, finally locating the canister he wanted. He opened it and scooped a heaping spoon of sugar. "You asked me if I could find a spot for her, and I did. You had to have known."

"I don't mind you puttin' me in danger. Fook, I've practically been beggin' for somethin' meaningful to do around here. But I have a choice, and I am choosin' to be involved. She didn't choose this!" Colin was infuriated, and he knew he would lose this fight. It was too late.

"Not yet she didn't choose it," Michael started. "But she will. 'Tis in her blood."

"And what did Uncle John say? Surely he's not in on this as well?"

Michael stirred his tea, still wary of its temperature. "No, he's not." The boys looked at each other in an awkward silence. "But he's no fool either," Michael continued. "He knows the Parsons. Good Christian gentry in every way save for their ancestral pillage of this land and their loyalty to a king who'd have us all in chains!"

"Michael," said Colin, "I'm askin' you, man to man, don't bring her into this."

Michael smiled. "A couple days shy of bein' a man, wouldn't you say?" He laughed, knowing it would be a knife to his cousin. "Oh, come on now, Colin. Why not? Is she not Irish as well? Of all people, Colin, she has paid a high price for being poor and Catholic in Ireland. You can hide her away all you want, but you cannot extinguish that flame within her."

Colin looked down at his boots. Sweat dripped from his forehead and onto the floor. "No," he said. His voice now sounded calm as well. He knew he had lost the point. "But I can delay it for as long as possible."

"You can't protect her, Colin, any more than you can protect the innocents of Bachelors Walk. None of us are long for this world, but we might as well make a difference while we are here. And besides, Ethan's not at the Parsons anymore. He's in Belfast making his mischief up there with his rich new wife, who as part of the dowry gave him his own regiment in the Ulster Volunteers. There's no business for him here these days."

"But you put her there for a reason," said Colin. "He'll be back."

"I pray he won't," said Michael. "Because when he's in town we all suffer more. But if he ever comes back—" Michael paused and looked at his younger cousin. "If he comes back, we'll have our little advantage."

"Don't call her that," said Colin.

"Everyone has a role, Colin. Everyone has to do their part," Michael said. "Call her whatever you want."

Colin abruptly turned to his cousin. "Every one has to do their part?"

"Aye, everyone," said his cousin.

Colin nodded. "Then I guess I'm headed to Wicklow."

"Fook you are. Right now you are headed to find that rascal Daniel before he gets us all killed."

"This conversation isn't over," said Colin. "I'll go and find Daniel so he doesn't get us all arrested. And when I get back, I'm gettin' ready to head south." He opened the door, but before it slammed behind him, he heard his cousin's galling response. "Fook you are."

The small bell clanged with excitement.

CHAPTER 18

July 29, 1914: The Liberties, Dublin, Ireland

Colin headed away from the Liberties and toward the Liffey by way of Francis Street. He crossed the Whitworth Bridge onto Church Street, where the houses began to look more and more dilapidated. The sun was finally setting on a glorious July evening—in the height of summer, the city stayed alight late into the night.

The previous summer, he had arrived in Dublin in the midst of the citywide strike and horrid lockout that had followed, leaving scores dead and the rest of the city near starvation. It didn't escape him that Ethan Parsons was a main proponent of that devastating lockout. At the time, his Uncle John truly was in a unique situation—a Catholic businessman who stayed afloat because of his wealthy Protestant customers. Few others had been so lucky.

The tenement population had almost doubled in the year since, and the historic buildings that had once each housed a single family now were home to hundreds of souls living in abject poverty. Colin had known poverty as a boy in Clare. He knew what it was like to lie awake hungry. But only since he had come to Dublin had he seen entire families starve to death or, if they survived, walk the city as hollow ghosts scavenging for food.

As he progressed up King Street, the stench of the infamous Henrietta Street tenement houses began to overtake the air. The warm, dry summer had been wonderful for rides on horseback through the Clare countryside, but the resulting low water in the city had exacerbated the overflowing water closets in the tenement homes, and it was common to walk across excrement throughout the yards and even interiors of the houses.

Colin had never quite gotten used to the tenements, though he had been inside of many to deliver free groceries no longer fresh enough to sell in the shop. Many of his fellow Volunteers hailed from the tenements on Camden Row, which Colin had thought were deplorable enough—until he had seen the horrid and almost inhuman state of Henrietta Street.

Colin knew he had arrived at Henrietta even without being able to read the street sign. The first hint of Henrietta Street was that the homes no longer had doors—instead there was simply a cutout where a door might have been a hundred years before, but which now remained open to the outside world day and night, summer and winter. Dirty children in ratty clothing scampered about the yards and street in front of the tenements, their only blessing being that they knew no other existence. Lone women, mostly middle-aged mothers, stood in the shadows where the doors should have been, waiting for their nightly customers.

He had seen Daniel here before, running about the yard at 437. But tenement children were wild and wandered throughout the north side of the Liffey by day. Daniel could be anywhere. Just because his family rented a room in the house didn't mean he would be home by evening.

Colin slowed as he approached the house where he had seen the boy before, but noticed that no young children were out playing. Sighing, he looked around and wondered if he should abandon his search until the next day. As he stood looking at the open doorway, behind which shadows darted about, he felt a small tug at his pants' pocket. Instinctively, he reached around and grabbed a tiny arm with his large hands. The culprit let out a squeal and thrashed wildly. Colin grabbed the boy's shirt with his other hand.

"Hey!" Colin began, but quickly let out a squeal of his own as a half-set of teeth sank into the flesh of his forearm. Colin yelled in pain, letting one arm go but holding the other fast.

"Let me go you piece of shite!" yelled a small child. Colin instantly recognized the voice.

"Daniel!" he said, "Look fella, it's just me!"

"I know who it is, you arse!" he said to Colin's surprise. "And I know you's got shillings in yer pocket!"

"So you staked me out, did you?" said Colin, half laughing. "Why didn't you just ask me for a shilling?"

Daniel stopped thrashing.

"I always give you a shilling, don't I?"

"Thought maybe you might have more than one," said the boy. "I followed you here from Church Street. Wanted to know what you were doing in me neighborhood."

"I was lookin' for you," said Colin. "Have a question that needs answerin'."

The small boy furrowed his brow. "Were you lookin' for me mum?"

"No," said Colin. "I said I was lookin' for you."

"Me mum's not home," he said. His eyes darted toward the open entryway of his house.

"All right," said Colin. "I wanted to chat with you. Is that all right?"

"Three shillings," said Daniel.

"Jesus, Mary, and Joseph!" said Colin.

"You shouldn't say that, you know," said the boy.

"You shouldn't be stealin' money. And why can't I say it, 'specially if the likes of you can call me an arse?"

"Because we aren't supposed to talk about the Virgin Mary," said the boy.

Colin looked at his hand and saw the imprint from Daniel's bite—with spaces where his front teeth should have been—along his wrist. "What's yer problem with the Virgin Mary?"

"Nothin," said Daniel. "Just another prayer to say."

"You don't like praying to the Virgin Mary?" inquired Colin. He tried not to let out a laugh. He wanted Daniel to think he was cross with him.

"Not if I don't have to. Saves me time, you see," said the boy.

"I see," he said. "And what does Father O'Brien say about that?"

"Don't matter," said the boy. "The Church of Ireland is teaching me now, and they say I don't have to say it."

"Church of Ireland!" exclaimed Colin. In his disgust, he accidentally took a deep breath and inhaled more of the tenement stench that hung like a fog all along Henrietta. "How's that?" he said, pulling his collar over his face.

Daniel never seemed to notice the wretched smell. "The Protestants pay me mum for me and me sisters to go there now. So I grow up to be one of them. And now she's not workin' at night anymore. So there's no need for you to come see her."

All at once, Colin understood. He had heard rumors of mothers across the tenements taking bribes to send their children to Protestant schools. It may have been a worse sin than prostitution, but at least the whole family could eat if the children's souls were sold to the Church of Ireland.

"Daniel," he said, "I'm not here to see yer mum. I don't even know who she is." He gave the boy a little smile. "And no matter where you go to school, you're still Catholic, and the government knows it, so you can bet the Virgin Mary knows it too."

Daniel wrinkled his face, and for the first time, Colin caught a brief glimmer of fear in his eyes. "You think?"

Colin nodded, laughing. "Extra penance for you." The boy frowned.

"Look Daniel," he said, his stomach still turning from the smell, "I'm here to talk to you about what you told me earlier today. I want to know how you knew that."

The boy began to negotiate a price.

"No, Daniel," he said, becoming quite serious. "I need to know. I need to know who told you and who else you've told."

Daniel shook his head. "I gotta live, too."

Colin stared at the small child in front of him with his missing front teeth. "I know, fella," he said sympathetically. "How 'bout I buy all yer information at a premium? And I'll pay you more if you don't go lookin' for it."

"How much?" said the boy.

"Jesus, Daniel!" said Colin. "I'm tryin' to keep you safe."

"And yerself safe!" said the boy, incredulously. "You don't want my information getting around!"

"Aye, I'm keepin' meself safe as well," he admitted. "But I'm a wee bit bigger than you. How about this," Colin thought quickly, "You can come by the store twice a week, and I will load you up with food. As much as you can carry home."

Daniel looked at Colin as if he didn't believe him.

"If I'm lyin' to you, then you can go back to smuggling yer information," said Colin. "But if I come through for you, I need you to give me yer word, Daniel. I need you to be a good boy and keep yer secrets to yerself. And you can tell yer da that I am givin' you the food, so he doesn't think you're stealing."

The boy laughed. Colin watched him breathe in the stench and wondered how he didn't notice. "Me da don't care if I steal."

"No?" said Colin. "I doubt that. Stealin' is a sin."

"Nah," said Daniel. "He don't care about nothin' I do. He's up in Glasnevin with me baby sister."

Colin sighed. Of course he was. A good portion of the men on this street who were sober enough to stand had been killed in the strikes the year before, or had starved or perhaps drank themselves to death in the aftermath. He looked to the open doorways along the street, many with women standing in the shadows, staring with blank eyes out into the hot July night. He wondered how many tenement kids grew up with no fathers. "Promise me, Daniel. This is important."

Daniel said nothing, but he gave Colin a slight nod.

Colin stood up and finally released the boy from his grip. "Come by tomorrow, about half eleven, and I promise you won't go hungry." He flipped the boy his last two shillings and started off back toward the Liberties and out of the rot of the tenements.

CHAPTER 19

July 31, 1914: London, England

Elizabeth nervously clutched the packet of pamphlets as her carriage rumbled through the streets of London. It was the Friday afternoon ahead of the August Bank Holiday, and the streets were practically deserted but for a few businessmen moving from one office to another along the sidewalks. In stark contrast, the coffee shops along Russell Street seemed absolutely packed with people, so much so that the patrons were huddled in the doorways waiting to get in. Empty streets and packed coffee houses usually meant only one thing—drama in Parliament. Elizabeth peered out of her carriage window and saw throngs of men outside the coffee houses, newspapers in hand, talking in excited voices and gesturing wildly. It was no wonder. All of civilized Europe was on the brink war.

Inside her gloves, her hands were sweating, not just from the heat, but also from the excitement of the day. On any normal day, she'd be excited to be headed to the Eldridge mansion for afternoon tea. Any chance to run into Edward was most welcome. However, today, even the thought of seeing Edward paled in comparison to the excitement of the coming days. *Would England actually go to war?*

She looked down at the pamphlets that she held in her hand. They were magnificent, indeed, and she had Gerald to thank for it. His scheme to introduce Viscountess Eldridge and her mother had been brilliant, but more than that, the viscountess was proving to be an asset to the literary campaign.

In one afternoon, she had devised a plan of outreach to the poorest London citizens and had even offered to host future meetings at the Eldridge residence. When Elizabeth had first met the viscountess earlier that week, she was immediately cured of her poor opinion of the woman. She seemed a fine, socially concerned citizen after all, and not nearly the bumptious snob she was gossiped to be. The pamphlets themselves, printed on fine parchment at the expense of the viscountess, advertised an evening reading class to be conducted in Aldgate, the first district the campaign would target. The adult classes would begin after the mill hours ended; volunteers would mind children to make it easy for parents to attend. Viscountess Eldridge, well versed in planning parties and social events, even devised a small menu to be served during the classes.

"You can't very well learn on an empty stomach, now can you?" she had said, to her mother's delight.

The first course was set to begin in early September. Now Elizabeth was delivering the pamphlets to the Eldridges for distribution, and she had been invited to stay for tea.

The carriage soon pulled up to the mansion, and Elizabeth was greeted by Francis, who looked sharp as ever in his top hat and tailored cloak. She was pleased he wore his top hat—she hated towering over all the men around her. "Good afternoon, Lady Elizabeth," he said, extending an arm to help her from the carriage.

Elizabeth clutched the pamphlets in one hand and took Francis's outstretched arm with the other. She reminded herself that she was in London, not New York, and tried more than usual to blend in with the social peculiarities of a world she had never understood. There were just so many rules, to no evident purpose. She was wearing a light pink dress that her lady's maid said flattered her skin tone. Under her fascinator, she wore her long brown hair partially up, but allowed some of it to fall down her back. She knew that her outfit suited her well, and she was hoping to run into Edward. Surely he would know that she would be attending tea.

"The viscountess is expecting you," Francis said as he escorted her to the double doors that opened onto the entrance hall. He removed his top hat, and Elizabeth awkwardly felt like she grew six inches. But he quickly diverted her attention away from her height—and his lack of it—when he leaned toward her and said, "And may I extend to you my warm thanks, Lady Elizabeth."

"Whatever for?" she asked.

Francis let out a small chuckle. "Just between you and me, ever since the viscountess returned from Lady Clarendon's charity event the other day, her mind has been entirely occupied by her charity work."

"Oh?" said Elizabeth.

"And for the first time in weeks, the house is at peace. On behalf of the entire staff, thank you."

Elizabeth giggled, then hastily covered her mouth. "You're entirely welcome," she said as they entered the doorway together.

In the entrance hall, they were met by the viscountess's secretary, Alice. "Good day, Lady Elizabeth," she said, smiling. Her words rolled off her tongue in a strong country accent as if she were reciting a poem. Her way of speaking fit perfectly with her personality, which was charming and bubbly, yet at the same time almost forcibly reserved. She always seemed to be trying to capture and stifle her own energy so as to not appear boisterous or impolite. Elizabeth immediately took to her, as she seemed so warm and welcoming.

"The viscountess is looking forward to your visit," she said. "Come this way, please."

Alice led Elizabeth to Lady Eldridge's sitting room, taking short, elegant steps that Elizabeth did her best to mimic. Alice's posture was picture perfect, and Elizabeth straightened her own slouching shoulders. Everything about the Eldridges seemed refined, even the staff. She felt awkwardly out of place.

When they arrived in the bright sitting room, Elizabeth marveled at how every detail of the room seemed meticulously planned. Each chair was upholstered in velvet and perfectly matched with the lavender drapes. Even the fresh purple and white lilacs adhered to the prescribed decor. Elizabeth saw three settings for tea—bone china patterned with deep purple violets—and around the table, chairs perfectly staged for conversation. *The third setting must be for Edward!*

She would feign nonchalance, of course, and so would he. Almost as if they barely knew each other—just acquaintances. The plan was working out better than she could ever have hoped. There was still time for an engagement this fall. It would be at least a month before the Parliamentarians began retreating to their country estates for the fall and winter seasons.

In the corner of the room, in front of the floor-to-ceiling windows, Elizabeth spied the viscountess, who practically burst from her velvety chaise and darted to greet her. "Oh, Elizabeth! So pleased you could make it today."

Viscountess Anita Eldridge was dressed in a radiant frock that seemed to melt away her advancing age. Her rose-colored dress was in exquisite taste, and layered skirts distracted from her plump midsection. Her graying hair was pulled up in an elegant coiffure that Elizabeth estimated must have taken hours to construct. She appeared, as always, intimidating. Elizabeth was slightly taken aback at the enthusiastic reception. "Oh, the pleasure is all mine, Viscountess Eldridge! Thank you for the invitation to tea."

"May I?" asked the viscountess, eyeing the pamphlets Elizabeth still clutched in her gloved hand.

"Of course!" Elizabeth handed the stack to Alice, then opened one example for the viscountess to inspect.

"Yes, a fine paper—so glad we decided on a sturdy parchment! September 1st, Aldgate, menu seems right. Oh these are just marvelous!" The viscountess produced a fan and waved it by her face. Elizabeth couldn't tell if it was the heat or the excitement over the pamphlets. "How many did we print?"

"One hundred."

"Brilliant. We'll start distributing them this week after the bank holiday. We'll need to get them to the foremen at the mills and other work centers so it can be advertised. I can enlist the help of both Gerald and Anna. It will be good for both of them to roll their sleeves up. Simply marvelous. Will you be assisting, too, with the distribution?" Elizabeth was caught off-guard. She hadn't thought about this.

"Certainly!" she replied.

"Wonderful. Let's arrange for you to ride with Gerald and Anna. It will be good for Anna to see an example such as yourself."

Elizabeth felt her heart sink a little. *Why isn't Edward available to distribute?* But she hid her disappointment. "Why, thank you."

"Come now. Now that we've attended to business, let's have some tea. Alice?"

"Yes, my Lady, the tea will be served momentarily," said Alice, springing to action.

"Lovely. Oh, and Alice?"

"Yes," she said, walking closer as Lady Eldridge beckoned to her. "Do see if Gerald can join us."

Elizabeth saw Alice's cheerful face fall into a blank stare. "Certainly," she said, and bustled quickly out of the room.

Elizabeth felt as disappointed as Alice looked—though she had no idea why the jovial secretary looked so bleak all of a sudden. She supposed she would be happy to spend the afternoon with Gerald. He was a nice boy, and he had certainly done her a favor. But she couldn't help but think how much better the afternoon would be if Edward had been invited to tea.

❧

Alice burst into the library where Gerald was sitting, studying a book on British military history. He had paid little attention to such things at university, but felt a sudden need to learn as much as possible about his new chosen path. The day was sweltering, and the dark wood panels of the library made the room feel warmer than the rest of the mansion. Even the open windows offered little reprieve.

At the sound of her footsteps, Gerald lifted his head and a broad smile came to his face. She always looked so sweet to him, no matter what the situation—note-taking for his mother, running errands for his mother, worrying over his mother, sneaking into the library to see him—she did it all so innocently and with such elegance—and perhaps just a little fear of his crazy mother. But he knew that beneath her sweet and proper exterior, she was just as mischievous as any girl he had known.

"Close the door," he said playfully.

Alice quickly obliged.

"Come, my dear." He patted his lap, and she shyly came over and sat on his knee. He put his arms around her waist and pulled her close, but she felt stiff and tense. "What's wrong, darling?" he said. "The heat, isn't it?"

"Oh Gerald," she said, bursting into tears. "We never should have deceived your mother!" This he hadn't expected.

"Deceived? I wouldn't say *deceived*. And she seems perfectly content with the outcome of her trip to the Clarendons."

But Alice continued, obviously upset by something. "This is why one should never be dishonest, it always comes back to haunt!"

"Whatever are you talking about?" he asked.

"Lady Elizabeth is here, right now, for tea."

"Yes, I know. Mother mentioned something about that yesterday. And? Is it not going well? Oh dear, that would be unfortunate."

"No, it's going just perfectly!" she cried.

"Then what appears to be the problem?"

"Your mother just sent me to invite you to join them for tea!"

"So?" said Gerald.

She tried again. "Not your brother—*you!*"

"Oh," he said, taken aback. "Do you think?"

"Yes, of course!" She gave him a dramatic look, and he understood that he had missed the obvious.

"All right, that is a small dilemma, but not one we can't solve. We just need to refocus Mother's efforts. Tell you what, my dear. I'll be perfectly uninterested, and I will bring up my brother at every possible opportunity. I'll tell Elizabeth what a charming idiot he is, and how well meaning he is for such a daft fellow. How's that? And remember, Elizabeth is in on this too, and she's already smitten with my brother, though Lord knows why. Mother's powers to influence are great, but limited."

An embarrassed smile broke on Alice's face. She often overreacted.

"You know—you should learn to control that dramatic side of yours," he teased. She hit him playfully on the shoulder. "On second thought—no. That's my favorite part about you." He wrapped his arms around her and kissed her.

But inside, he felt a familiar weight return—there was no chance of a future with Alice, and he knew it. This was only the beginning of such incidents. He had escaped his mother's matchmaking until now, but he knew she would relentlessly present young ladies to him until he chose a girl to marry—a proper girl. He couldn't protect Alice from the parade of women who would undoubtedly be showing up for tea. Alice's reaction had made him keenly aware that she was invested in their prohibited romance. *You're a coward,* he thought. *You should break it off, or...*He squeezed her a little harder...*or run away with her.*

He tried to force the thought from his mind. "Go now," he said to Alice. She hopped up from his lap, wiped her tears from her face, and hurried off to prepare the tea.

He reluctantly put on his day jacket, which had sat on the back of his mahogany chair, and walked out of the library to his mother's sitting room. Not only was he irritated at the prospect of spending the afternoon dodging his mother's matchmaking attempts, he also hated to be served by Alice, and he knew that she would be bringing the tea.

ॐ

"Hello, Gerald, dear!" exclaimed his mother as he walked into the sitting room. "How lovely of you to join us!" She turned to Elizabeth. "Gerald has been studying all day in the library. A keen learner he is. Always curious."

Gerald sighed. His mother was in fine form this afternoon.

Walking over to Elizabeth, he took her hand. "Wonderful to see you again, Lady Elizabeth. Thank you, Mother, for inviting me to tea."

"Oh, the pleasure is ours! What a treat!" said the viscountess.

Alice entered the room with tea and biscuits and began pouring. She made Lady Eldridge's tea with a drop of milk and sugar, just the way she liked it, and then proceeded to Elizabeth.

"Just sugar for me, please," Elizabeth said.

When Alice got to Gerald, she added plenty of milk and topped it off with a heaping spoon of sugar.

The viscountess frowned. "Alice, dear. You didn't even ask Gerald how he took his tea!"

Alice stopped short, immediately recognizing her error. Gerald felt himself stiffen. It was his error as much as hers. He and Alice had enjoyed tea together countless times when his mother was otherwise occupied, closed up in the library chatting over books and politics, and he knew all too well that she was quite familiar with what he liked—and not just as it pertained to tea.

He quickly came to her rescue. "I just got finished asking Alice to bring extra sugar and milk when I met her in the corridor. I always seem to require a lot of sugar."

"Ah," said his mother, apparently content with this answer. "Of course." When she turned her head to stir her tea, Gerald winked at Alice and watched her blush as she departed the room. His mother didn't catch the gesture, but he cringed as he saw that Elizabeth did. He had been careless.

"Now, Gerald," his mother's voice commanded his attention. "Elizabeth and I were just discussing the next steps in our campaign."

"Of course, the campaign. Brilliant." he said, still watching Elizabeth. She composed herself marvelously, as if it hadn't shocked her at all. She was probably used to scandals between aristocracy and household staff—it was so common that it barely warranted gossip. He felt his heart sink. Alice was so much more that that to him. *A coward,* he thought again.

"Elizabeth was planning to distribute the pamphlets starting on Tuesday of this week," she continued.

"Splendid," said Gerald, still distracted. Luckily, much of his life had consisted of participating in trivial conversations such as these, and he was used to pretending to be interested. He had his role memorized perfectly. He stared out the window, still consumed by his gaffe. Unlike the library, the breeze that came through the windows was refreshing. The lavender window dressings blew lightly, and he could smell the sweet scent of the lilacs.

"And to think, Elizabeth going to Aldgate by herself. I just can't imagine. Surely, we should be able to find someone to accompany her." She winked at Elizabeth. Gerald couldn't help but smile. His mother was perhaps more obvious than he was in her winking.

"Indeed. Perhaps Edward would be available?" Gerald offered.

At this Elizabeth smiled. "Oh, Edward! I didn't know he had an interest in literacy!" *Laying it on a little thick,* he thought.

But his mother frowned and discreetly wiped her brow. "Oh, he doesn't." She sounded annoyed. "Not Edward. And besides, Gerald, your brother is too busy these days, what with the conflict brewing and his orders to his unit imminent.

No, I should not think Edward would have the energy to devote to this."

Gerald heard Elizabeth audibly sigh. The light breeze continued and helped to cut the awkward tension that was building.

"But you, Gerald, you certainly have time to assist with the campaign!" his mother said. She seemed exasperated that she had to suggest the solution she sought. Gerald tried to voice a protest, but she added, "Ah yes, a lovely idea! And Anna can accompany you. It will be good for her to be involved in this sort of thing. What a lovely example the two of you will set for her. Yes, this will be just perfect. I will arrange it with Lady Clarendon." She beamed contentedly.

"Well, then I suppose there's nothing to discuss," said Gerald blandly.

"I suppose not," said Elizabeth, sounding equally unenthusiastic.

But his mother was not finished. "Oh, but of course there is!" she said. "I'll leave you two to iron out the details."

"But, Mother!" said Gerald, aghast that she, always concerned about proper social behavior, would depart to leave the two of them to talk. She certainly was interested in his getting acquainted with Elizabeth.

"I'll fetch Alice!" his mother called back. Apparently, Alice was her idea of a chaperone.

Elizabeth let out a laugh.

"I must say, Elizabeth," Gerald said, "My mother is quite taken with you. I do not believe she has 'fetched' anything or anyone in decades."

She laughed again, but he interrupted her. "Elizabeth—I need to explain—"

"Nothing to explain," she said. "Your secret is safe with me."

"It's not what you think."

"It doesn't matter what I think," she said. "And I won't tell a soul."

"Not even Edward?"

"Not even him," she said. "Cross my heart."

He sat back in his chair, still discontented. Elizabeth must have sensed it.

"Gerald," she started. "Having had the luxury—and I do mean luxury— of escaping this world for the past several years, I've come to feel that there is no one more imprisoned than the British elite. I mean, look at us. Playing ridiculous games just to be able to live the lives we want. To be able to love those we want. Edward and I—in America we could just marry. There would be none of this drama." Her voice became soft. "And you and Alice, even. Pedigree is less of an obstacle."

He shook his head. "That can't be true."

"It is true," she said. "Even the Catholics of Ireland—downtrodden as they are—have more freedom than we do when it comes to matters of the heart. It's ironic, really. Our families have the power to rule over millions, yet we can't make the most basic, natural choices for ourselves."

He found this to be a curious comment. He knew of no other family in his parents' circle who spoke of the Irish like this. Mostly it was *those damned rebels* or *the bloody papists*, but never *downtrodden*. This was precisely why his father would be aghast if he knew what Edward was planning. He took a sip of tea from the delicate china. There was a lot of wisdom to what Elizabeth had said.

He put his teacup down on its saucer with a clank. "Do you think me a coward?" he asked. He wasn't sure why he wanted Elizabeth's opinion, but he had spoken the words before giving them much thought.

She stopped midbite of biscuit in surprise at the question, but didn't hesitate to answer. "Not yet," she said, her mouth still full of biscuit. She swallowed and wiped her chin with none of the daintiness he expected from someone who went by *Lady Elizabeth*. "Ask me again in a few months, and I may have a different response."

He also didn't expect such a blunt answer. *Must be the American in her.*

❦

By the time Alice made her way back to the sitting room, Gerald and Elizabeth were deep in conversation, and Viscountess Eldridge would have been displeased to know it had nothing to do with distributing pamphlets, literacy campaigns, or a budding romance. "And what did the ambassador say?" Gerald was asking,

183

intently focused on Elizabeth's news.

Elizabeth, the first to see Alice, said invitingly, "Come, Alice, join our discussion."

At the mention of her name, Gerald looked up, and stood to pull a chair out for her. "Yes, Alice, please come sit with us. Elizabeth has news about Paris."

Alice daintily sat in the velvet chair previously occupied by the viscountess. For the past several weeks, she and Gerald had spent night after night hidden away in the library as they discussed the world events in whispers. Speculation was rife throughout the mansion staff about which way England would go in the burgeoning conflict.

"And so the French ambassador said that France will not enter the war at all unless it can do so with England as an ally," continued Elizabeth.

"And how can France ensure England will enter?" asked Gerald.

"I'm not sure," said Elizabeth. "But to think that they have come this close to war without a guarantee! Father said that no such guarantee would be given. How foolish! To provoke a war and then stand back to await our assistance!"

"Indeed," said Gerald pensively. "But why would they do this? It makes no sense."

"And Father even said that French troops were drawing back from the borders with Germany—can it be that they mean to back down?" Elizabeth shook her head. It seemed so unreasonable, after weeks of buildup to war. "Was it all a pretense?"

Alice shook her head. *Isn't it obvious?* she thought. "What if the Germans move first?" she finally blurted out, then immediately wondered if she should have kept quiet. She knew nothing about Elizabeth, save that Gerald's brother was smitten with her. Elizabeth was indeed quite beautiful, yet she seemed somewhat unrefined for someone of her status. Alice couldn't quite put her finger on just what it was.

"How do you mean?" asked Elizabeth. She didn't seem to care whatsoever that Alice had spoken up. *Perhaps this is why she seems so unrefined,* thought

Alice. *No other woman of her class has ever given me the time of day.*

Alice organized her thoughts. "If the Germans are allowed to be the first to strike, think of how the world will see it."

Gerald and Elizabeth thought about this for a few seconds. "They will be at fault for a continental war," said Gerald, thinking aloud.

Alice continued, feeling emboldened. "And what do you think will be their first move? Belgium, of course. They will enter through Belgium. The writing is on the wall."

Gerald began to nod. He looked at Alice, obviously impressed with her thinking. "I think you might have something here, Alice. Paris is waiting for Germany to invade, and then England will be bound by their word to Brussels to enter the war on the side of France!"

Elizabeth said slowly and softly, "If you are right, then we are going to war."

"Probably within the week," said Gerald. He scratched his chin and stared up at the ornate carvings all along ceiling, and Alice felt her heart begin to beat loudly. She knew that look—he was up to something. *Don't you dare*, she thought to herself, but she knew it was probably already too late.

CHAPTER 20

August 1, 1914: Dublin, Ireland

"Colin!" Michael whispered loudly and nudged his cousin's arm. Colin was deep in a drunken slumber in one of the small rooms above the store. He groaned, then rolled to his side. "Colin!" he heard again, this time a little louder.

Colin lifted his head. The room was pitch dark, and for a moment, he thought he was in his parents' cottage in Ballynote. He breathed in, and instead of the earthy smell of the cottage, with its dirt floor and drafty walls, he smelled the familiar musty wood scent of his uncle's shop. Instantly, he remembered that he was back in Dublin. His heart sank even before he became cognizant of his pounding head.

"Colin!"

"What is it?" Colin groaned. "It can't be time to get up already? The first delivery is not till seven."

"It's half five," replied Michael, "and it's time to get yer arse out of bed."

Colin sat up in bed, hitting his head on the low rafter in the corner where his bed stood. "Fook!" he yelled and rubbed his head.

"SHHHH!" said Michael. "You'll wake Da, you idiot!"

"What's the big deal?" asked Colin. His head was still cloudy, and his eyes hurt as he tried to focus them. "Why are we up so early today? Do you like to torture people?"

"Because it's yer birthday," said Michael. Colin forced his eyes to focus on his cousin. He was already dressed in a tunic with matching trousers and boots, which is what he usually wore when headed out for a meeting with the Volunteers.

"Aye," said Colin. "And yer present to me is to let me sleep off last night until at least seven." He lay back down on his straw mattress and held both of his hands to his forehead.

"It's yer birthday," repeated Michael. "And my present to you is a job…" he let out a big sigh. "In Wicklow."

Colin sat straight up in bed, his head again crashing into the wooden rafter. This time he minded less, as it distracted him a little from his hangover. "You're serious?" he asked, rubbing his temples. "'Cause if this is a rotten trick—"

"Very serious." Michael's voice was calm and his face humorless. "Now get dressed." Michael threw him a pair of pants and a cotton shirt. "We leave in five minutes."

Colin hurriedly dressed and pulled on his boots. He found his wash bucket and splashed cool water on his face, wishing that Michael had mentioned this to him the previous night, before he had emptied his flask. He quietly descended the stairs, careful to not wake his uncle, who would soon be rising to prepare the morning deliveries.

Michael was already waiting at the door when Colin appeared in the back room of the store. He eyed Colin's disheveled top. "Might want to button yer shirt."

Colin looked down and immediately saw that in his haste, he had missed several buttonholes.

"I trust you'll sober up soon?" said Michael.

"Aye," said Colin, and he fumbled to adjust his shirt.

"Let's go." Michael reached up to quiet the bell that hung over the back door, and the young men silently exited into the back alley. The cats, as usual, hung close to the back step, but then quickly disappeared at the sight of Colin and Michael.

"What made you change yer mind?" asked Colin, as they walked out onto the darkened street.

"You're eighteen now. Can make yer own choices," Michael said. For once, it was cool outside. Apparently you had to get up an hour before sunrise to catch any relief from the Dublin heat.

"I'm exactly four days older than I was the last time we had this conversation," he said to his cousin. He knew his birthday had nothing to do with this little excursion.

"There's another reason." Michael said nothing further, but kept up his brisk pace. Colin had to jog to keep up. With every step, it felt like some invisible demon was stabbing him in the eyes. *Fookin' whiskey.*

"Truth be told," Michael finally said, "I realized that you're eighteen and haven't had a date since you showed up on me father's doorstep over a year ago. I'm taking pity on you and trying to help you with the ladies." He cracked a smile. He seemed to enjoy nothing more than teasing his younger cousin. "The girls like a man with important work—I would know," he managed to say before Colin elbowed him in the ribs. It was a soft blow, done in jest, but Michael grimaced and Colin knew that it hurt. *Good.*

"Not true," said Colin. "What gives, Michael?"

Michael, still rubbing his side, became serious. "Look, Colin, we need someone who knows how to handle a small boat. That's all."

"What?" said Colin, "You can't be serious."

"You grew up near the Shannon, and I know for a fact that the McMahons are river pilots. I figured you've spent a decent amount of time on the water."

"'Tis true, I have," said Colin.

"Well," said Michael, lowering his voice, "we're taking the guns in tonight at Kilcoole, in County Wicklow. The harbor there is different—no pier for the offload. We'll need to meet the shipment out in the harbor and bring the guns and ammo in by boat. We've got only a few men who have any experience with boats. I told the boys you could help."

"I can!" said Colin. In his excitement, he tripped over a loose cobblestone. His balance was still a little off.

But Michael didn't laugh at him. "I hope you're ready for it," he said. "This one's not going to be easy, and judging from what happened at Bachelors Walk last week, if we get caught, there will be trouble." Michael stopped on the street and reached into his pocket for a cigarette. He didn't offer one to his cousin, but struck a match against the brick siding one of the row houses. He lit the cigarette and took in a deep drag. The light from the cigarette made him look older than he was—his cheekbones stood out, and the lines on his face looked deeper than they did in daylight. "We're not playing here," he said. "This is real, and it is dangerous. Just know that before you step foot in the house up there."

He eyed the row of ramshackle brick houses along the street, all in various states of disrepair. A century before, these homes were retreats for the wealthy. Today they were where the poorest of Dublin huddled in their misery. "Patrick wants to meet you before he trusts you with somethin' like this."

The smell of the cigarette was making Colin nauseous. "All I've ever asked for is for you to trust me."

Michael ignored this and continued. "The last thing we need is idiots yearning to die for Ireland. 'Cause that's just what they'll do. The ground is already chock full of dead idiots."

Michael's footsteps slowed as they approached a narrow, three-story row house. They were on the edge of Camden Row, and even in the cool morning air, the smell of filth and excrement on the streets was overwhelming. "How do you not notice the stench, Michael?" Colin asked.

"What stench?"

A gentle breeze exacerbated the fetid smell, which, when combined with Michael's cigarette, was more than Colin could take. He leaned on the side of one of the tenements and vomited onto the sidewalk. In the Protestant areas of town, this would have caused quite the commotion. But on Camden Row it was hardly worth anyone's notice.

"Jesus Christ, Colin! You think you could be in a little better shape for yer job interview."

"It's yer fookin' cigarette," he said spitting onto the cobblestone. He felt remarkably better.

"It's a fookin' idiot who can't handle whiskey," said Michael.

"I can handle the whiskey just fine," said Colin, standing up straight again. "It's the whiskey, the smoke, and the shite all at once that puts me over the top." His hand still rested on the row house. He leaned forward and let the cool bricks soothe his head.

"Well, I can't do anything about the shite," said Michael. "And I'm not goin' to stop smoking on yer sorry account. Perhaps you can lay off the drink once in a while? You sure you can sober up by this afternoon?"

"Aye," said Colin. "Feelin' much better now."

Michael spat. "If it were up to me, you'd be stayin' home. And one more thing," he added, "this isn't the typical work of a corporal in the Volunteers. And if you step through that door, you're no longer just a regular. The work we do is—" he looked at his cousin, "—different."

"I'm not pullin' some type of stable duty again," said Colin. With some effort, he lifted his head from the building.

"We're intelligence, you dumb fook," Michael snapped. "And it doesn't mean I think you're intelligent."

This got Colin's attention. "I knew you was up to something." He ran his hands through his messy hair then habitually reached for his flask before thinking the better of it.

"Up to my neck in something, that's for sure," replied Michael, grinning. He went ahead of Colin and bounded up a set of steps in desperate need of repair. The railing had long since fallen or broken off, leaving jagged stones along the edges of the steps. The second step was missing entirely.

Michael took a giant step up to the top stair and reached to knock on the large wooden door. Before his fist struck the wood—there was no knocker—Colin reached over and stopped him. "Do I know this Patrick?"

Michael replied. "I certainly hope so. He's Patrick Pearse."

"You bastard," replied Colin, smiling. "Up to yer neck for sure!"

"We'll hang if we fook this up, you know. If we push this movement far and don't quite make what we are aimin' for, King George will have our necks, and don't think I'm kiddin' with you. Best be victorious or go home now. We've got no other option."

Colin let go of Michael's arm, and his cousin rapped three times on the door. Colin stole a look at his cousin, with a creeping respect that made his stomach turn again. Patrick Pearse. Irish Republican Brotherhood. The so-called secret society. Fenians. Intelligence. And just as he had always suspected—closely connected with some of the Volunteers. All of a sudden, everything seemed real. Michael was right. Their necks were on the line.

A tall man with dark brown hair answered the door. It was Pearse. *Fook me,* thought Colin. His cousin wasn't just some arrogant bastard. He was running with the most infamous nationalists in Ireland.

"Patrick, this is me cousin, Colin. Don't be impressed—he's dumber than he looks."

"Mic, a gentleman as always. You've such a way with words. Good morning," said Pearse. He was energetic despite the early hour. He ushered them in quickly then shut the door behind them. Colin looked around. The old building was only slightly less dreary on the inside. The paperless walls were pockmarked with holes—the smaller ones were homes to the mice or rats that Colin assumed ravaged the entire street, but the more prominent holes were no doubt caused by drunken republican fists. But it seemed as though whoever had lent him the house had the entire space to themselves, which was more than most occupants of Camden Row could say. Patrick was dressed too nicely and had too good of manners to belong in such an environment. *Must be a safe house.*

"How do you do, Colin?" said Patrick, "Michael said you knew a thing or two about handling a boat."

"Yes sir, I do," replied Colin promptly. He tried not to focus on his host's wandering eye, which strayed to the outside, just as Colin had always heard in pub rumors.

"Just Patrick'll do," he said. "We're brothers in this." Pearse was less intimidating in person than Colin had anticipated. He had expected a soldier, but for a man who ran a clandestine organization to fight British occupation, he seemed frail and academic. He made frequent whimsical expressions in response to some deep conversation that must have played in his mind. He came across to Colin as poetic—more of a philosopher than a soldier—but he wasted no time laying out the plan.

"Colin," he said. "We're bringing in the shipment by boat at about midnight tonight. Kilcoole's a several-hour drive—give or take—from here, and we expect you to make it alone. Each of the boys will go down separately, taking different routes by car."

Colin nodded. He had been down to Wicklow the previous fall with Silas Smith and knew the road well.

"Can you drive, Colin?" Patrick asked with a sudden frown, as if he had just discovered a neglected detail in his planning.

"Of course," said Colin. For the first time, the fact that he was a grocer's apprentice was somewhat useful. He had spent the better part of the last year mastering his uncle's quirky delivery truck.

Patrick looked relieved. He returned to the silent conversation that must have occupied his thoughts, but he didn't share any thoughts with the Kildare boys. Colin watched him anxiously. He couldn't tell if Patrick was looking at him or off into the distance, as his wayward eye focused somewhere between the two.

"There will be several small crafts that will run the guns ashore," he finally said. "I'll need you to sail one of them. Can you do this?"

"Of course," Colin said again. He spoke loudly so as to sound more confident than he felt. He wished Seamus were in Dublin and not boarding a ship to America. Seamus could at least give him some advice. His heart skipped a beat when he thought of Nora. She, even more than Seamus, would be the perfect companion for this adventure. And she was certainly more qualified than he was.

"Brilliant," Colin heard Patrick say. "We're glad to have you, Colin."

Colin nodded. That was it. He was in. It had been so simple—Pearse might have taken any bloke off the street. The standards for entry into this secret clan seemed to be low. Why had Michael kept him away for so long?

"One more thing Colin," said Pearse. He put his hand on Colin's shoulder.

"Sure," said Colin.

"Yer girl…"

Colin looked to Michael, who smiled wryly. He made a conscious effort not to curse out his cousin front of Patrick. He felt his pulse accelerate—just what were they planning for her?

"The one we brought up from Clare to stay at the Parsons."

As if Patrick had to specify which girl. He wasn't his cousin, with a lady for every night of the week. *Yer girl*. This was really all about Nora—it finally dawned on Colin that he was only a small part of the real purpose of this visit to Pearse. He felt his left hand form into a fist.

"She reads and writes?"

"Aye," said Colin curtly. He glared at his cousin. Michael's little arrangement for Nora had been organized from the very top.

"Good. I'll want a full report, each week if she can. We'll set up a relay back and forth—time it with the grocery deliveries. Things are picking up. War, Home Rule, rifles—we'll need any and all information about those Ulstermen. You'll play a big role." Patrick squeezed his shoulder and emphasized, "This is yer chance."

Colin's heart sank. He had wanted so badly to do something worthwhile, and finally he had an opportunity. But Nora—his big break put her directly amid everything he needed to protect her from. Michael smiled with satisfaction, as if he was daring Colin to clobber him.

Pearse, his hand still on Colin's shoulder, must have felt how tense he was. He looked down to Colin's clenched fist. "Everything all right?" he asked.

"Just fine," Michael cut in. "He's just a bit hungover. Today's 'is birthday."

Patrick nodded. "Trust you'll be ready to go this afternoon?"

"Aye," said Colin.

"Good. Before you head out, though, a word of caution. We can't have you anywhere near the Parsons outside of groceries. For this to work, yer relationship with the Parsons has to be strictly business only. You'll deliver the groceries and any correspondence directly to Theo. You'll not have any contact with the girl."

Colin squinted his face. "What do you mean?"

"Ah—Theo is Ronan Dunham," said Patrick. "We call him Theo, after Theobald Wolfe Tone—one of my favorite nationalists. It's our little joke, and it keeps his actual name out of any written correspondence."

That wasn't Colin's question. But when he started to clarify, but Michael glared at him, so Colin closed his mouth and pursed his lips. *No contact with the girl.* It was a sucker punch on top of everything else.

"Theo will pass any messages to the girl, and then she will pass anything back through him. You'll be a courier back to Mic." Patrick nodded his head. The plan must have sounded just as good to him when spoken aloud. "But don't go readin' anything we send," he added, looking up abruptly. "'Tis strictly for our eyes only."

Michael laughed. "No need to worry! I tol' you, he's dumber than he looks!"

Colin could feel his face go red with embarrassment. But Patrick was kinder. "You could use some class, you know, Michael. He's yer kin, and he's saving your arse. If you could muster enough boys who can handle boats we wouldn't need yer cousin today."

It was some acknowledgement, and on any other day, Colin would feel somewhat vindicated by having the leader of Irish intelligence stand up for him. But today, on his birthday, it didn't resonate. He had just been told, in no uncertain terms, that he wasn't to have any contact with Nora. And it had come directly from the mouth of Patrick Pearse—one of the most influential rebels in Ireland.

"That'll do, boys," said Patrick. His lazy eye looked off into the corner, but he nodded at the door. Colin shook his outstretched hand. "Thank you, Patrick, for trustin' me."

"We'll see," said Michael. He slapped Patrick on the back. "I'll check in with you when we're back," he said.

"Godspeed to you," said Patrick.

&

"What the fook was that?" Colin yelled to Michael as soon as they had departed the row house. The sun was beginning to come up, and Colin knew the heat would draw out an even more potent stench. He started walking toward the Liberties, not caring if Michael followed. The street seemed even more depressing in the light.

"Happy birthday." Michael called from behind him. "I just set you up with everythin' you've been beggin' for. You're welcome." He snapped his head around. The motion made him dizzy. *I've got to cut back on the whiskey,* he thought as his eyes focused on Michael.

"Set me up all you like, Michael. I signed up for this. But Nora—" The cobblestones had become slippery with the morning mist.

"How can you be so sure yer Nora doesn't want a part of this? After all…"

"I know 'after all,'" said Colin, "'after all, she's got it in her blood,' I know."

"So what's the big deal?" asked Michael. He stepped over some rotting food someone had chucked from an upstairs window

Colin paused. *What was the big deal?*

"Why are you protecting her? She doesn't belong to you."

"No, she doesn't," admitted Colin. "But she's not pining for violence. She was raised by Eamonn—taught only about Daniel O'Connell's peaceful revolution. Taught that there isn't another way." But even as he said it, he knew his worst fear was that she might actually want to be a part of all of this. That it was in her blood, like everyone said.

"A couple months in Dublin'll change her mind. Particularly at the Parsons, and especially if Ethan ever pays a visit. Half an hour in that bastard's presence is enough to turn any Irishman, no matter how peaceful they'd like to be," said Michael. "Hell," he mused, "might even turn a bloody Englishman!" By now Michael had caught up to him.

"You promised me he wasn't there," said Colin.

"He's not," said Michael. "So there."

Colin felt dismayed. He could not convince his cousin to leave Nora alone. She'd be no good as a spy. If they knew anything about her, that would have been apparent. She was too good, too kind. "If you really wanted her help, you'd send her to Kilcoole," said Colin, though he wasn't serious.

"Fook I would." Michael spat on the ground.

"She's better suited for that, you know," said Colin, "than to be snoopin' around for us."

"Ha, now there's a thought!" said Michael.

They continued to walk toward the Liberties. The streets remained empty, save for the occasional drunk stumbling along the uneven cobblestones. "I'm just jokin' with you," said Colin, "but if you wanted to find somethin' for her to do, it's a better fit."

"I don't want her to have anything to do with us," interrupted Michael. "An' besides that, she's a girl."

"I'm well aware," replied Colin.

"Girls don't pilot boats, and if you think a girl would do better than you, we're going back to Patrick to tell him so."

Colin didn't reply. They just didn't know Nora.

"She's a Cullen. It might be her destiny, don't you know," Michael said.

Colin felt that strange sense of foreboding again. He wanted her to be destined to live in a free Ireland, perhaps more than he wanted it for himself. But at the same time, he had an ominous sense that many of those who would fight for a free Ireland wouldn't survive.

"Cheer up, Colin," said Michael, slapping him on the back. "It's yer birthday, and I just gave you the gift you've wanted for the better part of the last year. And you repay me by walking around like yer dog just died."

Colin forced a smile. "Thank you, Michael."

"You're welcome. You've got a good brain in there somewhere, and I think you're better suited for this type of work. Fits yer personality." He seemed energized by the morning's events and began to walk faster. Colin reluctantly kept up. The sight of the Liberties up ahead at least felt less depressing than the tenements. The markets were beginning to open, and the streets felt cheerful.

"Thanks," Colin said again.

"But I suppose we'll see how much yer thankin' me after you get back from sinkin' boats in Kilcoole," teased Michael, this time ducking out of the way to avoid his cousin's elbow jabbing him in the ribs.

"Now, get to yer deliveries before we have to shove off. An' don't you go anywhere near the Parsons. Patrick was serious. She's off limits to you unless I say so. I can't have you over there makin' anyone suspicious."

There it was again. That painful reminder. "I'll have to go back at some point," said Colin.

"Of course—but it will all be planned."

Colin adamantly shook his head. "I'm supposed to be back today! The missus needs an order for a delegation that's comin'. Mr. Dunham told me." He wasn't going to miss this chance to talk to Nora—he had so much to tell her.

Michael stopped dead in his tracks. "Say that again." he said.

"Mr. Dunham told me—"

"And why is this the first I'm hearin' about it?"

"No need to be cross Michael, they haven't even placed the order yet. That's me business today. Just a heads' up about their delegation."

"And he called it a delegation, did he?"

"Aye." A horse-drawn cart crossed directly in front of them, and Colin stopped to let it by.

"Fook. When will it be here?"

"How am I supposed to know? What's the big deal?"

Michael clammed up. "No big deal. Just next time don't let a few days pass before you relay news to me from Ronan."

The horse passed, and Colin began to walk toward the shop. "So I'll be headed over today," he said. Michael didn't follow him but called to him, "You just might be." Instead of heading to the shop, Michael turned on his heel and toward the markets. Colin watched him as he went and wondered what he was up to. "But keep to yer business and stay away from her," he called.

Colin heard him, but had no intention of following orders from his cousin—not when it came to Nora.

Chapter 21

August 1, 1914: The Liberties, Dublin, Ireland

Colin moved quickly along Ash Street toward his uncle's store. His boots were loud against the cobblestone, but he didn't care. He was too excited to temper his footsteps. He ran into the back alley and once again scattered the cats who waited for some scraps of food. "Michael's out today," he called to them. Their yellow eyes peered out from beneath the steps. "But perhaps I can find you something to eat." He quickly opened the back door, remembering a hair too late that his uncle had installed a bell over the doorway. He reached up to silence it, but the damage had been done. He heard footsteps, and soon his uncle appeared from behind the curtain that separated the front of the shop from the rear.

"Jesus, Mary, and Joseph, Colin!" he said, "what in Christ's name are you doing out at this hour?" He looked like a tired version of Michael. He had the same eyes and thick hair—though it was quickly graying—but his personality had no trace of his son's cheekiness. Colin wondered if this was a trait his cousin had inherited from his mother.

"Just out for a walk, Uncle," he replied. "Got used to morning walks while I was home."

"Aye," said his uncle, suspiciously. Colin said nothing, hoping his uncle would drop the subject.

But his uncle arched a brow and leaned one large hand on the wooden table. "Tell me," he said, "did you often go out to meet the Volunteers while you were back in Clare?"

"No, sir," said Colin. He looked at his boots. He felt a little embarrassed at having been caught in a lie, at his age. But his uncle did not seem very upset with him. "How did you know?"

His uncle smiled and walked toward him, his hand outstretched. He really had none of the traits that made Michael so annoying. He rested his hand on Colin's shoulder. It was a kind gesture and reminded Colin of how his own father might speak to him.

"Ah, Colin, me boy. I may be an old man, but I'm not so old as I don't hear two boys sneaking out in the middle of the night—in boots." A smile came over his uncle's face. He removed his hand from Colin's shoulder and smoothed his thick mustache. He took a step toward the counter and reached for a cup of lukewarm tea he had left on the counter earlier. "I don't know what you boys are up to, and I don't want to know." Winking an eye, he continued, "But I do want you to keep sneaking out at night, if you know what I mean." He took a sip of the tea. "It's better when it's warm, " he said in disappointment.

Colin felt his lips try to break into a smile, but forced them to remain stoic.

The elder Kildare pushed some old dishes out of the way and leaned on the counter. "I know Michael is in up to 'is neck with those Volunteers, though he'd never tell me the extent of it. Probably wants to keep the shop safe, and I'm grateful to 'im for it. But the Ireland we are fightin' for is ours to make, and I want me kin to shape it. Lord knows, we've lost enough over the generations to not have a say in her future." His voice sounded quiet, but he put his cup down with such force that Colin was surprised it didn't crack.

While it was no shock to Colin that his uncle was a nationalist, he was a bit surprised with at his unabashed support for Michael's membership with the Volunteers. Abandoning his tea, he added, "But I also want you to be safe. You're a young man, Colin. And you've got a future, though Lord knows it's not as a grocer."

Colin cringed a little. He had hoped his uncle hadn't noticed that his heart wasn't in the business. Colin looked at his boots again, this time noticing the dirt he had tracked across the kitchen.

"Come boy," said Uncle John. He didn't seem to notice the caked dirt that now littered the floor. It seemed to fit in with the rest of the mess in the living quarters.

Colin followed him up the steep stair that led to the second floor and then toward the back room where his uncle slept. The upstairs was sparsely furnished—and therefore much neater than the downstairs. At the foot of his uncle's straw mattress was a wooden chest covered in a gray woolen blanket. Uncle John carefully lifted the folded blanket and placed it on the bed. Then he reached into a crevice in the wooden rafter above and pulled out a small, silver key. A strong scent of cedar arose as his uncle opened the chest.

Colin peered over his uncle, who was withdrawing something linen partially wrapped in paper from the top of the chest. This his uncle placed on his bed, next to the wool blanket. "Yer Aunt Mary wore this on our wedding day," he said softly. "It was such a beautiful day." He dug around deeper in the chest. "One of those days where the sun doesn't stop shinin'. It lasts forever in yer memory, a day like that."

Now he brought out another item, wrapped in cloth. "This here, me boy, like all artifacts carries with it a story. Me hope is that you change the course of its story to a happier ending. It has a brother, which I gave to Michael last year, around the time he joined up."

Uncle John carefully unwrapped the cloth, stained yellow with time, and revealed a small handgun.

Colin's eyes got wide. "But these are illegal," he said.

"And since when have you cared if a firearm was illegal in Ireland?" His uncle laughed. "You think I was born yesterday? Take it," he said, putting the weapon into Colin's hand. "I'd rather be in jail for havin' it then be saying a prayer at yer grave because we didn't have it." Colin carefully held the firearm, running his hands along the smooth wooden handle and the silver barrel. His uncle returned to the chest, digging out a small box. "Here's some powder and rounds," he said. "We can get some replacements, if you need 'em. Can always trade some meat for goods such as that." He cast an eye on his nephew. "Being a grocer has its advantages, you know."

Colin eyed his uncle. Just what else had he managed to keep hidden all these years? He studied the handgun. Someone had carved what he assumed were letters on the wooden handle.

"This gun has history, Colin. Closer to you than you could ever imagine. It's part of our family's history, part of Clare's history. It carries with it a promise, which I intend to keep." He paused, reflecting, and carefully chose his next words. "Some say it's a bad omen to use a gun that failed in its mission, but I like to think of it as one act of a many-part play. The first act is over and done with. The dead have been silent and buried for more than a decade. Perhaps yers will be the last act and will end differently. That is me sincere hope for you, Colin, on yer birthday." His uncle rose and sat on the straw mattress. Colin saw him eying the linen dress he had pulled from the cedar chest and couldn't help but notice the sad look that overcame him.

Colin nodded and turned the gun in his hands, but no words came to him. In just one day, his life had been altered in so many ways. Between the two days that separated him from being a boy and a man, he had suddenly become charged with the duties of an adult and left his boyhood behind him. Perhaps forever. He scraped his fingers over the engraved handle. "What are these letters?" he asked. His uncle looked up sharply from the linen dress as if awoken from a dream, and Colin felt sorry that he had interrupted his thoughts.

"MJC. Initials of a dear friend," replied his uncle, snapping back into the moment. "A great patriot for Ireland. A man who wanted to right the wrongs that he saw. He had both wit and temper like this world has never known. But the time was not right for the change he sought. So we keep his promise." Uncle John sighed, and Colin thought he saw a small tear form in his eye. He looked at Colin, and a small smile appeared on his face. "You certainly know of him well. *Martin Joseph Cullen.*"

CHAPTER 22

August 1, 1914: Rathmines, County Dublin, Ireland

Nora had just settled down on her bed when she heard a knock. She knew it could be none other than the dreaded Finnegan, probably there to inform her that her break was being cut short. She looked out the window at the beautiful garden view. The last thing she wanted was to have to get up and answer her door. Her feet ached, and she wanted nothing more than to not have to stand on them for just a few minutes. The new shoes that the Parsons had bought for her were by far the nicest she had ever owned, but they still felt like chains, just like every other shoe she had slipped on her foot.

She slid off her four-poster bed and walked slowly across the wooden floor to the door. She opened it slowly, just a crack—but where Mrs. Finnegan's stern, beady little eyes should have been was the chest of a young man, dressed in a worn linen shirt with misaligned buttons. She looked up into Colin's face, buried under his old gray cap, and could barely contain her excitement. "Colin!"

she exclaimed. "What are you doing here?"

"Stoppin' by to get an order from Mrs. Finnegan. Thought I'd see how things were goin'." He looked over her simple black-and-white uniform dress with an admiring glance, and she felt herself blush. The uniform fit her perfectly and outlined her slender figure in ways that her normal attire never had.

"Let me get me shoes, and we can go out to the garden," she said,

"No," he said abruptly. "No one knows I'm here except Mr. Dunham. Probably isn't right for me to be seen hanging around with you. I'm sure ol' Finnegan wouldn't approve."

Nora nodded, realizing her mistake. She had never been so constrained by social customs before, and it was a constant reminder of how quickly her life had changed.

"Do you mind if I come in?" he asked, taking his cap off.

"If Mrs. Finnegan ever found out you were in here with me, I'd be walking back to Clare within the hour." She looked out into the long hallway but saw no one.

"I have it on good authority that we won't be bothered until half eleven," he said. "At least that's what Mr. Dunham told me. He brought me up and said he'd be back to get me then. Thought you might enjoy seein' a familiar face."

She smiled. "All right then, we can't very well have you hanging out in the hallway, now can we?" She reached out and grabbed his linen shirt, pulling him in to her room. She latched the door behind him.

As Colin stood marveling at how nice her accommodations were, she thought about what she was doing and whether or not she was technically breaking a rule. After all, Mrs. Finnegan had been explicit that she was not to fraternize with any of the hired hands, but technically, Colin was not an employee. She wondered if Mrs. Finnegan cared about technicalities.

"So you live here?" Colin finally said, peering out the window by her four-poster. He was careful not stand where he could be seen. He flung his cap on her four-poster bed. It landed on the soft coverlet.

"I do," she said. "Accommodations fit for a queen—though I'm a bit of a prisoner. I think they let me out for Mass, and that's about it."

"That's one way to make sure you get yerself to church every once in a while," he said. "And who lives there?" he asked, pointing to the second four-poster bed. "Are you lookin' for a roommate?" he teased. "I could get used to mansion life."

"Martha," said Nora. "And she's a lovely roommate, wouldn't trade her."

"Not even for the likes of me?" Colin asked, feeling the soft cotton of the coverlet on the bed.

"Especially not for the likes of you," said Nora. She smoothed the wrinkles Colin had made on Martha's bed. He didn't notice.

"And the work? They're not working you too hard, are they?" She saw him eye her red and swollen feet.

"No," she said, "no more work than on the farm. Different types of work, you know, but not more than I can handle. And besides—" She walked over to her wardrobe and pulled out a small envelope. "I'm making money!" She showed him a few coins she had saved already. "If I am very frugal, I should have plenty to send to Seamus by the spring."

He gave her a half smile, and once again she felt like he was hiding something from her.

"Has he told you he's not coming to Dublin?" she asked.

"You know 'im as well as I do. He's a free spirit. He'll go where the wind takes 'im."

She didn't like how his voice sounded. She knew he was avoiding answering her. "You'd tell me though, wouldn't you?" she asked.

He broke eye contact and looked back at her feet. Changing the subject said, "Sit, Nora. Rest a little while we talk."

She climbed back up onto her soft bed, sinking into the violet feather coverlet.

"So, if you don't have any news from home, what brings you by, Colin?" she asked. She tried to sound cheerful, but she couldn't shake the idea that he might be more loyal to Seamus than he was to her.

"Just wanted to say hello," he said.

"Just hello? Hardly believable. Why are you really here?"

"It's me birthday," he said. "Wanted to see you."

"Is it really yer birthday?" she asked.

He shrugged and leaned down to tie a loose string on his boot. "Maybe. Me ma always said it was the first of August, though I bet you she wrote it down wrong. But I figure today's as good a day as any."

She couldn't help but laugh. She had no idea when her birthday was either. Sometime in the winter. "Well then, happy birthday, Colin. I'll always remember it now."

He walked over to the writing table and pulled the chair over near the bed. "Actually there is somethin' else," he said, as he sat down.

I knew it, she thought.

He leaned in close to her. He smelled like the city—dust and whiskey. "Nora," he said, his voice low, "remember me cousin's letter?"

"Aye," she said, intrigued. It seemed he was going to let her in on a secret after all.

"The delivery in Wicklow—it wasn't about groceries. It's another shipment of rifles."

Nora felt her eyes get wide. More rifles meant more trouble.

"And..." he brushed his hair from his face and placed his hand on his waistband, which Nora knew meant that he was reaching for his flask. "And I'm going to help bring 'em back."

Definitely more trouble. He reached over and put his hand on her knee. "There's a lot of us going."

She swallowed hard. "When?" she asked.

"Tonight. The boys are taking small boats out to meet the ship that's carrying 'em. Should be a nice little adventure."

She looked down at his calloused hand, which still rested on her knee, gently moving back and forth while he waited for her to respond. *It did sound like a nice little adventure.* A chance to get away from Dublin, from the Parsons and her stiff uniform shoes, from Mrs. Finnegan and her strict rules that forbade boys like Colin from putting their hands on housekeepers' knees.

"I want to go with you, Colin," she suddenly said.

From the look on his face, she knew he was not expecting this. "A change of heart about rifles?" he asked, taking his hand from her leg and reaching for the dented flask in his waistband. He moved to the bed and sat next to her. She felt herself slide toward him on the soft mattress.

Did she have a change of heart? She wondered why she was so intrigued by the rifles. Was it just a chance to leave the city, or was there more? The last shipment had gotten four innocents killed—but perhaps, in the long run, those rifles would save lives. They'd keep those Ulster Volunteers at bay. Raise the stakes. *Was Colin right after all?* For this, she had no answer—she only knew that she longed for a reason to break away from her new life.

Before she could answer him, he tentatively reached for her curls, and said, "You can't come with me, Nora. It's too dangerous."

That was all the encouragement she needed. "And why would that deter me?" she retorted. "Can it possibly be any more dangerous than the life I have lived so far? An orphan, and every day since only one bad crop away from eviction? Only thing keeping me off the streets is the Parsons, and—"

"It's different, Nora," he interrupted. "The wardens will try to stop us if they find out. We could be arrested, even shot."

"Sounds a lot like Clare to me!" She took his hand, which was brushing aside her hair, and pushed it away. "You could get arrested and killed there, too! All you have to do is be Catholic."

She saw Colin grin. "You're sweet when you're mad," he said. She pursed her lips and jumped off the bed.

"Oh come on now," he said, sliding off the mattress and onto the hardwood floor. "No 'That sounds exciting, Colin' or 'I'm worried about you, Colin'?" he teased her. "Maybe a good-luck kiss?" he added. She scowled. His joking just made her more annoyed with him.

"There's no such thing as a good luck kiss. Just a good luck curse," she said, as she walked across the room toward the large windows. She opened one wider to let in some cooler air. "And I am worried about you!" she said, "But it doesn't mean I don't want a little bit of excitement, too. You used to take me everywhere with you."

"Yes, but it was easier when 'everywhere' was going for a swim in the river or taking a nap over by the cliffs. Worst thing that could happen to me was that your grandda would find out. And," he walked over toward the window, "you certainly never put up a fuss about kissin' me then."

"And what about yer sins?" she said curtly. "You'll have no time to confess a kiss before you get shot!"

"Oh come on, Nora, I thought you'd be excited for me," he said.

"I'll be excited when you stop treating me like a little girl," she said.

"I'm not treating you like a little girl," he said—then he winked, adding, "Though you are quite little. Might 'ave shrunk since I saw you last."

She knew he was never going to relent. "You can go, Colin!" she said, pointing the way toward the door. "Go and have yer adventure. Put a rifle in the hands of every teenager in Ireland! But do me a favor, and don't come to tell me about it and how much fun you had while I was locked away!"

"For Christ's sake, Nora, I'm just teasin' you."

"And I'm tired of you teasin' me," she shot back at him. "You never used to tease me."

"You never used to care," he said.

"Because you treated me like yer friend, not yer child," she said. "I haven't had a parent for over a decade, and I don't need one now."

He looked at her. "This wasn't how I wanted today to go," he said.

"What did you want, Colin?" she said. "Did you want me to be all wide-eyed and doting on you? Wish you well on your adventure while I sit here doin' nothin' useful?"

"Well," he admitted, "I kinda thought you'd be a little more dotin'—"

"I'll dote on you when you stop trying to protect me," she said.

He shook his head. "Nora," he started.

She stopped him before he could finish his sentence. "Don't come up with an excuse why, Colin," she said quietly.

Colin sighed and reached for his flask. He took a sip, never breaking eye contact with her.

"But answer me this," she said. "If you have no use for me, why did you bring me here? Why did you show me a world I can't be a part of? If that was yer intent, then you should've left me in Clare." She reached for the door handle.

"And what would have happened to you in Clare?" he asked. His voice was unexpectedly harsh sounding. She had struck a nerve with him, though she wasn't sure why.

"I would have—"

"You would have been homeless! And I know what happens to homeless orphaned girls in Clare." He looked down at the floor, and she knew he regretted saying it. But she was too frustrated with him to let it go.

She stopped herself from opening the door and instead put both her hands on her hips. "I'm glad to see you think so highly of me." The room felt suddenly stifling, and she could feel sweat begin to drip down her back.

"Nora, I—"

"You think it's impossible that I could have found honest work?" she asked.

"Not impossible," he said. "But to be honest, if you didn't end up in some unsavory job, more than likely you'd have been married off to the next poor farmer's son to come around."

She put her hands to her head in exasperation. "Is that what you thought you were protecting me from?" she practically shrieked. "Farmers' sons?"

"No." Colin laughed despite the tension between them. "Not exactly. Maybe I was being selfish in tryin' to bring you here."

"Why, Colin?" she asked.

He shook his head. "You think I am that drunk, at just a little after eleven in the morning?" He smiled at her. The blond tips of his hair were tucked behind his ears, making them stick out and giving his whole face a silly look. It was so hard to stay angry with him.

"Why won't you ever say it?" She dropped her hands back to her side and wished that a light breeze would cut the heat that was building in the room.

"Cause you already know," he said. "And you also know that that's precisely why I don't want you to come. I don't want you to get hurt." A breeze finally came in the open window, bringing with it the smell of freshly cut flowers. It blew his hair every so slightly off his face and neck, and she could see that he had been sweating too.

"So tell me," he said lightheartedly, "Am I going to get my good luck kiss or not?"

She wanted to say yes, but more than that, she wanted her adventure. "You're not," she said. "Unless you bring me with you."

"You're not coming with me, Nora." He put his cap back on his head and walked toward her. She stepped aside, letting him reach the door. But instead of opening the latch, he stopped, just inches from her. "You sure, now?" he asked. "It's me birthday, you know." He cautiously reached for her, as if he knew she might reject him.

She put her hands up in front of her and he stopped his advance. "Colin, you can't keep me locked away here." She was grateful that the breeze continued to come in through the window.

"You need to lie low while you are here," he said. "This place is not as safe as it seems."

"You don't understand me Colin," she said. "I'm not looking for trouble. But I'm also not going to sit around and wait for a bunch of boys to save Ireland for me."

Colin frowned. "Isn't that our best shot?" he asked, sounding serious.

She took a step closer to him and placed her hands on his chest. She knew it would get his attention. "I'm afraid that the plan so far seems to be to prepare for armed insurrection. That hasn't worked the last few times we tried it."

"What other choice do we have?" he asked, placing his hands on top of hers.

"What about Home Rule?" she asked. "What if that passes?"

"It'll pass because we're armed," he said. "Don't you see?"

"Perhaps," she said, but she wasn't sure she agreed with him. She didn't know what the right answer was, but she wasn't thrilled that Ireland's future was in the hands of a bunch of teenaged Irish boys with German rifles. He seemed to sense her misgivings.

"You'll come around to it," he said. "If only because there's no other way."

"Maybe if you let girls come with you on your gunrunnins', they'd have some ideas," she said, and she pushed him gently away. He stepped in close again.

"Maybe if the girls wouldn't be so stingy with their kisses, we'd have less time for runnin' guns," he said.

"Oh stop it!" she said, smacking him playfully. "Like you would ever do anythin' more than a kiss anyways, you wimp," and she put her hands on his stomach and prepared to push him away harder. As she shoved, she felt hard metal under his right arm. At first, she assumed it was his flask, but then she felt the handle of a gun. In one quick motion, she had pulled it out of his belt and held it up in the air.

His gray eyes got wide. "Give that to me!" he said urgently, reaching for it, but she quickly backed away.

CHAPTER 23

August 1, 1914: Rathmines, County Dublin, Ireland

Nora held the sidearm up in the air. It felt massive in her small hand. An eerie feeling came over her, and her hands began to shake. Her knuckles turned white as she clasped the wooden handle. She stepped backward across the wooden floor, away from him.

"Colin, what are you doing with this?" she said in alarm. "If anyone caught you with it…"

"I know, Nora." he said, "I wasn't jokin' with you —I'm involved with something dangerous." He started walking toward her as she retreated. She was quickly backed up against the corner wall, but Colin let her have a few yards of space.

"I hope you know what you are doing."

She ran her hands on the smooth wooden handle. Her tremor intensified. *Why did this old flintlock make her so uneasy?* The gun seemed to weigh much more than its size warranted, as if it held the burdens of those who had carried it before. She unexpectedly felt like she was going to cry. She bit her lip.

But Colin noticed everything. "It's just a gun," he said softly. "I know you've shot one before." He reached out for it, but didn't step any closer to her.

She couldn't help but think that Colin was marching down the same path as countless before him—with a hint of hope and a heap of arrogance, thinking his would be the generation to set Ireland free. She wanted so much to believe that they could be the ones to make life just a little better, but she knew better than to be arrogant about it. Their opponent was cunning and ruthless and knew how to use hope as a weapon and arrogance as a trap. After all, they had done it countless times before. The thought that everyone she had left—Colin and Seamus, wherever he was—were marching headlong into this world frightened her. *They are my hope,* she thought to herself, *but they are so foolish.* But she also knew that she didn't have any better ideas.

Reluctantly, she deftly flipped the flintlock around as though she handled one every day and presented the wooden handle to Colin. It surprised her how natural it felt in her small hands, despite its weight.

He reached out and took it, lifting his shirt to return it to an improvised holster above his belt. "It's made for a right-handed shot," he said. "I had to switch it around. Apparently no one thinks a heathen would have a flintlock." He smiled at his joke. The nuns had always told him his left-handedness was the work of the devil. Nora couldn't feign a smile.

"Come by when you get back so I know you are all right," she said. "I cut flowers in the front garden in the early afternoon. You don't need to stop, just let me see you."

A loud creak came from the other side of the door, and they became quiet for a moment.

"I have to get going," he said, pulling his tunic down over the flintlock. "I don't want to fight with you. And I don't want to part with you on bad terms."

"Then bring me with you," she said, but she knew it was a lost cause.

"Last chance to call off this curse," he said.

She shook her head.

"All right, Nora, I'll come by later this week." He lifted the latch on the door and, looking each way, peered out into the hall. Mr. Dunham was standing outside the door, just as he had said he would be, busying himself with a floral arrangement. He feigned surprise at seeing Colin. "Ah, Mr. Kildare," he said. "Right on time."

Colin looked back into the room and nodded to Nora. She listened to their footsteps as they left, Mr. Dunham's quick and sophisticated rhythmic steps, and Colin's trudging boots. When she couldn't hear them anymore, she closed the door and walked over to her bed. Her new leather shoes lay haphazardly on the floor, where she had tossed them earlier. She didn't notice the bright sunlight or the pleasant smell of lavender coming in through the window. All she saw were her tired, red feet, and she wondered if she could bear to shove them back into those wretched shoes.

She picked up the chair that Colin had moved and carried it back over to the writing table. Just like everything else in the room, the table and chair matched perfectly. The etched wood on both the chair back and the table drawers bore the same design. She sat on the chair and slowly loosened her shoes, opening them as wide as she could before squeezing her feet into them. She wiggled her toes until each hit the top of the stiff leather.

Back to work, she thought to herself. She took one last look out into the gardens. The stable hands were polishing tack out in the sun, chatting merrily with one another. They were boys of about her age, though she knew none of their names. They all looked like farm boys, probably brought in from the far corners of the island just like she had been. The Parsons had cleaned them up and given them new and dapper clothes, but she could see right though the façade. She could pick out a farmer anywhere—their mannerisms, their language, the way they didn't care that their faces had smudges of dirt or that their caps were askew.

She could faintly smell the leather cleaner as it came in through the window on a soft breeze. She longed to have a little more freedom—even the ability to work outside and not under the constant eye of Mrs. Finnegan.

A creaking sound interrupted her thoughts. She snapped her head and saw the bedroom door open every so slightly. *Colin*, she thought.

"Ah, Nora," came a friendly voice. Her heart sank. "Glad you're still here." Mr. Dunham said, and he slipped into the room.

"Is something wrong?" she asked

"No, Miss Cullen," he responded.

Her heart jumped, and she felt her eyes widen. *Cullen. How did he know?*

"But tell me this. Yer grandda made his living as a river pilot, did he not?"

"Yes," she said. She didn't let on how intrigued she was.

"And he taught his grandchildren a thing or two about sailing?" Mr. Dunham continued.

"Of course," said Nora with a smile. "Any soul with McMahon blood in Clare can pilot a boat or sail. It's been that way for generations."

"Mrs. Finnegan will be out this afternoon at the market," he said. "Yer absence will not be missed." Nora gave him a confused look. "Go and change out of yer uniform. We've got to hurry if you are going to make the departure."

"But where are we going?" she asked.

"You, my dear," he said, "are going to Wicklow. Because sometimes an old man knows a wee bit more than the boys who think they are in charge."

CHAPTER 24

August 1, 1914: Dublin, Ireland

The Lord will guide you, Nora, and there's not a thing you can do but follow. Her grandfather's words echoed in her head as she stared at the Pro-Cathedral. Here, only days before, Dublin had bade its murdered residents farewell amid a barrage of incense and Latin incantations, unchanging rituals with which Nora was only too familiar. The pendant around her neck felt heavy as she approached the church. Surely her grandfather, who guided his grandchildren toward discipline and ritual and prayed for boring but safe lives for them, would not approve of this path. He would have guided her to safer choices with that deep and steady voice of his, which in her memory was like a lullaby that rounded up wandering children and tucked them into safer places.

But on this day, try as she might, she could not imagine what words of wisdom he might call to her to coax her away from the trouble that beckoned. The barrier between the heavens and earth was a silent one. Such was the finality of death. She only had her memories, and already the wisdom he had preached was fading in her mind.

Would he see this massive house of worship, surely larger than any church he had ever seen, whose walls had witnessed more heartache and more pleas from the faithful than any church in Ballynote, and find evidence that the Lord called her to this point? Would he believe that she was being called to rebellion by God himself? Did she?

She closed her eyes and turned the pendant between her fingers. The groove on the back, where her grandfather's fingers had rubbed the soft metal year after year, fit her own hands perfectly. Did she rub the pendant because she had always seen him do it or because was it a natural tendency that was her own? She did not know where he ended and she began, so intertwined had their lives been until the day he had left her and Seamus to fend for themselves.

Since that day, her life had changed so quickly and so starkly that she had to strain to force the memory of him to follow her into her new existence. Just who was she becoming, and so quickly after he had been taken from her? Had nothing he had taught her over the past decade been memorable enough to last even a few weeks after he was dead and gone? Faith, peace, hard work, order. Those had been his tenets.

And yet none of his tenets, none of his words felt so natural as putting on her drab old clothes and setting out on an adventure, intent on breaking the rules she had been so diligently taught to obey. Maybe, at her core, she had always been a rebel. Now that he was dead, he couldn't keep her from discovering who she really was.

Beautiful white doves flew over the looming Pro-Cathedral. They majestically soared around the steeple on invisible updrafts and then furiously beat their wings as they landed, one after another, along the cathedral roof. From their perches, they fluttered their wings softly in motions that seemed to Nora as hands beckoning her closer. She dropped her pendant and felt it fall until it was caught by its chain. She focused her eyes on the side alley next to the cathedral, then stepped onto the street and strode confidently toward the massive stone church.

Nora blended easily into the normal midday traffic, a mix of pedestrians, carriages, and motorcars all weaving through the Dublin roads. They flowed through the street as though choreographed, each yielding and moving aside as necessary. Soon she was part of the lazy procession passing in front of the cathedral. There was no Mass scheduled for the afternoon, but the doors to the church remained open—as always—inviting the faithful in for a quiet moment. A few took advantage of the invitation, but most strolled past the open doors.

Nora walked in front of the church and peered in, but the stark contrast of the daylight against the dark interior of the church made it impossible to see anything inside. At the corner, she glanced to each side, then swiftly turned left down a narrow side street. She hoped she wasn't too late.

A series of black motorcars stood along the alley behind the church, unattended by any drivers. *Just as Mr. Dunham said they would be,* Nora thought to herself. She counted the automobiles: six in all. When she was convinced she was alone, she walked confidently up to the last car and placed her hand on the rear passenger side door.

But she had never been in an automobile before, and she struggled with the handle. A fear rose up inside her. Someone was sure to see her. She fiddled with the mechanism, while looking wildly about her. She took a deep breath and sank to her knees to investigate. *How does this damned thing work?* She yanked on it in frustration. It didn't budge. The bells of the church chimed one o'clock. She smacked the handle in frustration, and to her amazement, the door creaked open. With one more hasty look around, she quickly climbed into the rear seat and hid from view.

If Mr. Dunham had been right, a driver would come by any moment. She went over the instructions in her mind. *Stay hidden until you are well past the city limits. Estimate at least an hour.*

The interior of the automobile was stifling; sweat dripped from her forehead and pooled in the small of her back. She hoped the driver would come soon. Mr. Dunham's parting words came to her, and she smiled. *Frighten him a little, but not so much as he drives off the road.*

Just why Mr. Dunham trusted her with such an important mission, she did not know, but there was something curious about him that made her trust him too. And he had known she was a Cullen.

Footsteps came up the dirt street, and she sank as low as she could across the rear bench. Finding a blanket tucked under the passenger seat, she unfolded it and carefully draped it over herself, hoping that it would hide her if a rear door was opened. She heard the voices of men, but they suddenly went silent as they came close enough for her to make out what they were saying. Did she recognize a voice? She couldn't tell. She was so uncomfortable in the sweltering vehicle, covered by a woolen blanket, that she tried to concentrate only on her breathing, keeping it regular and controlled. How long would she have to wait here?

The boot of the car opened; with a clang, heavy objects were loaded into the rear of the car. "Courtesy of the Kaiser," a man's voice said. Others laughed. She felt a wave of excitement: these must be the Volunteers' newest acquisition.

She was relieved when the driver's side door opened and a gush of cooler air entered the car. With her hands she created an air pocket between her body and the thick blanket so she could benefit from the cooler outside air. But the relief was too tempting. Slowly, cautiously, she exposed the top of her head until her eyes peered out.

She could see the back of the driver's head. He was short, with jet-black hair. Her heart sank—she was in the wrong car. She carefully went over her instructions in her mind. She was certain that Mr. Dunham had told her to get into the last car.

The car engine suddenly roared to life, and Nora didn't know whether to continue hiding or flee. Again she heard some voices, but this time the sputtering of the six car engines drowned them out.

Then the black-haired man spoke to someone outside: "We'll see if you don't fook it up." A chorus of laughter followed. "She shouldn't give you any trouble. Just the occasional sound of grinding metal coming from the engine!" The driver's laugh got louder. "If you do all right, next time we'll get you a better car."

The black-haired man abruptly exited the automobile. A moment later, a familiar crop of unkempt dark blond hair came into view. *Colin.* The car lurched forward, and she lay back, enjoying the cool air blowing in from the open front window as the car made its jerky way through the Dublin streets.

CHAPTER 25

August 1, 1914: Road to County Wicklow, Ireland

Nora woke suddenly as the car jolted to a halt. For a brief moment, she was confused. She breathed in the hot smell of the wool that covered her face and realized her legs were cramped and uncomfortable. Blinking, she peered out from under the wool blanket.

"Jesus, Mary, and Joseph!" she heard the Colin mutter. She couldn't help but smile. She always associated that phrase with an older generation, and it sounded silly to hear coming from his mouth. As she lay there wondering whether to reveal herself or be discovered, Colin abruptly swung open the driver's side door and climbed out. His heavy boots trudged around the car and paused near the rear of the vehicle.

A loud thud against the side of the car, followed by an even louder "Jesus Christ!" She peered out her window. Colin sat on the dusty road, inspecting his foot. He had taken off his boot and was rubbing the front of his foot vigorously, all while talking to himself under his breath. She laughed to herself.

She slowly sat up and squeezed over into the front seat. A larger adult would not have been able to manage this without a struggle, but for once Nora's small stature was an asset as she slipped easily into the passenger side seat. Before her, a long dirt road followed along a cliff. Off in the distance rolled the waves of the Irish Sea. The countryside took her breath away, with lush colors that reminded her of Clare. The deep green hills and the bright blue sky were the same, and the salty sea air was so refreshing it felt as though she had jumped into the River Shannon on a hot summer day. Wicklow was much more the Ireland she knew than the crowded streets of Dublin, filled with the stench of the tenements.

She was startled by Colin's voice. "You chose the wrong car for a free lift, you know!"

He sounded angry. Nora stiffened and turned toward the driver's side door.

"What were you thinking, Nora?" he said. "Not only do I have a broken-down motorcar, but now I've got to explain to me cousin just why I brought a girl along with me. A girl I'm forbidden to see."

His words threw her off. *Forbidden?* But she recovered herself quickly. "Oh, get off it, Colin!" She sounded harsher than she meant to. "I'm here to save yer arse, and you know it." She had never spoken to Colin this way, though she and Seamus had often bantered back and forth. But she knew how to handle boys like Colin. "You fancy yerself a pilot, I hear."

"Can you fix a tire?" he asked.

"I suppose not," she replied.

"Then you aren't of any use here, now are you?" he replied. He sounded mad, but she noticed that his face looked more serious than it did angry.

"When we get to Wicklow—" she said.

"If we can ever make it there," he muttered under his breath.

Nora stubbornly crossed her arms in front of her and stood as tall as she could. *Why does he always think he knows best?* The argument from earlier in the day was still fresh in both of their minds. "Why do you want me locked up back in Dublin?" she said. "What makes you think that anything about me has changed? You can't keep me away from an adventure any more than me grandda could keep me away from you!" She felt her voice growing loud and out of control as she spoke, but she felt that just maybe she was getting through to him.

He kicked the dirt with his boots, and small stones scattered. But she could tell that he did it because he was deep in thought, not because he was angry with her. "Nora," he started, his hand on his flask. She could tell he was choosing his words carefully, "It's not that I don't want you here with me. It's just that I can't drag you into this world. It's not right. It's not like before when we could share adventures together." She slumped her shoulders. She had not gotten through to him at all.

"It's not Clare," he continued. "It's a different world. There's more at stake, and there's a real risk to what I'm doing." He kicked the dirt again. "We're not kids anymore, stealing away from chores. It's not Clare."

She tried another approach. "No, Colin," she said softly. "It's not Clare, but it's still you and me. We're still the same."

The soft tone of her voice had a calming effect on him, as she had meant it to. She knew how to argue with him and soothe him all at the same time.

"Are we?" he asked.

This took her by surprise. "Yes," she said adamantly. Now she kicked the dirt as well, but out of frustration. "Colin, the world around us has changed, but you and I are the same. And if you think we're not—if you think that geography and politics can change who we are—then what in God's name are you doing all this for?"

He looked up at the bright blue sky and took his cap off, letting the gusting wind from the Irish Sea blow through his blond hair. With his other hand, he took out his flask.

"Let me come with you," she said. "Let me help. This is my country, too."

"Let you come?" he said, throwing his hands in exasperation. Whiskey flew from his flask. "The decision's already made, now isn't it? You're coming whether I like it or not!"

"Why do you care so much?"

"Why do I care—" he said aloud, though it sounded to Nora more like a question he was posing to himself. He locked eyes with her and took a long swig from his flask. "Why do I care?" he said again. "Because I don't want a free Ireland if you're not here with me."

It was as close to an admission of his affection as she was going to get. "You still think you can protect me?"

"Aye, somethin' like that."

She walked toward him and reached up to put her hand on his shoulder. The gusts of wind made it impossible for her to tuck her long, auburn hair behind her ears, and she let it fly about. "But you can't. No one can. So you might as well let me come."

He didn't answer her, but she felt his shoulder tense as he gripped his flask tightly.

"Because this is my country too."

CHAPTER 26

August 1, 1914: Road to County Wicklow, Ireland

Colin at last broke his gaze with Nora. *It's my country too.* The words echoed in his mind. She had a point, but he wasn't going to let her know it. He didn't have time for that conversation. He was in a bind and he knew it. The gunrunning boats were to leave as soon as daylight expired. He looked up at the sun. There was plenty of day left, but they had miles to go, and they wouldn't make it on foot.

Over Nora's shoulder he could see the Irish Sea, its distant waters appearing to meet the rolling hills. The bright light of the day blended the blue and green such that they almost perfectly matched the shade of Nora's eyes. Mr. Dunham's words from earlier that day came back to him. Striking a much calmer tone, he said, "Nora, I don't know about you."

"And just what do you mean by that?" she asked.

"I don't know what to do about you," he said. He truly didn't, but again—he knew he didn't have time for that conversation.

"Well, like you said, there's not much you can do now," she said. He could tell she was trying to get him to reconcile with her. Or, worse, trying to get him to admit what she already knew. *Why is she so good at that?*

"Oh, I don't mean today," he said. One side of his mouth bent upward no matter how he tried to suppress it. "I mean tomorrow and the next day and the next day after that."

She had no ability to hide her smile. "So you forgive me?" she asked, in a tone that let him know that she had long since forgiven him.

He scratched his chin as if he were seriously contemplating a response, but Nora's coquettish expression had changed. She abruptly turned to face the road. A black motorcar was approaching, trailed by a cloud of dust. The direction of the wind meant they had not heard its motor until it was right upon them.

"One of yer friends?" Nora asked hopefully.

Colin looked intently at the vehicle. Each of the motorcars was to have left Dublin at different times to avoid tipping anyone off as to their mission or destination, and they each were to take different routes. How many possible routes were there from Dublin to the Wicklow coast? Surely this was not the only lonely country road that led there. "Not likely," he said.

The automobile began to slow, and Colin saw that the driver intended to stop. He knew that he had no good explanation for why he was out here on this desolate road with a young girl.

"Keep quiet, Nora," he said ominously. "Don't say a word. They'll know you're not from these parts."

The driver of the motorcar pulled it to the side behind Colin's parked automobile. "Hello there," called the driver, studying the scene.

Colin instantly recognized the Cockney accent and exchanged a nervous glance with Nora, who clearly had as well. He scanned the interior of the man's car. The driver was a tall, broad man of about thirty; his sole passenger was a red-faced, heavyset man of about the same age.

As the driver climbed energetically from the car, Colin recognized the uniform as British cavalry. He'd seen these uniforms on officers at the Royal Barracks in Dublin, as they mingled with the Dublin Fusiliers. He felt the blood drain from his face. What were they doing on this quiet road to Wicklow?

He nodded at Nora in a silent plea for her to refrain from speaking. He knew her quaint country accent would reveal her allegiances, if her faded homemade summer dress hadn't already given them away. Or would the soldiers recognize his own tunic and heavy boots as the telltale dress of an Irish Volunteer?

Another glance at Nora: Her demeanor was calm, but anxiety quietly built in her expression. She stood stoically near the driver's side of the motorcar.

"Hello, sir," called Colin casually. "God save the King." His stomach turned. A quick survey of the uniforms revealed he would be dealing with a lieutenant and a sergeant. An officer and a member of his staff. *Why so far from Dublin?* There could be no good reason.

"God save the King!" replied the lieutenant enthusiastically. "Troubles with your automobile?" He sounded cheery, and Colin had to remind himself to keep his guard up.

"Yes, sir, just a tire."

"Have you a spare in the boot?" he asked.

Colin could feel his pulse accelerate. *The boot.* A wave of heat crept over his face despite the refreshing sea air that whirled about them. The only items he knew for sure were in the boot were a pair of German Mausers, recently unloaded at Howth.

"These models all have Stepney rims in the boot, didn't you know that?" the lieutenant laughed lightheartedly. "We'll have you up and running in no time!" As the officer walked toward the boot, Colin quickly moved to intercept him. The lieutenant eyed him, and Colin knew he had made him suspicious.

Nora's voice cut over the gusting breeze. "Do you know much about automobiles?" The innocent Clare countryside rolled off her tongue. "Surely you must, you look quite handy." Her voice quickly evolved from innocent to flirtatious.

Momentarily distracted, the lieutenant looked her way and ambled toward the front of the vehicle. Nora said something, but he couldn't make it out over the wind. Colin furrowed his brow.

"We know a thing or two," the sergeant replied, as he lazily emerged from the car. He was larger than he had looked, and not so much fat as muscular. Colin surveyed the man as he walked, looking anxiously for a firearm. He didn't see any signs of one. He felt the cool barrel of Martin Cullen's sidearm in its makeshift holster in his waistband. He hoped his tunic kept it well hidden.

"Well that's a relief," he could hear Nora say. "Because me brother can be quite worthless at times. There's been something rattling in the engine since we left Rathmines." Colin rolled his eyes. She had gone too far. There was no way they could pull off Rathmines.

"It's amazing we've made it this far!" Nora continued.

Colin knew the damage had been done. But both soldiers allowed Nora to lead them around to the front of the car.

"What does the noise sound like?" asked the lieutenant.

"Like grinding metal," Nora replied. "It's a wonder we've made it this far," she repeated dramatically, and tossed her auburn tresses away from her face with one hand.

She smiled at the soldiers. Colin felt his stomach turn again, but this time from an unexpected bout of jealousy. He felt himself grow angry as the soldiers tripped over themselves to impress Nora with their knowledge of automobile engines. The two men disappeared under the hood and Nora peered over at Colin, who stood motionless watching them.

"Hurry up!" she mouthed.

He quickly reengaged and opened the boot. He saw the extra rim stashed beneath the Mausers and some loose ammunition. He rearranged the contents to get to the rim and within seconds pulled out the spare. It was remarkably heavy.

"Look and see if you have a wrench while you're back there," called the lieutenant to Colin, still listening intently at Nora's attempts to describe the nature of the grinding in the engine block. Colin went back into the boot and rummaged around until he came out with a wrench.

"Do you have one?" he called.

Colin looked over the open trunk as the lieutenant approached him.

"Aye," he called, hoping to stop the officer's advance.

Their eyes met and locked. Colin knew he must be growing suspicious. *Rathmines*, he thought to himself. *Why did she say Rathmines? Anywhere else.* Colin quickly slammed the boot closed and rolled the spare around to the damaged side. He placed the wrench on the ground next to the Stepney.

"Not sure what is wrong with your automobile," the lieutenant said to Colin. "What kind of noise was it again?"

"Um, sounded like something metal clinking around in there," Colin said.

"Aye, that's what your, uh—*sister*—said." He put too much emphasis on the family relationship. Colin knew their luck was running out. That damned Irish luck.

Without breaking eye contact, the officer reached into his shirt pocket and took out a cigarette. He lit it with difficulty in the gusting wind and looked Colin up and down.

"Just what are you two doing out here? On your way somewhere? There's trouble about, you know." He inhaled and held the cigarette between his teeth. He cracked his knuckles.

"Going to visit our aunt." He could have said anything or nothing at all—he knew the officer wouldn't believe any of it. But he went along with the game anyways.

"You don't say?" said the officer. "You don't say. And where does your auntie live?"

What would Michael say? Something vague. Something he wouldn't have to walk back.

"A couple miles south of here. On this same road." Colin watched as the officer smoked his cigarette. The wind had long since blown it out, but he kept pretending to puff on it, the same as Colin pretended that he and Nora had an aunt they were visiting.

"Perfect," the officer finally said. He went through the motion of extinguishing his cold cigarette. "Looks like we can't fix your vehicle, but we're headed south as well." He gave Colin a sarcastic smile. "We'll give you a lift."

Colin didn't answer. He felt the sergeant walk up behind him. Colin was used to being taller and stronger than pretty much anyone he had ever sparred with. But from the sergeant's shadow, Colin knew that he was outsized. His ears began to burn. He clenched his fists.

"What do you think there, mate, can we give these travelers a lift?" The lieutenant gave his partner a wink.

"Certainly," came a voice from behind. "Where exactly are you headed? We happen to know of some activity along the coast planned for later this evening. Maybe you were headed there?"

Colin said nothing. He sized up the sergeant out of the corner of his eye. His black hair was plastered to his head with pomade. Even the gusting wind didn't disturb it. *Did they know already about Kilcoole, or were they trying to get him to give up something?*

"An odd outfit for visiting your auntie," the officer said, and motioned to Colin's tunic and boots. "Did you steal it off a traitor or something?"

"Did you steal this here automobile, too?" he heard the sergeant ask. "What are you hiding from us, boy?"

Colin looked to the ground and saw the shadow of the sergeant approach him. He tensed just as the sergeant grabbed him from behind with raw and calloused hands. Colin tried to wrestle himself away, but was quickly thrown to the ground. He felt he sergeant's heavy knee plant squarely in the small of his back. No one had ever pinned him so quickly. He could smell the thick hair pomade—a mixture of peppermint and tar.

"I knew it!" he said. "I knew it when I saw you that you was filthy, lying Irish!" The solider grabbed Colin's right arm and wrenched it behind his back. There was so much tension on the arm it took Colin's breath away. When he regained his voice, he yelled, "Get off me you fookin' English whore!" Now they knew exactly who he was.

Before he could say another word, the lieutenant took two large strides over to Colin and kicked him square on his unprotected right side. The officer let out a yell as his foot struck a hard metal object. The flintlock. Colin grunted in pain.

"What the hell is this?" yelled the officer. He dropped to his knees and reached under Colin's shirt, exposing the flintlock pistol that had been in his waistband. The officer unholstered it and held it up in the light. It looked small in his massive hands.

"Where's the powder?" he asked. The sergeant, still holding Colin to the ground with his knee, reached into Colin's shirt and threw a small package over to his partner. Colin saw Nora duck to the ground near the Stepney spare. He wished she would just run. But he knew her better.

The officer caught the powder and slowly started to laugh. Colin's felt his anger become overwhelming. He began to violently twist and turn under the soldier, trying to free himself.

"Stop moving or I will break your arm!" said the solider. He sounded calm and methodical, and Colin didn't doubt what he said, but he didn't feel like he could control his rage.

"Harry, would you look at this," said the officer holding Colin's firearm. "This thing must be fifty years old!"

The soldier laughed again. "You thought you could take on the British Army with the likes of that?" he said. "Stupid Irish."

"My daddy had one like this," he said. He reached into the small sack and loaded the flintlock with powder and one round.

Colin stopped struggling for a moment to see what was happening. "Hold him there," he heard the lieutenant say. "I'm going to get the girl."

Colin once again began to thrash. "She's not your sister, is she?" the sergeant said. His cackling laugh echoed across the desolate road.

Colin's thrashing became wild, and the sergeant warned him again, "Don't think I won't break it!" But Colin did not heed the warning. He began kicking violently and managed to throw the sergeant off balance.

Rolling onto his back, Colin momentarily broke free of the soldier's grip. He grabbed the sergeant's pristine uniform with his right hand, and with his left, landed a punch squarely on the soldier's chin. Blood trickled out of the soldier's mouth, sullying the collar of his khaki coat. He spit the blood back at Colin, who swung again, this time missing. The two grappled for several seconds, rolling around on the dusty and rocky road.

From the front of the car, Colin heard a bone-chilling scream. *Nora.* Taking advantage of Colin's distraction, the sergeant grabbed Colin's left arm. "Won't make that mistake again," he said. Blood dripped from his mouth. "Imagine that, a left-handed Irish boy. I thought they beat that out of the papists." He twisted Colin's wrist and bent it behind Colin's back. Pain ripped through his arm, and he stopped thrashing.

"Move a muscle—" warned the sergeant a third time.

"Go to hell, you fookin' British whore!" grunted Colin. The soldier rotated Colin's wrist ever so slightly, in a precise way such that Colin knew this was not the first time he had executed such a maneuver. Above the sound of the whipping wind off the Irish Sea, a loud crack came from Colin's forearm, and searing pain shot up his left arm.

"I warned you," said the sergeant, matter-of-factly. He released Colin's arm. It fell to the ground and lay at an awkward angle. "But you Irish are too dumb to listen. Maybe now that the example is fresh in your mind, you'll heed my warning." While Colin lay stunned, the sergeant grabbed his other arm and twisted it in a similar way. "I'll break this one too if you don't sit still."

Colin lay motionless on the ground—not out of a sudden call to obedience, but because his attention was entirely consumed by his mangled arm. He closed his eyes. His entire left forearm burned. The pain radiated up to his shoulder. He clenched his jaw and tried to curl his fingers into a fist. He couldn't.

He opened his eyes, and through the dust that still lingered from their struggle, he watched the lieutenant lead Nora by the collar of her dress around the side of the car and past where he had lay the Stepney spare. Cocking her father's flintlock, pressed the metal muzzle against her delicate temple. The wind wrapped her hair around the barrel. The sunlight danced off the metal in sparks of light. Every motion seemed to last entire minutes.

"We'll try this again," the officer said. "Where were you two going?"

CHAPTER 27

August 1, 1914: Road to County Wicklow, Ireland

Nora swallowed hard. She didn't bother to lie to them. Instead she kept quiet and waited as the seconds ticked by. Her eyes locked with Colin's. The muzzle, pressed hard against her skull, felt warm against her skin, though she knew the metal barrel should have felt cold.

Colin slowly shook his head, imploring her to be careful.

"Where were you going?" the lieutenant shouted again. He was tall—so tall that he had to bend to yell in her ear. His hair and mustache were neatly trimmed, and had she seen him on the street and not in the vile uniform of a British officer, she probably would have thought him an attractive man. But he only impression of him, besides his towering height, was the rank smell of old cigarettes.

His rancid tobacco breath that sputtered toward her as he yelled made her nauseous.

"I'm going to take a look around," he said slyly. He lowered the gun and pointed it at the trunk. "Open it!"

Nora dropped her eyes to Colin, whose eyes had grown wide. "No," he mouthed.

The lieutenant, still clutching Nora by the collar, dragged her toward the boot. She made him work for every step, dragging her feet along the ground. She clung tightly to her only plan—the wrench that she grasped in her right hand. While the men were distracted, she had hidden it in her sleeve. How fortuitous that it had been forgotten there on the ground.

Frowning in concentration, the officer reached down toward the latch. She could see a small bead of sweat on his temple. *He's not as cool as he's pretending to be,* she thought. As he fiddled with the latch, she felt his grip loosen. *This might be my only chance.* She freed her right arm and pulled the wrench from her sleeve. She eyed the back of the lieutenant's neatly parted brown hair, and with all her might, brought the wrench down on the back of the officer's skull. It made a horrid cracking noise, and instantly a trickle of blood began to run down the back of his head and sully his uniform collar.

The lieutenant collapsed motionless to the ground, dropping the flintlock. Nora swooped down, seized the pistol, and pointed it directly at the sergeant, who looked on in shock. As soon as she grasped the handle, she felt a burning energy surge inside of her. Just like when she had grabbed it from Colin's waistband earlier.

"Let 'im go," she said. Her voice was loud and steady. She gripped the flintlock as tight as she could and closed one eye as she had been taught all those years ago. She aimed at the second button on the soldier's chest. The soldier released Colin and took several hurried steps backward. Despite his scuffle with Colin, his black hair was still perfectly arranged atop his head.

Colin staggered to his feet. His face looked gray. "Nora," he said quietly.

"I am not armed!" the sergeant cried. "Don't do something that you'll regret!"

Nora heard them both, but the words didn't resonate. The pistol, still pointed directly at the sergeant's chest, commanded all of her attention. These men had known nothing about them—just that they were Irish. It was just the same in Wicklow as it had been in Ballynote. *We're all just captives in our own country.*

Nora took a step toward him.

"You'll both hang!" he yelled desperately. *Hang.* The word resonated loudly in her mind, but worse, it triggered memories she didn't ever want to recall. Darkened, grotesque faces. Necks snapped so the heads fell at unnatural angles. Her last and most vivid memory of her parents. They had been good people, but too impatient to wait for the peaceful revolution that might not ever come. Her temple still stinging from the pressure of the flintlock barrel, she finally began to understand what drove good people to violence. Nora took another deliberate step toward the solider and with her thumb, cocked the hammer. The mechanism was difficult, but she was so enraged that she felt she willed the hammer back. Colin was out of her view—she only saw the solider.

The sergeant raised both of his burly arms high into the air. He didn't look so tough now. Until he had threatened them with hanging, she had no plans to pull the trigger. Now, she did not know what she would do, even as she stood just yards away. She didn't feel any sympathy for the sergeant—what he felt now was what she had felt for her entire life…to be at the capricious mercy of someone who didn't care if she lived or died.

As she rested her finger on the trigger, with no concept of passing time, she saw movement to her right. Before she could react, she saw Colin out of the corner of her eye. He lunged at the sergeant; the wrench held above his head and brought it down hard against the sergeant's temple. Like his partner a few minutes before, he fell in a heap to the ground.

Nora still held the gun pointed at the unconscious soldier.

"It's all right, Nora," she heard Colin say, almost in a whisper. "Put it down."

She looked from the soldiers on the ground, and back to Colin. Then, in a calculated move, she pointed the gun at the engine block of the soldiers' car and squeezed the trigger. The muzzle exploded with smoke, and Nora flinched at the shattering sound as a single shot ripped through the hood and into the engine.

"Jesus Christ!" yelled Colin. "Ever heard of ricochet?"

Engine fluid began to leak to the ground. Neither of the soldiers had even flinched. They were out cold.

"That's enough, Nora," Colin said. "Put it down." He spoke softly to her, coaxing her to listen. "Put it down."

The crack of the flintlock seemed to release the energy that brewed inside of her. All of a sudden she felt calm again. She slowly and methodically turned the pistol to the ground and handed the wooden handle to Colin. She watched him place it in his holster awkwardly. Something seemed odd about the way he did it, but she couldn't put her finger on it.

"Are you all right?" he asked.

She blinked her eyes. The wind seemed to be picking up, and it blew dust from the road into the sergeant as he lay on the ground. It stuck to the pomade in his hair, making his hair look gray instead of jet black.

"I'm fine," she said to Colin, for the first time turning to look directly at him. His expression surprised her—his face was twisted in pain and his complexion, gray. Then she noticed it—his left arm hung askew.

"Colin!" she cried, finally reengaging, "What did they do to your arm?" She reached out and gently took the arm in her hands. His forearm was bent at an unnatural angle, and the skin below the break had turned a yellowish tint. He grimaced.

"It will need to be set," she said. It was all she could think to say.

"Hurts like hell," he replied.

"We'll take care of it properly after Wicklow," she said. *After Wicklow.* Would they even get there now?

"Aye, after Wicklow," he said. She breathed relief. He wasn't going to give up on the plan.

Still holding his arm in her hands, she said, "Take off yer shirt, and we'll make a sling."

"Why my clothing?" He slipped easily back into teasing, but she could tell that he was distracted by the pain.

"Because it's yer bloody arm. And," she continued, carefully letting the arm fall to his side and walking toward the Stepney spare that still lay on the ground, "we can't use mine because you might not have time for confession on Saturday."

"Why not?" he asked, keeping up the game.

"Well," she said, "there's a high likelihood we'll both be in jail. Especially if we can't get out of here." The spare was resting against the car, and she straightened it and tried to align it to the bad tire. She had no idea how it worked. She looked over her shoulder and saw the tall grass between the road and the cliffs swaying back and forth with the wind. It was beautiful to watch. Ireland was always ironic in that way—no matter how unpleasant life could get, there was still raw beauty all around.

"Not quite sure why you shot out the engine on the automobile that still has four good tires, Nora," she heard Colin say. He gingerly began taking off his tunic and shirt, careful not to disturb his arm.

Nora feigned disinterest as he undressed, but couldn't help but watch him from the corner of her eye.

"To keep you from stealing their vehicle," she said. "It'd just get us in more trouble than we already are." The fact that Colin would be tempted to switch automobiles had played no role in her decision to fire the shot through the engine block—she did not know what had made her do that. But she was content with the result—they would have otherwise stolen the car, and she knew it would have only spelled trouble.

"You need some help?" She knew that Colin was watching her align the Stepney with the damaged tire. She kept an eye on him as he tried to fold his shirt into a makeshift sling.

"No," she said, though in truth she had no idea what she was doing. She lined the spare up against the existing tire. The size seemed off. "It's too big," she said. "It's not going to fit."

"I guess we'll just have to walk then," said Colin. "Come on, best be going." Smiling, he began to walk slowly down the road.

She frowned at him. He was too good at making his points. "Fine, Colin," she called. "You can help me."

"I have yer permission?" he asked.

She sighed. "Yes." The direction of the wind shifted and the smell of salt from the ocean surrounded them.

"You sure?"

"Just tell me what to do," she said dejectedly.

"You act as though it is painful to ask for help," he said.

"It is," she replied.

"From me?" he asked. His blond hair blew across his face and made him look younger to her. That was how she had always remembered him.

"Especially from you," she said.

"And why is that? Aren't we friends?" He kneeled down next to her, his left arm still hanging at his side. "Maybe more?"

"I suppose," she said. As he knelt right next to her, his shirt still on the ground a few yards away, she noticed his shoulders. His had none of the freckles that littered hers. They looked so much stronger than she remembered. "But the more I ask you for help, the more you treat me like a child."

"Nora," he said quietly, trying to align the spare with the existing tire, "if I thought you were a child, I wouldn't spend my time with you."

"You aren't spending yer time with me by choice," she said. She tried not to stare at him, but it was hard for her to turn away. The muscles in his right arm flexed as he adjusted the rim. But his left arm just hung there, turning grayer by the minute.

She continued her thought. "I'm a stowaway, remember? Because you didn't think I should come." She smiled. "But it turns out I was useful."

"Yes." He gave her a teasing smile. "I am a horrible flirt. Would have been difficult for me to lure those officers away from the Mausers all on me own."

"Or knock one out?" she asked, "While you lay pinned to the ground?"

"Small details," he said. "Now, help me—see, not painful at all to ask. Help me line this up."

Together they lined the spare rim up against the existing tire.

"Hold it there, like this," he showed her how to align it. "It will go over the existing frame. Use these clips." He pointed awkwardly with his elbow. "They'll be hard to open."

She pried one of the clips open and clasped it to the frame of the tire.

"Just like that," he said. "Now do the others, and we'll be ready to go again. It doesn't fit perfectly. Not supposed to go very far with one of these on. We'll have to move slowly."

With some difficulty, Nora attached the remaining clips. When the last one was securely in place, she dusted off her hands and stood up. By the look of the sun, it was late afternoon. They had lost at least an hour of time.

Colin put his good hand on the rim and slowly rose to his feet. "And now," he said, "I'm going to ask for your help again. Twice in one day, imagine that." He gestured apologetically toward his shirt on the ground. "I'll have to get dressed again at some point. Wouldn't want to have to send you to confession either."

She caught herself smiling and tried to stifle it.

"Nora McMahon, did I see you blush?"

She could feel her face turning red.

"I never thought I'd see the day. So the rumors are true," he continued. "You don't despise me."

"Of course I don't, Colin," she said. "Quite the opposite. But I think you already know that."

"All I know is that I asked you for a kiss, and instead I got some Irish curse, a broken vehicle, a broken arm, and about thirteen scowls since we left Dublin—" Over her attempts to protest, he continued, smiling, "I've counted them all. I'm afraid of what's next." Then, nodding back to the shirt, "See if you can't wrap it around me back." She picked up the shirt and undid the fold, rearranging it in a sort of triangle, and slid it under his arm so that the broken arm was cradled.

"Hold it tight to yer chest," she said, tossing one end of the fabric over his left shoulder. The other she passed under his right arm.

"Can you bend over, Colin?" she said. "I can't see to tie it."

He smiled. "Either you are going to have to start growing, or I will have to stop. I think you've shrunk four inches since last summer."

She scowled at him.

"Fourteen," he said.

Nora ignored him. She tied a square knot with the ends of the fabric and then inspected the sling. "It's not perfect," she said, running her hand along his shoulder, "but it should hold so long as you don't move around too much."

She handed him his tunic and helped him put it over his head. "There," she said, "That will help to keep it still."

Colin put his good arm through his right sleeve. "Can you tie up that other sleeve so that it doesn't flop around?"

As Nora began tying up the left sleeve, Colin put his hand on her chin, turning her head toward him. "Thank you, Nora," he said. "I'm glad Mr. Dunham sent you."

His hand slid down to her waist and he pulled her in closer to him. He rarely did anything like this—he was so afraid of anything that might warrant a confession. She leaned into him. She knew of two types of Irish boys—those who went to church and took every tenet seriously, and those who went to church twice as often and took none of it seriously. Colin fell squarely into the first group.

"How did you know?'

"'Cause I know you," he said. "And I know you wouldn't have done something I asked you not to do. And I know Mr. Dunham, too, especially when he gets an idea in his head…" She looked up at him, and he winked at her. "And now that I'm decently dressed again so as to not get you in too much trouble, I also know that you said you'd give me a kiss if I let you come with me."

"Why so brazen today?" she teased him back. "Do you think God can't see you on the road to Wicklow? Besides, if I remember correctly, you just take your kisses whenever you want them—or whenever you've had a bit too much whiskey."

He shrugged. "Not *whenever* I want them. I'd be in confession all day. Not fair to everyone in line behind me. Besides," he continued, pulling her in closer to him, "it's yer turn."

She had waited a whole year for a moment like this, but she reluctantly shook her head. Ever since he came back into her life she had wanted his affection, but she also knew she had to stand her ground, lest she remain locked up at the Parsons while a bunch of wild boys made decisions for all of their futures. "I said I'd kiss you when you let me come along. I'm holding out till you actually invite me and don't make me hide out in the back of your motorcar till it's too late to turn back." As she said the words, she wrapped her arms behind his back and laid her head on his chest. Her actions said everything her words didn't.

"You drive a hard bargain," he said. He sounded disappointed, but he didn't dwell on it. "But I hope at least you call off that bloody curse." He pulled away from her and started to walk toward the officers' car. "I've only one arm left, you know."

She watched him step over the bodies of the soldiers, still lying where they had fallen. Neither had moved, though the dust from the road had continued to collect in the sergeant's pomaded hair. His hair now looked almost entirely gray.

"Should we check on them?" she called after him.

"No," said Colin. "We should get going."

A sudden fear rose in her. "What if they die?" she said. Although she had clobbered one of them and had seriously considered putting a bullet through the other, now that her anger had quelled, she didn't want either of them dead.

"Then they die," said Colin. He didn't seem to have any remorse for knocking the sergeant across the face with an iron wrench.

"I thought you were afraid of mortal sins?" she reasoned.

He sighed. "I thought you weren't." He walked back to the officers and put his hand to each of their necks. One of them grunted.

"They both have a pulse—just out cold," he said. "They'll come to. Hopefully we'll be well on our way." He stood up and kept walking toward their automobile.

"What are you doing?" she asked, as he opened one of the doors.

"Nothin'," he replied as he rummaged through the front seat.

"Colin, let's just get going," she said. She didn't like that he was going through their things. It made her feel like a common criminal. She had watched her family be undeservedly treated like criminals for their entire lives, just for being Irish. She was better than that.

"Stand over there and just smack 'em over the head again if they start to move," Colin called from inside.

Nora picked up the wrench and looked at the men as they lay on the ground. Blood trickled down the backs of their heads, dripping onto the dirt road to form twin scarlet pools that soaked slowly into the dirt. Neither of them moved.

"Ready," Colin called from behind her. "Would you look at this?" Nora turned to see him beaming. "Notebook, cash, a baton, a whistle," he said, listing off his haul. "Official orders from headquarters. Quite a trove."

Nora frowned. "Colin, we can't steal their things."

"Nora, they stole yer damned country. What do you mean we can't steal their things?"

"'Cause that makes us no worse than them," she said disapprovingly.

"No," he said. "It makes us not complacent. I'm fookin' tired of being a victim day in and day out. We're soldiers now. Don't think for a moment they wouldn't have done the same, or worse, to us."

"I don't care what they would do!" she said. "Isn't that the whole point? That we're better than they treat us? That we're not dirty, lying Irish? That we're decent people?"

"You can't be a part of this if you don't start acting like this is a war, Nora. Because it is. And in war, you take the spoils you get." He thrust the notebook at her.

She reluctantly took it and leafed through the pages. In the neat handwriting of one of the men were written several cryptic notes. *Granby Street Pub, afternoon, July 15. Mr. Sean O'Malley, of 32 Pembroke Street.*

"What does it say?" he asked.

"These are notes from interviews, I think," she said. "Names, addresses, locations."

"Bet they are notes from snitches," he said. "We're keeping it."

He abruptly reached over to take took the book from her. She held onto it tightly. "Whose side are you fookin' on, Nora?" he said.

"Yers," she replied. "Leave the money."

"Nora—" he started.

"Leave it," she said, this time loudly.

He looked exasperated. "Like the way they left us alone?" he shouted over the sea breeze. "Like the way they left yer sheep? Like the way they left yer parents? They owe you somethin', Nora."

"And I'll get it," she said quietly, so that he had to stop yelling to hear her. "In one large payment. And it'll be worth more than a couple pieces of sterling. What we've lost is worth more than what a petty thief could take."

"Are you callin' me a thief?" he challenged her.

"I am," she said.

He walked over to the driver's side door and yanked it open, threw the coins and paper notes onto the seat, and slammed the door shut. "Fine," he said. "But we're keepin' the book and the stick. The whistle too. Anythin' they can use against one of us."

She looked at the whistle and raised her eyebrow.

His face fell.

"Fine," said Nora. Just as the word left her mouth, she became distracted by something out of the corner of her eye. The khaki uniform coats of the sergeant and the lieutenant blew in the wind. The blood still trickled slightly from their wounds. Then she saw it again. The lieutenant's hand moved slightly.

Colin must have seen it, too. "Do you want to come with me or stay here?" he asked, quickly stepping toward his automobile. "I'm sure they'll be even more pleasant when they wake up to find their heads bashed in."

Nora had no desire to stick around a moment longer. She rushed toward the motorcar, the book still held tightly in her hands. This time she had no problems with the latch to the door, and climbed right in, slamming it behind her. For the first time in an hour, she was out of the wind. She gathered her tangled hair and tried to run her fingers through it. It was no use.

"You decided to sit up front with me this time?" Colin asked.

"I suppose so," she teased him.

Colin started up the car. "No grinding metal," he said. Pointing to the shifter, he said, "Move this for me when I tell you to." She put her arm on the steering column and pulled the lever down to the first position.

"How did you know how to do that?" he said.

"I was watchin' you," she said.

"It's probably me who should be watching you," he said to her. "To keep you out of trouble."

"To keep me locked up," she replied. "Don't worry. If Mrs. Finnegan finds out I was gone, I'll never see the light of day again."

He pointed to the lever again, and she moved it down. The car picked up speed. The Stepney spare jostled the car around, but it held.

"You know, Nora," he said, changing the subject, "I still can't help but wonder if all this trouble could have all been avoided."

"How's that?" she asked, over the noise of the engine.

"If you had just given me that kiss instead of a curse."

"Not likely, Colin," she said. "There's no good luck to be had in Ireland."

"Someday, Nora," he said. "Someday."

CHAPTER 28

August 1, 1914: Kilcoole, County Wicklow, Ireland

Colin brought the automobile to an abrupt halt along the dark path. The sunlight was fading, though still perceptible, but the path felt as dark as night with its tall, thin pines and eerie silence. The trees seemed impervious even to the sea breeze Nora knew was all around them, and the silence felt ominous.

"Are you sure this is the place?" she asked as Colin set the brake.

She wondered how many narrow dark paths there were in County Wicklow. Probably hundreds.

"Of course, Nora," he said, confident as always. "My directions were clear. Drive a couple of hours south, and a little ways past Kilpedder turn toward the sea. Park the car where no one will see. Don't break your fookin' arm."

Nora frowned. "Well, no one will find us here. But will we find them?"

Colin shrugged. "Dunno. But if we don't, I won't be too upset."

"Why not?" asked Nora. She knew she was asking too many questions again.

"Because I'm going to get me arse beat when they see who I brought along." He opened the door and stepped outside. "You coming or not? You're welcome to stay here," he offered. "I'll come get you in a few hours." He winked at her.

"Not a chance," she said. She opened the passenger side door and stepped out of the motorcar into the cool night air.

"Figured you'd say that," he muttered loud enough for her to hear.

They walked to the back of the car and stood still for a moment, letting the twilight silence surround them.

"You have no idea where you are, do you?" Nora whispered.

"Nonsense," said Colin. He stepped onto a path that along the row of dark trees. His left arm was still wrapped tightly in his undershirt so that it fell across his chest. "I'm a several-hour roundabout drive from Dublin, fewer hours from a couple of soldiers with a blown-out engine and massive headaches—" he turned to her and smiled, "—thank you, by the way—and about fifteen minutes from being the laughing stock of all the boys I'm trying to impress when I show up to a midnight gunrunnin' with a girl."

He smiled and reached out his right hand for her to take, adding, "One wrong step away from prison—with a very fair and just sentence—from our British overlords." His voice dripped with sarcasm. When her hand met his, he grasped his fingers around hers and any anxiety over being lost fled from her. She felt as content as she ever had as he led her through the thick cover of trees.

He continued his thought. "I'm halfway to my next confession and holdin' the hand of a girl who hitchhikes her way into trouble and hits soldiers over the heads with wrenches and fires straight into engine blocks with no regard for ricochet." He glanced up into the dark trees. "But who won't kiss me just once. I know exactly where I am."

"But do you know where *they* are?" she pressed.

"No fookin' clue, Nora." He laughed. "Did you ever think I knew where I was going?

"Yes," she said, not seeing the humor. "Always."

"I never did," he said, and smiled. "But I always got you wherever we were goin' all the same."

They walked for a few minutes in silence, weaving in and out of the trees. The trunks were thin and bare, but the tops spread out in a great canopy above them as the limbs stretched out to compete for sun. The ground below them was dusted with pine needles. The forest acted like a dark curtain, blocking out much of the remaining light. Nora could smell the sea, but she could not see it.

After a few more minutes of wandering, Colin stood still. He looked around him for a moment and then down at Nora. Releasing her hand, he reached for his flask. "You hear that, Nora?"

She listened. "No."

"Listen harder," he said. "I hear the sea."

Nora listened intently and could hear the faintest sound of breaking waves through the trees.

"It's closer than you think," he said. "C'mon, this way." He quickly moved toward the sound of the waves, and she followed close behind. Soon the wood began to thin until, without warning, they broke out of the tree cover. The rising moon cast its reflection onto the dark waters before them. The night had a steady wind, and the Irish Sea churned with surface waves. As they stood on the top of an embankment that dropped down to a beach, Nora caught a glimpse of a lantern and could hear hushed voices carrying over the breeze.

"And here we are," Colin said quietly. "You ready?"

Nora nodded.

"You want a swig?" he asked, and offered her his flask.

"No," she replied.

"You sure? It will calm your nerves." He took a long drink. Moonlight glinted off the metal in his hand.

"What nerves?"

"Excuse me, Miss McMahon," he said to her sarcastically. "I forgot you aren't afraid of anything."

"Not if you're here," she said, and started down the embankment.

"That's what keeps you calm?" he said. He sounded a little surprised. "That wouldn't keep me calm."

By the time he caught up to her, she could make out several shapes along the beach, scurrying about between several small boats. Some of the boats had short masts, and others were just old, dilapidated hulls. Colin reached the rocky coast ahead of her and crouched behind a shale ledge. When she joined him, he whispered, "I want to make sure we've got the right gunrunnin'."

They listened for a moment and heard a man bark a set of orders, "Take every piece of unnecessary equipment out of the boats! The load will be heavy!"

Colin turned to Nora. "Yep, we've got the right place. That bloke barkin' orders but standin' with his hands in his pockets and doing nothin' would be me cousin, Michael." He stood up and walked toward the men on the beach. Nora followed. About hundred feet away and still unnoticed, Colin began to wave his good arm in the air. "Don't want to get shot," he explained to Nora.

Michael was the first to notice them. "About fookin' time!" he said to Colin. "What the hell did you do to your arm?"

"Lovely to see you, too," Colin replied. "We ran in to some trouble."

Michael walked toward him and immediately saw Nora. "Jesus Christ, Colin! What the fook do you think you are doin'?"

"Lovely to see you," Colin repeated.

"We can't have her here. Get 'er off the beach!"

"No choice, Michael, she's here now," Colin said calmly. "And she can help."

"She can't help!" Michael said. "I fookin' told you that you couldn't bring her."

Nora listened to this exchange with surprise. She had known that she would not be welcome, but she was intrigued to hear that Michael had, at some earlier point in time, told Colin that he didn't want her in Kilcoole. That meant that Colin had asked.

"Fook that," said Colin. "I didn't bring her on purpose."

Michael looked from Colin to Nora. "Get out of here."

Colin lowered his voice and leaned toward his cousin. "Mr. Dunham sent her," he said. "She was in the car when I left Dublin."

I can still hear you, Nora thought

Michael furrowed his brow.

Colin continued. "She's here now, Michael, and of all the things you could have her do, this one makes sense. If Mr. Dunham sent her..."

"That fookin' old bastard..." Michael began.

"That fookin' old bastard must know somethin' you don't," said Colin, still speaking softly. "And here's somethin' else you don't know. The Brits knew somethin' was up! They're looking for trouble tonight. They're going to be stakin' us out along the road home."

"And just how do you know that?" asked Michael.

"I asked them while they were breakin' me arm," Colin replied sarcastically. "So you better come up with a plan to get us all home."

Michael scratched his chin. He was obviously troubled by this information, but he still pressed Colin. "I'll come up with a plan just as soon as we get the girl out of here."

"And I'm not doin' this without her," Colin said. "She'll come with me. Won't be any trouble to you."

Nora watched this exchange intently. She had never met Colin's cousin before, but she could tell by the way they interacted that he was someone important. And Colin was right: he was an ass.

Michael was fuming. He turned to his cousin. "I asked you to do somethin' useful with her. You made a big stink about it. 'I'm not gettin' her in trouble' you said. And instead, you do this. This is the last time I ask you to do anything!"

"No, it's not," said Colin. "And you know it." He pushed past his cousin. "Come on," he said to Nora. "We've got some work to do."

Nora locked eyes with Michael as she walked by. His glare cut at her, but she stared back at him with all the intensity she could muster. It was he who dropped his eyes first.

Colin walked toward the farthest boat, which had no crew around it. It was a small sail craft with a rickety mast. "You know how to sail this thing?" he asked her.

She nodded and started to inspect the mast and sail. "Why are you suddenly stickin' up for me?" she asked.

Colin was trying to untangle some of the lines that lay in the bow with his right hand. "You can be pretty thick sometimes Nora," he said. "Isn't it obvious to you?"

Nora shook her head, daring him to say it out loud.

"Are you going to make me tell you?" he asked.

"Yes," she said.

He laughed. "Then you're going to have to wait." He turned back to his line. "If I get drunk enough to tell you, I'll not be able to run any guns." He looked at her and shook his head. "I don't know what I'm going to do with you, Nora. But for the time being," he said, tossing her a tangled line, "see if you can untie this knot. I'm not good for much of anythin' with only one arm."

CHAPTER 29

August 2, 1914: Kilcoole, County Wicklow, Ireland

The wind from the Irish Sea whipped across the open waters off Kilcoole as they headed back toward shore. Cool water splashed across the bow of the small boat and pooled in the wooden bottom. She thought she would feel exhilarated, but instead she felt an unexpected weight. Her grandfather's pendant, her most tangible memory of him, had broken in half somewhere on the road to Kilcoole. She couldn't help but think that it was a sign of his disapproval.

In the light of the moon, Nora saw ripples around her ankles as the water sloshed across her old shoes. Her heart sank further as she recalled a similar scene, just weeks ago, when she and Seamus had brought her grandfather to Inis Cathaigh to be buried. It was the last time the three of them were all together, as much as escorting a corpse could be considered "together." Now she didn't even know if she would ever see her brother again. Did he even care to come to Dublin? She needed him to. He was part of her, and the only one who knew her story. Everything about her childhood was slipping away, and there seemed to be nothing she could do to bring it back.

A flash of light caught her eye, and she looked up to the bow where Colin sat. The moonlight reflected off his flintlock every time the boat met a cresting wave. She remembered the energy she'd felt as she had held the heavy pistol in her hands. How satisfying it had been to fire it into the soldiers' automobile. The weight of it in her hand, the cracking sound, and the recoil. It was everything her grandfather had steered her away from since the day her parents were entombed on Inis Cathaigh. Why, since her grandfather's death, had her mother and father all of a sudden seemed more alive in her memory?

"Was easier than I imagined," came a voice over the wind. Nora looked up. The sails were full and the tiny craft moved quickly across the water. Land was fast approaching. She reached over and loosened the jib to tack directly into the offshore wind that now governed the direction of the boat.

"What?" she said.

Colin climbed over the newly acquired cargo toward her, as if it were the distance between them and not her meandering thoughts that had made her miss his words. "Wasn't too difficult," he said. "Was easier than I thought it would be." He smiled.

Even though he could never quite understand the thoughts that swirled in her mind and memory, he was the only tie she had to her old life. She smiled back.

"Don't say that, Colin. We're still a long way from Dublin." Nora turned her head from the sail and, hand still firmly on the rudder grip, looked behind her. They were in the middle of a trail of small craft making their way to the Kilcoole shore. Despite the strong winds, each boat was moving slowly under their burdens: almost seven hundred rifles in all, and countless crates of ammunition.

Nora's small boat in particular was weighed down. Small boards had been laid across the deck to keep the weapons and ammunition off the wooden deck. The full load disrupted the weight distribution on the boat. Nora tacked left and right to adjust to the changing winds and hit the surface waves at the right angles to avoid getting swamped. Wet ammunition was useful to no one.

As soon as the water became shallow, she pulled the keel up and motioned for Colin to jump out. He flipped his legs over the side and dropped out of the boat into waist-deep water. She saw him cringe when his feet hit the ground. It must have jostled his arm.

With one hand, he was able to guide the boat ashore. Nora pulled up the rudder, and she herself swung her legs over the side as well and dropped into the water. The cool water made the night seem cold, though it was the height of summer. It soaked her dress up to her ribs as her feet sank into the marshy bottom. Had it not smelled so strongly of salt, she could have closed her eyes and imagined herself in the Shannon.

She helped Colin guide the boat to the shore, but they could not pull it up together. The cargo was heavy, and Colin was of little use. Meanwhile, the rising wind began to swing the stern of the boat toward the shore. Colin and Nora struggled in the cold, crashing waves to keep the boat stable.

❧

At once, several young men came running toward the shoreline with ropes. "Quick!" one yelled. "Straighten her out!" Together, they realigned the boat so that it was perpendicular to shore and tied ropes to each side of the craft.

"What the fook happened to you?" said one of the men to Colin. It was the dark-haired man who had sat in the driver's seat of Colin's car back in Dublin.

"Got in a scuffle with some Brits," he said.

"Where did you find Brits in these parts?" asked the man.

"On the road to Wicklow. They knew somethin' was up."

"Jesus Christ!" said another. "How the hell are we going to get home?"

"Michael's got a plan," said Colin coolly. He looked at Nora, whose green eyes had grown wide. She knew as well as he did that Michael hadn't let on that there was a plan to get them all home.

"Let's pull this up on shore and get it unloaded," said the dark-haired boy. Each man took hold of one of the ropes, and together they tried to heave the boat onto the shore. But the soft, wet sand of the beach made moving the heavily laden craft a grueling task.

"We just need to get it so we can unload it," said Colin.

Nora grabbed a rope and began to pull with them. Colin saw that several of the men eyed her, but no one said anything. Within a few minutes, the boat was so entrenched in mud they couldn't move it another inch.

"It's far enough!" a tall, older man cried. "Half of you can unload it, and the other half can come with me." He pointed to the shore where the next boat was getting ready to land.

Colin jumped back into the small boat and began handing rifles down, one by one, with his good arm. *I'm fookin' useless,* he thought. Another man jumped up and began lifting the crates out.

"Bring them through the reeds and over to the road!" he yelled. "There's a car waiting!"

Colin looked at Nora and gestured toward the road. He smiled to himself as she kicked off her wet shoes, grabbed as many rifles as she could carry, and followed the others across the beach. *Any excuse to take off her shoes,* he thought.

"Who the hell is that?" asked the dark-haired boy.

"None of your business, Frank," said Colin as he passed another rifle over the side. His left arm felt like a dead weight, but it ached more than even the worst hangover.

"Oh, don't get me wrong, I'm not one to turn away free help," said Frank. "Especially when it's as pretty as that."

Colin wheeled around and grabbed Frank with his right arm. He grimaced. Every motion hurt. "I told you, it's none of yer business!"

"No need to get all worked up, Colin! I'm not going to fight you for her. Just was makin' an observation."

"Then make yer damned observations in yer own small brain. Don't trouble the rest of us with 'em!"

"Jesus Christ, Colin," Frank said. Colin said nothing in reply, but kept his eyes trained toward the tree line where Nora had disappeared. He didn't have the energy to have a conversation with Frank. He embodied common attributes of an Irish Volunteer—hard headedness and lots of opinions, few of them grounded in reality. None of these qualities made for good conversation.

Colin observed the myriad of shadows now returning down to the beach to get more rifles, but he only saw the tall and broad outlines of young men, darting this way and that. No long flowing hair, no dainty steps. Nora was nowhere to be seen.

"Is she the girl with the brother?" Frank asked. "The Gaelic League boy Michael sent to America?"

"Aye," said Colin, softly. His eyes still monitored the shapes emerging from the trees. "Him and another boy from Clare."

"You think they'll get the job done there?" asked Frank. He lifted the last set of rifles from the boat and handed them down to a Volunteer on the beach. "Get enough money to keep us goin'?"

"I don't know. But Michael's always got a plan," said Colin.

"What do you reckon Michael's gonna have us do?" asked Frank, as he passed the last crate of gunpowder over the side. "What's his plan for us getting this cargo back to Dublin?"

"I imagine he'll have us split it amongst a bunch of us. Maybe find some safe houses nearby."

Frank stepped onto the side of the hull and jumped down to the ground, his boots sticking into the marshy dirt below. Colin followed him and let out a loud grunt when he landed.

"Does it hurt you?" asked Frank.

"Aye," said Colin. "Feels like my whole arm is going to fall off."

"The Brits really broke it?" inquired Frank, with a mix of awe and disbelief.

"Aye," said Colin again. "Bent it around me back until it snapped."

"And why'd they do that?"

"Because they knew we was comin' to Wicklow."

Frank began to walk toward the next boat, already up on shore. "Then we better hope Michael's got a good plan," he called back. "The next time we run into them I'm pretty sure they won't stop at broken arms."

"I can guarantee they won't," said Colin, still watching the line of trees. Nora had not returned. Her shoes still lay on the beach where she had left them.

"You just going to stand there watching for her until the Brits arrive?" said Frank. "Did they break yer legs, too? We've got three more to unload!"

Colin looked toward the next boat, which was already a buzz of activity, with three volunteers handing rifles and crates over the side. Everyone around him ran, but he could only stand to walk. He stepped up to the side and reached up to receive a solitary rifle, then continued to run up toward the tree line, in hopes of running into Nora. She was nowhere to be found.

Nora quickly made her way back to the beach to pick up more rifles. The scene up at the road had been chaotic at best. Frantic boys had haphazardly loaded rifles and crates of ammo into tired old automobiles. Some of the drivers, too anxious to wait for the boats to be unloaded, left before their trunks were full, making other motorcars overloaded with contraband. Michael had run back and forth across the loading area, shouting directions amid the most inexhaustible tirade of swearing Nora had ever heard. Her initial impression that he was an ass had only been reinforced, but she couldn't help but be impressed with his fluent profanity.

The closer she got to the beach, the deeper her bare feet sunk into the thick mud along the shore. It was freeing to feel the earth beneath her feet. She approached the first boat she saw, a small wooden craft with a ragged white sail. Its inexperienced captain had been in too much of a hurry to properly tether the sail, so it billowed out, tipping the boat violently to one side and deep into the mud.

She spied the dark-haired man again. This time he was handing rifles over the side and barking orders to the boys who came up to retrieve them. She got in line with the rest of the men, and when it was her turn to receive cargo she lifted her hands up as high as she could to reach the rifle that he was preparing to hand over the side. She waited as he paused and examined her small hands, held high above her head.

"So you're back," he said. He didn't release the rifles to her. "How's it lookin' on the road?"

"A mess," she said, still breathing hard from her run back from the road. "Loadin' the automobiles as fast as we can. Some are full, but some are leavin' almost empty."

"Take a break," he said, and reached out his hand to help her into the boat. "Hand these out with me."

She grabbed his hand, and he lifted her over the side of the boat in one easy motion. She saw the disorganized pile of rifles and picked up the closest one to hand over the side. The line of boys waiting for rifles kept getting longer as they returned in droves from the road.

"Me name's Frank," the man said.

"Nora," she curtly replied. He looked as though he wanted to say something, but Nora turned back to the business at hand. She began handing the firearms over the side of the boat.

"Yer brother's a good fella," Frank said. His voice sounded strained as he lifted a large crate of ammunition and lowered it over the side.

"You know me brother?" Nora asked, surprised. She grabbed another rifle. "How?"

"I know of him," said Frank. "Doin' that mission for Colin over in America, takes guts to do that. Leave home and all."

Nora stood, still cradling the rifle in her hands. She gripped the barrel and stock tightly, sweat forming between her palms and the wood. Her heart was beating fast. She slowly digested the man's words. *Doin' that mission for Colin over in America. What mission?* She had been right—Colin was keeping something from her.

"How do you know about that?" she pressed, feigning that she already knew about the mission. At least her voice didn't sound like it was shaking. The rest of her body began to tremble. *He wouldn't have done that to me*, she thought.

"From Colin. He brought the money down to 'im when we was home to Clare. To buy the tickets for passage and all. Been plannin' this for many months they was." He heaved another pair of weapons to waiting hands below. "Real good of yer brother to do that for the cause. Once he gets some recruits in Boston, we'll be an international movement. And those Americans—they know how to hand it to the Brits!" Frank said knowingly.

Nora nodded. The words again echoed in her mind. *Been plannin' this for many months.* She continued handing the rifles over the side, faster and faster, as if she were trying to outrace her own pulse. When the rifles were gone, she reached for a crate of ammunition.

"That's a heavy one, leave that to me," said Frank.

Ignoring him, Nora grasped the case with both hands and yanked it upward and inch or two.

"Here," said Frank, and he reached over to help her lift it.

Nora shoved him away. "I've got it!" she yelled.

"Suit yourself." Frank took a step or two back, hand raised. "Charming personality," he muttered. She heard, but didn't acknowledge him. He hopped over the side of the boat and moved on to the next one without looking back.

Suddenly it all made sense. Why Colin had showed up with Silas that morning back in Ballynote. Why he and Seamus had whispered to one another throughout her grandfather's wake. Why he hadn't been able to look at her that night.

Nora bent her knees and with all her might heaved the ammo crate. The rush of anger that surged through her body powered her arms and legs. She rested the crate on the gunwale, then slid it to the waiting arms of two grown men who, with effort, lowered it and began trudging up the beach.

Still shaking, she scanned the tree line. The silhouette of a tall, muscular boy was making his way through the trees and onto the beach. The moonlight shone brilliantly all along the shore, revealing a left sleeve flapping in the wind. *Colin.* And then: *he thought I'd never find out...*

As he began making his way toward the water's edge, Nora slipped silently over the side of the gunwale, picking up two rifles perched up against the hull, overlooked by the boys as they had moved on to unload the next boat. She watched Colin approach the boat where Frank was conducting the next offload. When his back was to her, she ran up the beach in the opposite direction, holding her two rifles to her chest.

"Have you seen Nora?" Colin yelled to Frank. He held his broken arm tightly to his chest with his other hand. It was impossible to move without feeling a searing pain.

"She's somewhere on the beach," Frank said.

"I've got to find her, we're about to head out. This is the last boat, and one of the motorcars has already been stopped up on the road by the police. Luckily it only had a few rifles on board—and the boys were able to scatter. But we're out of time! This place will be swarming with coppers any minute!" It was all he could do to explain it to Frank. The pain was becoming unbearable. All he wanted was a flask full of whiskey and a long rest.

"I'd leave 'er here if I was you," said Frank. "She seems in a terrible mood. I guess gunrunnin' doesn't really suit the ladies."

Colin ignored the comment. He didn't have the patience to reply. "Grab everything off this one. I'm going to sweep the beach and make sure we got everythin'. Meet me up on the road. I'll be the last one!"

Colin ran along the line of boats beached along the marshy shore. All were empty. No sign of contraband, but hundreds of sets of footprints told the story of what had happened all along the muddy beach.

When he was sure he had left no equipment or Volunteers on the beach, Colin began to make his way back up to the road. He wanted to run, but the pain was too much. Out of the corner of his eye, he spotted a set of old leather shoes lying in the mud. He leaned down and picked them up. She hadn't come back for them.

He half-jogged up the beach and pushed through the reeds until he reached the narrow road. But the area that a few minutes before had been full of cars and shadowy men loading weapons was now abandoned. No last getaway car waited.

Something's not right. On instinct, he ducked low to the ground and backed slowly into the reeds. The broken stems below him made light snapping noises as he moved deeper into the marsh. He crouched as low as he could and observed. He could see none of the boys along the road. Not a person. The reeds blew softly in the wind. Something was up.

A tug at his shirt. He snapped his head to look and saw Michael, lying in the mud, motioning for him to get down and holding an urgent finger to his lips. Colin sank even further into the reeds and lay on his right side next to his cousin. His clothes soaked in the moisture from the marshy ground.

Michael put his mouth to Colin's ear. "They're onto us. I sent the last motorcar ahead and told all the boys to scram on foot and take whatever they could carry. I'm goin' back to the beach to clear it. They're patrolin' this area."

"I already cleared it. There's nothin' left. All the boys are gone. Did you see Nora?"

"Aye. I sent her runnin' with the others. I'll do a sweep of the woods nearby and regroup with any stragglers later tonight."

"I'll come with you."

"You can't," said Michael. "You've got to get yer vehicle back to Dublin. There's a can of petrol over on the beach by the rocks. Frank will go with you. I already sent him to fetch the petrol."

Colin pursed his lips.

"Don't argue with me, Colin. Just do as you're told. I'll find her."

Colin hesitated.

"Now scram!" Michael urgently whispered. "When you get home, park the car out by the train station and head straight home. I'll meet you there."

Colin looked his cousin in the eye. "Don't you dare leave here without her!" He rose and turned toward the beach.

"Don't fookin' tell me what to do," Michael whispered behind him.

&a.

Colin fumed at his cousin as he emerged back onto the beach. He hated that Michael ran everything in the predictably Michael fashion—arrogantly. It made him even angrier that his cousin was usually right. Just as before, the beach was empty. He made his way over toward the rocks where he and Nora had entered the beach a few hours before. Just as Michael had said, there was a can of petrol hidden among the grasses. Frank was crouched a few yards away.

"You ready?" Frank asked. "It's gettin' creepy here. Let's move out."

"When's the last time you saw her?" Colin asked him.

Frank scratched the stubble on his chin. "Now I sorta wish I hadn't given you the worst motorcar we had," he said. "Seems you're me ride home."

"When did you see her last?" Colin asked again, this time with urgency in his voice.

"I dunno." Frank shrugged. "What's it matter, she's probably halfway home to Dublin by now."

Colin picked up a rock and threw it as hard as he could with his right arm, which wasn't hard enough for how angry he felt. It landed just a few inches away from Frank. His broken arm throbbed with the motion.

"Jesus Christ, Colin! What's gotten into you? She's just a girl. Pretty, but with a rotten personality!"

"What are you talkin' about?" Colin said.

"I was unloadin' one of the boats with her, and I tol' her what a stand-up guy her brother was, you know, for offerin' to go to America—"

"Fook Frank!" Colin yelled.

"Shhhh!" Frank said. "I thought we was hidin' out here!"

Colin held his head with his one hand. "What else did you say?" he asked, this time quietly. He felt like the energy had just been drained from him. *She knows*, he thought.

"That you brought the money for the tickets down to Clare with you, that Michael was appreciative. And boy did she give me attitude!" Frank shook his head. "Not sure why you're mixed up with her."

Colin shook his head.

"Look at you," said Frank. "You look downright miserable. If you were smart—"

"If you were smart you would have kept yer damned mouth shut!" Colin yelled. He grabbed the can of petrol and trekked up the embankment toward the motorcar he had parked on the wooded path, swearing under his breath. He didn't care that anyone who was looking for the Volunteers would be able to pick him out. He didn't care that he had made enough noise to signal to the British where he was. And he didn't care that Frank was still crouching in the reeds, not understanding what had just transpired.

CHAPTER 30

August 2, 1914: Near Kilcoole, County Wicklow Ireland

Nora crouched atop a bed of straw, peering out into the night. Her breathing was rapid, and she could do nothing to slow it because it kept time with her pounding heart. With each breath, the straw beneath her bare feet moved ever so slightly. The rustling noise was soft in the night but deafening inside her head. She pleaded with her heart to slow. She knew she was being hunted, and her breathing would give her away.

Her cache lay behind her, within arm's reach, carelessly piled in a heap among the hay. The donkey kept watch over the nineteenth-century German rifles that her pursuers wanted so badly to find. He slowly chewed his hay and nudged the butt of one of the Mausers with his nose. He snorted curiously. It was not often that he had visitors after sundown.

The salty sea breeze whipped across the meadow and carried into the open barn the distinct sound of a tree branch snapping. Her attention turned to the tree line. The straw rustled. Was it a British soldier coming for her?

The moonlight shone brightly above. It was the same moon that had guided her hours before as she met her gunrunner amid the waves of the Irish Sea. That same pale light now silhouetted a lone man as he made his way across the rolling Irish field. He looked ominous, but the light of the moon revealed that he carried no large firearm.

Nora reached for a Mauser and a cartridge. She knew little about rifles, but enough to understand that these dusty weapons were antiquated. She carefully loaded the rifle, as she had seen her father do years ago, and aimed the barrel out the open window. Only the muzzle protruded.

She could hear her father's voice and for once, it was not faded or obscure in her memory. *Take yer time, Nora. Choose a spot well ahead of 'em. Settle yerself. Take aim. And just wait for 'em to cross.* Of course, he had been talking about the game that teemed along the Shannon. She was poised to kill a soldier in the King's Army. Only hours before, this would have seemed absurd. But the events of the day had made her question everything she thought she believed. She chose a spot just to the left of the hedge line, and waited for the man to come into her view. Her finger made contact with the trigger. The metal felt like ice despite the warm August night. She slowly increased the pressure but did not squeeze it.

She waited. A second felt like a minute. Two seconds, like a quarter hour. She blinked. The man did not cross the imaginary line she had drawn between the muzzle and the hedge. She peered to her right, careful not to reveal her position. Her heart suddenly stopped. He was no longer there.

She pulled the rifle inside the barn Standing slowly, she shouldered the weapon and steadied it across the open barn window, aiming it again toward the tree line. Her grandfather's old broken pendant hung heavily around her neck, its sharp edges reminding her that she was following a path he would have forbade. She took a step forward and kicked hay over the three rifles that lay on the ground. The donkey snorted again and his breath blew the hay off one of the barrels.

She listened intently, but heard nothing save the whipping sea wind, the pawing of the donkey, her own racing heart. Still shouldering the weapon, she peered further out the window. The summer grasses blew to the left and then the right like waves on the ocean yielding to onshore winds. The moon searched for the soldier like an enormous spotlight, but in vain.

Could the soldier have chosen to search the cottage instead of the barn? Did she have time to run to the shelter of the trees beyond? She didn't want to leave her rifles behind to fall into British hands. Many of her compatriots were also stranded and hiding throughout the Wicklow countryside, biding their time to make their way back to the Dublin safe houses. If the soldiers found her, it would put all of them at risk.

As her eyes scanned the meadow, the sound of a deep voice behind her took her breath way.

"Nora," it called in the distinct accent that marked Irishmen of the Pale. "Come child, 'tis not safe here." She swiftly turned and saw a face she recognized—a cocky smile that revealed a missing tooth. "Will be no easy task to get us home, but I've got a plan."

Only now did Nora recognize that the barrel of her Mauser was pointed directly at the man standing in front of her. Though he had dared to call her a child, she lowered it anyway. But she moved it slowly to allow him to sweat.

He tossed his head to the side, and his jet-black hair parted on his forehead, revealing dull gray eyes that hung with a fatigue uncommon for a man of just twenty-five. For the first time, he appeared to Nora to be human. Out here, he had no requirement to be braver, smarter, or more confident than every other boy around him. He didn't need to keep up an insufferable facade.

"Glad you don't mean to shoot me," he said.

"I almost did," she replied.

"I know, I saw you." Michael smiled..

"Are you ready for a bit of an adventure, Nora, in the name of Ireland?"

Now, it was Nora who smiled. "Always."

CHAPTER 31

August 2, 1914: Near Kilcoole, County Wicklow, Ireland

"Well, come then," said Michael. "It's going to be a long night." He walked into the barn and pushed the donkey aside. It brayed angrily at a second intruder. Apparently his first guest had been quite enough excitement for one night.

"How many of 'em do you have?" he asked.

"Four," said Nora, sifting through the hay to reveal the others. The donkey edged his way back to the hay pile, snorting to defend his territory.

"Just four," he said pensively.

"I'd have taken more if you had given me more," Nora interjected. "I'm small but not useless."

"Calm down," said Michael. He shook his head. "Don't think for one minute that I assume you can't pull yer own weight. Why do you think I let Colin bring you to Dublin in the first place? You didn't think I was in the business of charity did you? Quite the opposite," he said, as he examined the action on each of the weapons.

"'Twas me cousin who wanted you tucked away safely, stayin' out of trouble." He eyed Nora curiously, then muttered, "Except that we put you up at the Parson's and in the jaws of the enemy." He tapped his breast pocket looking for a cigarette, but found none. "But no one's ever been able to cram any sense into that thick skull of 'is."

"But you didn't want me in Wicklow!" she said indignantly.

"You're damned right I didn't!" he snapped back in a yell that startled her. "But it has nothin' to do with what I think you're capable of. You seem quite capable to me."

"Then why—"

"Me cousin warned me you ask a lot of questions," interrupted Michael. "Perhaps we best stick to business tonight and keep the chatter to a minimum. You jus' might learn as much with yer eyes as you do with yer mouth."

Nora fell silent and felt her cheeks turn red with embarrassment. She was glad the light of the moon didn't reveal that to Michael. *He is such an arse,* she thought.

"Come now, Nora," he said again, his tone calming. "I've got a job that only you can do. And I mean that in the utmost sincerity." He handed Nora a second rifle, gathered the other two and all the ammo in his large, burly arms, and without another word, walked toward the open barn door. Nora followed, only because she had no other choice.

As they approached the entryway, Michael brought his forefinger to his lips, motioning her to be quiet. *After that scolding, he needn't have worried about me speaking,* she thought.

A light emanated from one of the small windows of a cottage about two hundred yards away. A candle was lit, though previously the structure had been completely dark. Michael turned back to her and reached out his hand, signaling for her to hand him one of her rifles.

He took it from her, so that he now cradled three in his arms. Nora held tightly to the fourth.

"It is loaded?" he asked.

She nodded.

"Good." He peered back out the door, and Nora leaned close to look over his shoulder. He snapped back and moved away from the opening. He turned to her. "I'm going to go first. I want you to scan the trees. I don't know if they're out there, but if those British whores are in the woods, they're probably going to try to kill me."

Nora felt her eyes grow wide.

"I want you to watch the woods. And if they shoot at me, aim toward the flash and give 'em hell."

He handed her several extra cartridges. "If I get killed, fend 'em off as long as you can. Someone will come help you if they hear the fire. We've got boys scattered all about tonight."

Nora's heart was beating through her chest. She was certain that Michael could tell how nervous she was, but she didn't want him to know.

"Don't worry," he said, with a half smile. "The black powder in these damned rifles will only give away your position in daylight. Evens the score a little."

Nora stood as tall as she could and nodded.

"Oh," he said, as if an afterthought, "If you get hit before you run out of ammunition, throw the remaining cartridges in the water trough. I don't want them to be able to use them when they line us up in front of their firing squad. We'll make 'em waste good ammunition."

Nora refused to react. She knew he was trying to make her even more uneasy so she would be more inclined to listen to him. The wind continued to pick up and blew in gusts across the field. If she weren't so afraid, she would have found the moonlight on the swaying grass breathtaking.

"And you think I don't trust you," he said, winking. "You are going to cover me arse. Ready?" She nodded, and he took a deep breath, turned, and sprinted from the barn in the direction of the cottage.

Nora instantly raised her Mauser to her shoulder and scanned the woods. She heard nothing over the wind, not even Michael's heavy steps as he ran under the weight of three rifles and as much ammunition as he could carry.

The pines swayed. The grasses danced. The moonlight shone. No piercing gunshots broke the country silence. She watched the tree line intensely until Michael was almost to the cottage. She saw him kneel by the corner of the structure to return the favor of providing her with cover.

She turned to the donkey, who still eyed her curiously. "Here goes nothin'," she said aloud, and followed Michael across the field. Her bare feet pounded on the soft meadow. The waist-deep grass tickled her legs. She felt exhilarated—a feeling she hadn't experienced in what seemed like forever. There was nothing so wonderful as an Irish summer night, even in the midst of a gunrunning gone wrong.

She arrived, breathless, at the door to the cottage. It opened for her, as it had for Michael moments earlier, and a pair of calloused hands reached out and pulled her in.

Inside, several young men crouched out of sight of the single window, while one was posted guard there, facing the woods. The farmer who owned the property was boiling water over the fire.

"Can't let me guests go without tea," he beamed.

"You made it," Michael said, smiling at her. "We may have slipped by them. We'll lay low till dawn. 'Tis too early to know if we're out of danger."

Nora sat down and caught her breath. Everyone around her was covered in sand and mud from their adventure. It didn't matter though, as there was no harm in tracking dirt across a floor that was dirt to begin with. She relaxed as she looked around the cottage. It felt a little like home.

Michael slid down next to her. "You did good, Nora," he said. Though he was Colin's relative, he looked nothing like him. Where Colin was tall and fair, Michael was shorter, had a larger build, and had dark hair and darker gray eyes. In some ways, their mannerisms were similar. But though Colin, too, was emotionally reserved, he wore his humanity on his sleeve. She could not sense this quality in Michael.

"Hope you're ready for your next assignment," he said. "It starts tomorrow morning."

"So I'm in?" Nora asked. The farmer brought by a cup of tea, and she gratefully accepted it.

"You've been in since the day you arrived in Dublin," he said. He took a cup of tea from the farmer as well. His old, cracked cup was the same as hers, though it looked tiny in his hands. "We put you at the Parsons for a reason. You're there to be eyes and ears for everything that goes on between those walls."

Nora felt her heart flutter. "But what could possibly—"

"So he never told you?"

Told me what? She thought. *What else was he hiding?*

"I knew he hadn't. Mr. Dunham neither?"

Nora shook her head.

"Look, Nora," Michael started. "The Parsons aren't just regular old rich folk. The mister and missus—they seem harmless. But their home is the very seat of Ulster power."

Nora shook her head. "What do you mean?"

"They have a son."

"Five of 'em,"

"Aye," said Michael, "there are five. But one son, Ethan, is one of the leaders in the Ulster Volunteers."

"And how is that singularly different from any of the families in Rathmines?" Nora asked. "They are all Ulster sympathizers."

"Aye," said Michael again. "And you're all right with that?"

Nora didn't say anything. She wrapped her fingers around her cup and looked into her tea. Should she despise the Parsons just because they were sympathizers? She had struggled with this since Colin had told her about the Parsons. She knew they stood against everything she wanted—an Ireland free from English rule. Catholics with jobs and education and choices. And yet they were so nice to her—so charitable to everyone who worked at the manor. It wasn't so easy to hate when your declared enemy had shown you nothing but a kind heart and a full stomach.

"Ethan is a special case," Michael continued. "He played a large role in putting down the strikes last year. Lots of men died—needlessly. He was ruthless."

Nora looked at him. She took a sip of her tea. It was bitter and scalding hot. Nothing like the fancy English tea served every afternoon at the Parsons.

"He's sworn that he himself will put an end to Irish nationalism, if he has to execute each and every Volunteer himself." Michael reached into his pocket and pulled out a small flask of whiskey. He added some to his tea. "And he's no stranger to executions." He said the words slowly and deliberately. He must have known it would get Nora's attention.

It did. "So where do I come in?" she asked.

Michael smiled. He had piqued her interest. "You listen. And you report back. Let me know what he's up to, when he's visiting, what he's doing. What correspondence he writes. We can glean a lot from understanding what he does day in and day out. And when he's not home, keep an ear out for mention of the Ulster boys. It's that easy. You'll keep mental notes of the happenings around the house. Simple."

Nora's hand reached for the small notebook that she had hidden amid the folds of her dress earlier in the day. It was still safely stowed. She was sure that Michael would be interested in the contents, but she held back from telling him. She didn't trust him. She no longer knew who she could trust. For all she knew, she would hand off the book and hear nothing of it ever again. She wanted a chance to read through all of the entries and try to put the pieces together herself.

"So this is why you brought me here?" she asked. "It had nothing to do with charity?"

"Nothing," said Michael. "I arranged for you to come because I saw an opportunity to get someone we trust on the inside at the Parsons. Someone besides Ronan." He sipped his tea. "Ronan's got his own job to do."

Nora sensed that Michael wasn't being entirely straightforward with her. She clung to the little notebook in her dress. It was the only thing that might give her some credibility. If she could just figure out what it all meant—maybe she could get these boys to take her seriously. Let her make some of the decisions about her own role in this fight.

"And this was the plan the whole time?" she asked.

"Aye," said Michael. "But me cousin—"

"Colin," said Nora. A pit opened in her stomach. She was so angry with him.

"He didn't think you'd be up for it," Michael continued. "Thought you were—" he carefully selected his words, "too young to join in. Just not ready." He had chosen his words well. Nora felt her face turn hot. "And maybe he's right. Maybe a girl yer age needs protectin', but I tend to think you're ready. "

Nora clenched her cup of tea. She had been right—Colin still thought he could protect her, as if she was a child. *Protect me from what?* she thought. He should have known by now that he could not protect her from what fate had already chosen. But Michael—she knew enough about him to realize he made all the decisions but seemed to value utility. *The notebook.* She could make herself valuable to him. She tapped her fingers against the worn porcelain cup, chipped in multiple places around the stained rim. Seamus was gone. Her grandfather dead, and her parents only fading memories. She was a hundred miles from Clare and all alone in the world.

"Next time you need somethin' from me," she said, "don't bother to send the message through Colin. Tell me directly."

CHAPTER 32

August 2, 1914: The Liberties, Dublin, Ireland

"Colin," came a whisper. "Colin."

Colin opened one eye. The loft above his uncle's shop came into view. The dark wood ceilings and walls. He recognized the faint smell from the store below. His mind wandered back into a daze, and his head sank back into his mattress.

"C'mon me sleeping beauty," came the voice again. This time he recognized the distinct sarcasm of his elder cousin. A half second later he tried to throw his arms in front of his face, only to feel a shock of pain extend through his left arm.

Whack! Michael scored a direct hit with a pillow to the face.

"Jesus Christ, Michael!" Colin yelled. "Let me catch some sleep, will you?"

He sat up and cradled his left arm with his right. How had he gotten any sleep at all with the constant throb? He squinted his eyes. The hole in the floor that opened to the rudimentary stair was ablaze with the sunlight from below.

"What time is it?" he asked, confused.

"'Tis already evening, don't you know," said his cousin. "You slept the entire day."

"Did I?" he asked. "I got back just as the sun was comin' up. I'm wasted." He looked around, trying to concentrate. All of a sudden, he felt a rush of adrenaline and a familiar pit in his stomach. "Where is Nora? Did you find her?"

"Aye," said Michael. "I found her."

"And is she all right?"

"Of course. That girl of yers can take care of herself."

"So you dropped her off at the Parsons, did you? How did you get her back in? Is she fumin' at me still?"

"Did nothing of the sort," replied Michael. "Last I saw her was in a farmhouse in County Wicklow. The plan was to meet back in Dublin by tomorrow morning," he smiled. "And she is still fumin'." He seemed to enjoy his cousin's misery.

"You just left her there?" said Colin incredulously. He grabbed his shirt and pulled it over his head. He stood up, hitting his head against the low ceiling. "Jesus Christ!" he yelled again. Michael had an uncertain look on his face, as if he wasn't sure if Colin was swearing at the ceiling, in which case he should laugh, or at him, in which case he should duck. It appeared to be the former.

"You've lived here a year, and every single night spent at home—alone, I might add," Michael dared to laugh. "Seems to me you'd have figured out that you are taller than the ceiling by now."

"You just left her there?" Colin continued, not responding to Michael's jibe.

"No, there was a plan," came the cool reply. "I left ahead of 'er, under the cover of night. She followed after daybreak."

"You sent 'er out alone?" said Colin. "Even better, you idiot!"

"We had to get the cargo back, and to do that safely, we had to split it, Colin," Michael said. "You've got to start thinking with yer head. If you keep thinking with yer heart—or perhaps some other organ— you're going to get us all killed."

Colin glared at his cousin.

"It's not a knock on you Colin, it's just fact. We had a job to do."

Colin, having been reminded that every move was painful, moved slowly to the stair and stood, shaking his head in anger.

"You're the one who asked to bring her here," Michael said.

"It wasn't my ide—"

Michael cut him off. "It doesn't matter, you brought her. And we both know that she's a liability."

"She's not—"

He cut her off again. "She's a liability when you 're around!" Michael said sternly.

Colin instinctively tried to clench his fist, but his left hand didn't respond with anything but searing pain.

"It's the truth," Michael continued, evidently unaware of his cousin's suffering, "Because you will look out for her above everything else each and every time, and you can't. We look out for the mission and for the group—all of us. And I can't give a shite about your girl when we've got a job to do."

Colin moved toward his cousin, this time with his right fist clenched.

Michael held out his arm. "I'm not judging you, Colin," he said. "I like her. She's a nice girl, and she could be very useful to us. I'm just sayin' that I can't hold one person's safety over another. Or the success of the mission. I can't."

Colin felt his shoulders sag and tossed his head back. He stared at the dark wooden ceilings, pursing his lips. He did not want to admit that his cousin had a point.

Michael continued talking. "And so I did what needed to be done. We divided the haul, and every one of us who was left took a portion, and we decided to separately make it back to the safe houses."

"And then?" asked Colin.

"And then take a head count," said Michael. He rested his hands on the wall and made a face that let Colin know he didn't want to answer what would undoubtedly be the next question.

Colin asked it anyways. "And?"

"And," Michael obliged, "everyone is accounted for…except Nora."

"Jesus, Mary, and Joseph!" cried Colin.

"Not to worry just yet," said Michael. "She's resourceful. She'll figure it out."

"Of course she is, but—"

"But what?"

"But she's young, and she's pretty and—"

"Aye, she is," said Michael, "and she'll figure it out. You kids from Clare are just as good at getting out of trouble as you are getting into it. Besides that, she has till tomorrow morning to check in with me. Still a few hours yet."

Colin began pacing back and forth across the narrow room. His boots scuffed the floor loudly, making it sound as though furniture was being dragged across the floor.

"And Ronan is already movin' heaven and earth to find her," he added, "using 'is little network of contacts."

But Colin had made up his mind. In four large strides, he reached the stairwell. "I'm going to look for her."

"No you're not," said Michael. "She could be anywhere between here and there."

Colin said nothing and started to climb down. Michael rolled his eyes. "You're more likely to find her waiting right where you are."

He moved toward the stair and followed Colin. Just before he reached the door, Michael grabbed his shoulder. Colin shook him off. The movement made him wince.

Michael looked at his cousin's left forearm, and Colin followed his gaze. His arm still bent askew and his hand looked gray. "It doesn't hurt."

"Fook it doesn't. I'm sorry about that, Colin," Michael said sympathetically. Colin rarely heard his cousin sound so sincere. "We'll have to wait a day or so to see a doctor if you can manage. Don't want to draw attention to it. They might be lookin' for a boy with a mangled arm. It looks like it needs to be set."

Colin didn't respond. Instead he turned back toward the door.

"Look, Colin, I woke you up because I wanted to talk to you, not because I wanted to argue with you," said Michael.

But Colin was already walking out into the late afternoon sun, pulling his cap over his eyes. As he walked toward the River Liffey, he heard Michael close behind him, jogging to catch up. When he was alongside, he said, "I wanted to talk to you about Nora."

"After I find her."

"You're not going to find her. She's trying not to be found," said Michael.

"I don't care," said Colin. He started walking faster across the uneven cobblestones. Maybe Michael would get the message that he didn't want to talk.

Michael tried a different tactic. "Colin, I want to talk to you about Nora and the Parsons. Something's come up."

Colin almost turned his head but stopped himself. He didn't want to get into another argument with his cousin. One was enough. He continued to walk briskly toward the river. The evening breeze made the walk almost refreshing. He had no real plan; he just wished Michael would leave him alone so he could think. If Nora had made it back to Dublin, would she just head back to the Parsons? *The Parsons. Something's come up.* Michael's words still rung in his ears.

"What about the Parsons?" he finally asked, though he kept walking. He could see the Liffey on his left. The bridges had the typical evening traffic—women with parasols to keep the evening sun at bay, men on bikes, children scampering across as if being chased by invisible pursuers.

"About Ethan," said Michael. He slowed to a stop and waited for Colin to stop as well. He had gotten his cousin's attention.

Colin took a few more paces, then slowed and turned to glare at Michael, whose eyes were now cast downward. He felt his face get hot. "What about Ethan?" Colin said slowly. He kept his voice quiet and composed, though he felt an anger rising in him. "You tol' me—"

"I know," said Michael. "And I wasn't lyin' to you. But things have changed. There's a war on." Michael paused and looked up. The sun was only just starting to fade.

"You promised me—"

"He's coming home to Dublin." Michael interrupted.

"Fook," said Colin. "We have to get her out of there."

"Interesting," Michael let out a curt laugh. "I was thinking just the opposite."

"No!"

"Come, Colin, let's talk about it over a pint." He tried to redirect his cousin.

"Are you trying to get her killed?" he asked.

Michael cut in, raising his voice to drown out Colin's. "I'm trying to give us the best possible chance to get our country back. And I need every angle we can get."

"I get it, she's an angle to you," said Colin incredulously. "But she's more than that to me." The sun was casting long shadows into the streets. Colin felt a wave of anxiety as he realized Nora might spend another night out there all alone. How long had it been since she had slept? Since she had eaten?

"We're all fookin' angles, Colin! You, me, Seamus, Ronan—I will use anyone and everyone if it helps us. And since I'm in charge, I get to say how we use them. I'm sorry if can't handle that." Michael's voice was getting louder. "So yes, I will use every angle I can, including Nora. Especially Nora."

"So why are you so eager to have her spy on the Parsons—where she is a sitting duck if she gets caught—but so angry that she came out last night? " He watched his shadow become more animated.

Michael sighed. "You're not looking at the problem strategically, Colin," he said, and Colin shrunk at the thought that he was being naive.

"Colin, don't think for a moment that I don't want a pretty girl runnin' guns with us. Because I do. But I need her to be anonymous. We'll never get placement like hers ever again. She's the only one of us who can do that. We can run guns till the cows come home, but we will never have the impact she can have just by sitting there and listening."

Colin frowned and opened his mouth to speak, but Michael continued. "If she makes a habit of working with us—like yesterday—we risk someone noticing and tipping our hand. I can't have her doing anything that makes her look like a nationalist. I need her to just be a damned housekeeper. Uninteresting. Bland. But observant."

Colin clenched his teeth. As he saw it, the risk was much worse than what Michael had voiced. The real risk was that Nora could get tossed in jail, or worse, end up lying dead in a ditch.

"If you think I'm coldhearted, it's only because if I was any other way my heart would break open and nothing would ever get done around here. I'm not strong enough to feel any other emotion until this is over and Ireland is her people's again." This, Colin knew to be true. His cousin was a coldhearted bastard—or at least played that role exceedingly well. He hoped that in the end all the risk would be worth it. But the pit in his stomach told him that they would not all live to see the Ireland they dreamed about. "Now," Michael continued, "come have a pint with me while we wait for yer girl to get back. Plus, you'll want her to cool down a little."

"That bad?" asked Colin. He pulled his cap down over his eyes to keep out the evening sun.

"Aye, she's not happy with you."

"It's *you* she should be mad at. And Seamus."

"I know," said Michael, "but I wasn't about to tell her that while she was sitting with a rifle pointed at me head."

"What?"

"Never mind," said Michael. "Just come to the pub with me."

Michael put his arm around his cousin and turned him toward Mercer Street. "Come on, I'm taking you to me favorite pub to help you forget about yer troubles."

"How long have you known?" Colin asked.

Michael turned and looked at his cousin. "Since yesterday morning."

"Did Patrick tell you?"

Michael let out a laugh. "No, you did." He watched the confusion fall over Colin's face. "The delegation is Ethan. Whenever Ronan talks of a delegation, he's talking of the devil himself."

CHAPTER 33

August 2, 1914: The Liberties, Dublin, Ireland

The Mercer Street Pub was a frequent Volunteer hangout. The owner posted a burly, mustached guard at the door to keep would-be loyalist customers away. The pub also maintained several private rooms toward the back that allowed for a quick exit, if needed. In the year that Colin had lived with Michael, they had never once gone to a pub together.

"Will do you some good to have a drink. Will do me good as well. Fook, I haven't' slept in three days!" said Michael.

"You look like hell," said Colin, finally cracking a smile. "Worse than usual."

Michael jabbed his cousin in the ribs. "Ain't no amount of beauty sleep that will make either of us pretty."

"Speak for yerself," said Colin.

"You can live in yer fantasy world, the one where the girls come callin' on you every night. But to me, you'll always be me darling, ugly little relative."

"Thanks, Michael," said Colin. "That means a lot." Trading insults was the only form of affection the cousins could manage.

Michael nodded to the guard outside the pub, who said in a gruff whisper, "Must have some pair of testicles to show up here today, Mic."

Michael laughed. "Aye, all the ladies tell me that as well."

The guard eyed Colin and his injured arm suspiciously, but when Michael put his hand on his cousin's shoulder, the guard relaxed.

"If they put two and two together, you'll be a wanted man, Mic. But good job," the guard said, as he opened the door. "A Mauser in every nationalist hand is a good thing."

"Aye," said Michael, and he and Colin slipped inside. The guard closed the door swiftly behind them.

The darkness of the pub immediately struck Colin. He removed his cap, and when his eyes adjusted, he scanned the room. The bar was mostly empty, with only a few regulars huddled together in booths that lined the wall. The booths were small and intimate and reminded him of confessionals. Everyone spoke in whispers when the boys entered. A few nodded to Michael and smiled.

A lone bearded man sat at the bar. His white hair made him look ancient, though his beard still had remnants of the brilliant red it must have been decades before. A tall black hat sat atop the counter next to the old man. Michael strode up to the bartender.

"What'll it be, Mic?"

"What else?" asked Michael. The bartender pulled a tap handle, wiped the glass, and handed him a stout, all in one smooth gesture. He wiped his hands on his stained white apron and rubbed the graying whiskers on his chin.

Colin nodded toward the liquor. "A double," he said.

The bartender lifted an eyebrow. "Most of 'em prefer to start with a pint, no?"

"A double," Colin repeated.

"Trouble with the ladies," his cousin said and winked at the barkeep. "Give the boy a double."

"As you wish," the bartender said. "Anything for Mic Kildare."

The barkeep threw a copy of the evening edition of the *Irish Independent* on the bar. Colin eyed it but didn't react. He had no idea if the news was good or bad.

"Would you look at that, Colin!" Michael exclaimed. "You made the paper—nay, the front page! I don't come in until the bottom half of page one. You bastard!" Michael elbowed Colin, and he grunted in pain.

"'Officer and Solider Assaulted by Hooligans in County Wicklow,'" read the barkeep. "That's quite a headline. Nicely done, boy. As for you, Mic, 'Suspected Arms Arrive in Wicklow.' Not bad for a night's work!" He flopped a cleaning rag on the bar. "See, Mic— you can do some good when you take the night off from womanizin.'"

Michael took a long drink of his stout and licked the froth from his lips. "Only took half the night off."

Colin rolled his eyes at his cousin. No amount of attention was ever enough for him. He, on the other hand, felt a little uncomfortable at being so prominent in the paper. He felt sweat form on his brow, though the bar was cool for a summer evening. *Will they recognize me?* His arm throbbed, as if he needed reminding. Maybe Michael had been right—they might be looking for a boy with a broken arm.

He sighed and studied the interior of the pub while he half listened to Michael joke with the old barkeep. The wooden bar was old, but it had been polished so that it shone. The wall behind the bar was plastered in a faded paper, bright only in places where pictures used to hang. He looked up toward the cobwebbed ceiling and saw an old, faded painting of a white bird flying over a green ocean. It looked as though it had been painted directly on the wall by an amateur. The dimensions were off, and the wings were drawn but seemed incomplete, as if one was supposed to imagine how they looked.

Michael had drunk half of his pint in one series of gulps, but Colin held his glass, thoughtfully swirling the whiskey.

"Do you think she's all right?" he asked his cousin.

"Aye, I do," he answered. "She's a tough little thing. I suspect it'll take more than a few British soldiers to take her down. Plus, she's in a disguise of sorts."

"Oh?" said Colin, raising an eyebrow.

"I took care of 'er Colin. She'd have looked as innocent as a lamb as she carried those rifles north."

"Let's hope," said Colin as he took a sip of his whiskey. It tasted strong on his lips, and he savored the familiar burn in his mouth.

"Look, Colin," said Michael, "if it makes you feel any better, if I was you — and I thank God in heaven that I'm not, but that's another story entirely—I'd be worried about 'er, too. She kind of casts a spell on you, doesn't she?"

Colin looked at his cousin and grimaced.

"There's just somethin' about her. You're a lucky fook. And if she was my girl, I'd be worried about 'er too," he said again.

"I wouldn't," a voice cut in.

Michael looked over and seemed to notice the old man next to them for the first time. He shot Colin a look and rolled his eyes. Leaning in close to Colin, he whispered, "Crazy ol' codger."

Colin glanced toward the old man, when something caught his eye. Something about the man's wispy beard was vaguely familiar, but he couldn't place it. Shrugging, he turned back to his drink.

"I wouldn't—not quite yet," the old man said again. "Perhaps someday quite soon, but not just yet."

That voice. Immediately, Colin was brought back to that night in Ballynote, back to the fireside and Nora's old cottage. He snapped his head toward the old man and recognized him at once. It was the old storyteller.

"Halloo, boy," said the man. "'Tis interesting that we meet again."

"What are you doin' here?" asked Colin, surprised. "I mean, how—"

"I'm a traveling storyteller, my boy. I am everywhere and nowhere all at once." The old man laughed. "I make my rounds, have my routes. How interesting that our paths should cross again. Perhaps it is fate."

Colin raised an eyebrow. "Not sure I believe in fate."

"Ha, you can't be Irish then, can you? Perhaps you are Scottish?" he said, as if he were trying to irk Colin. "English, even?"

Michael let out a laugh. "I like this old codger."

"Take it back!" said Colin.

"Now, now, my boy. You'll come to respect fate one day, I presume."

"Did you follow us here from Ballynote?" Colin asked suspiciously.

"My boy!" the old man began. "I've traveled many a mile and everywhere in between and above and below since I saw you last. I've been to Cork and even up to yer despised Ulster before I made it here. What makes you think you are so important that I would follow you here?"

"I dunno," said Colin, sheepishly.

"Ah, but you are important," said the old storyteller with a gleam in his eye. "Don't let me fool with you! You travel along in life with some important associates."

Again Michael smiled. "I like this character more and more," he said.

But the storyteller was not interested in Michael's jokes. He kept his gaze on Colin. "So it seems that fate would have us meet again, and that fate would have you woven into its story in such interesting times."

Colin looked at him curiously. The old man took a drink from a copper mug and wiped his mustache with his sleeve. "Yes, interesting times," he repeated. Abruptly, he changed the subject: "Do you see that painting, young man?" He pointed to the faded bird on the wall.

"Aye," he replied. He looked up again at the bird, the wings still taking no real shape in his mind.

"Do you know what it depicts?" he asked.

"I suppose it's the story of Noah's Ark," Colin replied. "God sent a dove as a symbol of peace."

"That's one idea," said the storyteller thoughtfully. He smoothed his beard and took another drink. "But it seems the artist forgot the olive branch," he said. "The dove from the Bible is always carrying an olive branch."

Colin studied the picture again and shrugged. He cast a glance at Michael, who mouthed, "Crazy old codger" again.

His cousin turned to the barkeep. "Another stout!" The two began to talk quietly about Volunteer activities. Colin tried hard to listen in, but the storyteller kept talking.

"Did you listen to me story, boy?" the old man asked. "Back when I was in Ballynote?"

Colin swirled his glass and nodded, but his thoughts were elsewhere. Michael was making hushed plans to distribute the rifles evenly among the safe houses around Dublin.

The old man interrupted Colin's eavesdropping. "I think that is the dove from me story."

Colin adjusted his cap and turned to the storyteller, still half listening to Michael. "There was no dove in yer story," he said. "You told us a story about a white-haired girl who ran off with some solider."

The storyteller shook his head. "I didn't think you were listening to me. Too busy with the distractions of youth to notice the world around you."

Colin frowned. It was true—the best thing about that awful night had been the chance to sit quietly next to Nora. To lean his knees ever so slightly against hers. He didn't respond and returned to his drink.

"Where did I leave off in me story?" the old man asked. Colin shrugged. A memory from that night was etched in his mind, but it was not of the story. It was the incessant bleating of the sheep and the terrible look on Nora's face, her eyes aglow in the moonlight.

"I believe it was with the girl and her peculiarities," the old man continued.

"Aye," said Colin as he tapped the side of his glass. "She had white hair."

"Not only white hair, me boy!" said the storyteller, all at once coming alive. "Yes, that is precisely where we left off. She had the lightest blond hair, white as ivory, but she also had another curiosity about her. Her eyes were emerald, like the fields of Ireland. Eyes of the darkest green, of the sea during a storm."

Colin nodded politely to the old man, because he seemed so enthused about his story. "Curious indeed," he agreed. "And then she ran off with a soldier."

"No, my boy!" said the man with a laugh. "One might assume that. Her father thought so, if you recall. He went to the king to ask him to intervene and to return her to him. But he couldn't tell him what had become of her—it would break his heart."

"Why?" asked Colin. It was hard to avoid the storyteller's magic.

"Do you know anything about doves, boy?" asked the old man, again seeming to change the subject without prompting.

"Not really," said Colin. "Just that they're everywhere in Clare."

"That's a good sign, now isn't it? Did anyone ever tell you that doves were good luck?" asked the old man.

"There's no good luck in Ireland," Colin replied sullenly.

"Ah, you mustn't say that!" the old man said. "That's exactly what the Brits would want you to believe. That all of the luck on this island has long since died off or fled. But they don't know about our little doves, do they?"

Colin took another sip of his whiskey and stared up at the drawing. He hadn't a clue what the old man was talking about. The Brits must have noticed the doves at some point.

"And that's why the girl in me story is so important," the old man whispered. He watched Colin study the faded artwork on the wall. "She was that luck—that hope—when all else seemed lost."

Colin eyed the old man suspiciously. "How so?"

"The girl—she was the expression of all that existed around her. She was the wild river, the green meadows, the white glow of the summer moonlight, even the white dove that flew back and forth across the moors. And her family worried for her that she might not return, that she was perhaps even taken hostage by the enemy. But she was performing the duty that fate had given to her. 'Twas dangerous no doubt, and it required her to go in and out of enemy lines, never knowing what trip might be her last. The king could not bring himself to tell the father what had become of his daughter, because she was never to return to him."

Colin felt himself getting drawn in by the old man again. Just like in Ballynote. "And what was that duty?"

"To be the guardian of the future, of course! To guide the past to meet the future, to take the hand of fate! To avenge the invasion of the foreigner onto her beloved Irish soil! She couldn't be confined, locked away. Did you not listen at all to me story, boy?" the old man said. He began to chuckle. "'Tis no worry," he added. "As I said before, you keep important company, so I can forgive you for being distracted."

Colin felt a rush of adrenaline. The green eyes. The mission to rid Ireland of a foreign power. *But I don't believe in fate.* He shook his head. *Besides, she has red hair,* he thought. *Not white.* Then he scolded himself. *Pull yourself together. It's just a story!*

In the back of the kitchen, a phone rang. The shrill sound cut through the room and quieted the murmuring voices. It startled Colin from his thoughts. He jumped and disturbed his arm. The barkeep disappeared behind a curtain and a moment later, poked his head back through. "Got a call for you Mic. 'Twas Theo."

Colin looked up from his glass.

"Any news?" Michael asked.

"He says the package has been delivered. Safe and sound. And somethin' about the difficulties keepin' a pair of shoes on a girl from Clare."

A smile broke across Michael's face. He smacked his younger cousin on the back. "I told you she'd be just fine."

Colin threw his head back in relief then downed the rest of his drink. He pulled his cap tight over his eyes.

"What's your hurry?" asked Michael. "I buy you a double an' I expect it to last more than a couple minutes!"

"I'm headed up to see her," Colin said, wiping his face with his sleeve. His barstool squeaked across the floor as he pushed himself away from the counter.

"The hell you are," said Michael.

"I'll go unnoticed, I just want to chat with her for a minute, you know, about her new housemate. The one who wants us all dead."

"Ronan will take care of that for you," said Michael. "You can't be goin' up there."

Colin rolled his eyes. "Will I never see her again," he asked, "if you have yer way?"

Michael considered this. "Not up there, you won't. She'll be out and about once in a while, I'm sure. It'll be hard to keep her away from church. You can see her there," Michael added, and punched his cousin in the arm. "Keep you out of trouble."

"Since when did you become my warden?" said Colin.

"The day you joined up," said Michael.

Colin pounded his fist on the bar. They were right back where they had been—in complete disagreement. He turned back to the storyteller, but the stool he had occupied moments before was now empty. The copper mug, too, stood empty on the counter, a small scrap of paper neatly folded up against it. Colin looked about the room, but there was no sign of the old man. Most of the small confessional booths had emptied out. The old man must have slipped out.

Colin reached for the folded piece of paper and set it on the counter in front of him. With his right hand, he tried to undo the folds. But his hand was large and the paper delicate, and he tore it slightly in the process.

On the paper, the storyteller had written several words, and of course, Colin could not read what they said. He held it one way and then the next, not even sure which way was up.

His fidgeting caught Michael's eye. "What you got there?" he asked.

Colin shrugged, hoping Michael would take the bait and read it aloud.

Michael knew he was not educated, but he didn't know that Colin could not read at all, or even identify letters.

"Just a note from the old man," he said, showing Michael the text.

"A dove isn't a dove if she can't fly free..." Michael read aloud. "What the fook does that mean?"

Colin sat up straight and closed his right fist around the paper. He ran to the door as the remaining patrons in the pub stared. For a moment, he didn't care that the jostling made his arm hurt all the more.

"What's gotten into you?" said Michael loudly after him.

Colin didn't look back. He pushed open the heavy door and burst out into the street, taking the guard by surprise. "What's yer hurry?" he yelled as Colin pushed past. He pressed his arm to his chest with his right hand, trying to keep it still. It didn't help much. He turned around the corner, frantically looking for the old man with the tall black hat.

There were some people milling about, but no sign of the old storyteller. "Have you seen an old man come through here?" he asked a passerby. "With a long white beard and a tall black top hat?"

The man shook his head. Colin ran on to the next cross street, but it was useless. There were too many directions the old man could have gone. Breathless, Colin finally stopped and leaned against the side of a building. He could feel the heat from the bricks through his shirt.

A moment later, his cousin caught up with him. "What was that all about?" he asked.

Colin shook his head. "Nothin.'"

"Nothin'? You ran out of there like you stole somethin.'"

"Just somethin' the old man said," Colin said. "I had to ask him somethin,' but I can't find 'im now."

"Hope it wasn't important!" said Michael. He laughed, which irritated Colin. "'Cause you won't see the likes of 'im again. He's got one foot in the grave already."

"Thanks, Michael," said Colin sarcastically. "That's quite helpful."

He put his head back against the hot bricks and felt sweat run down the back of his neck. He had to find a way to see Nora.

CHAPTER 34

August 3, 1914: London, England

"Edward!" Viscount Eldridge's voice boomed up the back stair. "Edward?" No reply. "Now just where is that boy?" he murmured to himself. "Can he be relied upon for anything at all? Certainly not for his politics, certainly not for his punctuality." He eyed his pocket watch. "For folly and fool-heartedness, yes, I suppose." He cleared his throat and called more loudly: "Edward! The coach is departing with or without you!" He tramped loudly down the hall and past the parlor into the large entryway, where Francis awaited him, holding out his jacket and top hat.

"And young Edward, will he be joining you today?" asked Francis, pretending not to have heard the shouting.

"Maybe, maybe not!" said Viscount Eldridge. The frustration was clear in his voice. Just then, hurried footsteps echoed across the tile floors of the parlor.

"Well, at least he is moving with some sense of urgency," muttered Viscount

Eldridge. He took his jacket and hat from Francis and walked toward the front entrance. But instead of his eldest son, a sweaty and tousled Gerald appeared in the hall.

"Gerald!" he thundered. "Just where is your brother? We are due in Parliament! I cannot wait any longer!"

"He's coming Father, on his way just now," stammered Gerald. "Hold just one moment. He was tied up with some—military business. Not quite sure what, but you know, these days, quite urgent."

Francis frowned and looked disappointed. Usually Gerald had a good lie for any occasion. This was clearly not his best work. Catching his breath, Gerald said, "Come, Father, a quick refreshment before you go. 'Tis certain to be a long afternoon at Westminster."

"Yes, yes indeed it will be," he said, annoyed, but clearly distracted by the thought of an early afternoon nip of scotch.

"I'll join you, Father. He's coming—really—just sent me ahead to beg your pardon and ask your patience. He's really quite abashed at his tardiness."

Francis rolled his eyes.

"Five minutes, Francis!" Lord Eldridge announced. "And not a second longer! We will depart in five minutes."

Catching a glimpse of a familiar carriage coming up the drive, Gerald quickly escorted his father out of the entrance hall. "Mustn't waste any time," he said. "Just a quick sip and then you'll be on your way."

❧

Francis remained behind, holding the jacket and hat that Viscount Eldridge had redeposited in his hands before being whisked away to his scotch. He peered out the window as Edward's coach approached at a fast pace. The driver bypassed the front drive and pulled the horse around to the back, and Francis proceeded to the windows at the rear of the entrance hall to observe the scene. His job was usually quite mundane and predictable, and he relished the drama that seemed to follow the Eldridge boys, now that they were again full-time residents at the manor.

The carriage came to an abrupt halt, and Edward clambered out of it. He raced toward a back door and stumbled into the entrance hall. Finding no one there but Francis, with his father's hat and jacket in hand, he grinned.

"Just in time!" he said cheerfully to the butler.

"Quite late, actually," said Francis, unamused. "And you couldn't be bothered to make a visit to Westminster, as the guest of your father, while fully assembled?"

Edward looked down at his clothes and smoothed the wrinkles. In the process, he seemed to notice that something else was amiss. His shirttails hung below his trousers.

"Thank you, Francis," he said. "How about this?" He turned around.

"Marginal," came the reply. "Might want to fix your collar."

Edward was completing the necessary adjustments just as his father and brother came into view.

"Gerald, my boy," his father was saying, "I think that's a fine idea. I'll make the necessary arrangements at once! Good head on those shoulders, boy, and such a keen sense of duty. Must take after your father. Thank the Lord you got your mother's good looks, though." He laughed, then caught sight of his eldest son and frowned. "You can explain your tardiness while we are en route. It seems some of my children would be quite thrilled to join their father in session today, given this historic occasion. You don't know just how privileged you are, Edward. And that is the shame of it!"

Viscount Eldridge took his jacket and hat from Francis for the second time, and this time proceeded out the door to the waiting carriage. When he was just out of earshot, Gerald mimicked him: "And you can explain to him your tardiness while en route."

Edward smiled and playfully smacked his brother on the arm. "Thanks, Gerald. I owe you one."

"Nay, brother, you owe me two," he replied. "We mustn't forget the show I staged with Mother earlier this week. And I sure hope your excursion today was worth it. Father's raging. I'll be surprised if you survive your five-minute trip to Westminster!"

"She was worth it," Edward said. "Worth a thousand carriage rides with a mad hornet."

"EDWARD!" came a shout. Edward hurried out the door and disappeared into the carriage, which had already started to move toward the main drive.

Francis frowned. "You are lucky your father is so smitten with his drink," he said. "That story you concocted was rubbish, really. Not your best work."

Gerald smiled. "Just had to be good enough, Francis. No better than good enough. And you heard my brother—it was all worth it."

Francis nodded. "Though she really should press him to return home fully clothed next time."

Gerald eyed the old butler, as if trying to determine if he was making a joke. A second passed, and Francis let out an uncharacteristic laugh.

"Francis, old chap. Why don't we finish off where Father left off? Just a bit left in the bottle."

"In the words of your father, a fine idea, my boy. For once, a fine idea."

&⋅

"Now then, Edward," began the viscount after allowing several minutes to pass in silence. "I don't very much care why you disregarded my instructions to be ready to depart by two, but I do mind the mere fact that you did. A man's word is all that he has, and I expect you to honor your word, particularly when it comes to your professional commitments."

The elder Eldridge was calm in his delivery, which served to deliver his disappointment more piercingly than his usual shouting. Edward looked out the coach window. He knew his father was right, but he also regarded his father as a bit of a fool, which it made it easier to defy him.

His father continued. "And your brother made a spirited attempt to make your excuses, but I must say that I didn't believe a word of it. So, my boy—"

Edward turned, surprised. Father hadn't called him "my boy" since he had actually been a boy. Such terms of endearment were usually reserved for Gerald.

"You owe me the courtesy of telling me exactly what you were doing that made you so late today. Parliament will not wait for you, nor for anyone. And what you will hear there today will be historic. Your future career as a Parliamentarian will be shaped by the speech today."

"I had a social engagement with a girl, father. " He cringed. Surely, this would precipitate the shouted lecture he had been expecting.

"A girl? And for this you broke your word to me?"

Edward glanced at his father, but where he expected to see anger brewing behind his little brown eyes, instead he saw genuine curiosity. So he continued, "Yes, Father. I suppose I didn't judge it to be a choice between honoring my word to you and spending the morning with her. I thought I would manage to honor both commitments."

The viscount nodded while he processed Edward's response. "So no military engagement?" he asked.

Edward returned a confused look. "No Father, just a social engagement."

"I see," said his father. "Under normal conditions, Edward, I would have to relay my extreme disappointment in you."

Edward nodded. He was certainly used to that.

"But these are not normal times. And you can consider your morning dalliance as one of the last acts of your youth—when you are not beholden to the standards that are set for you because of who you are and can act on whims and fantasies. Because that time in your life is quickly coming to a close."

Edward was silent for a moment. The London streets looked so lively from the carriage. Had he not been privy to the political discussions for the past several weeks, he could have mistaken the excitement for a festival and not something much more somber. "Are we going to war, Father?"

"I do believe so," replied his father. "Though I can think of nothing that pains me more."

"It's our commitment to Belgium," said Edward. "We are bound to protect her."

"Rubbish," replied the viscount. "We are going to war for France. Belgium is just a façade. It's the only way Sir Edward Grey can justify a war without breaking his government into two irreconcilable factions. He'll put England's honor on the line and all the pacifists will cave."

"*All* of the pacifists?" Edward asked, raising an eyebrow.

"Myself included," replied the viscount. "Apparently every man can be backed into a corner, and Sir Edward has found mine."

"I hope you are right then," said Edward. The carriage bounced along the bumpy street. Even the velvet cushions couldn't absorb all the jostling.

"Pray I am wrong, Edward," his father said quietly. "Because it is your generation that will pay for this war in blood. Mine will legislate it from their comfortable seats here in London, but yours will pay the price on foreign shores."

Edward didn't want to get into this discussion with his father. Though he knew nothing about what the war would bring, he certainly hoped it wouldn't be as gloomy as his father predicted. But he could not be sure, and he didn't feel as comfortable as he had in previous weeks in debating the issue with his father.

"And what of your lady friend," asked his father. "How does she feel about war?"

"She is against the war," Edward said.

"A sensible girl."

"She's against the war for much of the same reasons you are," he said. "But she justifies a war because she sympathizes with the Balkans."

"The Balkans?" said his father, surprised. "Isn't it interesting how this conflict started over a scuffle in the Balkans, but all of the sudden looks nothing like a war over Austria's poor treatment of her empire? She thinks they should be out of the hold of the Habsburgs, no doubt," he said.

"Precisely," said Edward. He was surprised his father understood the nuance of Elizabeth's position.

"And perhaps that will be a side effect," the old viscount mused. "But mark my word, this war will be fought and won on French and Belgian soil."

As they rode over the Thames, the grand view of Parliament came into sight. It appeared ominous to Edward as they slowly approached. The massive structure peered down on the overcrowded streets below.

"Quite busy for a bank holiday," said Edward. He motioned toward the pedestrians and carriages that clogged the roads. "You'd think the masses would have headed to the seaside for the day."

"The excitement is here today, Edward, and not at the coast," replied his father. "And all of England knows it."

The carriage slowly made its way through the crowds, and Edward could hear the driver shouting at people to move to the side of the street so the carriage traffic could pass.

"And what of this girl, Edward?" his father suddenly asked.

He had hoped his father wouldn't broach this subject again.

"Is she from a good family?"

By this, Edward knew he was really asking whether or not she was of appropriate pedigree for him to be associating with. "I assure you, Father, she is," he replied.

"Do you wish to have her family invited to your mother's soirée this week?" he asked. At this, Edward was surprised. It seemed his father was truly making an attempt to reach out to him. First there was the invitation to Parliament, where he had certainly already failed to meet expectations, and now an offer to invite Elizabeth's family to the anniversary ball. He felt a pit in his stomach, as he knew that he would also fail to meet this expectation when his father learned just who Elizabeth was.

"Her family will be in attendance," Edward replied. "Alice showed me the guest list."

"Splendid," replied his father. "I look forward to meeting her family, and potentially making your social engagements with her more official."

Edward nodded. This would make him quite happy, if only Elizabeth wasn't the somewhat eccentric daughter of the even more unconventional Lord Clarendon. But still, he appreciated the olive branch his father was offering.

"Thank you, Father," he said. "I should very much like you to meet her." The two men sat together in silence; the elder scratched his chin and looked as though an invisible weight was chained around his neck, and the younger, for perhaps the first time in his life, saw his father in a new light.

CHAPTER 35

August 3, 1914: Westminster, England

Edward felt small, even minuscule, as he walked into the chamber behind his father. He had been to Westminster many times before as the guest of his father, but never on such an occasion as this. Never before had he seen so many people crammed onto the floor. Ushers scurried about, bringing in chairs to create as much seating as possible. Edward stepped aside as several wooden armchairs were placed in the corridor. He overheard an old usher marvel in a scratchy voice, "Not since 1893 have I seen the likes of this!"

"Home Rule," he heard his father say. "He's talking about Irish Home Rule. The first Home Rule Bill brought the same numbers. Your grandfather said he thought a riot might break out. Those damned Irish! Still causing us heartburn more than twenty years later."

Edward nodded. It was a rare topic on which both he and his father could agree. He felt a familiar dread in the pit of his stomach. The Clarendons had a soft spot for the troubled island.

"Go find yourself a seat in the Stranger's Gallery, Edward," the viscount said. "There will be no room for you on the floor today."

Edward slowly made his way into the gallery and pushed past throngs of men, all dressed in summer suits and sweating profusely, to find a narrow wooden chair.

"Can't see a bloody thing!" lamented a voice behind him. Edward turned to see a heavyset man with buttons on his shirt that looked like they could pop. *The most dangerous thing in here*, he thought to himself, *are those damned buttons. Hate to be near if one blows!*

Another gentleman chimed in, this one armed with only a cheery sense of humor and no imminent wardrobe failures. "Seems to be an empty chair up with the diplomats, if you want to venture there!" The two men laughed, and Edward craned his neck to look. The two prominent empty seats in the Diplomatic Gallery were habitually reserved for the Austrian and German ambassadors, who had returned home only days before. He smiled. *If that's not a sure sign we're headed for war, I don't know what is*, he thought to himself.

He took a deep breath. Anticipation was mounting in the air. England was on the cusp of monumental change, and Edward felt simultaneously excited and fearful. An unfamiliar feeling of nostalgia crept over him, and he felt a sudden longing for the boredom, the predictability, and the weeks and months of inconsequence he had passed over the previous several years. He had never before understood that those days, while monotonous, had been without care for the greater world, and without burden or ramification. Days such as those would likely not come again for him or his contemporaries.

The dull roar of the crowd suddenly dampened, as a gaunt and exhausted-looking Sir Edward Grey made his way to the lectern. The sounds of men hushing their neighbors flew through the various galleries. All in attendance recognized that the foreign secretary was about to begin what might be the greatest speech of his life.

303

On the government bench, Lord Asquith and David Lloyd George looked equally haggard. Now, despite the massive assembled crowd, the only sound that could be heard was that of someone in the hall tripping over the unexpected placement of wooden chairs.

The foreign secretary began to speak, and Edward leaned in intently. He spoke slowly, almost like a university lecturer, but Edward could sense the emotion in his voice, though he strained to hear each word. *Stand closer to the lectern!* Edward thought. All around him, the men in the gallery leaned forward to try to hear.

"What did he say?" asked one of the men behind Edward.

"Something about British interests and obligations," said Edward. "Nothing that sounds like a call to arms."

The heavyset man behind him groaned. "Figures. He'd call the entire city to attention just to drone on and say nothing."

"By God, he's going to do it," said the other. "Listen to him! He's just giving a history of British nonintervention. We know the damned history! Make your point man!"

A chorus of elderly men turned around to shush the rows behind them.

"You couldn't hear if you was sittin' in the front row!" cried the man with the buttons.

"Aye," said the other, "But where is our honor? We're sworn to protect Belgium, not sit back and let her be pummeled!"

"Hold fast there," said Edward, and they strained to hear Grey launch into a discussion of British naval commitments. "All is not lost." Edward closed his eyes and concentrated hard to hear. The squeaking sounds of the old wooden chairs filled the room. They were barely up to the task of holding the portly gentlemen who had gathered for the speech of the century. A smell of perspiration hung relentlessly in the hall. Even Edward was sweating through his day suit.

Grey was speaking passionately, still in his slow cadence, "*Could this country stand by and witness the direst crime that ever stained the pages of history and thus become participators in this sin*?" Edward breathed a sigh of relief. *Finally,* he thought. *We're going to fight!*

"He's quoting Gladstone!" cried a deep voice. "'Tis as good a declaration of war as any!"

Edward didn't need to hear the rest of the speech, which carefully laid out the stakes if England did not act to support France and defend Belgium; it passed by him as if he were in a dream. He felt almost dizzy in the hot, crowded room, and his mind drifted to Elizabeth and the precious few days he had with her. His window of opportunity to propose an engagement was closing. He, along with most of the young men his age, would be going to war.

He half-listened as his mind wandered, and before he knew it the speech was ending. The crowd leapt to its feet in applause. Even those who had arrived as dissenters now appeared to show unanimous support for the foreign secretary. The men behind him jumped up and down as if mice were scurrying across the floor. A moment too late, Edward remembered—*the buttons!* The last of the threads holding the buttons to the heavyset man's shirt began to fail, and where his jacket parted, three buttons, in quick succession, shot across the chamber and ricocheted off the wooden chairs. Edward might have been the only one who noticed. The entire hall had erupted in a celebration.

The cheers following Grey's speech went on for several minutes, and Edward stood on his toes to peer over to his father's seat in the chamber. Through the sea of people, he thought he could make out the back of his father's balding head, surrounded by other men huddled together in deep discussion. He wondered what his father was thinking, and though it caught him off guard, he realized he actually cared what might be going through his mind. Politically, the viscount had been defeated in this measure—and it was of no small consequence. He had staked his reputation on this issue, and yet, as he watched his father discuss the issue with his fellow parliamentarians, the smile on his face was obvious. Perhaps he had mistaken his father for a much lesser man than he was.

Edward slowly pushed his way through the crowds milling about in the corridors, discussing the future they faced—a war with Germany. As he approached the hall where the peers were still assembled, a familiar man caught his eye. It was Lord Gibbons, James's father.

"Edward!" Lord Gibbons said, shouting over the crowds. He was a cheerful, middle-aged man whose rosy cheeks made him look as though he were perpetually stepping in from the cold. "Edward, good to see you." The two men approached each other, and the parliamentarian held out his hand to shake Edward's.

"You'll be a busy man soon, Edward," said Lord Gibbons, still holding onto his hand. "Got the word this morning that they've called up the reserves. Have you heard? You'll have a telegram this evening, no doubt. Good luck to you, son!" he said. "Your country is depending on you!"

With that, Lord Gibbons turned on his heel and went off in the direction of the exit, and Edward stared after him, deep in thought. The energy that had filled him before had given way to an unexpected weight. He vaguely saw Lord Gibbons enthusiastically shaking hands with colleagues—liberal, conservative— it didn't matter. However divided they had been when they arrived, England was now, even if for a brief moment in time, united. A humorous thought came to mind: *Let's vote on the Irish as well, since we all seem to be getting along! Quash Home Rule for good!*

He stood in silence, enveloped by the swirling activity around him. The hall, with its deep wooden interior and heavy drapery, was as dark as ever, despite the bright summer day outside. He saw a familiar figure approaching—an impeccably dressed man with a comb-over that did nothing to hide a fat and balding head. His father was pushing his way up the aisle toward him. As he got closer, Edward could make out the tracks of perspiration on his father's temples. To his surprise, his father embraced him. He smelled of sweat and scotch. "Well, my boy," he said, "looks like you've got your war."

My boy. "Aye, Father," he said, smiling. Out of respect, he tried to hide his excitement.

His father took a handkerchief from his breast pocket and dabbed his forehead. From the looks of the handkerchief, it had been used many times that day.

"I just gave my pledge that I would support the vote, Edward." His father had a beaming smile.

What? Edward thought. *How could that be?* He wasn't able to hide his astonishment. "But did you need to in order for it to pass?"

"No, no, they didn't need my vote in the end." He leaned toward his son, and said, more quietly, "But I gave my support because I support you, and it will be you who fights this war on my behalf."

He had imagined he would feel exuberance at a comment like this—from his father, no less. But instead, Edward felt as though the weight of the world had fallen on his shoulders. The war would be his generation's responsibility to win. Not only that, but his father was placing his confidence in him. But perhaps most heavy of all was the realization that he had misjudged his father entirely.

CHAPTER 36

August 4, 1914: London, England

The next evening, Edward lounged in the parlor with his brother. Together, they sipped their father's scotch and waited for the sun to set and the temperature in the manor to cool. The parlor was a favorite room during the summer—the linen window dressings blocked the afternoon sun, and the tall windows along each wall provided a refreshing cross breeze. Upon hearing the heavy footsteps of their father as he neared the parlor, both Eldridge boys instinctively slid their scotch glasses under their respective chaises and straightened out of their slumped repose, but they were too late.

"Idleness! The work of the devil!" the viscount declared. Then his stern face broke into a smile. "But as much as everything is going wrong in this world, at least one thing is going right. Interesting how a war changes everything." He paused, clearly waiting for one of his sons to ask him to elaborate.

"What did you do?" Gerald mouthed to Edward.

What did I do? Edward thought. *Why is it always my fault?*

The brothers stared at each other in a silent standoff. The light curtains danced in the afternoon breeze. Their father arched an eyebrow, but said nothing.

"What is it, Father?" Edward finally asked.

"I expect you to be paying attention to these things, Edward," his father said. "You tell me."

Gerald coughed back a laugh. The only thing Edward had paid attention to all day, between naps and sips of scotch, was wracking his brain over his mother's impending party.

"The first round of mobilization seems to be in full swing?" said Edward. He had read it in the morning edition of the Times. He cringed, wishing he had voiced it more like a statement than a question.

His father shook his head and crossed his arms. Edward could feel his father's stare as he tried to think on his feet. The breeze blew his father's comb-over out of place, but the old viscount didn't seem to notice.

Edward did his best. "They are sure to appoint a new Minister of War now. Despite the threat of Irish mutinies, the war on the continent is now the focus." He knew he was reaching.

"No," said his father. His face conveyed great disappointment. The look was so familiar to Edward that normally it no longer fazed him, though after their heartfelt talk in Parliament the day before, it stung. Their lone moment of connection had clearly passed. Edward wracked his brain trying to resurrect that moment.

His father must have noticed that he was trying. "You mentioned the Irish, Edward," he said encouragingly. "So you got ten percent of the story."

How he hated this game his father always played! Just how was he supposed to guess what was on his father's mind, or what his father considered important? Blind luck was the only way to win in these situations. Except, of course, if you were Gerald. Edward shot a disgruntled glance toward his younger brother. Everyone loved and forgave Gerald. He could imagine his father's response if

Gerald had answered first. *Well, my boy—not precisely what I was thinking but you raise such an interesting point!*

Edward turned back to his father. *The Irish.* For Edward's whole life, his father had been befuddled by the Irish in a way that sent him either into a rage or to the liquor cabinet—sometimes both. Neither ever turned out well for those in the viscount's company. It either meant an afternoon sacrificed to an enraged soliloquy or an evening of watching the finest scotch in the house wasted at the expense of the bloody Irish.

"I just came from a meeting at Westminster," his father continued. Edward tried not to look at the way the wind was blowing his father's hair. It was a comical sight. "The House of Commons held session this morning, and do you know who had the audacity to stand up and give an oration?"

Edward shook his head. *Of course I don't!*

"Of course you don't!" his father said sternly. "Because you have been in here lounging all day!"

"With my brother," Edward pointed out. Gerald, as usual, took no criticism for his idleness.

His father smiled. "Ah, Gerald, yes." He winked at his younger son. "We'll get to you in a minute."

Edward frowned at this display of affection. For his part, after this clear sign of his father's good favor, Gerald leaned back and resumed lounging on his mother's favorite chaise.

The viscount's attention returned to his eldest son and the frown of disappointment returned to his face. "The Irish!" he boomed. "A constant thorn in the side of Mother England. We empty our coffers to support them when they continually refuse to take responsibility themselves, and all they can do to return the favor is rise up against us!"

He didn't have the energy for another of his father's rages about the Irish. And from the looks of it, his father's mood simmered on the verge of a boil, now that the topic had turned to his least favorite island. Already, bits of sweat were pooling on his father's round, balding head.

Edward looked out to the gardens, trying to look deep in thought. The linen curtains were forgiving—they blocked out the hot afternoon sun while still allowing him to see outside. Best of all, they allowed the fresh smells of the flowers to drift in with the breeze.

His father interrupted his thoughts. "They think they want self-government, but they will come running back for more currency the moment they lose their standard of living. And that will be the consequence of Home Rule, boys!" Viscount Eldridge was on the verge of slipping into a tirade. "A bunch of papists at the helm…we will see where that gets Ireland!"

Gerald must have sensed the urgency of the moment. He reached behind the chaise and grabbed the highball of forbidden scotch he had just poured and handed it to his father.

His father grabbed the glass so peremptorily that the amber liquid splashed on Gerald's hand. Gerald licked it from his fingers, again without any disapproval.

"Thank you, Gerald. Always on the spot, you are."

Edward rolled his eyes. Only his brother would get praised for getting caught stealing his father's beloved fifty-year old scotch amid such slovenly manners.

"John Redmond!" the viscount suddenly barked. He raised Gerald's glass animatedly. His sons looked at him in surprise at the sudden outburst. The old man began to cackle. Scotch spilled and dripped down his arm. The proud ruffled cuffs on his pristine white shirt seemed to wilt with embarrassment under the spreading, dingy stain. The elder Eldridge's eyes glowed like those of a sanitarium inmate.

Edward instinctively took a step back and cast a sideward glance to Gerald. "Gone mad?" he mouthed. Gerald raised an eyebrow and gave a quick nod.

"John Redmond, today in the House of Commons," continued Lord Eldridge with the booming voice of a disgruntled Parliamentarian on the floor, "got up and gave a heartfelt speech in support of the war." He took a long swig of the scotch. The beads of sweat dripped down his face and met the alcohol dribbling from the corners of his lips in little pools below his mustache. "About bloody time those wretched nationalists get in line behind something—anything— England advocates for!"

Edward was caught tongue-tied. He didn't know if it was better to respond or to stay quiet and ride out the storm. He got his cue from Gerald, who jumped to his feet and began pacing the floor, hand to his chin as if in deep thought.

That damned actress lover of his, Edward thought to himself, *made my brother an artist!*

"What is it, Gerald?" Lord Eldridge asked, "Have you a thought to add, my boy?" The viscount's wayward hair appeared to dance as he moved across the room. The closer he got to the window, the more the comb-over fell apart.

Edward rolled his eyes. Like his brother and father, he began pacing He refused to be overlooked.

"Nothing father, just—"

"Just what, my boy? Speak up! You can't be shy, not when you're an Eldridge, and your brother seems…" His voice trailed off for a moment. "…indecisive. Speak your mind, son. Don't be bashful!"

Having bought himself a few seconds to think, Gerald suddenly stopped pacing and lowered his arm to his side. He stood straight as he addressed his father. "The nationalists love their John Redmond, Father," said Gerald. "No doubt they will line right up behind him. We're about to have a few more regiments of soldiers, aren't we?"

A beaming smile erupted on Viscount Eldridge's face. He nodded his head. "Yes, my boy," he said. He swirled the scotch in his glass and nodded his head again, letting out a loud chuckle. "You have the instinct, Gerald! That killer Eldridge instinct for politics. You've got your mother's good looks and your father's keen mind!" His father drained his glass and wiped his mouth on his sad, ruffled cuffs.

Edward felt his mouth fall open. *I've never seen Father do such a thing!* Fifty-three years of etiquette training out the window after one speech by the blasted

John Redmond. The Irish insanity surely was contagious, and it had infected his father.

Viscount Eldridge smiled at his youngest son. He held his empty glass in the air, and it begged to be recharged. Edward made a dash for the liquor cabinet and filled it to the top. "Not too much now, Edward!" his father exclaimed. "One glass was quite enough!"

Edward felt exasperated. He couldn't win. When in his father's life had one glass ever been enough?

Gerald shook his head and cast his brother a sympathetic look.

"Yes," Gerald said, "Edward was just mentioning the idea of Irish regiments to me this morning. I thought he was crazy, but it seems he had a good point." He winked at his brother.

"So we'll be getting the Irish boys," Edward said. "Let's hope they learned some discipline from the ridiculous militia they are raising."

"Let's hope they speak English and know left from right!" his father said. "They will be raising Irish regiments so as not to taint our boys' discipline. What a thought! The Irish Catholics fighting alongside the English. Never thought that day would come!"

"But why?" said Edward. It was his turn to rub his chin, but he was not role-playing. "They must think they will get their Home Rule."

"Precisely!" said his father. "Precisely, Edward." Edward felt the connection return—though he was no closer to understanding what earned praise or scolding in the eyes of his father.

"I don't see that happening," said Edward. "You won't vote for it, will you, Father?"

"Not as it stands, Edward, but I can be convinced. There will be thousands of recruits to be had from that cursed island."

"What would it take, Father?" asked Gerald. He walked over to the liquor cabinet that stood proudly next to a set of large French doors that opened to the spacious veranda. He poured himself his own glass of the viscount's special collection. His father said nothing, even though the house rule forbade anyone from touching his special stock.

"We can't afford to lose Ulster," Viscount Eldridge replied. "If we can get something that looks enough like Home Rule for Dublin and enough like English rule for Ulster, I can support it."

"Those northern counties will never support it," said Edward. "They will never allow a Home Rule, and we have to support them. They are the only reason that island is not burning."

"You are right, there, Edward! I will never abandon Ulster, Edward," his father said. "The northern six counties are as good as English to me."

"And the other twenty-six?" Gerald asked.

"Papists." Lord Eldridge slammed his glass on the table. "Unruly and untamable!"

"But fighting for the British Army..." Gerald said.

"I pray their unruliness is a hammer on Germany and not on England," their father said. "It will take the untamable officer to tame them, but if it can be done, our boys will do it."

Gerald raised an eyebrow. "Which is a good time to bring up our conversation from the other day, Father."

This caught Edward off guard. *What conversation?*

Lord Eldridge chuckled again. "No, my boy—you are not untamable, you just have spirit! Two different varieties of energy. And I'll have no son of mine held back by leading a bunch of heathen rebels into war. No son, not you."

Edward felt his heart skip a beat. The room fell silent, save for the soft sound of the curtains as they blew in the afternoon breeze. Did his brother intend to seek a commission as well?

"But, my boy," their father said, "I am quite sure the King will happily accept your service in a regular English regiment to free another officer for duty with the Irish. 'Tis no place for an Eldridge." He sipped his scotch. "No, my sons will be accomplished officers." He smiled at Edward. "Both of them."

Why didn't you tell me? Edward silently asked his brother. The viscount raised what was now a hall-full glass.

"Congratulate your brother, Edward!" Lord Eldridge boomed. "He will be commissioned within the week!"

Edward could sense that his brother hadn't wanted him to find out this way. He wondered if perhaps he had been too wrapped up in his own world to notice that his brother wanted a part of this fight, too. *It shouldn't surprise me,* he thought. *Everyone young patriot will want a part of this war.* But instead of happiness, he felt a bout of jealousy. Would he ever be able to outshine his little brother, even for a moment?

"Congratulations, Gerald," said Edward, but he knew he didn't sound celebratory.

"Two sons in the King's service," Viscount Eldridge's booming voice cut like the strong summer breeze across the room. "I could not be prouder." He elbowed his youngest son. "But your mother will have my neck!"

The three men stood silently in the beautiful parlor, wrapped in the smell of the lavender that grew out on the veranda and a creeping solemnity. The viscount pulled both of his sons close. "This war will change both of you in ways none of us can predict. I can only pray that your spirits are preserved, and that England—Europe's beacon of light—can be preserved." Discussions of war and politics, combined with the finest scotch money could buy, had brought the viscount close to tears.

"It will be over in a few months, Father," said Edward, as he placed his arm around his father's stocky shoulders.

"I pray it is, Edward. Because more than that will break your mother's heart." He returned the gesture and wrapped one arm around each son and drained his glass. He apparently had forgotten that he hadn't wanted a second.

CHAPTER 37

August 5, 1914: Rathmines, Dublin, Ireland

Nora wrestled with her stockings, pulling them up and over her knees. She was grateful for the first time that Mrs. Finnegan required all the girls to wear them. She had often wondered, since her arrival at the Parsons, whoever had decided that stockings expelled indecency. But today, she felt differently. Stockings would do a marvelous job of hiding the scratches and bruises she had acquired in the marshes of Wicklow.

As soon as her stockings were satisfactorily on and her bruised legs duly hidden, she moved on to her hair, which was an unkempt mass of tangled auburn curls. Her hair fell halfway down her back and twisted itself in every which way. She ran her fingers through it, doing her best to tame it, and then pulled it into the tight bun that Mrs. Finnegan required. No matter how tightly she tried to twist it into submission, certain strands were not meant to be tamed, and they protruded in whatever direction suited them best and irritated Mrs.

Finnegan the most.

Content that she was as close to regulation as she could be, Nora stopped fiddling with her hair and looked into the mirror. She smiled with satisfaction, but her impish grin took three years off the image in front of her. She sighed and looked at the little notebook that stood on the dresser. She had read through it several times since returning from Wicklow. It was filled with names, addresses, and cryptic notes. *Mr. S. C., 54 Marlborough Street, Mulcahy's Tavern. Brother-in-law. Mr. J. L., Distributor. Tuesday—Dairy. Granby Street Pub, afternoon, July 15. Mr. S. O, 32 Pembroke Street.* She had read it enough times that she had it memorized, but it meant nothing to her. The grandfather clock in the room struck six. She took the notebook and wedged it under her mattress.

As the clock struck the sixth bell, Martha came crashing into the room. Martha, as Nora, hadn't quite achieved the level of sophistication that Mrs. Finnegan asked of her staff. She was clumsy, and she was loud. She tripped over things and plodded around on feet that reminded one of a young puppy who had not yet grown into its massive paws. When she laughed, she took over a room. When she ate, she spilled.

Everything about her that made Mrs. Finnegan cringe made Nora smile. Martha was the best thing about the Parsons residence. Today, the look on her face exuded everything but the subtlety she intended.

"Good morning, Martha," Nora said. She pretended to putter around the room for a few seconds, until Martha began tapping her foot on the floor. The slap of her leather shoe on the wooden floor echoed in the large room.

"All right, Martha, what's on yer mind?" Nora finally gave in.

"You've been keepin' a secret from me," she said, pretending to be irritated. But her eyes were bright with excitement.

"I have?" asked Nora, wondering what it was that Martha knew.

"Absolutely everyone is talkin' about it!" said Martha.

Nora's heart skipped a beat. What exactly was it that "everyone" knew? Did they know that Colin had visited her the other day and broken one—or two, depending on how one counted—of Mrs. Finnegan's cardinal rules? Or worse, did they know she had sneaked out to Wicklow? Either way, she was in trouble.

"Why didn't you tell me?" asked Martha, in a voice filled with excitement and a hint of betrayal. "I though we was friends!"

"We are friends, Martha, but I couldn't tell you because it was a secret."

"I know! And that's precisely why you should have told me!" said Martha, exasperated. She flung herself on her bed and lay there for a moment. "Secrets are my very favorite things in the whole world," she said wistfully, "except for perhaps gossip."

"Tell me, Martha, what exactly is this secret of mine that you claim to know?" asked Nora, sitting down on the bed next to her.

"What do you mean, what is it?" she asked. Then her eyes got wide. "You've got two secrets, don't you?" she asked.

"I might have more than that," Nora admitted.

"Well, I'll tell you my secret that I know about you if you tell me yer other one," said Martha. "Even trade."

"Sounds fair," said Nora. "You go first."

"You're famous!" blurted Martha.

"I am?" asked Nora. "Do you mean infamous?"

Martha scrunched her face. "I have no idea what that means. All I know is that the whole of the city of Dublin is talking about you."

Nora frowned.

"In the papers yesterday—so James from the stable tol' me—was the story of a girl who, two days ago, in great disguise and in the company of nationalists, delivered some special cargo." Nora felt her eyes widen and the blood drain from her face.

"Shall I continue?" asked Martha.

"Tell me everythin' that you know," said Nora. "An' everythin' that was in the papers!" Her mind churned with all the possible problems this news brought.

"She carried a load full of ammunition to our Volunteers, all of it disguised as a baby in a pram!" exclaimed Martha. "An' when James tol' me this, I said to 'im, 'now that is one crazy girl, and I should like to meet her.'" When Nora didn't respond, Martha continued. "An' do you know what he said to me?" she asked.

"No," said Nora, cringing. "What did he say?"

"He said that he saw the story in the papers and would have thought nothin' of it except—"

"Except what?" Nora asked. She wasn't sure she wanted the answer.

"He said he would have thought that it sounded like just a silly story except that he saw a motorcar drive up to the stable in the evenin' a couple days ago. And he saw you get out of it, and he wondered what you was up to."

"And?" asked Nora again. She felt slightly ill.

"So he looked into that motorcar, and do you know what he saw?"

"A pram," said Nora flatly.

"A pram," said Martha. "And he put two and two together and started a rumor all around the residence that the girl from the paper was you."

"So this is just a rumor?" asked Nora.

"It might as well be fact," said Martha. "Or at least it will be until you tell me otherwise and offer specific proof as to where you were." She sprang up from the bed and onto her feet again so that she could once again tap her loud leather sole against the wooden floor. She stood there tapping with her arms crossed.

"'Tis true," said Nora cautiously. "It was me."

Martha covered her hands with her mouth and let out a shriek. "Are you kiddin' me?" she exclaimed. "I thought it was just a story!"

"But you just said you thought it was fact!" said Nora, confused.

"I didn't actually mean it!" she said. Martha started pacing, the sound of her plodding leather soles loud on the floor. "I can't believe it!"

"Well, believe it," said Nora. "But how is the whole city talking about it?"

"They're talking about the gunrunning and a girl who was stopped by the warden and fooled them because they thought she was pushing a baby along the road to Dublin," said Martha.

319

"But they don't know it was me!" said Nora.

Martha threw her hands up in the air, almost knocking over a vase. She didn't seem to notice. "Of course they don't know. But I know it was you! An' everyone else here thinks it was you, thanks to James. You're famous!" Martha said again. "An' you're a hero!"

Nora felt ill. This was not going to go over well with Michael. She was supposed to be anonymous. "Do the Parsons know?" she asked nervously.

"Nah," said Martha. "No one trusts them. Don't get me wrong, I like the mister and missus, but they aren't to be trusted. They are the enemy."

"The enemy?" asked Nora. "Aren't you exaggeratin' just a bit?"

"Well, perhaps a nice enemy, but the enemy nonetheless," said Martha.

There it was again—that conflict she could not internally resolve. "Not all Protestants are enemies, Martha," said Nora quietly.

"Ones that produce an Ethan Parsons assuredly are," said Martha. "You'll see once you meet the bastard."

Nora joined Martha in her pacing, trying to decide what to do. The sun was coming up—they were going to be late for work. *It's not as bad as it could be,* she told herself. Despite the fact that the whole staff knew of her escapade, she was quite relieved that the Parsons didn't know yet. It was only a few minutes after six in the morning, and the day was already more exciting that she had hoped.

"Well," she said, "let's get downstairs. No need to bring more attention to meself by showin' up late."

She headed toward the door but again heard the inescapable tapping of Martha's shoe.

"What?" said Nora as she reached for the door handle.

"I tol' you the secret I know," she said. "Now you have to tell me the secret I don't know."

"Oh yeah," said Nora. "After your secret, mine seems quite silly." She could see Martha's disappointment. "I had a boy in me room."

Martha perked up, a grin sweeping across her face.

"And...I closed and locked the door," said Nora, smiling. She quickly slipped out into the hallway, but could still hear Martha slap her hands to her mouth to muffle another shriek.

Nora had counted to three in her head when she heard Martha's galloping steps behind her. "What do you mean a boy?" she said too loudly for Nora's comfort.

"Shhh!" said Nora. "Unless you want a new roommate when I get sent packin.'"

"Who is he?" whispered Martha.

"A friend," said Nora.

"Just a friend?" said Martha. "Do you often close and lock a door to hide a friend?" She leaned back against the wall and almost disrupted one of the many oils paintings that decorated the second floor of the manor.

Nora felt ill again. "It doesn't matter now anyway. I'm fumin' mad at him, and I don't much care to see him anytime soon." Martha tried to adjust the painting so that it was straight again.

"You lied *again*," said Martha, "this is not a secret...it's better than that."

"I know," said Nora. "Gossip."

"Gossip." Martha looked quite intrigued. "You've just got to tell the rest now," she said. "Or I'll just assume the worst." She began walking away from the painting. It looked as though it was about to fall. "But let's hurry."

She scampered down the hall in her typical, clunky fashion. Luckily, ornate Oriental rugs lined the length of the hallway and muffled her steps. They were almost late for the morning meal preparation.

"Is he married?" Martha asked as they rounded the corner toward the stair. Nora pulled her in close to avoid knocking another vase.

Nora shook her head. "I should think not. It's really not all that exciting, Martha."

Martha gasped and put her hands to her mouth. "I know!" she exclaimed. She stopped walking and whispered loudly, "He's a Protestant, isn't he?" Even in a whisper, her voice echoed down the stairs.

Nora laughed. Martha always managed to make her feel better. "No, Martha, he's certainly not."

"Then what?"

Nora thought how she could explain this quickly. She placed her hand on the top of the polished banister. "He treats me like…" she paused.

"A sister?" Martha suggested.

"No."

"A mother?" Martha tried again.

"No, not at all." Nora searched for the right words to describe her situation. She picked up her hand and noted with chagrin that she had left a handprint. One more thing to clean.

"A dog?"

"No!" said Nora. "He treats me like a child."

Martha looked confused. "Is that all?" she asked. "I mean, it certainly beats the others."

"But I'm not a child, and I haven't been one for a long time. I can make me own decisions. For God's sake, I just ran ammunition up from County Wicklow and got through the very checkpoint that was supposed to stop me. I even made the papers! I'm not a child!" She started down the stairs.

"No, I suppose not," said Martha. She looked surprised that her friend was so animated.

"He brought me here to Dublin after me grandda died with the idea that he was goin' to keep me locked up here and safe. And then I snuck down to Wicklow—"

"You snuck down there?" asked Martha. "This gossip just gets better and better. "

"Well, yes," said Nora. "And we had a crazy adventure, and I thought finally he was seein' me for who I am…" She kept descending, though Martha waited at the top.

"And then?' Martha had to practically yell.

"And then…" Nora paused, still not able to put her thoughts to words. "…and then I find out that before he brought me up here, he orchestrated a scheme to send me brother to America, and away from me. I may not ever see him again!"

"And?" Martha finally started walking down the stairs.

"And he just never even tol' me. Hid it from me even when everyone else knew."

"That's not so bad now, Nora," Martha said. "I mean, there are worse things."

"Yes," Nora admitted, "I suppose there are. But I always trusted him to be honest with me." Nora stopped on the bottom stair and looked both ways to see if anyone was in the hall. One of the sitting rooms was across from the staircase, but it, too, was empty.

"And so your brother is in America, is he?"

"I think so. Or on his way, at least."

"Might be better off there," offered Martha. "America is the place where the Irish go when they have nothing else."

"But he had me," said Nora.

"Aye," said Martha. "Perhaps that's the real issue, isn't it? Perhaps it's yer brother you are mad at and not yer…" Martha stopped midsentence.

"Colin," Nora said. "His name is Colin." She looked at the corner clock to see that it was already five after six. She walked quickly down the hall, hoping to pull Martha along.

"Well, maybe Colin is not totally at fault." Martha said from behind. It was very hard to get Martha to hurry when she was chatting.

"Maybe," said Nora. "But I am still angry at him."

"Is he handsome?" asked Martha.

"I suppose," said Nora, though it was a little bit of a lie. *He's the most handsome boy I know,* she thought.

"Then I wouldn't stay mad for long," said Martha. She paused to look at herself in a gold-framed mirror. *Hurry up!* Nora thought. Martha fixed her hair

KATRINA NOWAK

in the mirror and added, "But if it makes you feel better, I'll be mad at him as well, until you decide not to be cross anymore."

Nora smiled. "Thanks, Martha. Now let's go!" It still amazed her that the residence was so large it could take minutes to traverse from one room to another.

"And I would write that brother of yers a nasty letter," she said. "It was more his place to tell you than yer Colin's."

Nora hadn't considered that before, but Martha's logic made a lot of sense. She slowed her step.

"Did he just up and leave?" Martha asked.

Nora thought back to her grandfather's wake and his burial. Seamus had certainly hinted that he was going to America. Maybe she should have paid closer attention to him. "He might have. He was tryin' to convince me to go, but I was so scared at the thought of having to leave Ireland altogether—"

"—that you didn't listen to what he was really sayin'," Martha chimed in.

"Right. In truth," Nora admitted, "it doesn't really surprise me that he left."

"Just hurt you that he didn't tell you," said Martha. "I don't judge you, Nora. But I, for one, wish at least some of me brothers would head to America. I've got nine of 'em, you know. An' if they didn't eat so much, who knows, maybe I could be livin' at home still."

Nora looked at her roommate and smiled. Before she knew it, a laugh escaped.

"I'm tellin' you, it's like feeding a pack of wild animals," Martha said, lightheartedly. "No food and no peace. I'm serious!"

"Good morning Miss McMahon, Miss Murphy!" Nora jumped at the sound of Mr. Dunham's cheerful voice.

"Good morning, Mr. Dunham," said Martha.

"On yer way to the kitchen, I presume?" He said, checking his pocket watch.

"Yes, Mr. Dunham," said Nora, her face blushing. "We're running a little late."

But Mr. Dunham didn't seem to care. "You're in luck. Fresh biscuits this morning," he said. "And how are you this morning, Miss McMahon? Feeling all right?"

"Yes, of course," Nora replied. He winked at her, and the ever-observant Martha grinned. She had noticed the wink, too. He put a finger to his lips and smiled again.

As he was about to depart he turned again and looked at Nora. "Miss McMahon, dear," he said, "your little pendant has broken." He pointed to the small piece of metal that remained on the chain around her neck.

"I know," she said sadly. "It happened during our little adventure."

"What a shame," he said. "I could see if I could get you a new one. The Twelve Apostles of Ireland are not hard to come by."

"But it was me grandda's," she said sadly, "And Senan is gone now. That was his saint."

"Well let's look to see who's left," Mr. Dunham said, and took the small piece of metal in his hand. The break in the metal was jagged quite sharp.

"Seems he must have rubbed it between his fingers for years, the way you always do," he said. "Wore the metal right down to nothing. 'Twas not just because of your adventure, it would have probably happened anyway." Nora wasn't convinced.

"Let's see," he continued. "We still have Brendan the Navigator, Ninnidh, Ciaran, Mobhi—he's a Dublin man, you know. We've got Glasnevin cemetery right here in Dublin, named after his order." He looked closely at the pendant. "And it appears we also still have Columba." He stared intently at the remains of the pendant. "'Tis hard to see." He turned the pendant over in his hand.

"Which Columba?" asked Martha.

"Excellent question," said Mr. Dunham thoughtfully. At last he smiled. "Looks like Columba of Iona. What good fortune to still have 'im on board with you."

Nora looked down at the pendant in Mr. Dunham's calloused hands. It looked more natural in his hands, as that was how she always remembered it—

in the rough and gnarly hands of her grandfather.

"But no Senan," Nora said.

"Perhaps not," replied Mr. Dunham. He released the pendant, and it fell again around Nora's neck. "But Senan was your grandda's protector. Who is yers?"

"I don't know," said Nora.

"Well, you've got a few to choose from. One of them is surely looking out for you." His voice got quiet, and he leaned down close to Nora. "There's not too many other explanations for how you returned to us without a scratch. Particularly when they were searching high and low for you and yer cargo." He stood up again. "Might want to figure out who it is who is watching out for you. Always good to know these things. I, myself, am rooting for Columba." He winked again.

"Aye," said Martha, whose eyes were wide.

"Well, girls, I must be going. Go and enjoy a few biscuits before they all end up on other peoples' breakfast plates," he said and laughed.

When he was out of sight, the girls continued the last few steps toward the kitchen. Although they were unenthusiastic to begin another day of work, the delightful aroma of biscuits enticed them into the kitchen.

"So who do you think it is?" asked Martha, wide-eyed, as she stepped into the black-and-white tiled floor. The tiles were covered in flour and footprints. More cleaning.

"I don't know," said Nora. "I'm not sure I even believe in all that."

"What?" shrieked Martha.

"Shhh!" said Nora.

"How can you not believe in it?" she said.

"I don't know."

"If it was good enough for your grandda, it is good enough for you!" she replied. "He surely thought someone was protectin' him." Nora watched as they tracked flour behind them.

"Aye," said Nora, "but our world is different. We live in different times."

"But some things are still worth believin'," said Martha. "Ain't that why we're in the situation we're in anyways?"

"What do you mean?" asked Nora.

"If our religion wasn't worth believin' in," said Martha, "we wouldn't be here in the first place, would we? We'd be like the English, and we'd go to proper schools, and we'd be like Ulster, content to be ruled by London. But we aren't, are we?"

Nora stopped short. Martha's comment had taken her by surprise. Though her friend had not spent a single day in any formal education, this was the second time that morning she had challenged Nora's thinking. It was that ancient Irish wisdom she had been missing since the day she buried her grandfather.

Chapter 38

August 5, 1914: Rathmines, Dublin, Ireland

Nora stared at the countertops near the oven. They were caked with crumbs and flour, but no sign of biscuits. She frowned. "It seems this room was recently occupied by a bunch of stable hands!" said Martha, sounding annoyed. Dirt had been trekked across the floor of the baking room and mixed with the flour from the morning baking, the rear door still swung slightly, and most telling—all of the warm biscuits were gone.

"Late again!" said Martha in an exasperated voice. "If only you had spilled yer gossip right away and not made me work for it. Now, no biscuits!"

Nora put a finger to her mouth. "Shhhh!" She walked up to the swinging door and put an ear to it. "They're still here!" she mouthed.

Martha grinned impishly and tiptoed—though it still sounded to Nora like heavy, boot-laden footsteps—toward the door. She peeked through the crack. "It's James," she whispered. "You want some biscuits?"

Nora smiled and nodded.

An instant later, Martha crashed through the door. "All right—hand 'em over!" she said. As one of thirteen children, Martha was well practiced in fighting over food.

Nora waited on the other side of the door and anticipated a commotion. When she heard nothing else, she peered around the corner. She spied a group of the stable boys and Martha, all huddled around a copy of the *Irish Independent*. James slowly read aloud to the group between mouthfuls of biscuit. "With Prime Minister Asquith's ultimatum unanswered by Berlin, England declared war on Germany, effective four August. England has begun preparations for full mobilization. The King's Army will begin to depart for the continent before the month's end, and all reserves have been called to service."

"And what of the Irish?" said Martha. Her eyes were wide.

"Redmond promised our services—the bastard," said Joseph. "Keep reading, James."

"That's all it says," said James, and he shrugged his shoulders.

"Read another article," said Martha. "How about this one?"

"I don't have the energy to start another one," said James. "And I certainly don't have the energy to go to war on behalf of the bloody King! No, thank you, I'll stay right here. I'll shovel Irish shite over British shite any day."

"Aye," came a chorus from the stable hands.

"Have a biscuit, Nora," said James, handing her a plate of what remained of the morning's baked goods. "Need to keep you well fed for the next gunrunnin'." He winked at her.

"Let's keep that to ourselves, shall we?" she said, taking a biscuit. She had never spent any time with the stable boys. She barely knew their names, thanks to Mrs. Finnegan's strict rules on socializing. As she bit into her biscuit a loud bell sounded across the residence. It took everyone by surprise.

"What on earth?" started Nora.

"The bell," said Martha. Her eyes were wide. "They only ring it when there's trouble."

"What kind of trouble?"

"Usually trouble with the staff," said James. He eyed Nora and wiped the biscuit crumbs from his chin.

"Someone's gonna get fired," said Joseph. "And we'll all have to stand around and watch as they parade 'em by. Remember when Lucille got caught stealing jewelry? The coppers drug her out screamin'." The boys nodded. A horrified look came over Martha's face.

Nora felt her heart sink as all eyes rested on her. *They know,* she thought to herself. *The Parsons know.*

"Maybe they only know some of yer secrets," Martha said. She didn't sound too hopeful.

"We'll protect you, Nora. If they try to fire you, we'll all quit!" said James.

"Aye!" said Joseph.

"That's silly," said Nora. "You all will stand there with yer mouths shut and pretend to be shocked an' horrified. Otherwise they'll suspect us all!"

"You should hide, then," said Martha. "Don't show up."

"Nonsense," said Nora. "I'll take what's comin' to me." In her mind she began to think how to protect Michael and his Volunteers. They would find out pretty quickly that she was connected to them through Colin. Would Mr. Dunham be implicated too?

In the hall, they could hear staff members scurry along the tile floors.

"We best be going," said Joseph. "Can't be late."

"Maybe it's something else," said James. "But I'd hang in the back all the same, see if you can make a run for it."

The stable boys quickly departed the pantry via the back entrance, leaving Martha and Nora by themselves. "Well, come on then," said Nora. The girls made their way through the kitchen and into the main hall, where a crowd of house staff were gathering in front of the main staircase near the entrance. Nora had never seen the entire staff assembled in one area before. There were almost two dozen employees, including the stable hands and gardeners.

Nora and Martha were some of the last to arrive and hung near the back. Nora stood on her toes and tried to make eye contact with Mr. Dunham, who nervously twirled his fraying mustache as he reviewed the assembled crowd.

Nora felt a tug at her sleeve. "Girls!" Nora saw Mrs. Finnegan's beady eyes glaring at her. "To the front!" She and Martha reluctantly obeyed and made their way to the very front. Nora looked over toward Mr. Dunham. He nodded to her, but she didn't feel reassured. Around her, everyone chattered in hushed whispers. The entire group seemed nervous. Nora slumped and eyed the ground. Already her new shoes looked scuffed. It made her feel a little better— they felt more familiar now that they were no longer shiny and new. Less rigid, less confining.

She thought of Colin. Would she see him when they brought her in for questioning? Would he have time to run? She looked around the entryway and remembered how she had felt when she first walked through those massive doors just a week before. So much had happened in such a short amount of time. She could clearly remember what Colin had said to her that day. *Don't ever, ever be ashamed of who you are or where you came from.* She looked up at the staircase and stood up straight. She was glad she was in the front. She wanted them to know she was not afraid.

Over the lull of the hushed voices, she heard Mr. Dunham clear his throat. Instantly, the murmurs and whispers ceased, and an eerie silence fell over the hall. A lone set of footsteps—firm leather soles on the polished tile above— sounded through the hall. Mr. Thomas Parsons came into view on the floor above them. He surveyed the crowd below and descended halfway down the stairs.

He had an air of authority over the staff. He stood tall and dignified and commanded everyone's attention. Nora had seen him several times throughout the residence, but she had never before heard him speak. His voice boomed in a low, confident tone. "Good morning. I address you this morning because something unprecedented has occurred."

Nora could feel her heart beating fast. A week ago, she had been a new, obedient member of the staff. Now, she was probably the first young girl on the staff who had beaten a member of the King's Army with a wrench or helped to arm Ireland's young men for insurrection. Unprecedented was probably the right word.

"Yesterday afternoon, in the great halls of Westminster, our government declared war on Germany."

Martha breathed an audible sigh of relief and murmured, "Oh, thank the Lord. Just the war."

Nora tried not to laugh at how ridiculous that sounded, though she couldn't help but feel the same. She glanced at Mr. Dunham, who looked no less serious. Clearly, this news bothered him.

"Please recall that we are one Ireland under the Crown," continued Mr. Parsons, "and we will follow our King to war as loyally as our brothers across the Irish Sea." He paused as if he expected applause or agreement with this statement, but the entryway remained quiet. Even Mrs. Finnegan, who usually commanded the housekeeping staff to follow every Parson instruction with vigor and enthusiasm, stood quiet. The stern crookedness of her face looked even more angry than usual. Nora smiled to herself. *So she does have a heartbeat—at least when it comes to Ireland.* She tucked this bit of knowledge away.

Mr. Parsons continued. "And every able-bodied man on the staff is highly encouraged to enlist to support the King's Army. We, too, shall make our sacrifices for England! Any staff member who enlists will be returned to his full employment upon completing his enlistment term. I give you my word." Murmurs erupted among the crowd but were quickly hushed by Mr. Dunham.

"We hope to be finished with this business of war by the new year. With your fervent support of this effort, I have no doubt that the manor will be returned to its usual operations by early spring." Appearing to sense that his staff was less jubilant than he, Mr. Parsons immediately turned and ascended the staircase.

Again, the clip of his leather soles against the tile floors sounded across the quiet hall.

As soon as his footsteps faded, Martha turned to Nora. "So let me get this straight—his sacrifice is to be light on staff for a few months, and ours is to fill the ranks of the King's Army." She shook her head. "Something seems off—I can't quite put my finger on it..." Nora smiled and suppressed a laugh. She expected them to feel the glare of Mrs. Finnegan, but although the old lady had obviously heard Martha, she had chosen not to respond. Nora eyed her. Perhaps she had not given old Finnegan enough credit.

"There is one more announcement!" Mr. Dunham was standing on the first step of the staircase. "One more announcement, please!"

Again, the chatter died down. There was a common respect for Mr. Dunham across all of the staff—one that Finnegan did not seem to command.

He looked around the hall and smiled. "Speaking of sacrifices," he said quietly, then raised his voice: "Mr. and Mrs. Ethan Parsons will be passing an extended stay at the residence beginning Friday, and they intend to stay for the duration of the conflict."

An audible moan ran through the staff. "Maybe enlisting isn't such a bad idea," one of the boys said loudly. Neither Mr. Dunham or Mrs. Finnegan corrected him, and laughs echoed across the hall.

Mr. Dunham raised his hand to silence the group. "I understand if your... patriotism, shall we say, therefore calls you to enlist," he said. "But for those of us who must stay, due either to age or gender, please be mindful of this arrangement, and assist in what will be a monumental preparation for their arrival and stay."

Mr. Dunham looked quite serious, and a depressed silence hung over the hall. Nora, in contrast, felt so relieved that she wasn't in police custody, she almost felt guilty.

"What a way to destroy a perfectly good day," said Martha gloomily as the staff dispersed. "Don't get me wrong, Nora," she said, "I'm glad you aren't going to jail and all, but I'm not sure I can live through another visit by the likes of Ethan and Suzanne Parsons."

"What's so awful about them?" asked Nora.

Martha rolled her eyes. "Everything. Has 'is own regiment in the Ulster Volunteers. Got blood on his hands. Practically orchestrated putting down the strikes last year and fillin' Glasnevin Cemetery with the sufferin' families of Dublin. Rumor has it that he's killed a man with his own hands just for bein' poor and tryin' to do somethin' about it. But if all of that's not enough to make your stomach turn, he's just an arse. And 'is wife could keep the entire staff busy all day with her silly requests. 'More tea, less tea, open the windows, close the windows!' I could go on and on."

Nora's thoughts returned to her little notebook, hidden away under her mattress. The Ulstermen were keeping tabs on the Irish Volunteers—but who was keeping track of the Ulster Volunteers? Surely, two could play at this game.

"Oh—and one more thing," said Martha. "He's got a bad case of wanderin' hands, if you know what I mean. Likes nothin' better than a young housekeeper who can't say nothin' for fear of losin' her job and her reputation."

Nora heard Martha as she droned on, but her mind was focused on her little notebook and the opportunity that Ethan's arrival presented.

CHAPTER 39

August 6, 1914: Dublin, Ireland

It was a brilliant summer morning. The grasses were speckled with dew, and the heat hadn't yet cast its pall over the city. Once the sun heated the streets, the smells of the tenements would again fester and overtake the neighborhoods along the Liffey.

Mrs. Finnegan marched her housekeepers in orderly columns along Sackville Street. The looming steeple of the Pro-Cathedral stood in the distance. This long walk from the Parsons to town was the only time Nora had been on an authorized excursion since arriving at the Parsons. With the exception of her midnight crimes on behalf of Ireland, she had found herself quite locked away in Rathmines. It was an odd existence, after living her entire life outdoors. The Parsons would likely not consider her quaint Clare cottage to be an actual, habitable building.

Though it was a Thursday morning, Mrs. Finnegan was in her Sunday best, save the same stern look that adorned her face every day of the week. Whether she was scolding girls for lackluster dusting, greeting guests to the Parsons residence, or undertaking her favorite duty—walking the girls to Mass—Mrs. Finnegan always looked like a hornet ready to strike.

"Step lively, girls!" she called. "We shan't be late for the Lord!" The five girls of the Parsons housekeeping staff walked along obediently, though perhaps more leisurely than Mrs. Finnegan would have hoped.

Nora relished the cool morning air. She breathed it in, hoping that it would rid her of the knot that had plagued her stomach since the night of the gunrunning, when she'd learned that Colin had helped to send her brother to America when she needed him most. Maybe forever.

Martha stepped along next to Nora and tapped her lightly on the shoulder, waking her from her thoughts. She gestured to the column of boys about a hundred yards behind them. The stable hands and gardeners marched along in a decidedly more jovial manner, led by Mr. Dunham, who ran a looser, more lively procession to church. At that moment, he looked toward Nora and smiled. She smiled back weakly. Had he known about Seamus as well? She shook her head. He wouldn't have kept that from her—or would he have? She had been tricked before into thinking that she knew someone's character. She wasn't sure if she could trust her intuition anymore.

Usually the staff attended a local church closer to the residence, but with the war on, Mr. Parsons had granted the morning off because he had it on good authority that Father McKinney at the Pro-Cathedral would be devoting his homily to John Redmond's promise—that Ireland would supply its boys to the war effort. It was a controversial promise at best, and Nora was certain that it would hold no sway with the ardent nationalists whose company she kept. Some of the boys, particularly those who had avoided politics up to this point, could likely be persuaded by the promise of adventure and a full belly. But many knew better.

Mrs. Finnegan, on the other hand, had happily accepted the responsibility of leading the staff march to the Pro-Cathedral to get their daily dose of Jesus, and was not dissuaded in the least by the fact that the service would double as a call to arms.

Staring up at the high steeple, Nora recalled how, just a few days ago, she had stood almost at that very spot and thought of her grandfather, just before mischievously sneaking into Colin's automobile. She touched the pendant that hung around her neck, now just a broken piece of what it had been. St. Senan was completely gone, and just a few of the Twelve Apostles remained. *I've almost nothing left of Grandda*, she thought. She felt no more assured that she was following the right path, or any identifiable path at all for that matter. The weeks since his death might as well have been a lifetime.

Mrs. Finnegan marched up to the door of the cathedral and ushered the girls in one by one. As Nora took her turn and stepped into the church, the bright summer day disappeared, replaced by the dark, dreary interior of the church. With a slender, bony finger, Mrs. Finnegan pointed to one of the pews in the back, and the girls obediently genuflected and slid in. They seemed relieved for a break from the long walk into Dublin proper. When the first pew was full, Mrs. Finnegan motioned for Nora and Martha to file in behind the rest of the girls. Martha smiled at Nora, not believing their luck, but quickly wiped it from her face under Mrs. Finnegan's stern look, which warned them that no one was going to be having any fun.

The girls mechanically got to their knees as they waiting for the opening processional. The various stages of a church service were so ingrained in their minds that every step was habit, and they thought not at all about what they did. Each action was rote.

The church was full, but it felt unnaturally quiet. Everyone sat in anticipation of what the priest might say to lure their men to a foreign war. The old pews creaked as their occupants waited restlessly. The row behind her was especially creaky as the boys clumsily moved into the pew, shoes scuffing the kneelers and wayward elbows and knees bumping against one another.

The organ broke the silence with dreary tones that signaled the beginning of the Mass. The girls rose from their kneelers to their feet and watched as the priest and altar boys in their long robes, much too hot for a summer day, slowly made their way up the aisle to the sanctuary. The stern look on Mrs. Finnegan's face had finally relaxed. This place that brought Nora such internal conflict seemed to be Mrs. Finnegan's only source of peace.

As anticipated, the priest seemed eager to discuss the opportunity for Ireland's boys to enlist in the British Army. He opened in English to ensure the young men in the pews understood his message. "We welcome with joy the youths among us and pray that they might be drawn to fight for the righteous and the oppressed!"

"So much for waiting for the homily," Martha whispered to Nora, rolling her eyes.

"No vocations?" whispered Nora. "I thought we were to pray for vocations on Thursdays!"

Martha stifled a giggle. "I'll pray for yer vocation if you pray for mine."

"Don't you dare!" said Nora. "If you pray for a vocation for me, I'll pray for you to marry an Englishman!"

The organ interrupted their jests, reverberating a melancholy sound throughout the congregation as the opening song began and the church was filled with soft, mumbled singing. Only Mrs. Finnegan seemed to be singing with any volume, her overly enthusiastic soprano drowning out the less eager parishioners around her.

Nora stood and listened to Martha's soft voice singing, and though she knew all the words by heart she could not bring herself to participate. She was watching Mrs. Finnegan's starched black dress move in rigid, wrinkle-free motions as she belted out the song. A light tap on her shoulder startled her attention away. She turned to Martha, but she was still dutifully singing, paying no attention to Nora.

Nora reached her hand to her shoulder, wondering if she had imagined it and felt another hand lay gently on hers.

She snapped her head around. Colin stood behind her, an apologetic smile shining through his several-days-old beard.

She felt a scowl come across her face and abruptly turned back to face the altar. *How dare he?* Her face felt hot as she stewed.

"I need to talk to you," he whispered. She didn't turn, but instead shook her head firmly. "No," she said aloud.

Martha glanced over and stopped singing. "What?" she mouthed. "Am I way off key?"

Nora again shook her head and gestured over her shoulder. Martha looked back, but turned back with a puzzled face.

"Colin," Nora mouthed.

At once, Martha's eyes lit up and she turned back to Colin.

"Tell her I need to speak to her," he murmured to Martha, though it was obvious Nora could hear him as well. "It's important."

"The hell you do," whispered Martha loudly. Then, turning to Nora, and thinking she was whispering, "You're right! He's a handsome bloke!" Nora felt her face turn even redder as Martha turned back to her songbook, which she couldn't read a word of, and began singing loudly. Mrs. Finnegan turned around at the sudden volume coming from behind her, and seeing Martha's nose in the music, nodded approvingly and faced the front again.

The song came to an end, and the service began. Nora opened her Bible to the appropriate page and tried to forget that Colin was a mere three feet behind her.

"Want me to smack 'im?" Martha whispered to Nora.

"No," she replied. "Not just yet."

At the next prayer, Colin knelt as far forward as he could on his kneeler and again whispered. "Nora, I need you to talk to me. This is the only place where I can see you."

Nora looked back at him. She wished the sight of him didn't make her heart beat faster. "If you weren't so afraid of your cousin, you could see me any time you wanted!"

"I'm not here to fight with you," he whispered.

Mrs. Finnegan wheeled around in time to see the girls kneeling in prayer, but nothing else. She cleared her throat.

Colin redoubled his efforts during the next hymn. "Nora, I'm sorry. Please talk to me."

By now, all the boys in the pew behind Nora were quite interested in what was going on. She wanted to melt into the floor, but she knelt as tall as she could with her short stature.

"Nora," he said softly. "Please. There's somethin' goin' on that you should know about. Meet me after Mass, and I'll tell you about it. And then I won't come lookin' for you again. I promise."

Nora could hear the seriousness in his voice. For once, he was trying to include her in what he was up to, but she was too angry with him to hear him out. She turned around. "You've done enough Colin. You've robbed me of my family, you've lied to me, and worst—" Martha elbowed her, and Nora snapped back to the front.

Mrs. Finnegan looked over her shoulder again and scanned the pews. All the young staff seated behind her had their music books over their faces and appeared to be singing. Nora, peeking over her hymnal, caught her frown, but couldn't tell if that was a normal frown or a more serious frown. They all looked the same. Mrs. Finnegan returned to her singing.

"And worst—" Nora continued, snapping back around without regard to Mrs. Finnegan, "you didn't think I was grown up enough to know what you were planning for me brother. I had a right to know. I've earned me right to know and to make me own decisions!"

James, who was sitting next to Colin, whispered, "Damned right, Nora."

Colin looked at him incredulously, as if wondering who had the gall to both swear in church and challenge him all in one breath. James just nodded and

340

returned to what was becoming a rousing rendition of *Saint Patrick is our Hope* as the boys did their best to drown out Colin's attempts to speak to Nora. She was, after all, now famous among the staff and, in their eyes, deserving of this gesture.

"Nora—" Colin began.

"Leave me alone," she said. "Just leave me alone. You've done enough."

At this, Colin finally fell silent.

Father McKinney, once he apparently felt he had inspired his audience with a Gaelic verse of the popular Irish song of Saint Patrick, began to speak again about the war. By now, all of Dublin was aware John Redmond had promised that Ireland would supply boys to the British war effort. It was a politician's barter meant to secure Home Rule for all of Ireland. But Parliament had yet to respond with a vote. Many in Dublin thought it was another ploy—just another trick by Westminster to get Ireland to behave in return for nothing. Father McKinney was clearly in the John Redmond camp. Many of his generation were. The pew behind Nora, however, which consisted mostly of ragged boys from the far corners of the island who had wandered to Dublin because they had no other choice, were categorically opposed. As the priest spoke, Mr. Dunham did nothing to quiet their grumbling.

Midway through the priest's carefully crafted homily, Colin leaned forward again. "Would you have me join up? Put on a British uniform?"

Without thinking, Nora said, "If it means you'd leave me alone, yes. Go off an' fight for yer enemy."

Martha looked at her with big brown eyes. She looked horrified. Nora instantly felt awful. She turned around just in time to see the cathedral door close and Colin's seat vacant. She slumped in her pew.

Martha was still gazing at her wide-eyed. "You don't think he's going to do it, do you?"

Any other day, Nora would have no doubt that Colin would stay in Ireland. But today, she could not be so sure. "I don't know, Martha," she said.

Mrs. Finnegan cleared her throat.

Nora looked down at her pendant and wanted to cry. She felt a pair of eyes on her, and turned around to see Mr. Dunham, watching her as she clung to her pendant.

CHAPTER 40

August 7, 1914: Rathmines, Dublin, Ireland

Nora dipped her brush into the wash bucket, shook off the excess water, and resumed her scrubbing. Despite what Mrs. Finnegan had claimed, the library floors simply could not shine. No matter how often she cleaned them, within the hour they looked dull and trafficked.

She looked at her swollen, pruney hands. *That's it*, she muttered to herself. She dropped the brush back in the bucket and wiped her hands on her apron. The floors would have to be good enough.

She got to her feet and picked up her cleaning rags. The French doors that led to the veranda were wide open, and the room swirled with a refreshing outdoor breeze that carried in the sounds of the outdoors—the birds, the carriages that drove by. Outside the walls of the manor, Rathmines was a pleasant neighborhood.

As she walked toward the massive doors that opened into the hall, she heard a faint raspy noise from the front drive. Her heart raced, and a chill ran down her spine. She stopped and listened. Nothing.

Perhaps she had imagined it. She took another few steps and then heard it again—the distinct raspy bark that had echoed in her nightmares since she had been a child. She froze in her steps and heard a crash. Water seeped into her shoes. She looked down and saw that she had dropped her bucket. The dirty water spilled across the floor.

"Nora!" came an angry shout. "What is the meaning of this?" Mrs. Finnegan stood at the library doorway.

"Sorry, Mrs. Finnegan," she stammered. "I wasn't paying attention."

"Get it cleaned up!" she said, frantically. "They have arrived!" Mrs. Finnegan quickly disappeared from the doorway, and Nora could hear her tiny footsteps echoing down the hall. *Ethan Parsons.*

As the cleaning rags absorbed the water, she ran over to the open window. A motorcar, laden with trunks, was parked in the drive. A tall, well-dressed man stood in the front yard. Puffs of smoke from his pipe rose above his top hat. Mr. Dunham opened the passenger door to the automobile, and a woman, dressed in a spectacular lavender dress and matching fascinator, stepped out into the bright sunshine.

But Nora saw all of this from the corner of her eye. Her attention was focused on the dogs that frolicked in the yard. Red and white setters. Her hair stood on end.

"Pssst! Nora. Nora!" Martha stood at the open door. "What are you doin' in here? Are you crazy? Now's the time to be scarce, not hangin' around askin' to be noticed! Quick!" Martha tugged at Nora, who tore herself from the window. "Hangin' out the window, gawkin'. You're goin' to end up with a mountain of new chores. Come on!"

The girls were escaping toward the back of the house when they ran directly into Mrs. Finnegan, who was still scurrying about, this time on her way she to greet the guests.

"Nora!" she called in that choking little voice that always seemed to turn any name into an obnoxious noise. "I trust you've cleaned up yer mess."

"Yes, Mrs. Finnegan," Nora replied. Martha pulled on her sleeves, urging her to keep moving down the hallway.

But a frown descended on Mrs. Finnegan's face. "Glad I ran into you again. I'm not sure what you've done, but for some reason, God only knows, Miss Evelyn has taken a liking to you." Mrs. Finnegan looked Nora over disapprovingly. "You'll need to fix yer hair, Miss McMahon," she said. "It looks half wild!"

Nora was tempted to say, "Thank you," but was able to stop herself.

But she must have grinned, anyway, because Mrs. Finnegan erupted. "What are you smirking about? Best wipe that silly smile off yer face," she said. She lowered her voice to almost a whisper. "Because you have been selected to serve as Suzanne Parsons's first maid while she is here on her visit." For a moment, Mrs. Finnegan looked almost sad for Nora. "And the woman is not, shall we say, easy to wait on," she said. "But I expect nothing less than the finest service you can offer. It would be dangerous to get on her bad side, if you know what I mean."

Nora nodded. She knew exactly what Mrs. Finnegan meant.

"Follow me. Both of you." The girls obediently followed behind, but at a distance. Mrs. Finnegan's frail little legs moved at an unnaturally quick pace.

"Suzanne is a real treat, I'll tell you," Martha said quietly. "There's not a thing you can do to be on her good side. I was her first maid the last time they had an extended visit. Thought Mrs. Parsons was goin' to send me home."

If the excitement and bustle of the previous week had been unusual, in a matter of minutes, the mansion had sprung into a frenzy. The staff scurried about, many trying just to get out of the way, while still others jostled to take their positions in the entrance hall, ready to receive the enormous amount of luggage that was sure to accompany the junior Mr. and Mrs. Parsons. Nora witnessed a gardener jumping out a window to avoid the scene, not trusting himself to get to a back door in time to avoid the grand arrival.

Mrs. Finnegan positioned the girls in the entry hall with the gathering staff just as the massive front doors were flung open. Nora jumped, then froze as the three setters ran into the house, barking and howling as though on the hunt. The man she had seen in the drive entered the home, arms outstretched.

"Oh, my dear Ethan!" cried Mrs. Parsons as she descended down the stairs. "How lovely to see you! And you are early—what a wonderful surprise!"

"Wonderful, indeed," Martha murmured, sarcastically.

Half a second later, the woman in the lavender dress walked through the doorway, led by Mr. Dunham. Nora had never seen such fancy attire, and for traveling at that. After her came the luggage—trunk after trunk, piled high.

"Mother, dear," Ethan finally spoke. His voice was deep and his posh, drawling accent seemed contrived. "I hope you haven't put me in the Gardenia Room. I was dreadfully uncomfortable there last year."

"Darling, take whatever room you like!" said Mrs. Parsons. "I want you both to be comfortable."

Just then, Mrs. Parsons made eye contact with Nora. "Suzanne!" she said to the woman in the lavender dress, "You must meet our new housekeeper, Nora!"

Nora felt herself shrink. She wished she could disappear into the wall behind her. Instead, she heard herself say, "How do you do, Mrs. Parsons?"

"Nora, is it?" the woman in lavender said, in a soft voice, almost inaudible. Nora had to lean in close to hear her. "I trust you are more skilled than your colleague." She cast a judgmental eye toward Martha, whose cool gaze remained unchanged.

"Lovely to see you again," Martha said.

Ethan frowned.

"Nora will be your first maid for your stay, dear," said Mrs. Parsons. "I'm sure you'll find her just lovely."

"Let us hope," said Suzanne, smiling pretentiously at Nora. The girls watched as mother and daughter-in-law strode up the massive staircase arm in arm. The men followed, and Mrs. Finnegan snapped at the girls to grab the handbags that sat in the entry.

"Not you!" said Mrs. Finnegan, glaring at Martha. Martha backed away from the bags. Nora grabbed what looked to be Suzanne's bag, and, as she ascended the staircase, overheard Ethan say to his father, "Why is that dreadful Martha still employed here?"

Nora had never used these stairs before, and by the time she got to the top, she felt dizzy looking down over the banister. But she moved as quickly as she could through the upstairs hall, given the load she was carrying.

Mrs. Finnegan stopped at the Lilac Room. "Ethan will be staying here," she said, motioning toward the room. "And Suzanne will be staying in the Rose Room."

Both rooms were massive suites with a private connecting hallway between them. Nora had thought her own bedroom was the finest she had ever seen— until she had begun her housekeeping duties and seen the larger suites in the house. They were dazzling, each decorated with the finest window dressings and matching paper on the walls. Best of all, every room had large windows or verandas to look out on picturesque gardens in the rear of the residence, which is why, Nora supposed, they were all named for flowers. How someone could not be comfortable in one of them was beyond her.

"Thank you, Mrs. Finnegan," Nora said, approaching the Rose Room doorway. "Mrs. Parsons," she said from the doorway. "I have yer handbag. We'll have the rest of yer luggage to you shortly. Where shall I place it?"

Suzanne, who was propped carelessly on the pink satin bed linens, gave her an exhausted look. "Please place it in the wardrobe."

Nora quickly obeyed, hoping to make her exit as soon as possible. She reached for the brass handles on the mahogany door and slipped the leather bag inside. "Will you be needin' anything else, Mrs. Parsons?"

"Not at this time," she said. "Now, please leave me to rest."

"Of course, Mrs. Parsons," Nora said, happy to be leaving.

"Laura!" Suzanne called after her. Nora decided she wouldn't correct her.

"Please inform my husband that I am too tired for tea today. I wish not to be disturbed until dinner. You can unpack my luggage while I am dining."

"Yes, Mrs. Parsons," she said, exiting the room. She walked briskly down the hall to the Lilac Room. The door was still open, so she knocked gingerly. Her breath caught as she spied the dreaded dogs milling about the room. They growled a cold greeting.

"Excuse me, Mr. Parsons?" she said, peering around the door. Ethan appeared at the sound of her voice.

"Nora," he said, "what can I do for you?" His baritone voice was hair-raising.

"Mrs. Parsons wished me to tell you that she is too tired to join you for tea but will be happy to join you for dinner later this evening."

"Very well," he said. "Thank you."

"Yes, Mr. Parsons." She turned to leave.

"Nora," he called, stopping her. "Do come here for a moment. I wish to be properly introduced to you. Where are you from? You weren't here when I last visited."

She swallowed hard, never looking away from the dogs. "County Clare, sir."

"Clare, is it?" he asked, but Nora knew he didn't intend for her to answer. "Is that where that lovely little brogue is from?"

Again, Nora remained silent. She hoped that Mrs. Finnegan would call her or that Martha would crash into something—anything that would give her an excuse to leave.

"All the way from Clare?" he said, almost in disbelief. "I've been down there just once. A long time ago—maybe a decade. Unpleasant business." The floor-to-ceiling windows were wide open, but no breeze fluttered into the stale room. "No housekeepers to be found closer than Country Clare? Well, never mind, then, you are here now."

She nodded, hoping he would ask her to leave.

Instead he beckoned her toward the window. "Come here for a moment, Nora. Cast your eyes on these beautiful gardens."

Apprehensively, she walked over to him, hugging the wall and keeping half an eye on the setters. She peered out the closest window and into the garden below. Rows and rows of carefully manicured flowerbeds spread out all the way to the stables. The flowers were in peak season, and the colors were dazzling in the afternoon sun.

"I have spent many, many afternoons of my life looking out at these gardens," he said. "And each year, they seem to me more spectacular than the last. There really is nothing like home, is there Nora?"

"No, sir," she said. To her, the view looked more like a painting than an actual landscape. Nothing about the Parsons seemed like real life. Before she knew it, Ethan had moved close to her. She could feel his hot, alcohol-laced breath on the back of her neck.

"I am pleased you've come to stay here, Nora," he said softly. His voice had turned eerie and soft. She looked over her shoulder as the dogs approached him.

"Are you afraid of my dogs?" he asked.

Nora did not know how to answer his question, but wanted to end this encounter as quickly as possible

"You mustn't be afraid of them." She cringed as his hand touched the small of her back, then glided up toward her shoulders and instinctively swatted his hand away. He caught her wrist and gripped it tightly, then twisted it to get her attention. She stood perfectly still as he looked down at her. A look of rage descended on his face, but then subsided. He continued his previous thought, pulling her in close to him and speaking in an unnerving whisper. "They'll not hurt you, Nora, so long as you treat them well. They're really quite docile. And best of all, they're from Clare, like you. Second generation given to me by a dear family friend."

Nora felt her body tense. "I must be tending to Mrs. Parsons." She abruptly stepped to the side and almost into the purple and white drape.

"No need to rush away," said Ethan indifferently, as if this type of exchange with a housekeeper was routine for him. He released her from his grip. "I'm glad to have been properly introduced to you, Nora."

Nora felt a surge of anger. She stood as straight as she could and stared up at him, matching the intensity of his gaze.

"My God," he said, in astonishment. His voice was suddenly meek. "You have the most beautiful eyes."

With no regard for protocol, she turned and walked toward the door. She could hear his footsteps following her. But before she reached the doorway, his hand seized her arm and whirled her around with such force that she almost fell to the ground. She found herself face to face with him once again. His stale, alcohol-laced breath was nauseating.

"Please come fetch me for tea, Nora" he said quietly, his soft voice in terrifying contrast to his brutal grip on her arm. "I should be so pleased to see you again this afternoon."

She forced herself to say, "Yes, Mr. Parsons."

To her surprise, he let her go.

CHAPTER 41

August 8, 1914: London, England

Elizabeth took a deep breath as she stepped from the carriage and into the late afternoon sun. She was at the Eldridge residence for the second time that week, which was more time than she had ever spent at Edward's family home in the year since she and Edward had made their acquaintance. She looked down at her soft blue dress, a color selected specifically because it was Edward's favorite. Her father next held out his arm to assist her mother down the step. With his wife on one arm and daughter on the other, he began to walk toward to the front entrance.

Francis's smiling face greeted guests from the massive door to the interior. The music from a string quartet playing just inside filled the carriage drive.

"I still don't know why we accepted this invitation," said Lord Clarendon in a slightly irritated voice.

"Now, Phillip," Elizabeth's mother said, "The viscountess was kind enough to invite us, and she has been so good for our social work. How could we not come?"

Elizabeth nodded in agreement. Her mother winked at her.

"And besides," Lady Clarendon continued, "the Eldridge sons are quite accomplished and are exactly the type of young gentlemen I wish our daughter to associate with."

Elizabeth nodded again, worrying that perhaps her mother was laying it on too thick. Her mother's American upbringing made it very difficult for her to be subtle or refined about anything. That was an art form reserved for the English.

"With a war erupting across the continent, I'm not convinced now is an appropriate time for our daughter to be associating with any young man, particularly one who is certain to soon be a soldier," her father began. But seeing a cross look descend across his wife's face, he added, "But my dear, I am happy to accommodate your request, as always."

Elizabeth walked carefully across the packed stones of the carriage drive. *Not only do they expect us to dress in these ridiculously cumbersome gowns, but they think we can prance across the drive in heeled shoes!* She thought to herself. She jealously eyed her father's much more comfortable-looking flat leather footwear.

Her father leaned toward her and said, "And, judging from the lunacy of Viscount Eldridge's politics, I'm sure he must be under the influence of an extensive liquor cabinet, and so the evening certainly won't be entirely for naught!"

As Elizabeth stifled a laugh, they reached Francis. The old butler bowed his head slightly, then took Lord Clarendon's top hat. Two other members of the staff took the ladies' coats. Then Francis loudly announced into the hall, "The Earl and Lady Clarendon and Lady Elizabeth Clarendon."

How I hate these stupid formalities! thought Elizabeth. "I'll never get used to the English way of life," she heard her mother mutter.

❧

Edward, milling about with his brother and a few friends, had his ears tuned to the goings-on in the entrance hall, so he heard the announcement of the Clarendons. He grabbed Gerald by the arm, and the two of them raced to the hall to join the end of the receiving line. His father nodded to his sons, smiling slightly. He then turned and recognized Lord Clarendon and his wife, with a young and beautiful daughter in tow. Edward's heart sank as he watched his father frowningly put together the significance of Edward's sudden entrance and the arrival of the Clarendons. As his father tensed up, his mother bumped his elbow sharply and gave Lady Clarendon a sincere welcome and smile. The viscount followed suit, and Edward watched the two men shake hands briskly.

Gerald leaned over to his brother. "Well, at least he didn't take a swing at him. I'd say that's a good sign."

"Hardly," moaned Edward. But he smiled as the Clarendons approached.

"So lovely to see you again, Gerald," said Lady Clarendon. "And this must be Edward! I am so pleased to make your acquaintance," she said, grabbing both of his hands as well. Edward marveled at how easily she threw convention to the wind. It was such a breath of fresh air among an evening of stiff formalities.

"And you know Elizabeth," she said, presenting her daughter and winking at Edward. Edward felt his face turn flush. As the elder Clarendons proceeded toward the ballroom, Gerald murmured to Edward, "Did I just witness that? Is her mother in on this as well?"

"She is," Edward said. "She absolutely is."

"I need to find an American mother-in-law," said Gerald. "They seem quite handy to have around."

❧

Elizabeth, overhearing the Edward's conversation, couldn't help but agree. Her mother's down-to-earth personality was rare in London's high society. For

Elizabeth, it helped to make the London scene tolerable. She caught Edward's eye one last time before catching up to her parents.

The viscountess had considered every last detail. Each long hall they passed through on the way to the ballroom was decorated with beautiful white lilies in perfect bloom. "The entire residence smells like a garden! How wonderful!" exclaimed her mother. As they walked the long corridor to the ballroom, Elizabeth saw many familiar people, all dressed exquisitely. The men wore variations of the season's formal evening attire, each so similar that they looked as though they could have been in a prescribed uniform. The women, however, were dressed in beautiful pastel evening gowns. Some were obviously burdened by intricate corsets, but a few dared to dress in a modern fashion that threw convention to the wind and forewent the oppressive undergarments. The ladies wearing the old and the new were easily told apart by those who moved slowly and erectly, and those who fluttered about the ballroom floor with enough air in their lungs to manage laughter.

"Everyone who is anyone is here," remarked Lady Clarendon as they entered the ballroom, which was already filled with mingling aristocracy. She gestured as discreetly as she knew how toward the duke and duchess, who were surrounded by several Parliamentarians eager to catch the duke's ear for even a moment.

"I'd expect nothing less from the viscountess," said her husband. "She measures her status by her guest list."

"Now, Phillip," Elizabeth heard her mother scold, "no need to spoil what is poised to be a wonderful evening. She's no different from half the others here. You know as well as I do how this scene works. You yourself would be a product of it, had I not wrenched you out of it years ago."

"That is true, my dear," he said. "I do have you to thank for a different perspective."

Before the Clarendons could begin mingling with the other guests, the chatter around the ballroom fell quiet, and the string quartet, which had relocated to the entrance of the ballroom, struck up a few notes to get the attentions of the guests. All the attention fell to the entrance to the grand hall, where Francis now stood. Elizabeth noticed that the butler was the only one in the room who didn't seem to be enjoying himself. He looked not at the guests, but at the far corner of the grand room and, with a distinctly bored expression, cleared his throat. Perhaps he had seen one too many anniversary balls. "We are happy to present Lord and Lady Eldridge," he announced wearily, "on the blessed occasion of their thirtieth wedding anniversary." Elizabeth stifled a laugh. He didn't seem happy about anything.

CHAPTER 42

August 8, 1914: London, England

Gerald peered over the heads of the throng of ladies who crowded around him vying for his attention. While he was quite tall, the elegant coiffures atop his pursuers' delicate heads towered so high that he could barely make out his brother across the room. *Is that fool my brother?* Gerald thought to himself. *Jumping up and down like a lunatic?* He strained to see. *Ah! Must be time!* He thought excitedly. *We'll see if this little plan of his worked.* At that very moment, the towering blond tresses of Lady Abigail obstructed his view.

"Oh Gerald!" she was saying, "Such a spectacular party! Your mother has such an eye for every detail!" She stepped directly into the only open path out of the gaggle of women.

Before she could finish her thought, she was interrupted by Lady Delores. "And you look so sophisticated in your suit. Your tailor should be commended, and—"

Yet another interruption came from Delores's younger sister: "And how handsome you would be in uniform, Gerald!"

Lady Abigail took offense to this. "Oh, Gerald can't go off to war! By the time he got a commission, our soldiers would be on their way home." She clasped her hands to her face as delicately as one could possibly clasp. "You aren't thinking of such a thing, are you Gerald?"

Gerald smiled slightly, feeling claustrophobic among his crowd of admirers. He tried to back up but bumped into Lady Delores, who had moved to his other side. He thought to himself, *If you only knew.* For the first time since he could remember, he was annoyed by the endless chatter of his band of ladies. He usually egged them on and loved to return their flirtations. But today, his mind was occupied by distractions—Edward and the looming war. His heart sank at the thought. War meant he would soon be saying good-bye to Alice.

"Ladies, if you would excuse me," he said. Spotting an opening between the coiffures of Ladies Abigail and Delores, he began making his way across the ballroom to his brother.

Gerald pushed with difficulty through the crowded room, and his crowd of young ladies scattered now that his attention was not on them. He spied a less trafficked shortcut via the veranda. Quickly, he stepped out into the afternoon air and stood still for a split second of peace, relishing the quiet. He knew his brother was waiting for him.

"It's wonderfully quiet out here, isn't it?" came a familiar voice. Alice stood next to him on the veranda, dressed in a festive version of the household uniform. His mother had evidently chosen the colors—a soft gray trimmed with her favorite pastel pink and a flowered fascinator. He half smiled and bit his tongue not to laugh. It looked ridiculous. *Poor Alice*, he thought. *Every other woman here gets to dress like an exotic plant and my girl, like a...*Even in his thoughts, he couldn't put words to her outfit. *Primped donkey*, he decided.

Without thinking, he reached out his arm and invited Alice to come closer. "Wonderfully quiet" he said, belatedly answering her question.

Alice quickly stepped away. The glasses of champagne she was carrying wobbled on their tray, and the flowers in her absurd fascinator danced in the afternoon breeze.

"You trying to get me fired?" she asked. She furrowed her brow and adjusted the fascinator, balancing the tray in one hand.

"Give me that," he said, pointing to the tray. He hated watching her slave under the weight of such a platter. He knew it was gilded and had to be heavy.

Her face fell into a scowl. "You are, aren't you? Wouldn't that be a lovely scandal for your mother's party?"

He laughed. "Not trying to get you fired. Trying to—"

"Make yourself feel better?" she interjected.

"Exactly," he said quietly. He looked through the tall and ornate windows to the party. He no longer saw his brother wildly trying to get his attention, but happily, none of the guests seemed to be taking any note of the activity on the veranda.

"Will it always be like this, Gerald?" she asked.

When he didn't answer, she said quietly, "I'd better get back to the party. It was nice to see you." She studied him. "You look as handsome as ever. And I—" she looked down at her ensemble. "I'm not quite sure what I look like."

"You look beautiful, Alice," he said, and he wasn't lying. Her clothes were silly, but it couldn't hide the fact that she had pretty features. Her hair, pulled up tight in a bun with little ringlets freed on either side, her plump face and smooth neckline—he thought it was all quite beautiful.

"I was going to say 'a jackass,'" she said, "but I prefer your description."

"You look beautiful," he said, and despite the throngs of people who might see, leaned over and kissed her.

❦

"Gerald! Pssst, Gerald!" Edward called to his brother. He had spied him chatting up one of the staff on the veranda. *Does that boy ever stop gabbing?* Edward wondered. *I mean, he's practically talking her ear off. Poor Alice. Probably thinks she needs to stand there and listen just to be polite.*

"Gerald!" he called again. Gerald turned toward him and hastily took a glass of champagne from the tray Alice held, abruptly cutting off his conversation. Alice's face looked flushed. Edward did a double take when he noticed Alice's uniform. *Who the hell chose that ridiculous outfit?* he thought to himself. *Someone who is obviously mad.*

Alice curtseyed and began to take her leave when Edward, trying not to be distracted by the bizarre fascinator, said, "No, Alice dear, you must stay for this. Based on what I've just seen and heard, I may be in possession of the best gossip floating around London—and it involves you, Gerald!" The fascinator jumped as Alice took a great step backward.

Edward frowned. *I didn't think it was possible for her face to become redder,* he thought. "So you already know?" he said dejectedly. He had wanted to be the one to break the news.

"Know what?" asked Gerald, in a cautious voice.

"The gossip, of course!" said Edward. "How is it that you already know? I just discovered it myself a few moments ago!"

"Gossip?" inquired Gerald. "Is it about me?"

"Gossip is just that—unsubstantiated rumors," interjected Alice.

Edward was becoming annoyed. "Why does everything have to be about you?" he asked his brother.

"Why are you so worked up?" asked Gerald suspiciously.

"Because I have some important news for you!" said Edward. "I want to make sure it doesn't catch you off guard!" Edward watched his brother and Alice exchange worried glances.

"Tell me this, Big Al," said Gerald, becoming quite serious. "Does mother know?"

"Of course she knows, you dunce! Mother is the originator of all gossip, you know that. She witnessed it herself!"

"Oh dear," said Alice. Her face went from bright red to ghostly white.

"What the devil has gotten into you two?" Edward asked.

"Nothing, Al—it just sort of happened, you know," said Gerald, almost frantically, "Not overnight, but over time. Does Father know?"

"Of course!" exclaimed Edward excitedly. "He said he was going to take care of it tonight!"

"Oh Jesus!" said Gerald, clasping his hands to his face. Alice dropped the tray of champagne. A dozen dazzling crystal flutes personalized with a gaudy letter "E" plummeted to the veranda, taking with it their holdings of the viscount's prized 1895 champagne.

At the sound of shattering crystal, the orchestra paused to allow the staff to locate the source of the crash. But the music quickly resumed as the wait staff went on full alert and bustled over to the distraught-looking Alice to assist with the cleanup.

As the staff cleaned the mess, Edward pulled Gerald aside; but Gerald's attention seemed focused on Alice, who was fleeing the scene. He began to follow, but Edward pulled him back. "Seriously, Gerald. What is wrong with you?"

"Nothing is wrong with me!" he said, "People just fall in love, you can't help whom you fall in love with!"

"Exactly!" exclaimed Edward. "Exactly!" He threw his arms up in exasperation.

Gerald looked confused. "So tell me this, Al. Is Father going to kill me or not?"

"What in God's name are you talking about?" asked Edward. "Why would Father kill you over me getting engaged to Elizabeth? He doesn't care about our little scheme to trick mother. Gerald, grow up! It's not always about you, you know!"

Edward stared at his younger brother as Gerald put a hand to his forehead and began to laugh like a maniac. The scene on the veranda was among the most bizarre he had ever seen: half a dozen staff members, all dressed in matching light gray suits and trimmed with pink, on their knees picking up broken shards of crystal, against a backdrop of a magnificent afternoon sun that put his mother's most valiant efforts at decorating to shame, and his younger brother, extravagantly dressed yet typically unshaven, laughing like an inmate at an asylum.

"What the hell is wrong with you?" Edward asked. "How much have you had to drink? You're certifiable!"

"Al, forgive me!" His little brother regained his balance and put an arm around Edward's shoulder. "Forgive me, but your news is wonderful. Not at all what I expected—"

"What were you expecting?" asked Edward. "What other news could I have had? Isn't this what we've been scheming for weeks?"

"It doesn't matter," said Gerald. "But damn, I have to go find Alice!"

"No!" exclaimed Edward. "You have to come with me! Father is meeting with Lord Clarendon as we speak in the parlor. He asked me to join him in a quarter hour." He hastily took his gold pocket watch, engraved with EABE, out of his jacket. "Now."

"This is it, then!" said Gerald. He flung his arm around Edward's shoulder. "Come on!" he said excitedly, pulling him off toward the parlor.

Edward followed his brother's lead and couldn't help but think that anyone watching would assume Gerald to be the older brother and not him. As much as he felt in constant competition with Gerald for his parents' approval, he couldn't deny that Gerald was the best friend he'd ever have.

CHAPTER 43

August 8, 1914: Rathmines, Dublin, Ireland

Colin pulled his uncle's delivery truck up the drive to the Parsons residence. As he eyed the massive structure, he felt his pulse accelerate. It had only been a day since his run-in with Nora. Not nearly long enough for her to cool down, but still—he had to see her. But the manor and grounds were so expansive, he had little hope of running into her by chance. As his heart pounded, he thought, *I have equal chances of running into Ethan.* He wasn't sure which he wanted more.

He wanted to set eyes on Ethan and have his anger and resolve renewed. The strikes, the crackdown, men like Daniel's father now lying in Glasnevin. And Nora. *Did she know yet?* The greatest secret they were all keeping from her. He wanted to be able to, as sure as day, pick Ethan out of a crowd and know who to target. In his mind, the man was a hulking, ugly, burly figure, the evil within him unable to hide itself.

As expected, Ronan Dunham came to meet him in the drive, and his thoughts turned to the immediate business at hand.

"Hallo, Mr. Dunham!" he called. "Sorry I'm late. We've been quite busy this week, what with the declaration of war and all. Seems everyone wants to stock up out of fear of what's to come."

Colin jumped from the truck onto the stone drive and walked around to the rear of the vehicle. Together, he and Mr. Dunham opened the back door, and Colin reached in to grab packages of wrapped meat.

"Lamb. Prepared specifically for the delegation," he said and smiled.

"You didn't poison it, did you?" Mr. Dunham asked, winking.

Colin frowned. "Wished I had thought of it."

"It best be the finest cut John Kildare could muster," said Mr. Dunham. "He can't afford to lose this customer. Too much at stake." He looked through the cool brown paper packages.

"Aye," said Colin. "Fat only around the edges, but plenty of it. Thick roasts. The likes of most of Dublin will never know such fine meat exists." He shifted his weight to reach into the back of the truck. "Probably best that way. There'd be a riot for sure."

"Not forever, Colin," said Mr. Dunham quietly. "It won't be like this forever. Someday…" He turned to Colin. "Best hurry—the chef has been waiting on these all day. Why don't you bring it into the house for me?" He winked again.

Colin eyed him curiously. He rarely set foot in the mansions of Rathmines. Carefully, he piled the packages in his right arm. His left dangled awkwardly at his side. The throbbing had become a constant feature of his day. He could not longer feel much of his hand, which had taken on the color of a corpse.

"Jesus Mary and Joseph, Colin!" said Mr. Dunham. "What has happened to yer arm?"

"Gunrunnin' and British soldiers," he said, trying to find humor.

"Did I read about you in the paper?"

"You did," said Colin. He couldn't conceal his smile.

"And why are you walkin' around with a mangled arm?" Mr. Dunham shuffled across the stones to get a better look.

"Michael thought it best that we wait—you know—till things calm down."

"Michael's an arse. You get that fixed. Today! You hear?" Colin had never heard him sound angry before. "And until you do, keep it hidden!"

"Aye," said Colin, pulling the fabric of his sleeves over his discolored hand. He hadn't the slightest idea of how to go about getting his arm mended.

Mr. Dunham took the remaining cuts and put his hand behind Colin to guide him toward the back entrance. It was a friendly, fatherly gesture, but he scolded him as they walked. "It's dangerous for you to be walkin' about like that. Just brings attention. But more than that—if you don't get it tended to, it'll never heal. You're a young man yet—would be a shame to live the rest of yer life with a crooked arm."

They crossed the drive, kicking the loose stones as they walked, and entered into the kitchen, where a space on the countertop was already cleared for the delivery. The space was massive—almost unimaginable. The ceilings were high, and the floor tiles sparkled. The kitchen alone was larger than his uncle's shop. Colin marveled at how he could hear the echo of his own footsteps.

He laid the packages on the counter, wiped his good hand on his trousers, and pulled a slip of paper out of his pocket. "Here's the bill, Mr. Dunham. Uncle John asked for payment today, if possible, what with the uncertainty of everything."

"Of course, Colin, of course," said Mr. Dunham. He examined the bill with some difficulty. Clearly, middle age had begun to rob him of eyesight. "Everything looks fair," he said. "Come with me."

They walked down the hall and up the back staircase toward the offices on the second floor. A crystal chandelier hung above the stair and cast sparkling reflections all along the walls.

"Stop gawking, Colin," said Mr. Dunham. "Can't have the delegation take note of you."

"Then why'd you bring me in?" he asked in a whisper. "This place is incredible."

"Amends."

"Amends?"

Mr. Dunham looked over his shoulder. "You need to make good with Nora."

"*She* needs to—"

Mr. Dunham stopped. "No. You need to. You boys need to figure yerselves out. We can't have Michael's ego and yer petulance ruin our chance for another generation. I assure you, we'll not get another go. The world will never present this opportunity again in our lifetime."

"What opportunity?"

Mr. Dunham sighed. "War, Colin. Mother England won't be able to give a shite about Ireland while she's tangled in a continental war. Stop and think once in a while. Come now. We have but little time."

As they neared the top of the stair, they heard the scurrying of fast and light footsteps.

"Hell," said Colin. "Her again."

Mrs. Louise Finnegan came into view. As usual, she looked irritated. Her dreary uniform and large apron only made her appear more unfriendly.

"Good morning, Louise," Mr. Dunham said. His voice sounded much cheerier than Colin felt was warranted.

Mrs. Finnegan's face turned from annoyed to cross. "That grocer's back again, I see."

"Yes ma'am," said Colin, doing his best to hide his arm.

Mr. Dunham cut in. "He's here to bring by the lamb for the *delegation*," he said quietly. Colin was taken aback by the mention of Ethan in Finnegan's presence. Mr. Dunham must have slipped. Mrs. Finnegan didn't seem to notice.

"Late, I see," she said to Colin, eyeing him in the most disapproving way.

"We're just settlin' the bill, and then he'll be off," assured Mr. Dunham.

"No need to bring him in the house in the future." She looked frowningly at Colin. "He can wait outside like all the others."

Mr. Dunham checked his pocket watch. "Please excuse us, Louise. We're behind schedule. Want to get the boy on his way." The two passed by Mrs. Finnegan's disapproving stare and walked quickly toward Mr. Dunham's office. They stopped at a small closet-looking space along one of the interior walls. Either side of the plain wooden door was decorated with marble busts on ornate white stands.

Mr. Dunham opened the door and ducked his head into a cramped space. Colin followed, feeling as though he was stepping into a simpler world. Mr. Dunham's office had none of the opulent decor that adorned every other space in the manor. After Colin had ducked into the room, Mr. Dunham closed the door lightly behind him, and took a small key from his pocket. Under his desk was a small wooden lockbox with the letter P ornately carved on it and fastened to the hard wood floor. Mr. Dunham turned the key and opened the box to count out the payment for Colin.

"Mrs. Finnegan doesn't miss anything, does she?" Colin asked.

"No, my boy, she doesn't," answered Mr. Dunham with a smile, "but she's not as harsh as she comes across."

"I'm not so sure about that," said Colin. "She seems downright cruel."

"Ah, but you don't know her, my dear boy. You don't know the experiences and the life that made her this way. I can assure you, she has a big heart."

Colin was silent. The Mrs. Louise Finnegan he knew did not have a kind bone in her body.

"She acts that way to protect the girls," Mr. Dunham said. "She thinks she knows what is best for them. They're the closest she'll ever have to a family of her own. Do me a favor and give her the benefit of the doubt."

"Anything for you, Mr. Dunham."

"Excellent. Now, I'll point you out of the mansion in the roundabout way."

"But—"

"You'll pass by Nora on yer way out. And I expect you to walk out of the residence in her good graces again."

Colin sighed. "You make it sound like it's easy."

"It's both the easiest and hardest thing to do. Just say that you're sorry."

Colin pursed his lips. It was his cousin who should be apologizing. Seamus's departure was part of Michael's scheme. He'd just gotten caught in the middle of it.

"It's not easy to be an adult, Colin. But I need you to grow up fast. You've got a good head and a good heart. Yer cousin—I'm not so sure about 'im. But we can't always choose our boss, now, can we?"

Mr. Dunham opened the door and peered out. "Coast is clear, my boy," he said and stepped into the hall, Colin close behind him. Mr. Dunham leaned in close to Colin. "Turn that corner by the vases, then follow the hall to the end. Turn right, go by the oil painting of Westminster—it's as big as you are—you won't miss it, then the first room on the left is the Gardenia Room. You'll know it by the sign on the door."

Colin gulped. He wouldn't know a damned thing from a sign. "First room on the left, you say?"

"Aye. I'll be by in about fifteen minutes to get you. If you need a quick exit, use the back staircase. It will let you out by the kitchen where we came in."

Colin nodded.

"What are you waitin' for? Time isn't goin' to give you any more courage. You have to make do with what you've got."

Colin managed a smile, then headed off around the corner. *First room on the right*, he said to himself.

CHAPTER 44

August 8, 1914: Rathmines, Dublin, Ireland

Nora lazily made her way to the Gardenia Room. Her charge was out for a late afternoon carriage ride, and she had the luxury of spending a relaxed afternoon cleaning. The complaints from Suzanne Parsons had already begun. Something was wrong with the Rose Room. Too cold, too hot. Too much light, not enough light. But Nora was pretty sure her problem was really too much Ethan. Whatever the issue, Mrs. Suzanne Parsons had loudly and rudely announced that morning that she was to be moved to the Gardenia Room, where she could have some peace.

The Gardenia Room was the smallest of the guest suites and was located at the far end of the residences. Secluded and quiet indeed, it also had the luxury of no private adjoining hallway to any other suite. Nora's task for the afternoon was to move Suzanne out of the Rose Room and into the Gardenia Room. *Would be much easier if each garment, shoe and book didn't have such specific tastes about how they had to be stored*, Nora thought as she rolled her eyes. Nora had learned from her first day with Suzanne that there were hundreds of ways to get something entirely wrong, and likely no way to get something entirely right.

She entered the Gardenia Room with the first of many loads of Suzanne's garments and hung each dress in the wardrobe. The satin fabrics were so soft and the pinks, yellows and blues so vibrant—Nora loved the soft swishing noise they made as the fabric flowed. She recalled how on her first day here, she had thought her black-and-white uniform the finest garment she had ever seen. Her perspective had changed so much in a few short weeks. There seemed no end to the wealth in this family.

As she carefully hung each of the dresses, a noise rumbled at the door. "Hello, Nora."

Her heart skipped a beat. She turned slowly and faced the open door. The figure of a cheerfully smiling young man took up almost the entire doorway. The walls sounded as three exuberant tails thumped against them.

"Halloo, Mr. Parsons," she said as blandly as she could amid her sudden vigilance.

Ethan walked into the suite, closely followed by his ever-present setters. "So lovely to see you again, Nora."

She said nothing, but instead hastily hung the last two evening dresses in Suzanne's wardrobe then moved toward the doorway. He immediately cut her off.

She looked at him. Her eyes felt like they were on fire.

"Perhaps we got off on the wrong foot the other day. Sit down," he directed. "Let's have a conversation. I'd like to get to know you." His words were probably meant to sound kind, but his gestures made them sound threatening.

Nora protested. "I need to finish readying this room before Mrs. Parsons returns."

He frowned. "I'm sure whatever you need to do can wait just a few minutes." He walked closer toward her, and she backed away, but she was quickly cornered between him and the large four-poster bed. "Have a seat, Nora," he said. "No need to be wary of me. I only wish to make your acquaintance."

She looked from him to his dogs, all standing before the door, the only exit. They were bigger up close than she had remembered from growing up. Each of the setters had immaculately groomed coats and polished leather collars. They practically shone. She felt her face scrunch with aggravation. *These dogs have had luxuries denied to living, breathing people!* Reluctantly, she walked toward the bed, staring directly into his dark cold eyes in a way that seemed to startle him. His icy eyes widened. She sat stiffly on the soft coverlet and folded her arms tightly across her chest.

"So tell me about Clare," he said. He sat next to her on the soft mattress, so close that she sank toward him. As before, he smelled strongly of alcohol, and not in the faint and familiar way that Colin did, but like a drunk. "I've never known of anything pleasant to have come from Clare, and yet you seem to be quite a pleasant girl."

"Clare is quite beautiful, Mr. Parsons," she said defiantly. "Beautiful people and beautiful land."

He nodded. "It was anything but beautiful when I was there last. Full of rebels and rain clouds." He smoothed the satin bed linens around him. "Does it rain there every day?"

"No," she said. *What an idiotic question.* "Not every day."

"And the insane radicals?"

She shrugged. "I know of none." Then to herself, *Only the insane think freedom is a radical idea!*

"Well, that is reassuring," he said to her. "So tell me then, what makes it beautiful?" He edged closer and she sank nearer to him.

"Small things," she said. She looked warily at Ethan's dogs. It was the bigger things that made Clare ugly. Like the Crook and his estate. His agents. His dogs.

"Such as?"

She exhaled loudly. He was not going to let her out of this conversation.

"Green," she finally said.

"Green?"

"The green hills. The green Shannon when it turns into the green ocean. The faint smell of the Atlantic. That's what makes it beautiful."

"Green eyes?" he said. "Like yours." Ethan's hand curled around her waist. She shuddered, though she had expected this. "I haven't been able to stop thinking about those eyes."

The sudden eruption of a flock of birds drew the dogs to the window, barking and sending a frightful chill up her spine that even Ethan could not inspire. Amid the distraction, she lunged for the door, but he clasped his arm tightly around her and pulled her back with a laugh. "Oh no you don't."

She began to protest, loudly, and just as quickly, his other hand closed over her mouth. He was holding her so tightly, she felt like she could not breathe. The smell of alcohol on him was almost overwhelming.

"Best you not be so loud," he said. "We wouldn't want Mrs. Finnegan to hear you, now would we?"

Nora stood perfectly still, not acknowledging his threat. She tried to break away from his grip, but he held fast. He suddenly became agitated and tightened his hold on her so that it hurt. "Since you seem to be in such a hurry, I'll be straight with you, Nora. We pay you very well," he said to her. "Room, board, clothes, shoes, and if I'm not mistaken a stipend on top of all of that."

Again, Nora didn't move. He squeezed her ever tighter. She felt as though she could hardly breathe. "It's true, isn't it, Nora?" She nodded slightly and he softened his grip. "And if you weren't here, if we didn't treat you so well, where do you think you would be?" He paused for a moment to let it sink in. "You certainly wouldn't be living in a mansion in Dublin, with three meals a day and the luxuries you have now, would you?"

Learning from the last time, she softly shook her head, though she could feel the rage building within her. "Of course you wouldn't," he said. "You'd be like every other girl who no one else wanted. Living on the streets. A whore perhaps." She tensed up at this accusation.

"But instead, you found your way to us," he continued. "And we are perfectly happy to provide you with all the things we give you. But sometimes, I am going to want a little bit more. And you will give it to me," he said, almost in a whisper. "Because if you don't, I guarantee you, I'll make you wish you were a whore working the streets of whatever wretched little village you came from." He paused. "Now then, are we clear?"

Nora felt a magnificent heat rising from her eyes. She was so angry that her whole face burned. She refused to respond to him, and he forcefully pushed her head up and down so that it nodded.

"Good then," he said, apparently satisfied that this constituted an agreement. "I'm going to take my hand away, and you are going to be very quiet. Do you understand?"

Again, he forced her head to nod, and just as he had said, removed his hand from over her mouth. She did not scream. He slowly released his hold, and she stood still. He put his hands on her shoulders and turned her to face him. "There," he said. "That wasn't so hard, now was it?"

Staring back at him, Nora could still feel the heat of her anger in her eyes. She had never felt a hate so fierce—not even for the Crook.

He must have noticed it, too. "I've seen that look before, Nora," he said in a peculiar voice. "If I didn't know any better, I'd think you wanted to hurt me." He laughed an eerie laugh. His eyes seemed dark and empty. She did want to hurt him.

He sat down on the bed again and pulled her close to him. He put his hands on her hips, then ran them up her back, looking for the tie to unfasten her dress. When he found it, he loosened the strings. She wondered how many other housekeepers he had treated this way. How many times had he taken advantage of the poorest, most vulnerable in Dublin, either for financial gain or for his own entertainment?

A stark realization came to her. Everything about the relationship between

Dublin and Belfast and London enabled him and others like him to this entitled existence. Those who had robbed her ancestors of land and rights and freedom all those generations ago had no reason to change. All of a sudden, a political solution to any of the Irish problems felt naïve. Why would someone like Ethan willingly give up his powerful position? At last she understood why Colin had said there would be no peace without outright revolution. She finally knew what had driven her parents to armed rebellion.

"Green, you say," he said and laughed again. The words interrupted her thoughts. "When I think of Clare, I think of green, too. It's ironic, really." He fiddled with the strings on the back of her dress. "I once knew a man from Clare with green eyes. Angry, defiant green eyes."

Nora's body tensed. A queasy feeling came over her. Her knees began to shake. But she didn't resist him. She thought only of how sweet revenge would be.

"Does everyone from Clare have green eyes?"

"No," she said firmly. She heard the tremor in her own voice.

"Just the characters I meet, I suppose. Well these eyes were nothing like yours. They were evil." He loosened the cloth around her shoulders.

Nora's mind raced. She barely noticed Ethan's hands. She stood perfectly straight and felt entirely disassociated from her surroundings. A thought entered her mind—so dark she didn't want to consider it—yet she explored it anyway. *The dogs, the rebels, the green, Clare. Of course.* Before she even asked the question, she knew the answer. "What was yer business in Clare?"

"Acting magistrate," he said. "My father is too busy for some of his duties."

"And you met men with green eyes?"

"One man," Ethan corrected her. "A criminal. A stupid, backward papist not smart enough to understand his place."

Her queasiness turned to an eerie calm. It finally made sense—why Colin was so squeamish about her being at the Parsons. She felt oddly collected and her mind was clear.

"What was his crime?"

Ethan seemed to study her face and her suddenly calm demeanor. "Murder."

Nora nodded slowly, and even felt a small smile break.

"In cold blood."

"And what did you do about it?" she asked. Her voice was so calm that it scared her.

"I sentenced him to die. And then I hanged him myself. And even after he was dead, those ugly, soulless eyes glared back at me. Pure evil."

He resumed untying Nora's dress.

CHAPTER 45

August 8, 1914: Rathmines, Dublin, Ireland

First door on the right. Colin cautiously turned the corner toward the main residence according to Mr. Dunham's instructions. The huge painting of Westminster came into view and he knew he was in the right place. The left side of the long corridor was lined with multiple doorways. But about halfway down the hall was a sole door on the right-hand side. He took a deep breath and gathered himself. He did not know if Nora would even be willing to see him.

As he walked past the first door to the left, he saw movement out of the corner of his eye: a man and a woman were seated on the bed. He quickly scurried by, then turned and watched the doorway, but saw no further movement. Had someone seen him? He quietly crept toward the door on the right and darted in and out of sight. He listened. Nothing.

Sighing in relief, he looked about the spacious room. The walls were lined with books. Ceiling-length windows opened to the front lawn of the residence.

A light breeze blew the white curtains in gentle motions. It felt so peaceful and so quiet. But there was no Nora.

Colin kept out of sight and walked along one wall of the room, running his hands along the shelves of books. He slid a book off the shelf and touched the gold embossed letters. None of the shapes meant anything to him. When they were in Clare, Nora had always promised to teach him to read. Someday. But it was a promise made in a time and place where one day ran mindlessly into another, and time ticked by slowly. Back then, they had not understood that one day, time would cease to stand still. Childhood didn't last forever.

He wedged the book back into the crowded shelf. Nora wasn't where she was supposed to be. What was he to do now? The path to the back staircase was blocked by the occupants of the room down the hall. He sat on the floor and decided to wait for Mr. Dunham. Resting his left hand across his lap, he pulled the fabric away from his swollen arm. A blue-gray hue spread from his elbow to his fingertips. He pressed his fingers lightly against the injured arm. In some places he felt intense pain, and in others, no sensation at all.

He leaned his head back against the bookcase. Voices came from the room across the hall. He wondered whom he had happened upon. For all he knew, it was the dreaded Ethan and his wife. He rolled his eyes at his bad timing.

And yet the girl had been much more plainly attired than the wife of Dublin elite—dressed in a simple black dress and hair tightly pulled back into a bun. And younger than he'd expected.

His heart skipped a beat.

An instant later, a loud crash echoed down the hall, followed by the frenzied raspy sound of barking dogs. He jumped to his feet and ran toward the sound of the crash, not caring who saw him or what questions they asked.

Bursting through the door, he saw Nora, a piece of a broken vase in her hand, waving it at a tall, well-dressed man. Shards of blue and white pottery littered the floor. Blood dripped from the man's forehead. Both turned their attention to Colin.

He ran toward the bloodied man and put himself between the man and Nora. He needed no introduction—Colin knew this man as sure as he knew his own brother.

Ethan changed his stance to engage Colin, throwing up both fists and readying for a fight. Colin raised his own right hand in return. He heard Nora scamper into the far corner, away from Ethan and away from the dogs.

A smile came across Ethan's face. He laughed and relaxed his stance. "Boy, you've wandered into the wrong room. One step further, and your employment here will be terminated. Go back to the stables."

Colin stopped his advance. *He thinks I work here.*

Ethan smiled. "There's a good lad. Best be on your way."

A little more than two arms' length from Ethan, Colin hesitated, contemplating his next move.

"I promise you, you will regret any choice that isn't leaving immediately." Ethan pulled a small blade from his sleeve and turned it this way and that in his hand so that the metal gleamed in the afternoon light.

But Colin didn't move.

Ethan walked slowly toward him. "You can consider yourself unemployed," he said. "And blacklisted. You'll never work in Dublin again." Usually, a threat like that was enough to make any blue collar Catholic in Dublin reconsider. Hundreds had starved the year before because Dublin's elite had made it impossible for men to return to work—long after the strikes had ended. Ethan held the blade up a foot or two from Colin's face.

Colin took note of his surroundings. He was slightly taller than Ethan, but his left arm was entirely useless, and every movement was painful. He knew this was a fight he could never win. He slowly stepped backward, buying time and wishing Nora would run for the door.

As he moved one step closer to the wall, a dog's distinctive low growl came from behind him. Almost before he had time to think "dog," sharp teeth tore into his right leg. Pain seared up the leg as he shook the dog off.

But an instant later, he felt a pain much worse as Ethan jammed his pristinely polished black shoe into his injured arm. Searing pain ripped up his arm, the same way it had when the British sergeant had broken it. He bent over in agony, and ducked his head, trying to anticipate where Ethan would strike next.

Suddenly the room echoed with the sound of another crash. Colin watched as Ethan fell to the floor and landed next to him, appearing to be unconscious. He lifted his head and surveyed the room.

Nora was herding the dogs from the room. When the last exuberant tail had been shoved into the hallway, she slammed the door. The setters howled from the other side, and Colin knew it was only a matter of moments before someone investigated. He hoped it would be Mr. Dunham.

The immediate danger had passed, and he knelt on the floor, cradling his arm. "Nora, what did you do?" he asked, though it was obvious. In her hand, she held a wooden post that moments before had served as the decorative top to one of the bed's four posts.

"Saved yer arse," she said. "Again."

"You have a knack for that, it seems," he said. He wiped sweat from his forehead and caught his breath.

She reached toward him. He thought she was reaching for his hand to help him up, but instead she grabbed the flintlock and kit from his waistband. Pouring a small amount of powder down the muzzle, she removed the ramrod.

His heart skipped a beat. "Nora, stop," he said.

She didn't listen to him. He staggered to his feet. He could see that she was singularly focused on the task at hand. "Nora," he said urgently. He eyed Ethan, who lay still. The wooden floor beneath him began to darken as it soaked in blood.

Nora looked up at the sound of her name, but continued ramming the powder and bullet down the muzzle. "Did you know?" she said. Her voice was cold and angry.

Know what? he thought. He knew a lot of things that he didn't want to have to tell her.

"Did you fookin' know, Colin? He killed me parents!" She was almost hysterical.

His heart sank. *How did she find out so quickly?* He reached out his hand to stop her, but she had finished loading the weapon. She pulled back the hammer, and he cautiously stepped away.

"I knew." His voice was quiet. He was ashamed to admit it. "I've known for a while."

She began to speak, but he held his hand up. "I didn't tell you because I hadn't found the right time. But I didn't know he was coming here. Certainly not that he was going to stay."

"But you put me here!" she screamed.

"Michael put you here," he corrected. "I never wanted you here."

"But you agreed in the end!" She sounded unhinged.

Colin chose his words carefully. "Was the only way I knew of to get you to Dublin. I couldn't leave you by yerself in Clare. And Seamus wanted you here."

"Seamus?" she said, her voice rising. "He wanted me here so he could run off to America without me knowing! So I couldn't stop 'im! And you were his accomplice! And then you decided that the best thing for me was to put me up in the very home of the man who murdered me father and mother!"

Colin wanted to object to this characterization, but she was technically right. "Nora," he started, "I know you don't believe me, but I did this because I wanted to protect you."

"Protect me from what?" she cried. He regretted his choice of words. "You can't protect me from a world that I am already up to my eyeballs in! You can't protect me from poverty or from people who want to do us harm. That is Ireland, for Christ's sake! It's chalk full of poor people who have to make bad choices and the bloody rich folk who want nothing else but to live their luxurious lives on the backs of those very same poor people! You can't protect me from that, Colin, whether it's in Clare or Dublin. That is Ireland!" She put her hands to the side of her face, and he didn't know if she was going to scream or cry. Instead, she closed her eyes and softly said, "Until we change it."

"You're right," he said. "I can't lie to you. But I wanted to do right by you, and in me small brain this was what I thought was best." The dogs, which had remained quiet for a few moments, began to whimper out in the hallway.

"How about letting me think about what is best for me," she said, lowering the flintlock so that it was pointed directly at Ethan. "Nobody fookin' thinks I have the right to make me own choices." She started to look as though she were possessed.

"All right," started Colin. He didn't know how to calm her down. "But can I at least weigh in on this one?" Ethan began to twitch and cough. "Killing him may not be what's best for you—though don't get me wrong, I want him dead, too. But he's worth more to us alive."

"Do you have any more secrets, Colin?" she asked. Her finger rested on the trigger and was beginning to turn white. He knew she was applying pressure to it. "Are you keepin' anything else from me?"

"Aye," he said, cautiously, speaking softly to try to calm her. "I'm keepin' two things from you."

She seemed surprised by this answer and turned toward him. Her finger slid off the trigger, but she kept the weapon pointed at Ethan.

A step in the right direction, he thought. "Give me the gun, and I will tell you," he said. He reached out his hand. She shook her head.

"Give it to me. I have to show you somethin'. Please trust me."

She kept shaking her head.

"Nora, I'm sorry. Just know my heart was in the right place."

The dogs began to bark incessantly on the other side of the door. Colin knew it was only a matter of time before someone came crashing in. He prayed it would be Mr. Dunham and not Finnegan, or worse—one of the Parsons.

"Yer brain wasn't in the right place!" Nora interrupted his thoughts and slowly handed him the flintlock. He grabbed it from her, but realized he couldn't release the hammer with only one hand. It was still cocked.

"Keep yer fingers well away from the trigger," he said, "but look at this. My second to last secret." He ran his hands over the wooden handle. *MJC.*

He heard her gasp as she put her hands to her face. "Is it?" she whispered. All of the anger fled her voice and her face took on a look of astonishment. The dogs started to howl.

"Aye," he said. "'Twas yer da's. Me uncle ended up with it."

"Do you think this was the gun?" she stammered, stepping backward across the shards of broken pottery.

"There are two," he said, stepping toward her as she retreated. "Michael has the other. 'Twas one of 'em, we'll never know which." He held the gun so she could reach it.

She brought a quivering hand forward and touched the letters carved into the wood, probably by her father's own hands. "Do you want it?" he asked her.

She shook her head vehemently. "No, and you shouldn't have it either. We should throw it into the damned Liffey. It's probably cursed."

"These things are hard to come by these days. A shame to send it to the bottom of the Liffey. I'll keep it for you. And anytime you want it, it's yers." He slowly put his hand on her shoulder. It rested on bare skin. Looking closer, he saw that her dress was partially untied and hung loosely on her. It dawned on him, finally, what had been taking place in the Gardenia Room.

And this time it was she who had to stop him from putting a lead ball into Ethan Parsons.

CHAPTER 46

August 8, 1914: Rathmines, Dublin, Ireland

The door swung open, and an out-of-breath Ronan Dunham stood panting in the corridor. Three dogs burst into the room and stood over their master, who was still out cold on the floor. Nora nonchalantly finished tying her dress, then took her father's flintlock from Colin. She released the hammer and blew the powder from the pan to disarm it. Without a word, she handed it back to Colin.

"What on earth?" Mr. Dunham stammered.

"I was about to murder the bastard who killed me parents," said Nora, coolly. All of the adrenaline had drained from her and left her feeling tired and queasy. "Then Colin stopped me." She surveyed the room. It looked as though it had been ransacked. Broken blue and white pottery lay all across the floor. One of the bed toppers was missing. Ethan lay in his own pooling blood.

Mr. Dunham's eyes got wide in alarm as he saw Ethan sprawled out face down on the floor.

"There's a little more to it," said Colin.

"He's breathing still, I presume," said Mr. Dunham urgently. He pushed the dogs out of the way and bent down to put his hand on Ethan's back, which softly rose and fell.

Sadness crept over her as she watched. "Did you know, too?" she asked. *Can I trust any of you?*

"Of course I knew, child," he said. "And you were to know as well. It was no one's intention to keep it from you. You've barely settled in here—I didn't want to throw you right into the fire. We're not heartless, and certainly not when it comes to you."

His voice was oddly soothing, and she instantly regretted the way she'd spoken. "I'm sorry, Mr. Dunham," she said. "It just—took me by surprise, that's all."

A shriek came from the open doorway. They all turned to see a pair of familiar beady eyes aghast at the scene in the Gardenia Room.

"Christ," muttered Colin.

But Mr. Dunham seemed less concerned by the new arrival. "Let's control the damage, Louise," he said. "Surely we can concoct a story. Won't be the first time." He turned to Nora. His tone was serious. "What does he know?"

She thought about everything she had told him since he arrived. It had all been about her home. "He knows I'm from Clare."

"Did he make the connection?"

"I don't know," said Nora. "He recognized me eyes I think."

"Jesus, Mary, and Joseph!" cried Mrs. Finnegan. "I told you not to bring her here. Anywhere but here! She's a liability! And the boy—he should never, ever—"

"Yer opinion is known Louise," said Mr. Dunham. "And you may have been right all along, but we are where we are. Let's do what we can to get him off the scent."

Colin and Nora exchanged puzzled glances. Nora turned to Mrs. Finnegan.

"You know me story?" she asked. It felt odd to address her directly, unprompted.

Mrs. Finnegan pursed her lips and squinted her beady eyes. "Yer fame—or infamy, depending on who you ask—precedes you. But don't think you're the only one who's had a rough go of it! This history belongs to all of us!"

"Then why do you hate me?" The question was sincere, but again she instantly regretted voicing it.

Mrs. Finnegan's voice softened. "Nora, child, I could never hate you. But yer very presence here puts us all in real danger. And Michael—he gets an idea in his head…" her voice trailed off.

"So you don't hate me either?" asked Colin, hopefully.

The accustomed frown reappeared on Mrs. Finnegan's face, and she did not answer Colin's question.

Ethan made a gurgling sound, and Mr. Dunham rolled him onto his back. Ethan's blade fell out of his hand and onto the floor. "What else?" asked Mr. Dunham. "Did he see Colin?"

"Aye," said Nora. "Got a good look at him."

"Jesus!" said Mr. Dunham.

"But he thinks I work here," said Colin. "Said he would have me fired."

Mrs. Finnegan's face lit up. "That's lovely," she said. "We'll have you fired. And what do you do here, besides fraternize with my housekeepers?"

Colin's face hardened, but he answered her. "He thought I might be a stable hand."

"Brilliant," said Mr. Dunham. "Louise, announce to the staff today that we've fired Colin the stable hand."

"But his name shouldn't be Colin," interjected Nora. "Call 'im something else."

"Of course, Nora," said Mrs. Finnegan. "We'll fire some poor sap named—Emmet? That's a nice name for a nationalist if I don't say so myself. An Ulsterman will naturally hate a name such as Emmet."

"But what of me?" said Nora. "He'll want me fired, too." The dogs again became distracted by something out the window and scurried over to resume their barking. She closed her eyes and wished it would stop. That dreadful noise!

"No," said Colin. "He won't know it was you that knocked him over the head and out cold. He could think it was me."

Mr. Dunham didn't look convinced.

"Nora," Mrs. Finnegan suddenly interjected. "Your dress is askew."

"Aye," said Nora, flushing as she adjusted it. *Of course Mrs. Finnegan would notice.*

Mrs. Finnegan's eyes grew even beadier. Mr. Dunham's mouth dropped.

"And that's the rest of the story," said Colin.

Nora felt warm all of a sudden. Her rage began to return. "I'll be fired for sure," she said. She was annoyed at herself for letting her voice shake.

"No," said Mrs. Finnegan sharply. "Ronan and I have been on staff here for years. Our word carries some weight. He's always been a spineless arse. My bet is that he'll keep his mouth shut."

"We need to get you both out of here," said Mr. Dunham suddenly. "Until the dust clears. You shouldn't be here when he wakes up."

Nora took a step toward the door, but her knees buckled. Her whole body had begun to shake. Colin stepped toward her but she held up her hand and he didn't come any closer.

"It's just nerves," he said softly. "It'll stop in a minute."

"Come on," said Mr. Dunham, jumping up from the floor and giving the dogs room to crowd around Ethan again. "Follow me. The women will be back from their carriage ride soon, and we'll want you both out of the house."

"Aye," said Mrs. Finnegan, leaning down to pick up shards of the broken vase. "I'll try to wake 'im before his wife finds 'im. I'll do me best to plant the proper story in his mind. How his head was bashed in by a wayward stable hand."

Colin and Nora quickly stepped out of the room and followed Mr. Dunham into the hall. Nora found her feet and scurried behind him as he descended the wooden stairs and moved toward the back entrance. Their hurried steps echoed loudly in the corridor. She felt relieved to leave the scene behind her.

"Bring her to yer uncle's, Colin," Mr. Dunham said over his shoulder as they hurried through the kitchen. "I'll come fetch her tomorrow. Ethan will have cooled down and sobered up by then."

Colin put his hand on her back and rushed her through the kitchen "It will all be all right," he said softly. For the first time in all the time she had known him, he didn't sound convincing.

Near the back door, they ran straight into Martha, apparently trying to sneak her way to the baking room to steal an afternoon snack under the guise of delivering afternoon tea. She stopped dead in her tracks and dropped the tray that she was carrying. The sound of the shattering bone china teacups filled the hall. She saw Colin, and a dutiful scowl came over her face.

"What's he doin' here?" she asked.

"Never mind, Martha, never mind," said Mr. Dunham, stepping over the broken pieces of china. "As soon as you tidy up this mess, please run up to the Gardenia Room, and help Mrs. Finnegan straighten it up."

Martha looked curiously at Nora but obediently reached for a broom.

"I'll be back tomorrow," Nora said, as they rushed out the back door and onto the stone drive.

A small smile emerged on Martha's face. "Until then, everything will just be a rumor," she called. Nora knew Martha hated to wait for what was obviously spectacular gossip.

Colin's truck was where he had left it, parked out behind the rear entrance to the residence. Mr. Dunham looked around, and when he was convinced there were no onlookers, he opened the passenger side door. "Quick now," he said, and he helped Nora climb in to the cab. "I'll see you tomorrow. Everything will be as good as new."

Nora sat in the passenger seat. The air felt cool to her, though she knew it was warm outside. She slipped her hands into the pocket of her dress. "My notebook!" she exclaimed. "I've got to go and get it!" She moved to jump out of the cab, but Colin pulled her back in. She squirmed out of his grasp. "Jesus, Nora!" he yelled and clutched his arm.

"I'll get it," said Mr. Dunham.

"Under me mattress," said Nora.

"Lie low," Mr. Dunham said and hurried back into the residence.

Colin looked nauseous as he held his arm. The skin around his hand looked like it belonged on a corpse.

"I'm sorry, Colin," she said.

"Get down," he said.

"I didn't mean—"

"Get down!" he said again, loudly. Nora peered through the windshield and saw a familiar carriage approaching. She ducked her head below the dash and laid her head on the seat. Colin fidgeted and put his hand on his flask. He unscrewed the cap with one hand and took a drink, his gaze fixed on the drive. Evidently, he had quickly adapted to only using his right hand to open it. "Do we have to wait?" he asked her.

"Aye—I should have given it to Michael before."

"They're just a little ways away," he said. Nora could hear the horses' feet slow on the packed drive. "Just stay still." He put his flask back in his waistband, reached over, and took her hand. "I'm sorry I never tol' you about Seamus, Nora," he said. "And I'm sorry I never tol' you about Ethan. It wasn't fair to you."

"I just want you to stop tryin' to keep me safe. Let me make me own choices. Like you said, we're not in Clare anymore."

"Fook, don't I know it," he said and laughed. "And Michael wants you to be a full-fledged spy." He released her hand and brushed the hair away from her face, tucking it behind her ear.

"An' no one ever asked me," said Nora.

"What do you want, Nora?" he asked. "An' I'm being sincere. What do you want?" He kept his eyes trained on the drive, where by now Nora assumed the carriage passengers were disembarking.

Without hesitation, she said, "I want to squeeze every last bit of useful information out of Ethan Parsons, and then I want to kill him. And I want the last thing he sees to be my rebel green eyes." He stopped running his hands through her hair and took her hand again, this time squeezing it hard.

"I think we finally want the same thing, Nora," he said. He looked down at her for a moment and smiled, but Nora was taken aback by how sad his gaze looked. He let go of her hand and went to his flask again.

"Mr. Kildare!" came a call across the drive. It was Mr. Dunham's distinct, cheerful voice. "I have yer payment!" he said loudly.

"He's putting up quite an act for the Parsons women," Colin said softly. He reached out the window of the truck and took a leather-bound book from Mr. Dunham.

"Paid in full," said Mr. Dunham. "Thank you for bringin' by the lamb roasts. Surely the finest cuts we've seen from yer uncle. Thank him for me." He leaned in the cab and said, "Now be on your way. I'll be by tomorrow to pick you up."

"Thanks, Mr. Dunham," said Colin.

"Anythin' for you, Colin," he said, and winked. "Now, you tend to that arm of yers, you hear?"

Colin nodded and awkwardly put the truck into gear with his right hand. The truck jostled as it picked up speed. Nora kept her eyes on Colin, who looked stern as he concentrated on the road, using his knees to steer instead as he shifted gears.

"Is it clear?" she asked.

"Aye, it's clear."

She sat back up and slid into the seat. Out the window, the mansions of Rathmines seemed to look on in disdain as the sputtering old delivery truck rumbled past. Nora reached for Colin's waistband.

"What are you doin'?" he asked.

"Relax." She smiled and pulled the flask from beneath his belt, opened it, and took a long drink. The warm liquid burned and ran out the corners of her mouth as the truck navigated the uneven road.

"Jesus, it's not water, Nora," said Colin. "Take it easy."

She lowered the flask and swallowed, her eyes watering. It burned her entire throat and mouth. But she said nothing as she screwed on the cap.

"Since when do you drink whiskey?" he asked.

"Since today," she said and turned to look out the window. The wealthy streets of Rathmines slowly faded into the ramshackle old buildings of the city proper. The shells of once opulent homes teemed with dirty, ill-fed Dubliners who had been stripped of all reason to hope for a better life, yet who clawed their way through each day, hoping nonetheless. They were the type of people the Parsons turned up their noses to or even pretended didn't exist. They lived far worse lives than Ethan's dogs. They were her people, and though she lived in a comfort most of them could never even imagine, she belonged to them.

"Pull over, Colin," she said suddenly. "Right over here." She pointed to a lonely lane ahead. He pulled the truck into the dirt road and reached around with his right arm to shift the truck into neutral. Tall grass stood on either side, overgrown amid the decaying buildings. Swarms of birds were not deterred by the creeping smell that signaled they were approaching the tenements.

"What?" he said. She leaned over and kissed him. Unexpectedly, he laughed. "What the hell was that for?"

"Overdue," she said.

"I'd say so," he said. "Imagine the trouble we could have saved if you just had kissed me earlier. No curses, no broken arms, none of it." He took his flask back from Nora and shook it.

"How do you have any left?" she asked. "Every time I see you, you are sippin' on that thing."

"Jameson's is right around the corner from the shop," he said and took a drink. "And he's a customer of me uncle's."

"It's awful," she said, peering out the window to see if there was anyone walking along the lane.

"Blasphemy!" Colin laughed. "You didn't like it?"

Nora shook her head. A skinny stray cat poked its head out from the grass. It eyed the truck warily, then scooped up a tiny kitten by its scruff and scampered across the dirt and to the other side.

"It calms me nerves," he said. "And you get used to the taste of it."

"Why do you need to calm your nerves around me?" she asked. "If there's anywhere you can be yourself, Colin, it's with me. I won't judge you." She moved closer to him.

He half smiled at her. "It helps me relax a little. No harm in that." Colin adjusted his left arm so that it lay safely across his lap, and then with his right, he reached over and placed his hand on the curve of her jawline. He kissed her again, but she didn't let him pull away. She laced her hands behind his head.

"Reminds me of Clare," she said. "Before you decided to leave."

He nodded and guided her head to his shoulder, wincing as her weight pressed up against his left side. "I didn't want to leave, you know."

"Why not?" she asked, smiling. "Tell me."

He shook his head. "Up to your tricks again. You won't trap me that easily," he said. "But I will tell you this—I don't know what it is about you, Nora McMahon, but I can't tell if you're an angel or a mortal sin in the makin'."

"Nowhere near an angel or a mortal sin—yet."

He laughed and sat back in his chair. He put his right hand out the open window and tapped the roof of the delivery truck with his fingers.

She took the flask from him and shook it. "Wonder if we have enough whiskey left for a mortal sin?"

"We don't," he said and brought his hand back inside the cab to take the flask from her. "Get that grin off yer face." He turned and looked out the window. "You ready to get goin? Or do you have more trouble in mind for me?"

"Trouble?" she asked. "I don't bring you any more trouble than you already make for yerself."

"You are only trouble, Nora," he said, teasing. "Take this week for instance.

Twice I saw you hit a grown man over the head with a blunt instrument. If that's not trouble, I don't know what is."

"Aye, 'tis quite an effective skill, isn't it?" She untangled herself from him. It was getting hot inside the cab. The afternoon sun beat down on the weathered black truck. "You've only got one arm these days, so it seems you are in great need of my trouble." She wiped the sweat from her forehead and picked up his gray left hand. She slid the ratty fabric sling over his wrist so she could see his entire arm. It was still bent askew at an odd angle, and the bluish tint was spreading higher up his arm.

"Do you think he broke it further?" she asked him. "When he kicked you?" She rested his arm on her knees and slowly followed her hands along his forearm, starting at his elbow, feeling for a break. When she approached his wrist, he winced. She held her fingers over the bulge on his forearm and pressed slightly. She felt the bones move. He let out a yell.

"Seems to be just one break," she said. "But it needs to be set. The bone is snapped clear through."

"Michael wanted to wait a few days so that we wouldn't draw attention to it." He tried to blow the hair from his eyes, but the sweat on his forehead kept his hair plastered to his skin. .

"He's an arse," she said. "If they don't set it soon, it'll never heal the right way. And it's the hand you always use."

"Maybe I can learn to use me right hand," he said. "Finally stop being a heathen."

"You're not a heathen, Colin. Nothing of the sort. But I suppose you'll be headed to confession this weekend." She winked at him and lifted her thick curly hair off the back of her neck. The heat was becoming unbearable.

"Probably," he said. "Though I have to find a new priest. This one is gettin' tired of hearing the same ol' story from me week in and week out."

"So give 'im something a little more exciting this week," she teased him, gently moving his arm aside. She began unbuttoning his shirt and slipped her hands under the garment.

"Nora," he said, "What are you doin'? You're goin' to get me a one-way ticket to hell."

"Just givin' you some new material," she said. "Keep that priest of yers on his toes."

"Stop it," he said, but winked at her. He took her hand and lowered it along his stomach and toward his belt. "No more." When she didn't balk, but instead went further, he sat up straight, bumping his head on the ceiling. "All right, really, stop it."

"Why?" she said. She wiped his forehead to stop the sweat from trickling down his temples.

"Because hell is going to be chalk full of bloody Englishmen, and I don't want to hang out with them both here in Dublin and for all eternity."

She slowly took her hand off his stomach and buttoned up his shirt. "Can hell be as hot as this truck?" she asked.

"I don't know, but Christ. Nora, just confessing this itself will be a sin," he said teasingly.

"So don't," she said. "It's nothin' that every single other boy isn't already doin'."

"How do you know?" he said, sitting all the way up. "If you're not careful, you'll be spending eternity burning with the English."

"Eh, you'll be right there with me," she said.

"What's gotten into you anyways?" he asked, taking another long sip from his almost-empty flask. She gritted her teeth and felt anger building inside her again. He brought his hand to her mouth. "Shh," he said. "You don't need to say it." She felt a tear forming in her eye, and he reached over to wipe it away.

"It's only because all I ever wanted was to be with you," she said. "And then— that filthy murderous bastard—"

"We don't ever need to talk about it again," he said, cutting her off. She sat back in her seat and leaned her head back. She wanted to think of some happy memory. But she could only think of revenge.

"Let's get out of here. Get some air moving." With some effort, Colin put the truck back into gear and backed out onto the main road. As the truck jostled forward and the cool breeze once again began to pour through the cab, he said, "You really only ever wanted me?" he asked. "Nora McMahon, the girl who is afraid of nothing, who can run guns with a bunch of boys?"

"Of course, Colin," she said. "You're an idiot if you didn't already know that. And I know you're smarter than that." After a moment passed, she said, "And you can stop calling me Nora McMahon. It's not my name."

He eyed her curiously.

She nodded. "When I pull the trigger, I want the papers to report that he was murdered by a Cullen."

CHAPTER 47

August 8, 1914: The Liberties, Dublin, Ireland

Colin gingerly opened the back door to the shop, doing his best to avoid ringing the bell that sat above the doorway. Despite his best efforts, the bell sounded a light clang that attracted the attention of his cousin, who was manning the front of the shop. Before they could ascend the stairs to the second floor, Michael appeared from behind the curtain that separated the front of the store from the back.

He looked at Colin, then at Nora, then back to Colin. "Are you crazy?" he exclaimed. "I thought I was clear—"

"You were clear, you arse," said Colin. "She just needs a place to hide out for a while, Michael."

"I've got a store full of customers—she can't be seen here!"

Nora scowled at him. "Don't speak as if I'm not standing here in front of you," she said.

"I'll hide her upstairs till we close," said Colin. "She'll be gone tomorrow."

"Tomorrow?" yelled Michael.

Colin turned his back on his cousin and led Nora up the stairs to the loft. Stepping off the top stair, Nora looked around the sparse living quarters.

"Not quite a mansion, but it's what we call home," Colin said.

"He's right," Nora said. "I shouldn't be here."

"Just hang tight up here, Nora. I'll talk to him." She plopped down into the sole chair in the loft and stared out the small window. Colin watched her for a moment. A sliver of evening sun shone through the small window, bringing out the red in her auburn hair and reminding him of how she had looked when they were children in Clare. It didn't seem so long ago, and yet so much had changed. He wanted to always be able to remember how they had been. With difficulty, he turned away and descended the stairs to deal with Michael.

As soon as he emerged from the loft, Michael bellowed, "What the fook do you think—"

"Shhh!" said Colin, stepping off the bottom stair and walking across the cramped space to the kitchen. "Keep your voice down. I was over there this mornin' deliverin' the order."

"And you were supposed to check in with Ronan an' be on yer way!" Michael followed him. His heavy boots tramped over the creaky floors.

"And that's what I was doin'—"

"Seems likely," said Michael, as he pounded the counter. "That's why she's sittin' up in our loft."

Colin ignored his cousin. "But somethin' happened," he said. "Ethan had her cornered in one of the rooms, and there was a bit of a scuffle—"

"What do you mean?" asked Michael. He lifted his hand and readied it to pound again.

"She knocked him out," said Colin.

Michael's mouth dropped instead of his fist, revealing the awkward spacing of his teeth. The gap where his missing tooth should have been was the only disorderly thing about him.

"But Mr. Dunham is working to control the damage," Colin quickly interjected, "He'll be by tomorrow to get her, so long as they can convince Ethan that it was some rogue stable hand that knocked him out, and not a girl."

Michael ran his hands through his hair, leaving it uncharacteristically ruffled. He paced back and forth. Colin hadn't seen him so anxious before. "Do you think he'll believe it?"

"Dunno. Depends on how hard she hit 'im." Colin couldn't help but smile. Nora certainly had proven that she knew how to take care of herself. He observed his cousin as he nervously paced across the room, and noticing a rare silence from his cousin, took the opportunity to broach another topic "We're going to have to have a gentlemen's agreement over what we tell each other. I need to know who is on our side."

"What do you mean?"

"Finnegan," said Colin. He thought about pounding the counter to get his cousin's attention. Instead, he walked toward the door to feel the breeze. Since leaving the Parsons', every space had felt unbearably hot.

"Her," scowled Michael.

"I need to know who is friendly. How can we work if we don't know who we can trust?"

Michael nodded. "Did he see you?"

"Aye," said Colin. He knew the details would only incense his cousin, but he elaborated anyway. "And I might have taken a few swings at 'im. I'm to be the rogue stable hand."

Michael shook his head angrily "You always manage to fook things up, don't you?" The tension between them only added to the heat.

"Don't think I can take credit for this one," said Colin sullenly. Above him, he heard Nora's footsteps pacing along the floor. He lowered his voice. "What would you have done? The whole damned reason I want a free Ireland is to have it with her. I don't know what version of freedom you are lookin' for, but that's what I want. What would you have done?"

"Colin," said Michael. For once, he sounded earnest. "I would have done the same thing. Look, I can find another place for her. Maybe this was too much to ask of her. Maybe it just won't work."

A creak from the stair interrupted Colin's reply. "Stop it!" Nora stood in defiance on the top step. "I'll not have you sittin' around and decidin' what is best for me. I'm going back there. Mr. Dunham is coming to get me tomorrow, and I'll be ready. We'll carry on like nothin' happened—"

"Nora," said Michael, "there can be other options." Colin eyed his cousin. *Finally—some sense!*

"No!" she said, slipping down the staircase to stand on the last step. "I want to go where I am needed most. Whether that is runnin' guns in Wicklow or runnin' information at the Parsons. I can make me own choices. And I choose to fight."

Colin pursed his lips but held his tongue. He knew there was now nothing he could say that would change her mind. It was too late. *Why couldn't Michael have just relented earlier?*

Even standing on the bottom stair, Nora's stature was quite small. But she looked right at Michael with her glowing green eyes, and Colin saw that even his normally arrogant cousin had trouble keeping eye contact with her.

"Well then," Michael said softly, clearing his throat. "It's decided. Let's get you ready,"

"Aye," said Nora. She now turned her glance to meet Colin's eyes, and a softer look came over her. "But first we're taking Colin to a doctor. He needs to have his arm set." She stated it as a fact, and Michael made no protest.

Colin smiled to himself. *So in the end it'll be Nora who knocks sense into Michael. Of course it would be that way.* He watched his cousin nod obediently. Even he was not immune to her spell.

"And then we'll come back, and you'll tell me about whatever it is that you brought me here to do. The whole story." She gave Michael a hard look.

"All right, Nora." Michael turned to Colin. "Let's get you to a doctor. I'll call Cian and set it up."

CHAPTER 48

August 8, 1914, London, England

The parlor was thick with the smoke of cigars. The last embers on Viscount Eldridge's cigar fell to the mother-of-pearl ashtray, and he snuffed out the stub. Francis, the only member of the staff senior enough to decline the evening's ridiculous prescribed uniform, entered the room and pulled back the long drapes to open one of the floor-to-ceiling windows.

"Sir, your sons have arrived," he said. Francis discretely replaced the ashtray with an identical clean one.

Edward stood with Gerald at the door and thought he saw the flicker of his mother's skirt out of the corner of his eye. Gerald leaned toward his brother and whispered, "You couldn't keep Mother away from the parlor—even if the Queen herself were in the ballroom!" The Eldridge brothers looked into the dimly lit room on a most peculiar scene.

"Never thought I'd see this day," said Edward quietly. Before them sat avowed political rivals Viscount Eldridge and Lord Clarendon, sharing cigars, the finest scotch anywhere in London, and what looked to be a cordial—if forced— conversation.

"Edward," boomed the viscount before Gerald could respond. "Why don't you come and join us!" He sounded sterner than Edward had expected. Gerald smacked his brother on the back. "Good luck, Al," he said as Edward feigned a confident step and walked into the parlor.

"Have a seat, my boy," his father said, opening his hand to the empty upholstered chair by the fireplace. "Lord Clarendon," Edward said, greeting Elizabeth's father.

"Edward," he said in return, lifting the last bit of cigar to his mustached mouth. Expectedly, Edward saw a flutter of activity by the far door. Both his father and Lord Clarendon were facing the opposite direction, so they couldn't see his mother and Gerald listening in from the door on the other side of the room.

"So tell me, Edward," started Lord Clarendon "Where's your unit currently stationed? Duke of Cornwall Light Infantry Reserve, I hear. A fine unit with a brilliant young officer corps."

"Yes, sir. Both Gerald and I begin drill at Bodmin in a few days' time." he replied. "Our train will depart tomorrow. The word is that we will depart for the continent before the end of October." He wondered if he was being too talkative. He awkwardly clasped his hands in his lap, wishing his father had offered him a cigar as well.

"And my three sons are already with their units. They are military men by career, you know," said Lord Clarendon, this time picking up a highball glass filled to the brim with his father's finest scotch. "These are interesting times we live in," he said.

Edward nodded in agreement. He didn't dare take the bait and strike up a political discussion. He was quite confident he could not referee any fight that might break out between his father and Elizabeth's. He eyed the two. Elizabeth's father certainly had the height advantage, though the viscount countered that with his burgeoning girth. The question would be, could his father roll up off the floor if he was knocked down first?

"My daughter, Elizabeth," Lord Clarendon said, catching Edward's undivided attention, "has been quite successful with her literacy campaign, and I can't help but thank the viscountess for her assistance with the effort. Please, gentlemen, give Lady Eldridge my sincere thanks for her support."

Edward's father gruffly nodded and grabbed his own highball. Edward sat uncomfortably and stared at his father. *Can you at least acknowledge the compliment?* he thought. His father sipped his scotch and adjusted his gold cufflinks.

"Thank you, Lord Clarendon," said Edward. "I'll be sure to let my mother know." He tried hard not to look to the far end of the room, where his mother stood partially obscured in the doorway by a strategically placed potted tree.

"Has Lady Clarendon discussed her plans for the campaign this fall?" he asked. It was a perfect topic of conversation—politically benign and centered around Elizabeth. Surely it would naturally lead to the conversation he had come to hear.

"With London mobilizing for war, I'm afraid it will take a back seat," said Elizabeth's father.

"That's unfortunate," said Edward. "There's a great need for such a campaign." He shot a glance toward his father, who had drained his glass and was now looking quite bored.

"'Tis unfortunate, Edward, that's a perfect description. Literacy is a sign of an educated population, a thinking population. And we must work to create a world where the citizenry can benefit from the wide variety of information that is readily available." Edward nodded in understanding, still wishing he had either a glass of scotch or a cigar in his hands.

"I couldn't agree more," he replied. He stole a look at his father, who must have noticed his glare and mumbled a half-hearted agreement. "Yes, of course," grunted the viscount.

And while Edward was lulled into complacency by the benevolent conversation, Lord Clarendon fired the first shot across the bow. "Which is precisely why Elizabeth will be headed to Ireland by month's end!" Edward, who had been nodding his head to establish his firm agreement, suddenly stopped and looked first to Lord Clarendon and then nervously to his father. *Not Ireland!* he thought. *Any topic but Ireland!*

Viscount Eldridge suddenly looked agitated. Edward took a deep breath.

"Why would she waste her precious time on that confounded island?" his father said. Edward closed his eyes. If there was any topic that made his father instantly belligerent, it was the Irish. He opened his eyes and saw Gerald shaking his head violently from the door. He knew he had to redirect the conversation, and quickly.

"Surely an educated Ireland can only be a good thing, Father. And she'll be staying with relatives?" He hoped that would be sufficient.

"Yes, her mother's cousin is a great philanthropist in Dublin."

"Ah, Dublin," Edward said. *The very heart of the nationalist movement.* "Brilliant."

"Have your relatives been there long?" his father asked. Edward knew it was a loaded question.

"For years," said Lord Clarendon. "So long that he calls himself Irish." Edward cringed, but Lord Clarendon continued. "He's a magistrate by some generations-old birthright. Feels very connected to the place."

"So very pro-Ulster," said Edward, going out of his way to make it quite clear that Elizabeth's relatives were not the type to harbor any nationalist sentiments.

"Yes, indeed," said Lord Clarendon, and Edward saw his father break into a small smile.

Defused. Edward smiled to himself and saw Gerald dramatically wipe his forehead form across the room. A close call.

"Yes, indeed," Lord Clarendon repeated. And then he launched the fatal shot.

"The bloody bastard." Had Edward been given a glass of scotch, he would have choked on it.

"Excuse me?" said the viscount. He held his glass to his mouth—it was now empty, but still convenient for a prop—and abruptly put it back down on the table.

"I said he is a bastard," said Lord Clarendon matter-of-factly. "A people must be free to determine their own future. He will blindly support Ulster and their misguided attempt to hold the rest of the island under their thumbs. It's not right any more than it is right to allow Austria to rule over the Serbs!"

Edward readied himself to stop his father from pounding his fist on the table. He had to say something. *What would Gerald do?* He thought frantically. He jumped to his feet and began to pace the parlor floor the way he had seen his brother do days before. "Very interesting," he said, scratching the stubble that was not on his chin. "Which is precisely why it is so important that Elizabeth go to Ireland," he said.

"Why?" asked his father, sounding about as belligerent as he expected.

"Well," said Edward, "Perhaps a more educated Ireland is a more sensible Ireland...perhaps they will find a more peaceful solution to government." He knew he had to walk a fine line between his father's hatred of all things Irish and Lord Clarendon's obvious soft spot for the island.

"Yes, Edward!" said Lord Clarendon. "An educated Ireland might finally have peace!"

While he was pleased that Elizabeth's father agreed with him, he knew that this would not sit well with his own father.

"Yes," the viscount chimed in, and Edward knew that things were about to get ugly. He looked frantically toward the half-empty bottle of scotch perched on the bar to try to determine how much his father had had to drink. "An education might teach those foolish Irish how fortunate they have been to be subjects of the Crown!" Edward saw his brother put his hands to his head. It was as good as over.

Yet his father continued. "It's not as if England *enjoys* their caretaker status! No, quite the opposite!" His father was now bellowing out his words, and there were little beads of sweat forming on his bald head. "It is a burden we have shouldered in order to bring a backward society into the twentieth century. And the very least they could do is show some gratitude to Westminster!" Edward thought he heard the potted plant let out a little shriek.

At once, the two men were on their feet, and Edward stepped precariously in between them. "Gentlemen," he said, holding his hands up to keep the men separated. "I think we all know we are not going to reach an agreement on this tonight. Our government has not been able to solve it over hundreds of years—perhaps we can revisit it another time?"

Both of the men stared intensely at one another, but they grunted an agreement and sat down in their respective chairs. "Now I believe," Edward continued, "that we are here to discuss another topic."

"It's been discussed, Edward," said his father.

"Yes," said Lord Clarendon gruffly. Both men reached for their empty highballs. Edward took a few quick strides over to the bar and returned with the bottle of scotch, generously refilling each glass and grabbing a third for himself. He placed the open bottle in the middle of the table, next to Lord Clarendon's smoldering cigar, and sat back in his upholstered chair. By now, his mother had emerged entirely from behind the potted plant.

He took a most ungentlemanly swig of the scotch and leaned back into the chair.

"Edward," said Lord Clarendon. "You are a fine young man." Then he muttered, "A great feat, considering the household you grew up in." Edward cringed. He imagined that this would be the mood of every family gathering after he and Elizabeth were married—an ambiance more fit for a pub brawl than an English estate.

"I couldn't imagine a better match for my Elizabeth."

Edward finally felt a wave of relief. He looked to his father, hoping for at least a smile, but instead the old viscount stared angrily at Lord Clarendon. *You know how to spoil just about everything*, Edward thought.

"But as I said before," Lord Clarendon continued, "we live in interesting times." A strange sense of foreboding crept over Edward. He gripped his highball glass. "A war is no time to make any sort of long-term decisions. There are just too many unknowns."

He felt his heart sink, and a cold sweat break out on his forehead. Though he had had but one drink of scotch, he felt like the room was spinning.

He vaguely heard Elizabeth's father say, "Now, when this war comes to its conclusion—which I pray is sooner rather than later—we can revisit this subject again. But now is decidedly not the time."

Lord Clarendon finished off his glass of scotch. "Don't look so downtrodden, Edward. You are about to embark on the greatest adventure of your life. Focus on that, and when you get back, you can focus on my daughter. One thing at a time."

He rose from his chair, and Edward followed suit. "Thank you, Lord Clarendon, for your consideration," he said.

"Of course, Edward. Now, if you'll both excuse me, I believe there's a party going on. You'll both be wanting to get back."

"Of course," said the viscount. "We'll speak again in a few months."

Edward didn't watch as Lord Clarendon left the room, but the sound of his footprints let him know that he was headed down the hall and toward the ballroom. He slumped back into his chair, highball still in hand. He rested one arm on the upholstered arm of the chair and drained his glass. He felt his father put his hand on his. "Edward," he said. "I'm sorry. I did my best."

"I know, Father," he said as he stared up at the ceiling.

"Try to enjoy the party. It'll be the last grand affair until this war is over," he said. The viscount stood and exited the room. Edward took a deep breath, then stood and slowly walked over to the potted tree, which was shaking with the viscountess's sniffles.

"Mother," he said, holding his arms out. "Don't be upset. You'll get your engagement—just a few months more to wait." He feigned a smile.

"Oh Edward!" she said, sobbing into his pristine uniform. "It was perfectly arranged! An engagement announcement on my anniversary, and then that scoundrel Clarendon had to go and mess it up!" she had quickly turned from sobs to anger.

"There, there, Mother," he said. "There's still a party to enjoy."

He glanced over at Gerald, who mouthed, "Go, I'll take care of her."

Edward nodded, relieved, and awkwardly released his whimpering mother to Gerald. Once she was safely in Gerald's arms, he quickly moved down the hallway, taking a roundabout route to the ballroom. He passed his mother's office, and on a whim jumped inside. He strode over to her great mahogany desk and rummaged for a quill and some parchment. Ripping the corner off a large sheet, he penned a quick note, then folded it into his fist.

He quickly emerged back out into the hallway and toward the staff entrance to the ballroom. As he walked among the maids and butlers, he spied Alice, wiping the crumbs from a tray of hors d'oeuvres. "Alice," he said urgently. "Have you seen Elizabeth and her mother?"

"I just saw them leave," she said. "Lady Clarendon looked mad as a hornet, and Elizabeth…" her voice trailed. "Not well."

"Damn!" he said, and ran back into the hall, hoping to head them off at the front entryway. He ran down the hall, his dress shoes holding no traction on the waxed and polished floors. Sliding around the final corner to the entryway, he saw Francis handing a top hat to Lord Clarendon. He burst into the entryway, not caring that he was probably about to make the type of scene that would feed the London gossip mill for weeks to come.

"Elizabeth," he cried. She snapped her head toward him and let go of her mother's arm.

She reached for his hands but instead of taking them, he slipped the piece of paper under the glove of her left hand.

"It'll be all right."

"But I won't see you—"

"It'll be all right," he said. "Good night, my darling," he whispered to her. He glanced at Lord Clarendon, who viewed the scene with abject disapproval.

He nodded his head in deference to her father, then returned Elizabeth to her mother's arm.

Francis guided the party out the door and to the waiting carriage, and Edward watched sadly as the three departed down the carriage path.

CHAPTER 49

August 8, 1914: Dublin, Ireland

Nora peered out the window of the home at Fitzwilliam Place. Cian O'Brien stood at the doorway, looking out. The streets had fallen dark, and the lamp keeper was making his way through the streets, lighting the lamps.

Cian gestured sternly to Nora. "Shut the curtain. The last thing we need is for anyone to see you lookin' out and think that somethin's up."

Nora quickly shut the curtain and gazed back into the foyer of the home. It was nicely fitted with furniture that was probably a generation old, but was well kept and matching. The walls were papered with a floral print that had faded over the years into a blurred pattern of pink and green.

Her thoughts were interrupted by a door opening from the back bedroom that, in this house, was used primarily to examine patients. Cian had found a bona fide doctor, a Protestant—as most Dublin doctors were—but with a soft spot for Irish nationalists. He had treated quite a few in recent times. Business had been so good that he had begun to keep office hours late at night to treat patients looking to avoid attention from the authorities.

"Well," Doctor Fabian announced to the room in a loud, booming voice, "It's broke right through. A compound fracture."

"Is that bad?" asked Nora.

"Quite bad. And it's an old wound." He looked at Cian. "What's the meaning of keeping him suffering all this time? Come to me as soon as possible—no matter the circumstances. Don't wait. It could have gotten infected—he could have lost the arm."

Cian looked a little sheepish. "Michael didn't realize it was that bad."

"As it is, it's begun to heal a bit, and I'm going to have to break it again to set it. It's going to be painful. The worst of it is that I'm fresh out of chloroform," Dr. Fabian continued. "We'll have to do it on whiskey alone. "

Cian cringed. "When can you get some chloroform?"

"There's a war starting up. It's going to be a while, and we can't wait."

"All right then, let's do it." Cian said, as if he were in charge. He offered the doctor his own flask. "Just topped it off. There should be enough to get 'im tipsy."

Dr. Fabian opened the metal cap and smelled the contents. He set it down on an antique end table in the sitting room. "And a massive hangover. You boys really need to drink better whiskey less often. It'll cost you the same and save you the trouble of the hangover. Are you a nurse, girl?" he asked.

"Nah, she's just 'is girlfriend," Cian broke in, answering for her.

Nora glared at him until Cian dropped his eyes to the ground. She addressed the doctor. "No, but I've worked on a farm. Stitched up sheep and the like."

"That'll do just fine," he said. "And girls are good in these situations. It'll toughen him up to have you in there. Makes things easier on me. Come with me. And you—" he gestured to Cian. "Wait out here, and let me know if anyone is hanging out too long outside or coming up the walk. And douse the lanterns in the front rooms."

Nora grabbed the flask from the end table and followed Dr. Fabian across the creaky wooden floors into the dim but comfortable bedroom. Colin sat on a bed among a pile of white linens. Dr. Fabian pulled a thick, black curtain over the window, then lit a gas lantern on the small table that held his leather medical bag. "Light the other one, Nora," he said, pointing to a lamp on one of the bedside tables. Nora struck a match on the bedside table and adjusted the wick.

"Here, boy," he said, handing Colin the flask. "Drink this."

Colin took the flask uncertainly. "Is it medicine?" he asked.

The doctor laughed. "Sort of, my boy. When you've drunk half of it, let me know." He turned to Nora, "Come and get me when he's lit," he said to her quietly. "I'll be reading in the study." Then he turned and left the room through a small side door.

After the door had shut behind him, Colin took a sip, then smiled. "This is the best medicine I've ever had." He patted the bed next to him, and Nora sat down beside him. "Do you want some?" he asked her, offering her the flask.

"No thank you," she said. "I'm not the one with a broken arm."

"Aw, come on," he said. "It'll grow on you." He shook the flask. She apprehensively reached for it and took a small sip. Again, she felt a burning sensation in her mouth and throat. She tried not to cough.

"Any better?" he asked, though he must have known her response from the repulsed look on her face.

She stuck out her tongue and shook her head. "Not yet. I suspect it'll take a lot of getting used to." The awful taste still lingered in her mouth. "How is it that everyone seems to actually like this stuff?"

Colin laughed. "It's not so much the taste—which does grow on you—it's the after effect. Makes the day a little bit better."

No amount of whiskey is going to make your day any better, Nora thought to herself. She turned away from Colin. The mere thought of what was coming made her a little sick to her stomach. The room around her glowed with the orange light from the two gas lanterns. Though the home had electricity, the doctor had lit the back bedroom only with the old lanterns. For the first time, it occurred to Nora the risk he was taking in treating Colin. Doctor Fabian was no fool—he knew exactly what Colin had been up to. No doubt he had read the papers and learned the details. And yet he was willing to risk his practice and his livelihood to help the Volunteers. There was still goodness in this city—though it was always hard to know who to trust.

"What did the doc say he was going to do?" Colin interrupted her thoughts.

Nora didn't know how to respond. "Best you don't know, I think," she said.

"Brilliant," said Colin. He brought the flask back to his lips. Instead of sipping it, he took several large gulps. "I suppose I want to be good and drunk."

Nora laughed, though she felt very sorry for him. "Yes, you do."

He put his right arm around her and pulled her closer to him "You really want to go back to the Parsons?" he asked. "You can tell me the truth." He offered her the flask again. "Take another swig, think about it, and tell me."

Nora put her hand up, refusing the drink. "No, Colin, I've made up my mind," she said. "You're not going to change it."

"I was afraid of that," he said. "Why do you have to be so tough?"

"Would you like me if I wasn't?"

"That's a good question," he laughed. "I guess I don't mind you being tough once in a while. I just wish you chose another battle to fight me on."

She tapped her fingers on her knees. "Are you good an' drunk yet?" she asked.

"Not yet," he said. "It'll take a little while at least." He drank more. "Plus, I never get to see you anymore. I'll drag this on as long as I can."

"Not too long," she said. "The worst is yet to come. Might want to get it over with and not have it hangin' over your head."

"You sure you don't want any more?"

"Positive," she said.

"There's an easier way to drink it, you know," he said. "Not sure why I didn't think of it before."

"How's that?" she asked. "Does it burn the same?"

"Not at all." He took another long swig from the flask and swallowed. "Funny thing is, I like the burn." He handed her the flask. "Here's what you do," he said, pointing to the flask in her hand.

She followed his gaze, waiting for the next instruction. When he didn't say anything further, she looked back up, only to find his face right up next to hers. He held her chin with his right hand, and kissed her softly on the lips.

"There," he said. "You can taste it without the burn. Was that better?"

She scowled at him, not pleased she had fallen for his game. "I'd say you're good an' drunk now," she said. "In all the years I've known you, you've never ever had the guts to pull a trick like that."

"Not true," he said, setting the flask on the night stand and wrapping his arm around her. "But you sure you don't want to try it again? I swear it'll grow on you."

"You're lucky you're sick," she said, smacking him lightly on the shoulder. "Because you are an intolerable drunk."

He laughed, then something caught his eye. "Nora," he said. "Your pendant is broken."

"I know," she said. "It happened somewhere on the way to Kilcoole. I looked down and half of it was just gone. It's a sign from me grandda, I think."

"A sign that you should stay away from the Parsons, probably," he said knowingly. She felt herself frown. "But maybe somethin' else. Who's left on it?"

"Brendan the Navigator, Mobhi of Glasnevin, Columba of Iona—"

"Columba?" asked Colin. He took the pendant in his hand and examined it. "Jesus, Mary, and Joseph, of course he would be," he muttered under his breath. "Do you know who Columba is?"

"No," admitted Nora.

"You've always been a lousy Catholic." His smiled looked troubled. "He's the dove of Ireland, don't you know?" He dropped the pendant and reached again for the flask. "Of course he would be left," he muttered again. He turned to Nora and kept his eyes locked with hers as he drank the last of the flask. "Why don't you go and get Dr. Fabian, and let's get this over with, whatever it is."

§♠

"So, you're ready, my boy," the doctor said. Colin was beginning to look quite groggy. The doctor picked up the flask. "I said half of it, not all of it," he said. "You'll be in tough shape tomorrow. Broken arm and broken head." He set a pillow up against the headboard. "Lie back," he instructed Colin.

As Colin settled in on the bed, Doctor Fabian beckoned to Nora. "Come here, my dear," he said to Nora. "I'm going to have you help me. Here," he gave her a rolled-up bed sheet. "Tie down his legs." He motioned to the foot of the bed.

Colin's face immediately turned serious. "Is that necessary?"

"Very," said the doctor.

Nora ran the cotton bed sheet under the mattress and then over Colin's trousers, as the doctor had instructed, then tied the ends of the sheet in a double knot.

"As tight as you can," he said, while he rolled more bed linens. "Right above the knee."

He took a second sheet and ran it across Colin's chest and right arm. "I want it so tight that you can barely breathe," he said. "Have I got the balance right?" he asked.

"I'd say so," said Colin uneasily.

"This is the part where I'd usually give you something to help relax you," the doctor said. "Except that I don't have anything. That was the medicine, shall se say, that you drank earlier. Let's hope whatever Cian had is strong."

He gave Nora a wooden baton, and told her to put it in Colin's right hand. "I want you to squeeze this as hard as you can," the doctor said. "When I tell you to."

"And Nora," he said, "I need you to restrain his upper left arm," he motioned to Colin's limp arm. "Between the shoulder and elbow, and give it everything you've got."

He pulled her aside and spoke quietly into her ear. "I'm going to tell him that I'm going to count to three, but I'm really going to break it on two," he said. "Be ready. And then after the initial holler that he's no doubt going to give, I'm going to go right in and set it. The whole thing will take less than five seconds. Are you ready?"

Nora tried not to look horrified, but she wasn't sure she succeeded. "Yes," she said. "I'm ready."

She walked over to Colin, but she couldn't look at him. She placed both her hands against his bicep and pressed as hard as she could into the mattress.

"Put all your weight into it," he said to her. "Now Colin," he said, "I'm going to count to three, and when I hit one, I want you to squeeze that baton with all your might. I took it off a British warden, so don't be afraid to give it hell." He winked at his patient.

"Are you ready?"

Colin nodded and took a deep breath.

"One," said the doctor. Nora could feel Colin as he tensed up and squeezed the wooden baton. "Two!" the doctor said, and Nora pressed down on Colin's arm with all her might. She heard a snap and Colin let out a yell. As soon as he relaxed just a little, she felt the doctor grip Colin's forearm and set the bone. Again, Colin yelled.

"Atta boy!" the doctor said. "Now don't move a muscle. We're going to splint this up properly. Come, Nora." He directed her over to a table where he had laid out all the supplies. "Just hand me what I ask for," he said. "We'll be done in no time."

"How are you doing, Colin?" he asked. "The worst is over now. In about two months this arm is going to be looking very good." The doctor pointed at the bed sheet that covered his chest, and Nora gathered it up into a bundle.

"You told me you were going to count to three!" moaned Colin.

"I know," said Dr. Fabian.

"Did he tell you he was going to do that?" he asked Nora.

She looked away.

"How's that whiskey treating you, Colin?" The doctor asked as he positioned the pasteboard and linens for the splint.

"I think all right," he said, sounding quite relaxed all of a sudden. "Everything feels good now."

"Hopefully it'll help you sleep," he said. "You did a good job, Colin. I think that arm is going to be just fine. It's a pity you're left-handed though—you might not ever gain all the strength back in it. Time will tell."

He finished his work quickly and turned to Nora. "Excellent work, my dear. I'm going to keep him here overnight. Not so much for the procedure, but more that I don't want him causing a drunken ruckus on the way home. Why don't you stay here with him?"

Nora raised an eyebrow.

"Come now," he said. "Don't look so alarmed. I'm a Protestant, remember?" He laughed. "And all men are really boys at heart. Sometimes they just need someone to dote on them. He'll recover quickly, you'll see. Come and get me if he needs anything."

Dr. Fabian left, and Nora could hear him talking to Cian outside the room. A few moments later, the front door shut as Cian left, and Dr. Fabian's slow footsteps climbed the stairs to his own room.

The two gas lanterns were still lit. She looked at Colin. His eyes were open, but he didn't seem very alert. Untying the remaining bed sheet from his legs, she covered him with it, then found a blanket on one of the chairs and draped that over him as well. She wondered if Colin had ever slept in a bed as nice as this one.

She turned out the first gas lamp, then picked up the other one and brought it to the table next to the bed. She sat down beside him and looked at his arm. The color was returning to his hand. It no longer looked gray and dull.

From the pocket of her dress, she pulled out the leather-bound book and went over its cryptic notes again. *Mr. S. C., 54 Marlborough Street, Mulcahy's Tavern. Brother-in-law. Mr. J. L., Distributor. Tuesday—Dairy. Granby Street Pub, afternoon, July 15. Mr. S. O, 32 Pembroke Street.* She knew so little about Dublin. None of these places were familiar to her.

Colin rolled onto his side. "The notebook," he said. "Read it to me." His eyes were open.

"Do you know any letters or numbers, Colin?"

"I know numbers," he said. "Had to learn them to be able to get around the store."

"So you can learn when you need to," she said. "Letters won't be that much more difficult." She put her fingers under the first printed address and showed the book to him. "5, 4" he said.

"Aye 54. 54 Marlborough Street. Do you know where that is?"

"Aye," he said. "Not far from here."

"How about this one?"

"3-2" he said.

"32 Pembroke Street."

"Know that one too," he said.

"Granby Street Pub?" she asked.

He closed his eyes and laid his head back down. "Yes," he said.

"We should get a map," she said, "and mark these places with dates and people."

He nodded, not opening his eyes. She put her small hand inside of his left palm, and he lightly closed his fingers around it.

"Haven't been able to make a fist since it was broken," he said. "I guess that's progress."

She nodded, then stood up and walked to the other side of the bed. He turned his head to look at her as she climbed in next to him.

"Oh no you don't," he said smiling. "You're just going to get me into trouble."

"I don't think you are capable of getting into trouble tonight, Colin," she said.

"I'll risk it."

She doused the last gas lantern and put her head down on the pillow next to him. She wrapped her arm around him, feeling his bare stomach with her hands. It was trim and muscular, just as she had always remembered it. His side was still scraped from their encounter with the British officers, but mostly his skin was smooth. At last she settled her palm on his hip bone. He turned toward her and kissed her forehead. He ran his hand through her curls, brushing them away from her face.

She listened to his breathing turn soft and rhythmic and assumed that he had fallen asleep until he spoke. "Do you remember the other night, Nora, when you asked me why I was stickin' up for you? When we were on the beach?"

She had thought about that question many times since then. "I remember, Colin," she said.

"An' I told you that you would have to wait for an answer," he swallowed, "because I hadn't had enough to drink to tell you?"

Nora didn't say anything, but she ran her hand from his hip to his left hand, and put her fingers back into his palm. Again, he loosely wrapped his hand around hers.

"I think I've finally had enough tonight," he said. "The damned room is spinning. And if tomorrow goes anythin' like I think it will, this might be the last time I am drunk enough for a while." He lay there silently for a moment, running his hand through her hair. "I love you Nora," he finally said. "I always have. And that's me last secret."

CHAPTER 50

August 8, 1914: London, England

Elizabeth was stunned. On what should have been the most perfect evening of her life, when all the pieces had come together so beautifully, her father had declined to agree to a marriage. Her father! Who had always been on her side and always acted with compassion! She had been hoping for some sort of excitement in her life, but certainly not this. She fumbled with the piece of paper that Edward had hidden in her glove. She was dying to know what he had written.

She sat directly across from her father on the bumpy carriage ride to her family's London estate, but she couldn't bring herself to speak to him. She didn't even want to look at him. Her mother sat beside her, and for once, held her American tongue. No amount of arguing was going to change his mind.

"Now, Elizabeth," he said after some time, "you will thank me in time. The eve of a war is no time for an engagement, much less a marriage."

She was a rational person, but she would not yield this point to him. Matters of the heart didn't follow logic, this he must know. She played with her gloves, inching the little piece of paper closer to her palm.

"Edward must be able to focus on the job at hand and not worry about things back at home. It is important for our boys to be fully engaged in the war effort," Lord Clarendon continued.

"Not possible," she replied, angered into breaking her silence. "Edward will think of me regardless of whether we are engaged or not."

"Perhaps," Lord Clarendon said.

"You know that it's true," she said. "Surely you thought of Mother when you were separated." She looked at her mother for assistance, and her mother raised an eyebrow to her father.

"'Tis true, I did," he said. Since both women were quite cross with him, he was clearly trying to choose his words carefully so as not to incite an explosion within the carriage. "But your mother and I were different."

Lady Clarendon rolled her eyes, which told Elizabeth that they had not, in fact, been any different.

"You were not!" Elizabeth replied. She surprised herself at the harsh tone of her voice, but her neither of her parents objected to her outburst. "You were not," she repeated, composing herself. Why did all adults of her parents' age believe that their experience of love was singular and unique? How did one forget so quickly how it felt to fall in love, particularly when the emotion was so strong?

"When you are older, you will recognize that I did this to protect you," he said.

"You did this because you do not like Viscount Eldridge," Elizabeth replied defiantly.

"I will grant you that I absolutely do not care for the viscount. But Edward is different. I quite enjoyed our conversation tonight, if I can be frank."

Elizabeth stared at him, her face still hot with fury. She quieted her hands, lest he discover that she was preoccupied by something in her glove.

"Elizabeth. I know you are upset, but please listen to me. You have not lived through war. You do not know what it can do to a man or, for that matter, what it can do to those left behind. Not one of us will be the same when this is over. I do not want to chain you to a memory of someone you once loved."

"I will always love Edward!" she said. "There is nothing that would make me change my mind."

Lord Clarendon nodded. "We will discuss this again when the war has concluded. You may not have long to wait."

Elizabeth scowled. She wished she could control her temper, but she couldn't. She could feel energy coursing through her entire body, and she had no outlet. It was useless to argue further with her father. He had already made up his mind. They passed the rest of the trip in silence.

As soon as the carriage pulled into the drive and came to a halt, she jumped out and scurried across the gravel walk into the residence. When she entered the manor, she darted toward the spiral staircase to the second floor. Her father continued wordlessly into the dining room to pour himself his customary glass of cognac, but her mother caught up to her at the top of the stairs.

"Elizabeth, dear," she said, taking her aside. She spoke quietly. "Listen to me. I will try to talk some sense into him. All is not lost yet. But you mustn't lose your temper with him. Don't do anything rash. Try to be patient."

Elizabeth did not respond but watched her mother descend the stair to follow her father into the dining room. Her thoughts immediately turned to the slip of paper folded inside her glove.

She ran across the halls of the upper floor to her bedroom, where she shut the door and pulled the latch over the handle. She pulled off her glove and carefully unfolded the crumpled paper. It was a note in Edward's handwriting that simply said, "*Stables. 10:00.*" She stared at the note for a moment, then folded it back up. Then she lit an ornate lantern in her room and burned the small piece of paper. She was tempted to save it as a keepsake, but didn't trust that no one would find it. She looked at the clock that stood in the corner of the room. It was already quarter to ten.

She removed her remaining glove and slowly unpinned her intricately curled updo so that her long brown hair fell down her back. Seeing in the mirror that her cheeks were still flushed from anger, she splashed water on her face and combed back her hair. She removed her heeled shoes and slipped off her dress so she could untie the corset underneath. She stepped out of her undergarments and took her first deep breath of the night. Leaving her dress in a heap on the floor, she darted toward her wardrobe and picked out a summer dress that didn't need a confining corset and some slippers that made her sore feet feel like they were stepping on clouds. Satisfied that she was ready, she headed for her open bedroom window.

She had done this many times before, but as a young child, when she and her brothers would sneak off to the garden on summer nights to explore. Something about the night had always made the garden much more interesting. Once in a while they would get caught, and other times their parents would let them have their adventures. She was much larger now, and she did not realize how much she had changed in her years away at school. She was surprised at how difficult it was to fit through the window. She quietly put her feet out onto the ledge and moved slowly across it until she reached the lattice by the side chimney.

As a child, the lattice held her weight without a problem, but she wondered how she would fare now that she was an adult. It creaked as she put her slippered feet onto it and swayed slightly as she balanced her full weight on the tresses. She held on motionless and with eyes closed for a second, waiting for the lattice to break off the side of the exterior wall, but to her relief, it didn't. She descended foot over foot as quickly as she could and ran off in toward the stable. Before she slid the large door aside, she looked behind her. She heard nothing but the crickets and a distant carriage rumbling through the streets. She moved the door slightly ajar and disappeared into the stable.

It was pitch dark inside, and she stumbled into the tack room to find a gas lamp. Surrounded by the deep breathing of the horses, she fumbled around the room until she found a box of matches. Once a match was struck, the small room became visible, and she lit the lantern. All was quiet. By now, it must be close to ten, but there was no sign of Edward.

She took the lantern and walked into the main part of the stable. A horse whinnied curiously at this nighttime visitor, so she placed the lantern on the floor and reached over the door to her father's gelding's stall. He nickered and approached the door, and she felt sudden regret that she hadn't thought to bring a treat for him. As she scratched the horse's ears with one hand, with the other she traced the wooden lettering on the door, "Albert." She smiled at the memory of her introduction to Edward, but the sight of the horse made her feel intensely sad.

As Elizabeth absentmindedly smoothed Albert's forelock, the gelding's ears suddenly pricked forward, and Elizabeth felt a firm hand on her back. She whirled around, surprised. Edward stood directly behind her, only a few inches away. She hadn't heard him come in.

He was a tall man, but still she was almost his height, and she only had to lift her lips slightly to kiss him. As their lips touched, he wrapped his arms around her waist and slowly pushed her up against the stall door.

"So you got my note," he said in jest, and pressed his forehead to hers. "Glad I didn't have to scale the wall to see you." He smiled sadly. "Though I would have."

He took her face in his hands and ran his fingers through her hair, brushing it slightly away from her eyes. He looked down at her feet. "Interesting choice."

"A bit more practical than wearing a full military dress uniform in a barn." She laughed, happy for a chance to be more lighthearted. "And if you had to wear heels, you would understand."

"Let's go for a walk," he said.

She shook her head and took him by the hand. "Come." She had no intention of going for a walk with him. She picked up the lantern and led him to a ladder on the far side of the stable.

He peered up into the dark space above. "A much better idea," he said. "After you."

She stepped onto the bottom rung and handed him the lantern before climbing up to the top. When she was on the platform above, she sank to her knees and reached down to take the lantern back. She held it as he climbed to the top. She wished he wasn't wearing his uniform. It was going to get dirty.

Elizabeth placed the lantern on the wood floor and sat on a bale of hay. He sat down next to her, and she watched the light-colored fabric of his perfectly creased trousers grow dusty from the hay.

He leaned over and kissed her again. "Elizabeth," he said, "I am leaving in a few hours."

"I know," she replied. She looked into his dark brown eyes, which looked almost black in the dim light of the loft. What could she say? Their parents had spoken for them. There would be no engagement.

"I mean to marry you, Elizabeth Clarendon," Edward finally said. "If you'll have me."

"I'll have you," she answered. "I will wait for you. For as long as this war lasts, I will wait for you."

He stroked her hair. "It will be over in a few months' time, you'll see."

She shook her head. "Do you really think that? Germany is a force to be reckoned with. I don't think I'll see you for the better part of a year, perhaps longer."

He opened his mouth to protest, but he didn't speak. She knew he suspected the war would last a long time too.

"You aren't so confident, are you?" she said.

"I don't know," he said. "I just don't know what will happen."

Unexpectedly, she laughed.

"What could possibly be funny?" he asked.

"This whole situation," she said. "It's not funny, but you have to admit, these past few weeks have been fun." His face furrowed. "This whole scheme to trick your mother," she went on, "getting her to join the literary campaign…Gerald. My God, that was funny! You can't deny it. It's the most fun I've had scheming anything in quite a while."

"It was entertaining, I suppose," admitted Edward. "Though all for naught."

"Nonsense," said Elizabeth, shaking her head. "We didn't quite reach our objective, but now we know something about ourselves."

"And what's that?"

"That we're rather good at scheming together," she said. "So it gives me the confidence to scheme a little more."

"How so?" he asked.

"Marry me," she said.

"I just told you—"

"No," she said, "in a scheming way. Without anyone knowing. Before you leave for the continent."

He shook his head. "You don't want to invite that kind of trouble," he said.

"Yes," she corrected him. "I certainly do."

Now, he laughed. "Fine then. *I* don't want to invite that kind of trouble—for you. I'll be long gone fighting a war on the continent, and you'll be here, fighting your own war with your father. I'll not do it."

All at once, he stood and lifted her from the hay bale where she was perched, and she let out a surprised laugh. "Let's forget it for just a moment," he said, "Pretend tonight never happened."

He placed her down on the rickety boards so she was facing him. The lamplight flickered, and all of his features looked shadowy. She slowly began unbuttoning his waistcoat and shirt. "Is this the kind of trouble you came here for?" But he grabbed her hands to stop her, and she could see that his eyes had a serious look. "What's the matter?"

"Elizabeth…" He held on tightly to her hands while she tried to free them, gently pushing her away. "There's a chance that I might not come home. I may never see you again after tonight."

"It doesn't change my mind. It's all the more reason to marry now."

"No, quite the opposite," he said, and his face grew sad. "Elizabeth, even if people survive wars, I'm not sure that love always does."

"And what is that supposed to mean?" she said. She stopped fighting with him to let her undo his buttons and brought her hands to her hips.

"What if I come back a different person? Is it fair for you to be married to a shadow of the person I am today?"

"Remember the other day, when we watched the sunset from the cypress grove?" she said.

He nodded.

"I have to believe that a future exists for us. You have the luxury of making that future—I don't. I have to sit here and wait while others decide and others act. I don't have a say in my own future, except for you. I can choose you, here and now. But if you leave without marrying me, I may never again have the ability to choose something that I want for myself. Even if it is just for a few days or weeks, I can make a choice for my own happiness. I'll not be guaranteed that ever again."

She watched him digest what she had said. Never before had her predicament been so clear to her. She had everything at her fingertips—wealth, prestige, and yet no real freedom.

"And if I don't come back?" he said. "To be a widow at such a young age is a horrid thought."

"It's all horrid, Edward. I'd rather be your widow than your lover, whom no one will recognize if you should die."

"All right then," he finally agreed. "Before I leave for the continent, I will marry you." He took her hands back into his.

For some reason, she didn't feel as content as she had hoped. He was still leaving within a matter of hours. "Enough of this talk about you not coming back," she said, running her hands along his arms, trying to memorize each part of him. She continued unbuttoning his shirt, this time without any protest.

"Let's just be young and in love and doing what every other soldier and lover around the country are also doing tonight."

"And what's that?" he asked with a smile

"Saying good-bye," she said. "In shadows and hidden corners and up in haylofts—wherever they can steal away to be alone. Wrapped up in each other, making promises for a future world that may never come."

He reached over and extinguished the lantern. The loft instantly turned as black as the night. He pushed the loft door further ajar and the moonlight swept into the barn. "We can't risk that anyone will see the light. Or I'll be dead long before I ever get to Belgium."

"Don't be so dramatic," she said. "You can certainly outrun my father." She laughed, but in her mind she couldn't stop hearing his words: *Even if people survive wars, I'm not sure that love always does.*

CHAPTER 51

"You look like hell," Gerald said as Edward emerged from his bedroom. He sat in the upstairs sitting room, his bare feet propped up in the suitcase he had packed for the train to Bodmin.

"'Tis early still," Edward sleepily replied.

"I took that into account," said Gerald, "and even still, you look awful. Have trouble sleeping?" Edward walked over to the table in the sitting room and lit the lantern. It reminded him of Elizabeth and the hayloft. He could still smell her on his undershirt.

"Something like that," he muttered, answering his brother as pithily as he could. He wasn't ready for a conversation just yet. He wiped the sleep out of his eyes and refocused on his younger brother, who was smiling. "What's up with you?" he asked. "And what in God's name are you doing up this early?" He plopped down on the sofa next to his brother.

"Couldn't sleep," Gerald replied, a silly grin still stamped on his face. "Some bloke sneaking around and stumbling down the hall about an hour ago woke me. Doesn't look like he stole anything, so I suppose we'll be all right." He pretended to survey the room for missing items.

"Don't know what you're talking about, Gerald," he replied sleepily. "Now, do me a favor and go back to bed. I want to be miserable in peace."

"What were you up to?" he asked.

"What do you think I was up to?" Edward replied, annoyed. He nudged his brother's feet over and propped his up on the suitcase as well. "And I assure you, were you in my shoes, you'd be up to the same thing." He threw his head back and rested it on the wooden edge of the sofa.

"I would have to agree with you," Gerald replied. "So," he continued, oblivious to the fact that Edward was not in a chatty mood, "what a surprise that Lord Clarendon pulled last night! I couldn't believe it myself. To think, Father putting his differences aside, which would never happen in normal times, and then Lord Clarendon snubbing him that way. At his own party! Mother was inconsolable after you left. The whole party fell apart. Mother may never throw another one!"

"Oh Gerald, don't remind me. I am sick about it." He put his hands to his face and rubbed his eyes, yawning.

"So what are you going to do?" Gerald somehow knew that this wasn't going to be the end of the drama.

Edward looked Gerald up and down, from his scraggly hair and unshaven face to his ugly, bare toes. "You must swear to never tell Mother and Father. I will tell them in my own time, but it will be mine to tell. Do you understand?"

"Of course, Big Al. I helped to get you into this mess, after all. I won't tell a soul." He put his arm around his older brother. "You smell like a girl, Al," he said.

Edward ignored him. "We're going to marry against her father's wishes."

Gerald went pale and, for once, avoided striking a humorous tone. He sat up straight, knocking Edward in the face with his elbow. "I think that is a horrible idea. Edward! Get ahold of yourself. Her father will be hopping mad. He could sideline your career in Parliament before it even begins! And you heard him as clearly as I did—he'll rethink it when the war is over!"

"Can you watch your flailing arms for once?" Edward said, rubbing his nose. Satisfied that it wasn't bleeding, he said, "I can't wait that long, Gerald. I'm in love with her."

"So?" Gerald walked over to the window and opened the drapes, letting in the first rays of the morning light. "You'll be in love with her when you get back," he said. "This war won't last forever."

"I already promised her I would marry her before I left for the continent. And I intend to keep that promise."

"And how will you will that off?" he asked, walking to another window, which, conveniently, had a small liquor cabinet adjacent to it. "Want a drink?" Gerald asked, as he began pouring one for himself.

"I'll have her out to Bodmin some weekend before the unit departs. We'll take care of it there." He watched his brother haphazardly pour a glass of scotch. "And no, I don't want anything to drink. It's six in the morning, for Christ's sake!"

"Suit yourself," he said, licking some errant drops of alcohol from his fingers. "And then what?"

Edward paused. "And then she'll come home. And I'll go to Belgium or France or wherever. With your ugly mug in tow, no doubt. And I guess we'll keep it a secret."

Gerald replied. "Al, think about what you are doing. What difference does it make if you marry her now or in a couple of months?"

"What if it lasts more than that? Everyone says we'll be home in a matter of weeks. But we don't know that. And," he heard a creak in the hallway and lowered his voice, "I don't know that I will ever return. What if this is my only chance?"

"So you would prefer to make her a widow?"

"It's complicated. What would you do?" Edward asked his brother, who didn't answer right away but stood in the middle of the room, sipping his scotch. "Not so easy, is it?"

"I would want to be man enough to do the right thing."

"And what is that?" He could tell his brother was suddenly conflicted.

"We get so few chances at love, Al. Maybe you are right." Gerald plopped back on the sofa.

"When did you get to be such a philosopher?" he asked. He sniffed the air and smelled a faint, unfamiliar perfume. "I hate to say it Gerald, but you smell like a girl, too! What do you have to say for yourself?"

"Nothing," said Gerald, clamming up.

"Well surely you remember who at least one of them was?" asked Edward, happy at the chance to tease his brother, for once.

"I do," said Gerald.

"And who were the lucky ladies?"

"Just one lady," said Gerald.

Edward looked incredulous. "Not my brother! Just one?"

But Gerald turned serious. "Just one, Al."

"I don't believe you. Sometimes I wish I had your spunk, Gerald," Edward said, this time putting his arm around Gerald's shoulder.

"And sometimes I wish I had your courage," Gerald said, slapping his brother on the shoulder.

"Courage?" said Edward. This comment took him by surprise. He always considered Gerald to be the one with the better qualities.

"Aye. Courage to do right by her and marry her."

"I can't tell if it is courageous or foolish. It's not easy to be young and in love, is it?"

"It's hell," said Gerald grimly.

Edward let out a loud laugh. "I never thought of it that way, but there is truth to that. And just who is your girl, Gerald, who makes your life such hell? I've never known you to have just one love interest. Do I know her?"

"I believe you do, Edward," Gerald replied.

When he offered no additional information, Edward decided not to press his brother.

"Probably time to get going, wouldn't you say? The train leaves Victoria Station in a few hours. Mother's already downstairs waiting for us, no doubt. You're going to break her heart, you know."

Edward turned his head at the sound of approaching footsteps. His father's figure came into view. Like his sons, he also looked like he had spent a sleepless night. "Edward's right," the viscount said. "Your mother's already waiting for you—already gone through about four handkerchiefs this morning. Gerald, why don't you run downstairs and talk to her. Tell her only good things—the war will be short, you'll write every day—the things that might not be true but that she wants to hear."

Gerald popped to his feet and brushed Edward's legs off the suitcase, carrying it with him into the hall.

The viscount came into the room and slowly walked over to the sofa, lowering himself into it gracefully. Edward couldn't recall a time in his adult life when his father had sat so close. Before he could say anything, Edward said, "Father, I don't want to talk about last night."

His father put his hand on Edward's knee. "Me neither," he said and let out a chuckle. "Me neither. But I do want to tell you something, Edward, while your brother is out of earshot. Listen, because I'll only have the nerve to say it once." His father leaned back into the sofa, and Edward followed.

"Edward," his father said, sounding almost as though he were reading from notes, "I look at you, and it is a mirror to my past. I can see myself in so much of you. And if I could give myself at age twenty-five advice, this is what I would say: Time will change you, but don't let it embitter you." A tear welled in his eye. "Edward, this war will shape the man you become, but remember that you still have control over your decisions, and therefore some control over your future. Don't let this experience steal your dreams and your passion. Lock them away for a time when you can return to them. Keep them safe, no matter what you see or experience. I hope to God that war will be kind to you," he stopped and put his hand on his son's shoulder, "but I know better."

CHAPTER 52

August 9, 1914: Dublin, Ireland

Early the next day, Colin awoke to the smell of coffee—not the bitter, acidic drink he had known his whole life but real, aromatic British coffee. The smell made his stomach growl with hunger. In that first moment or two of consciousness, he felt only pleasant comfort—the luxurious bed, the slight morning breeze from the bedroom window, and the smell of the coffee.

Half a second later, the pain hit. He squinted, which only made the sensation worse. It was as if someone had shoved a metal spike behind his right eye. The smell of the coffee—that rich, coveted drink—made him nauseous. His arm throbbed with a dull pain from above his elbow down to his littlest finger. And Nora was gone.

Colin half opened his left eye—the one that didn't feel impaled—and saw rays of light coming through the curtained window. Someone had removed the black curtains that had concealed last night's procedure from any nosy British sympathizers passing by. The pale dawn light cast gentle rays across the room. Any other morning, he would have marveled at how comfortable a dwelling could be, but this morning he could only groan.

The door creaked, and he opened his other eye, the eye with the metal spike. Nora crept in, carrying a tray with a biscuit and the offensive brew. The hall was dark. The sun as yet only shone on the eastern side of the house. He lifted his right hand to his head. "Why so early, Nora?" he asked. "Couldn't you have given me a few more moments of peace?

"It'll just get worse the longer you let it fester," she said. "I brought you three servings of coffee. And a bit of aspirin."

"I'll take three servings of aspirin," he said, "but hold the coffee." He was intrigued by the medicine. He had never had it before but had heard of its powers to alleviate a hangover.

"Here." She put down the tray and held out her hand, and he reached over with his right hand and took the large, white pills. "Doc said just to swallow them with a drink of coffee."

"Is he up, too?" asked Colin. "'Cause I have a bone to pick with 'im. And that bastard Cian. Fookin' cheap whiskey."

"He did say only to drink half of it," she said. "And the whiskey was no worse than what you're used to."

"Fook that." He shot a glance at Nora to see if he had offended her. He swore around her all the time, but never at her.

"Sorry," he said.

"It's the least of your sins," she replied and let a small grin escape. He could tell that she wanted to suppress it. He left it at that.

She handed him a delicate white porcelain cup, trimmed with gold and filled with dark black coffee. He turned his head away. "Not a chance," he said.

"It'll make you feel better," she said.

"It won't," he said.

"Have you ever had it? It's quite good."

"Have you?"

"Of course," she said. "I live with wealthy Protestant tyrants, remember?"

"Is that why you brought it to me in the King's dinnerware?" he asked. He nodded toward the cup and saucer. "Pour it into somethin' more fittin' for the likes of me, and I'll consider it," he said.

"Oh, quit bein' a snob," she said sarcastically, "What's good enough for the King is good enough for you."

She sat down on the bed next to him and again handed him the cup.

"Come a little closer, and I'll think about it," he said. He reached his good arm around her and scooted her closer.

"Not a chance," she said.

"It'll make me feel better," he offered.

"It won't," she said and stood up. Her bare feet landed lightly on the wooden floor.

He closed his eyes and listened as she walked across the room. Her footsteps fell so softly—nothing like the tramping noises he and his cousin made on their wooden floor.

"Doctor Fabian will be back from his rounds soon," she said. "He'll give you a quick check to make sure you're breathin', and then we have to get over to the store. Mr. Dunham will come for me this morning."

Colin opened his eyes again and began to speak, but she cut him off. "It's already decided, Colin." And then, for emphasis, "I've already decided. I'm going back."

She slid out the door and into the hallway, closing it behind her. He exhaled. His head throbbed. He reached over to the night table and picked up the white porcelain cup. It looked out of place in his large, clumsy hand, which wrapped entirely around it. He raised it to his mouth and breathed in the smell. It was delicious and nauseating all at once. He took a small sip. Nora was right—it was good. Really good.

He finished all three servings before Doctor Fabian entered the room. "Ah,

Colin!" He said. "Good to see you up and moving. Let's take a look at that arm, shall we?" He walked over to Colin, whose left hand still rested on the bed. Most of his forearm was covered by the pasteboard and linens the doctor had wrapped it in the night before.

"Hand has good color all the way to the fingertips. That's an improvement since yesterday. Does it ache more or less?"

"Certainly less," said Colin.

"Can you wiggle your fingers? Excellent!" Doctor Fabian smiled at his handiwork and turned the arm gently to the side.

"It must stay set in that cast for several weeks, but come back around the end of the month so I can take a look at it. If you're careful with it, you just might regain full strength. Time will tell."

"Thanks for yer help, Doctor," Colin said. "I'll be forever grateful to you."

"Do me one favor, Colin," said the doctor. "When the arm is good and healed—say four months or so—give that cousin of yours a solid left hook to the jaw, will you? He had no business letting you suffer like that. Not when there's help right around the corner."

"Would be my pleasure," said Colin.

"Excellent!" said Doctor Fabian. "And when you do, send him my way so I can set his jaw properly." The old man laughed loudly. "That cousin of yours is something else. A heart of gold, he has, but only for one thing at a time. I reckon that one thing is not you, Colin."

"I reckon not," said Colin.

"Well then, off you go my boy, no worse for the wear."

"No worse for the wear?" said Colin. "Me arm may be better, but me head is the worst it's ever been. I think I'd rather just stay here. Looks to be daylight out there." The mere thought of the bright sunshine made his head ache more.

"A small price to pay to get your arm back. Off with you both, now. Can't have you here when my patients begin to show up. I'll show you both out the back." Doctor Fabian led Colin and Nora toward the second exit to the room, which led into a narrow hallway filled with medical supplies. Bandages, soaps, gauze. Colin spied several bottles of aspirin. Doctor Fabian followed his eyes.

"You can have one dose," he said. "There's a war on, you know. I'll have to ration it for who knows how long."

"The war will be over in a few months' time," Colin said. "Perhaps two doses."

Again, the doctor laughed, but this time it seemed less jovial. "This war will last years, my boy. These things are never simple affairs. You can have one dose."

Colin held out his right hand, and the doctor gave him the tablets.

"There's more here if you need it for something besides a hangover," he said, then he opened a small rear door to the house.

"Run along now, and don't forget to stop by at the end of the month. The more careful you are, the more likely it will heal properly."

"Aye," said Colin. "Thank you again for all you've done."

"Thank you, Doctor," said Nora. "We're very grateful."

"Thank you, Nora, for your help. If you ever decide that housekeeping's not for you,"—he winked at her—"this city is in short supply of nurses."

"Aye," was all she said. Colin wondered what profession she had in mind for herself. He hoped it wasn't a rebel, but he knew it was probably already too late.

She and Colin quickly made their way to the main road and set off toward Kildare's Grocery.

❦

They walked in silence for several minutes. In addition to his head and his arm, his calf had a mild throb from the dog bite the day before. He had always hated those damned red and white setters. He had never met one that he liked. Everything seemed to hurt. The morning sun was now shining brightly, and Dublin was waking from its slumber.

"How's yer head?" Nora asked.

"Rotten," said Colin. He was thankful they weren't in the tenements. The middle class areas of the city were clean—and without that awful stench. "But I would wake to this head every day of me life over yesterday," he said.

"The arm—that sounded so painful. The snap." She shuddered. "You did good, Colin."

They turned the corner onto a small side street. The laundry hanging from the upstairs apartments shielded his eyes from the sun. "I wasn't talking about the arm."

Nora's mood instantly turned dark. "Forget about it, Colin. I have."

"You have not!" He looked at her sternly. "Everything that happened yesterday will shape what comes next. And Michael is probably secretly thrilled, because it makes his life easier. He'll get what he wants—his loyal spy on the inside. But —" He turned to her. "Make sure you're gettin' what you want. Whatever that is." He wondered if she still wanted to put a bullet through Ethan's skull or if her anger had quelled.

Nora looked down for several strides. Her new leather shoes sounded loud against the cobblestones. "You know what I want," she said in a quiet, determined voice.

"Not peace? Not political solutions?" he pressed.

"Aye," she said, "I did want those things. But there's nothin' peaceful about Ethan Parsons. Maybe you're right—maybe peace isn't possible. But more than that I want to make me own choices."

Colin nodded. "You've made that perfectly clear."

"And I may adore you in every possible way, but I'll never let you make decisions on me behalf. Ever."

Colin stopped walking. The trudging of his boots had become a steady beat to their conversation, so when it stopped the streets sounded eerily quiet.

A few paces ahead, she stopped and looked back at him. "What?" she said. "Can I not ask that of you?"

He held back a smile for a couple seconds, but then let it escape.

"What?" she said.

"I do believe, Nora *Cullen*," he said, emphasizing her name, "that you just said that you adored me in every possible way."

"As if you didn't know! 'Twas nothing like what I got out of you last night."

"Aye, but I was drunk," he said. "You are absolutely sober, and you have been for sixteen and a half years. That's worth twice, you know."

"So you remember what you said then?" she said.

"I absolutely remember," he said.

CHAPTER 53

August 9, 1914: The Liberties, Dublin, Ireland

Colin and Nora approached the shop through the back alley. As usual, the cats scattered under the steps of the store. Colin slowly walked up to the door and opened it gently, then propped the door with his foot and reached up to silence the bell.

"No need," a voice from inside came. It was Michael. Colin turned to Nora and motioned with his head for her to follow him in. He released the bell, and its clang sliced through the peaceful alley.

As they entered the room, they saw that Michael was not alone. "What's this?" asked Colin.

Michael stood up from the table, walked over to the small kitchen, and took the water he was heating off the stove. "I thought it might be best if we brought in a few more for our conversation."

Nora recognized Michael, Cian and Mr. Dunham—already there to get her—but the fourth was a stranger.

"Nora," said Michael, "this is my father, John Kildare. He wanted to meet you—"

"To see you—" John Kildare interrupted. "We've met before."

"We have?" she asked.

"Aye, on a sad, sad day 'bout ten years ago. Inis Cathaigh."

Nora felt as though the wind had been knocked out of her. "You knew me parents."

"Aye," he said.

It shouldn't have been so surprising to her. Colin's family was their closest neighbor in Ballynote. And he had somehow ended up with her father's old flintlocks after the arrest. "And me grandda?"

"Of course, God rest him."

Mr. Dunham interjected. "We all knew yer family, Nora."

Nora furrowed her brow. Colin's family made sense—but Mr. Dunham did not. "How?"

Colin pulled a chair out from the table and brought it toward her. She sat down. The room fell silent as everyone looked from person to person. Finally, Mr. Dunham spoke.

"Many years ago, yer father and I were boys together in Ballynote."

"We grew up together, went to the same hedge schools, listened to the same homilies, and were shaped by the same events."

"You really knew him?" she asked. A strange sense of hope came over her, almost as if she would be able to recapture some of her parents from Mr. Dunham. She had rarely ever spoken about them to anyone but Seamus over the past ten years.

"Aye, he was me dearest of friends."

Nora recognized the sad look in Mr. Dunham's eyes—it was the same look she seen in him when she first arrived at the Parsons'. "So that's why you've taken care of me," she said.

"Aye," he said. "Though things have been turned on their head a bit."

"When did you come to Dublin?" she asked.

He looked down, and Nora wondered if he was ashamed, then he quietly said, "Ten years ago. Exactly."

Again, Nora felt weak. "You were there, then?" she whispered.

Mr. Dunham didn't respond, but she saw a tear form in one of his eyes.

"You were there," she said aloud, then immediately wished she hadn't. He *was* ashamed, though she couldn't fathom why.

"Till the end," he finally said. "Till the rope was tied around their necks, till they fell and—" his voice trailed off. He was beginning to sweat, and he wiped his brow. "I watched from a distance, you see—hidden in a grove of trees, though I should have been hanging right there with 'em. And until a few weeks ago, I wondered why fate had let me escape and survive."

Nora felt everyone's eyes on her. Her face felt flush, and her heart beat so fast she could hear it. She had never met anyone who had been present for the hanging who hadn't been there to jeer, and certainly not anyone who might have been an accomplice and was willing to talk about it.

"And then you arrived at me door," Mr. Dunham continued, "And I wondered if perhaps fate still had a story to weave. Maybe their story is not over. And those eyes—they brought me back."

"What is it about the eyes?" she said quietly. "Everyone says that to me."

Mr. Dunham laughed, but it was not his usual cheerful laugh. It was a sad, whimsical chuckle. "They're yer da's eyes, don't you know? A peculiar shade of green against that crop of almost white hair. Everyone knew 'im because of those eyes. 'Twas one reason why he couldn't hide like the rest of us..." His voice trailed off. "Was what got 'im killed in the end."

Colin's eyes were wide. He looked spooked, as if he had seen a ghost.

Nora had never before imagined her parents' final moments, though she distinctly remembered the image of their bodies lying days later on the ground under the tree. More than that, she remembered her grandfather trying to change her fate, change her course by bidding her to ignore the wild streak within her that he knew would call her to the same cause. She thought of her parents, so full of life, so twisted and mangled from their tortuous deaths. Of her childhood, of winters close to starvation. Of her massacred sheep. Of her brother leaving for America—driven away from his home by a government that had never cared for him, that had abused his ancestral land until it had nothing more to give. Of Ethan Parsons and the stale smell of liquor as he breathed over her. Of his dark and empty eyes.

Was this the path her grandfather had steered her toward, hoping to quell her wild streak? Could fate be so easily fooled?

She closed her eyes and searched for more peaceful memories. She thought of her cottage and its dark and earthen smell. She thought of her wind-whipped fields in Clare. Of the thrill of being out at sea bringing in the cache of rifles. She thought of Colin and the blond tips on his unkempt hair and how he brushed it out of his eyes when he was deep in thought. The Shannon and the doves that soared overhead.

"Nora," came a voice. "Nora, are you all right?"

She opened her eyes to a room of faces staring intensely at her. "I'm fine Mr. Dunham," she said. "And I'm ready."

She realized she was shaking and leaned back in her chair. The room was still silent. In a crisp, surprisingly loud voice, she said, "Michael, we took a notebook off the two British soldiers down in Wicklow. It's got notes and names and locations in it. It gives us a place to start, to weave together what we are up against. Find out what they were up to and how they knew we would be there." She pulled the small, leather-bound book from a pocket and handed it over to Michael.

He reached over and took it from her, allowing the pages to fall open. He looked as though he was about to say something but held his tongue. Colin's Uncle John stood up and looked over his son's shoulder at the open book. "I know these places. But the names are obscured. They were careful."

Michael at last spoke up. He had managed to control his temper. "Next time you come across somethin' like this—"

"*We* need to be more careful," Colin interrupted. "Can't be correspondin' the way we have been—writing everything down and sending it through the post." He was obviously referring to Michael's letter that their Uncle Lawrence had intercepted.

Michael shot a look back at his cousin "How 'bout we can't be hangin' out with Nora so much, either?"

The distinct sound of a muffled sneeze came from behind the tattered curtain that divided the front and back of the store and interrupted the brewing argument. Michael and Colin quickly jumped to their feet, but John Kildare was first to duck behind the curtain and chase down the retreating steps that echoed across the wooden floors of the shop.

"Let go of me, you piece of shite!" cried the high-pitched voice of a small child.

"You bit me you little thief!" Colin's uncle yelled.

Colin, who was already on his feet, lunged toward the curtain. "Don't hurt 'im!" he yelled.

Nora looked at Michael and could see that he was as confused as the rest of them.

Moments later, Colin's uncle emerged from behind the curtain holding a skinny little boy by the back of the collar. Nora noticed that his dirty bare feet barely touched the floor as Colin's uncle held tightly to the back of his shirt. "Caught this little shite listening in on our conversation!" he said. "I've seen you snoopin' 'round here before!"

"Don't worry about him," said Colin. "'Tis only Daniel." Nora looked from Colin to his uncle. *Daniel?*

John Kildare loosened his grip on the boy, who instantly sank his teeth into his captor's forearm.

"I didn't mean to let go of 'im!" cried Colin. "Hold tight to 'im"—he paused and winked at Daniel—"just no need to kill 'im!"

The blood drained from Daniel's face. He began to thrash again.

"Now hold up, Daniel," said Colin, reaching over to assist his uncle. "You've got no right to be offended. You got caught red-handed! Take yer punishment like a man." Colin laughed. "I told you to come by twice a week for food, and you just got yers yesterday."

"You feed this little urchin?" asked Colin's uncle, eyeing his nephew. Nora looked at the boy's dirty face and felt bad for him. She knew what it was like to be hungry.

"Aye," chimed in Michael. "We employ 'im, if you will. What's the deal, Daniel?"

"You give me food, and I keep me mouth shut," the boy said quietly.

"Aye," said Michael. "And here's a new rule. You keep your mouth shut, and you only come here twice a week, you got it?"

"Aye," said Daniel.

"Now what did you hear?" asked Colin. *He probably heard it all*, thought Nora.

A mischievous smile came across Daniel's face. "I heard that you was gonna all be spies like me," he said.

"You're not a spy Daniel, you're a snitch," said Michael, "of the worst kind." *My God*, thought Nora, *Michael is such an arse!* He seemed to be void of empathy.

"Not anymore," said Daniel, looking offended. "I'm keepin' my end of the bargain."

"You are?" asked Colin. "Then why are you here?"

"Because I was gonna tell you somethin', and then I couldn't find you in the shop. So I heard some people back here, and I didn't know the voices, so I waited to make sure it was you."

"What were you goin' to tell me?" asked Colin. Nora watched him speak softly to the little boy. He had a lot of practice with younger brothers, and seemed to know how to get Daniel to cooperate. This tactic was much more effective than Michael's demeaning tone.

Daniel shook his head and frowned. Dust flew from his dirty-blond hair.

"They're all right, fella," said Colin. "You can say it in front of 'em."

Daniel looked around the room and made eye contact with each person. He clearly thought he was intimidating. "Ulster is gettin' ready to fight," he finally said.

"There's a war, Daniel," said Michael. "Of course they're gettin' ready to fight."

"They is gettin' ready to fight the likes of you," he said, looking right at Michael. His little lips were pursed in anger. "The devil is back."

Colin looked to Michael. "Ethan," he said. Nora felt her heart skip a beat.

Daniel nodded defiantly. "He's back."

"How do you know this, Daniel?" Colin asked.

"None of yer—"

"How do you know?" Michael yelled.

Uncle John tightened his grip on Daniel's collar. "I seen someone who seen him this mornin'," said Daniel. His voice sounded as though he were holding back tears, but he seemed resolved to be tough as any boy of eight could be. "And I jus' thought you would want to know."

"Let 'im go," said Nora suddenly. She'd had enough. "Let 'im go. He's any one of us, were we to be a child in Dublin!"

Daniel stared at Nora, his little mouth slightly agape. John Kildare released him and raised his arms out of the reach of the boy's teeth. But Daniel didn't go after him. He kept his eyes on Nora.

"We do want to know, Daniel," said Colin softly. "Thank you for coming and tellin' me."

"I won't ever ag—"

"Yes, Daniel," said Nora. "Come by any time you like to tell Colin what you know."

"But otherwise keep yer trap shut!" said Michael.

"He's a child!" said Nora, looking angrily at Michael.

"He looks like a child, but he schemes like a seasoned criminal," said Michael.

"He knows only what his life has taught him." She knelt down and took the boy's hands. The grime on his face hid a palate of dark freckles.

"Daniel," she said. "After Daniel O'Connell no doubt."

A smile broke across Daniel's face, revealing all his missing teeth. "My da named me after him," he said excitedly.

"You and an entire half of this island," said Michael under his breath.

But Nora ignored him. "What a lovely name," she said. "You can come back any time you like. Just to chat if you want to."

Colin nodded. "Any time you have stories that need tellin', come here first," he said. "I'll find you somethin' to eat." He looked at his uncle, who nodded.

"Does she live here?" he asked, and pointed at Nora.

"No," said Michael. "She's just visiting, and she's leaving today."

Daniel frowned. "Will she be back?'

"No," said Cian. "Never."

Daniel sighed the way he had undoubtedly seen countless adults sigh. It was comical to watch him imitate grown-up mannerisms. Nora smiled at him.

"Too bad," he said. He seemed sad.

"Da, get the boy somethin' to eat," said Michael, motioning toward the front of the store.

Colin's uncle directed Daniel through the old curtain and toward the front of the store.

He momentarily broke away. "Will I see you again?" he said to Nora.

"Of course," she said. "I'll make sure of it."

The two disappeared behind the curtain. Cian and Michael returned to the small table. "Not a good start," said Cian.

"As we were sayin'," Michael started. "We'll all have to be more careful. Keep your voices low. That boy can't be trusted."

"We'll have to keep 'im close," said Colin. "He'll be my responsibility."

"Can you handle that?" asked Michael. He sounded doubtful. "That *and* stayin' away from the Parsons'?"

Nora shook her head. Michael took every opportunity to poke at his cousin. The tension in the room again bordered on a fistfight.

Mr. Dunham interrupted the feud before it got too hot to dampen. "No need to worry, Colin's been fired by Mrs. Finnegan." He laughed his deep rolling laugh. "He won't be back at the Parsons' anytime soon."

Cian and Michael looked at him, confused. Both failed to find any humor.

"Louise—that's Mrs. Finnegan, the housekeeper, to you—helped to wake Ethan from his stupor yesterday," Mr. Dunham began. "She wove a great tale of a stable hand who had been caught red-handed in assault. Ethan, the aggrieved, was as mad as a hornet and demanded that the stable boy who struck him be fired and blacklisted. Louise of course, was incensed and immediately fired one Emmet Sullivan." Mr. Dunham eyed Colin. "She can be quite the actress when she needs to be. Had some of the girls frantically looking for some new hand named Emmet, who of course, existed only in name."

"Finnegan," said Colin. "She's good."

"There's more there than meets the eye," said Mr. Dunham. "But that's a story for another day."

"Hard to imagine her stickin' up for the likes of me."

"Because you are too interested in the likes of her," Mr. Dunham said, gesturing toward Nora. "And she's not stickin' up for you, she's sticking up for Ireland. Just be thankful. Without her you'd probably be in jail. The police are now searching high and low for poor Emmet, who is quite good at being on the run. Not a trace of 'im anywhere." Mr. Dunham laughed again, so hard that this time a tear ran down his cheek.

Michael looked at his cousin. "Emmet, you say. Seems quite an apt name for an Irish rebel. I guess that's what we'll be callin' you from now on, Colin." He scratched his head. "It'll be good to mask all of yer names." He turned to Mr. Dunham. "You still all right with Theo?"

He smiled. "Wolfe Tone was always my favorite rebel."

Michael rolled his eyes. "Theo it is. Though I feel like it's blasphemy. And you, Nora?"

They looked from one to another. No one seemed to have any ideas. *Surely there have been famous female rebels before,* she thought, though none came immediately to mind. She could hear Daniel as he chattered away in the next room. It sounded like he was negotiating for more food.

"My mother's name was Eleanor," she finally said.

Cian shook his head. "No, too obvious. And too close to Nora." He reached up and touched one of the low rafters in the kitchen, stirring up years of dust.

Mr. Dunham looked at Nora. "You're not an Eleanor. She was a good soul, but so meek and mild. Followed your father anywhere and everywhere. Even to the grave. That's not you."

"Maybe we don't use a name. Maybe a code," said Colin.

"Like what?" said Michael. He began pacing across the wooden floor.

"Maybe a dove," he said quietly. "Like yer pendant." Nora's hand instinctively grasped the sharp edges of her broken pendant. *Columba of Iona.*

Mr. Dunham looked at Colin and nodded slowly. "She is a little dove, isn't she?" he said. "Like the white doves of the Burren. Quite Irish."

"Like Columba," he said. Then almost in a whisper, "Or perhaps like a girl in a story I once heard." Nora's ears perked up at this. She eyed him curiously. He still looked somewhat pale. Something about the conversation was making him uneasy.

Michael frowned. "You guys are terrible at this."

"Do you object?" asked Mr. Dunham.

Michael shook his head. "So you will be our little White Dove. And you two"—he motioned to Colin and Mr. Dunham—"will be our Irish rebels. Quite the names to live up to. Let's hope it ends better for you than it did for your namesakes." He smiled grimly at his cousin. "So it's decided. Now let's get down to business."

Cian finally spoke up. "If we're going to be a real ring, we're going to need basic rules of operation. Michael and I are already known to the authorities. All the heavy liftin' will have to be done by the rest of you."

Nora nodded. That was just how she wanted it to be. The less Michael was involved, the better.

Mr. Dunham cut in. "Usually when Ethan's home, he's spendin' his time out and about in Dublin. If he's not harrassin' the locals one by one, he'll be sure to be organizin' trouble for all of us with his Ulster boys. But he never leaves home without his damned briefcase. We'll be needin' to know the contents of it inside and out," he said.

"We'll see if we can start to build a web of his contacts. Use the book we lifted to see if we can find any connections," said Nora. "We'll need a map to outline the places and people." She drew in the air with her hands.

"Aye, and the first step will be to see just how entrenched the Ulster boys are with the local authorities," said Colin.

"Fully entrenched, no doubt" said Michael.

"But more than that, we can try to understand their plans moving forward," said Nora.

"Aye," said Michael. "He's still going to be leadin' that regiment of Ulster Volunteers, most likely. We'll want to know everything about them that we can. Some of them will go to war, no doubt. But not all of them. Their real business is here."

Cian nodded. "Aye, just like ours. We'll have to use a place for our headquarters. Somewhere Nora can get to regularly that isn't out of her routine."

Mr. Dunham nodded. "I was thinking about this. Let's use the safe house by the market. The market would be a logical place for her and Colin to be." Nora found it interesting how much more productive things seemed when Michael wasn't the only decision maker.

"Aye, cause there's no way we can use the shop," said Michael. "And," he added, "there's no way you two can be seen together outside of the safe house. We can't have you connected in any way. It's too risky."

The group became silent. They looked from one to another. Nothing would ever be as it had been.

"It's decided then," Nora finally said.

Mr. Dunham nodded. "Aye, for now," he said. "We'll have to be gettin' back, Nora. Louise can't cover for us all day."

Colin and Mr. Dunham stood up from the table. The only sound in the room was the wooden chairs moving across the wooden floors.

Mr. Dunham said, "I'll be outside waitin' for you, Nora. Give me a minute to get the automobile up and runnin'." He nodded to Michael. "You two probably need to check on our little snitch." Michael and Cian understood the hint and moved the curtain aside as they walked to the front of the store, their boots plodding across the old wooden floors.

❧

When they were alone in the back of the store, Nora said, "Mr. Dunham always looks out for us, doesn't he?"

"He looks out for you," Colin corrected her. He ran his hand through his hair to brush it from his face. "And now we now why." He managed a small smile and slowly made his way toward her. "Well, this is the worst part of me day."

She nodded. He opened his good arm, and she walked slowly into his embrace. He held her closely.

"I wonder what my grandda would think of this path," she said.

"Maybe it is fate, Nora," he said quietly.

She glanced up at him. "I thought you didn't believe in fate?"

He laughed. "The idea is growing on me." Stroking her hair, he added, "Someone once told me that Irish Catholics are afforded some flexibilities in their beliefs."

"Some heathen told you, no doubt," Nora said.

"Indeed," said Colin. She rested her head on Colin's chest. Her ear was perfectly aligned with his heart, and she listened to it for a moment. It was slow

451

and steady, yet strong. It beat a comfortable rhythm, like footsteps. Like a guide.

"So this is it," she said. She released herself from his embrace and walked toward the open window. As usual, it was hard to find any relief from the heat of the Dublin summer. "I shan't see you for quite some time."

"Nonsense!" said Colin. He followed her toward the window. "I'll see you on Saturday at confession."

"I've nothing to confess," she replied. She thought she saw the dusty old curtain move and leaned forward to try to feel the breeze.

"No?" asked Colin. "Perhaps spending the night with a boy?"

"Not the whole night," Nora argued. She could hear the automobile running out on the street. "And there were no other beds. A practical solution and hardly a sin."

"No impure thoughts?" he questioned. "That's always good for a few Hail Mary's."

"Not a one," said Nora. She heard a door slam out on the street. Mr. Dunham was no doubt on his way back.

Colin reached out and grabbed her hand, pulling her close to him again. He leaned forward and kissed her softly. For once, she couldn't smell any whiskey on him. "How about now?"

"Perhaps a small impure thought," she said. She reached up and brushed his hair away from his face.

"Perfect," he said. "I'll see you Saturday then."

She sighed. "You know you won't, Colin."

"Pretend with me."

"If I'm goin' to pretend to be somewhere with you, it sure isn't goin' to be at confession."

"Then where?" he said.

She smiled, though she suddenly felt sad. "Clare," she said. Just voicing it made her homesick again. "Along the Shannon. That place where there's a small bend and a little tower of stones left over from who knows when. Where the purple flowers grow and the birds fly above the water and ride the currents of the wind."

"Those are doves, Nora. Like you." He smiled at her. "And I know the place."

"The first place you ever kissed me," she said. She heard Mr. Dunham's footsteps out in the back alley.

"And if we don't wind up dead or in jail, I'll take you there every day as an old man until the day that I die. And it'll be the last place that I kiss you too."

"Do you think we'll live to be old together Colin?'

"Of course I do. I have to believe it."

"It's hard to believe it sometimes." She looked over her shoulder, but the door stayed closed and the brass bell silent.

"Why is that?"

"Because we're about to start a war, Colin, and even if people survive wars, I'm not sure that love always does."

"Of course it does," he said. "Otherwise what the hell would we fight for?"

"Remember that always," she said and wrapped her arms around him tightly so that her ear was pressed up against his heart. She wondered how long it would be before she saw him again. After a long moment she pulled away. "Good-bye for now, Colin," she said. He leaned toward her to kiss her, but they were interrupted by small footsteps coming. The curtain that divided the back room from the store flew open.

"You're still here!" exclaimed a little voice.

She laughed. He held a half-eaten apple in his hands, the little bite marks in the red skin were uneven due to his missing teeth. "Only for a moment, Daniel."

"I have to ask you somethin'!" he said urgently. "Why did you come here? Why did you come to Dublin?"

"To Dublin?"

"Was it to fight for Ireland?" he asked, excitedly.

Nora finally smiled and leaned down so she was at his height. "I suppose it was, Daniel, in a way."

"I knew it!" he said. "I knew you did!"

The bell over the back door began to clang, and Mr. Dunham appeared in the doorway. Nora felt her heart sink. "'Tis time, Nora," he said. "We have to get goin'."

Nora stood. Time was up. "Good-bye, Colin," she said. "And good-bye to you, too, Daniel. So happy to have met you."

The little boy beamed.

✻

Colin watched as Nora and Mr. Dunham stepped out into the alley. For an instant, the midday light wrapped around her auburn hair like a sunburst. And just like that, she was gone.

"Thanks, fella," Colin said to Daniel. "You have very bad timing."

"You were kissin' her weren't you?" he asked. He bared his toothless grin.

"Was tryin' to, you little shite," he said. He put an affectionate hand on Daniel's shoulder. "But that's all right, fella."

"I had important business, too," said Daniel.

"Oh yeah?" said Colin incredulously.

"I had to know. She's the girl in a story me da used to tell me. About war and armies and Ireland. I just know it."

Colin felt his heart beat loudly in his chest. His hand on Daniel's shoulder grew clammy and cold. He swallowed hard. "I knew we had somethin' in common, little fella." He knelt down and brought the little boy in close to him. "I know that story, too," he whispered.

The loud engine of the Parson's motorcar roared to life, then faded down the street. Nora's words echoed in his head: *Even if people survive wars, I'm not sure that love always does.*

CHAPTER 54

September 1, 1914: Massachusetts Bay, Atlantic Ocean

To the east, the vast blue ocean met the sky just where the sun broke the horizon. The dawn sky glowed in a rose color that seemed unnatural against the slate of the sea. As the breaking daylight streaked across the sky, a small, dark strip appeared to the west. At first, it seemed an aberration, perhaps a distant ocean region the morning light had not yet touched. Then it began to grow.

Seamus trained his eyes westward and squinted. The whipping wind blew white-blond strands into his eyes. He quickly brushed the hair away and focused on the western horizon. The dark area began to spread across the ocean.

"Land," he whispered. He grabbed the rail of the ocean liner and leaned far over the side. "Land!" he yelled. "Land!"

Only a few passengers stood on the deck, but they, too, began to train their eyes westward.

"Land ho!" a man cried.

Silas, who had been peering off the port side, half ran, half stumbled across the deck to Seamus. Looking up, Seamus saw the large hats of women on the upper decks as they gathered, graceful arms pointing toward Boston harbor as it came into clearer view.

"We made it!" Silas yelled, jumping up and down. "America!"

"A beautiful sight!" said Seamus. He felt his throat tighten and his face get hot, almost as if he might cry. "Everything I knew she would be!"

"You haven't even seen her yet," said Silas.

"I don't care," said Seamus. "She's beautiful to me. And no one there will care if I'm Catholic or Protestant or anything else. I'll just be Seamus McMahon, and I'll be a damned millionaire."

Silas shook his head. "You think you'll stumble across a fortune the moment you step off the boat, do you?"

"Somethin' like that. Who cares, so long as I'm as far as I can get from fookin' County Clare, Ireland? And farming. And the Crook. And three hundred years under the thumb of the bloody King."

"I'll drink to that," said Silas, pulling a flask from his pocket. "Got a splash left."

"You were holding out on me," said Seamus, reaching his hand out.

"Nah, just waiting for the right time." He handed Seamus the last sip. "Enjoy it. Who knows when you'll have your next?"

Seamus opened the screw cap on the metal flask and brought it to his lips. As he finished the last of the flask, something caught his eye. "Would you look at that, Silas," said Seamus. His chin-length hair, almost white after a summer in the sun, blew every which way in the wind, and he brushed it from his pale blue eyes. "'Tis a little dove, coming out to meet us. Look at how she rides the wind over the waves! Just like back home."

"I guess they have doves in America, too," said Silas.

The boys watched the dove fly low over the water and then glide high up above the ship's steam stack. She flew higher and higher until she, too, was a speck in the distance.

"She's headed the wrong way," noted Silas. "Boston is west."

"Hope she's not headed to Ireland. 'Tis nothing there for any of us but misery." As Seamus said the words, his heart sank. *Except for Nora,* he thought. *The only good, pure-hearted thing left in Ireland.*

The boys watched until they could no longer see the bird.

"And just like that, she's off," said Seamus, a little saddened. He turned back toward the looming shore and smelled the sweet, salty smell of freedom for this first time in his life.

END PART I

A Request and a Peek!

Dear Reader,

I very much hope you enjoyed *White Dove*.

If you did, I would greatly appreciate it if you could leave a review on either Amazon.com or Goodreads.com. Just zip along to the sites, find the book, and use the '*Leave a customer review*' option.

If you *really* enjoyed the book—I have great news!

White Dove is the first novel in the three-part series, *Shadows in Drab and Green*. To keep up to date with the progress of the series, please register for the Scribble & Spark Bookworks mailing list at www.scribbleandspark.com: you'll also be the first to know about the release of *Book II, Forever England*.

Until then, here's a sneak peek of *Forever England*…

Katrina Nowak - May 2018

Preview of Book II: Forever England

1915: The Western Front

"Major...Major? Can you hear me?" Someone was screaming in agony. "Major!"

"We've got to move him. There's no time!" yelled another voice over the volleys of fire.

The medic protested. "He's not stable!"

"He'll not survive if we don't move him!"

Major Eldridge slowly opened one eye, and the world around him began to come into view. Darkness. Mud. And then the dreaded whistling noise of a German artillery shell flying through the air.

"Incoming! Incoming!" came the shouts. He closed his eye again and listened to the whistling shell. He had memorized how they sounded in flight. The rhythm of the gun, the shrieking and whining as the shell pierced through the air. And then the silence.

Three...two...one, he counted, and another explosion ripped through the trench and deep into the mud, throwing up an explosion of dirt. In his delirious state, he mused that this earth had been buried below the earth's surface for thousands of years but had now been freed and sent skyward. He imagined what it must feel like to be imprisoned for hundreds of lifetimes, then launched into liberty by an artillery strike. He watched with a strange calm as the dirt soared into the air and began to rain back down. He lay still, propped up against the side of the trench. His medic hunkered down, his hands over his helmet, trying to shield himself from the debris.

Major Eldridge laughed. "Don't fear, Baker!" he tried to say to his medic, although what erupted from his mouth were only moans. He continued the thought in his head. *'Tis only deliverance, falling down on us from the sky.*

He lay back and closed his eyes again as the soft earth landed all around him, covering his body in a cold, wet tomb. As the cool dirt spattered his face, he felt nothing but relief. He opened his mouth and let the wet mud fill in, finding comfort in its dampness—his canteen had been empty for at least a day, maybe longer. His relief was so great that he didn't panic as he was trapped by the avalanche of mud. He continued to suck the moisture from the dirt, even as the weight of the mud slowly forced the air from his lungs.

Hands. Hands everywhere, burrowing down toward him as he lay in his earthen grave. Hands that poked his neck and face and grasped for his clothes.

"Leave me!" he shouted, but again his words emerged only as a series of groans and coughs. He wanted to be free, like the mud that had just risen fifty feet into the air and found a resting place along the walls of his collapsing trench. "Leave me," he said again, softly.

But the hands would not listen. They continued to scrape the soft mud away from his face and pull on his tunic, trying to drag him out. "He's still breathing!" a voice shouted. "Medic!" He looked to where his medic had been sitting just moments before, and he saw nothing but piles of dirt and soupy, dark, red mud.

"The medic's dead!" called a voice. "Get the major to the rear!"

"Is it worth the risk?" shouted a private. "He's got but moments left, and we'll have to bring him up over the top! He'll slow us down and get us all killed!"

Major Eldridge shook his head. *No*, he thought. *It's not worth it. My life is not worth any risk. It is ending.* He had witnessed countless men sacrificed to save a man with one foot in the grave. Hell, he himself had ordered it at least a dozen times—enough to know it was never worth sacrificing a living, breathing, vibrant man to save a corpse.

But a sergeant smacked the private across the face. "He's a senior officer, you fool! And a human soul. We'll carry him out if it's the last act we do on this earth!" Despite the major's silent protests, the soldiers pulled him onto a rickety stretcher. With effort, they dragged him up over the top and toward the rear along with dozens of their comrades who were also evacuating.. Their trench network had completely collapsed in the latest artillery volley, and the only way out of certain death was exposing themselves on the ground level as they fled toward the rear line.

The soldiers diligently carried the major along on their makeshift stretcher. For the first time, he realized that he was in excruciating pain. The men stopped frequently as bursts exploded all around them.

Was it night? Was it day? He could not tell. It didn't matter. Whatever time of day, he was certain he would never see a tomorrow. This was what the end felt like.

He had seen it so many hundreds of times now. He knew what death looked like when its shadows came to collect soldiers. It collected men unsparingly, men who had once been the very essence of life. They had been fathers and sons. They had been lovers and hooligans and dreamers. They were young, for the most part, stolen away from life in disgusting, dismembering explosions when they should have been dancing and laughing and stealing away on lazy afternoons to meet with forbidden lovers.

They had been England's future, and they were now rotting whispers of dreams beneath the soil of a foreign land. England could never reclaim their vigor or passion or spunk. Death found them when they were tired or scared, or when they were joking with their backs turned, and stole them away while they still yearned to live, while they prayed and screamed in agony and called for their mothers. It turned them from boys to corpses with sheared-away faces and limbless, disemboweled bodies. It transformed youthful laughter to incessant, possessed screaming and hollow, guttural death rattles.

If he ever saw home again, he wanted only to tell his mother that these memories and ghosts and rotted human marrow were his best friends, and that the war was not worth their lives. No praise he could utter would ever do their lives and their loss justice. He wanted to tell her that Father had been right. War was hell.

After several long and agonizing minutes, the men carrying him took cover from a barrage in a crater created by an exploded shell. *Just hours ago this was a death trap,* Major Eldridge thought. *And now it preserves and protects.* His brother would appreciate this irony.

In a moment of lucidity, he had a panicked thought. "My brother!" he gasped.

The private who had questioned the utility of trying to save his life said, "He's trying to communicate!"

"My brother!" Major Eldridge said again.

"Your brother?" said the private. He turned to another soldier. "Which Major Eldridge is this?" he whispered.

The solider shrugged. "Dunno. But there are no more survivors."

"Sir, your brother is back in the trench," the private relayed.

"Go and get him!" screamed Major Eldridge with all of his strength, though the words emerged as a whisper.

The private just shook his head. "Can't recover the body, sir," he replied. "Not just yet."

The words hung in the air. *The body.* The major retched. Before he could recover himself to order them back again, a call came across the multiple craters, all filled with Tommies who had fled their entombed trench and their comrades still buried in the mud. They had left the medic, Sergeant Baker, with whom the major had shared cigarettes and stories and laughs. They had left his dear brother, with whom he had shared his youth and his mischief and his soul. Who was more important to him than life itself. And they had left countless others who would now live only in the nightmares of the survivors.

"Gas! Gas! Gas!" came the call. He watched as his rescuers frantically pulled on their gas masks. As he reached for his, his arm scraped uselessly against his left leg, and he felt an agonizing pain.

He no longer had a left hand.

The private pulled his bloody stump away and placed the major's mask over his nose and mouth for him. Before the mask could make its seal around the remnants of his facial flesh, Major Eldridge took a deep breath, hoping to inhale enough of the vapor so that he wouldn't have to wait to join his brother, and so the men would abandon their suicidal effort to save him. His life was no longer worth living and he couldn't bear the thought that any able bodied man might die trying to save him.

About the Author

Katrina Nowak is an Indie author who specializes in historical fiction. She studied European History at the University of Rochester and Russian and East European Studies at the University of North Carolina at Chapel Hill. Her academic research includes twentieth century European conflict and political transitions. She is an officer in the United States Navy and a former faculty member at the National Defense University where she designed and published academic wargames. She is a wife of one and a mom of three, and in her spare time, an avid runner.

In 2017, she founded Scribble & Spark Bookworks as an independent press.

www.scribbleandspark.com

Acknowledgements

This book was made possible by a fantastic group of friends, family, and strangers who believed in me and in this project and supported the Kickstarter campaign to fund a professional editor for my manuscript and first edition publication. Without this group of crazy, positive, and enthusiastic supporters and their constant encouragement, this novel would remain a draft hidden somewhere on my desktop. Thank you for helping to breathe life into this project, for your constant words of encouragement, for your friendship, for your patience, and for your fantastic senses of humor...

A heartfelt shout-out to my gang of superfans:

Maggie

Joe Nowak and Pete Nowak

Anthony Nowak (Peachy)

Kathy and Paul Dusek

Michael and Jaclyn Zona

Sue and Marty Kornonowski, Ryan, Brooke and Natalie

Sam and Stephanie Phillips

Krishnan

Jim and Jan Harvey

Aunt Jane, Uncle Dan, Danielle and John Luc

Aunt Elsie and Uncle George Stec

Heidi Stec

Chris Kofron

The Ladies of Gilbert 4: Delilah, Andrea Murphy, Julie Czupryna,
and Honorary Member of the G4 club, Jenny

Grace Kraay Simmons, my lifelong partner in crime

Sue Kenny and Dawn Kenny

My Tarheels: Karen Lloyd and Drew Steen, R. Williams, Erik Russ,
David Marshall, and Jeff G.

Mr. Sanjeet K. Deka, a Superhunk and Exceptional Texan

Eric

The Smith Family

Christina

Chris Paternostro

Carl Kammerer

Matt Tierney

Jay Boyles

Pete

Crystal Bergemann

Kate Durant

Colin Tse

A handful of silent supporters

The countless others who have cheered me on, and

My life and my love, Greg

CPSIA information can be obtained
at www.ICGtesting.com
Printed in the USA
FSHW01n2042240418
47226FS

9 781732 038103